I0622287

Pilikia

Is My

Business

Mark Troy

Ilium Books

College Station, Texas

Pilikia Is My Business

by

Mark Troy

First American Edition

Published by Ilium Books

ISBN 978-0-578-06966-1

Previously published in Canada in both paperback and electronic
format by LTDBooks

Ilium Books
1002 Rose Circle
College Station, TX 77840
http://www.marktroy.net

Cover design
David L. Shackelford
http://www.idrawbooks.com

DEDICATION

To Mary Fran with love.

ACKNOWLEDGMENTS

This book would not have happened without the support of friends and fellow writers in the Brazos Writers who read and criticued the early drafts. I also owe thanks to the great editors and publishers at LTDBooks, Laura Adlam, Terry Shiels, and Dee Lloyd, who had enough faith in Pilikia to publish the first edition and to nurture a new author.

1 *PILIKIA* IS MY BUSINESS

My name is Val Lyon. *Pilikia* is my business.

   Pilikia means "trouble" in the Hawaiian language. You pronounce it *pi* as in what children do in the swimming pool, *li* as in the Confederate general, *ki*, an instrument to open locks, and *ah*. At one in the afternoon, two weeks before Christmas, I had an appointment with an attorney about some *pilikia*.

   Brian Magruder had worked six years in the Honolulu Public Defender's shop before striking out on his own. When he struck, he struck big, locating his office in a marble and glass downtown high-rise favored by the moneyed and powerful. The building directory listed the law offices of a former governor, two former mayors and a US senator. Magruder hadn't been in the building long enough to be listed in the directory. A security guard directed me to a middle floor.

   The hallway outside his office was wider than my apartment. It had a deep carpet and green trees in planters. The walls bore paintings of Hawaiian women in languid poses done by a local artist who had acquired a measure of status among the state's trendsetters. All of the doors were marked with fancy nameplates except Magruder's. His had a five-by-eight card taped crookedly to the center.

   The scene inside was one of disarray. Boxes were

everywhere. I announced myself to a middle-aged woman in a yellow muumuu. She looked up from the file carton she was unpacking and shouted, "Your detective is here!" To me, she said, "Don't mind the mess, honey. We're just moving in, that's why. Go on back."

I went through a conference room with more boxes to a third office and Brian Magruder. My first impression, as he came around his desk, was of a young Captain Kangaroo. He had a round face, thick dark hair worn longish, and a droopy mustache. Mid-thirties, my age or a couple of years older, with the layer of fat young men often acquire when they cease being active. I figured him for six feet and two hundred-forty pounds. His clothes, faded cotton twill slacks and Aloha shirt, fit him badly.

"Hey," he said, "it's the distaff shamus! Good to see you."

His handshake was firm but not crushing. His eyes, warm and brown like Hershey's Kisses, stayed on my face.

"Mr. Magruder," I said, "you have a job for me?"

"Call me Brian," he said.

He directed me to a visitor's chair. The view, through the window behind his desk, looked towards the ocean but it was partially obstructed by the rest of downtown. I let my gaze wander around the room. There were no unpacked boxes here. The furnishings spoke money: polished hardwood desk and tables; chairs, like the one I sat in, upholstered in green leather with little buttons sunk deep into the padding. Framed photographs hung on the wall nearest me, kudos pictures of famous and powerful people posing with a man I didn't recognize.

"I don't see you in the pictures," I said.

He made an embarrassed smile before settling into the chair behind the desk. He said, "My Dad. All this was his. It still is. You're looking around this office and thinking fat cat lawyer, right? Well, it's not me. Okay, I'll own to the fat part. Dad happened to have this space. He sublets it to me for a nominal fee. If not for that, I'd be in Mo'ili'ili. You know the kind of place - two rooms next to a dentist, noodle shop down below."

I nodded. If not for his Dad, we might have been neighbors.

I said, "Not the kind of setting your family's used to, I imagine."

"Good insight. You've done your homework," he said.

In truth, it was a hunch based on common gossip picked up here and there, but if Magruder wanted to believe I'd checked him out, I wasn't going to tell him differently.

He continued. "I did some homework on you. You were with the San Francisco Police Department - six years on patrol and three years as inspector. Right?"

I nodded. "What else did you find out about me?"

"That you're stubborn and you don't take shit from the people you work for."

"Such glowing recommendations. Did your sources mention that my performance ratings were high?"

"They did. They also told me you got involved in something that had the brass pissing acid and that you were terminated two years ago."

"A career readjustment."

"What did you do after that?"

"I was in prison."

"Prison? No kidding?"

"No, it's a figure of speech. Yes, no kidding, Brian. I was in prison for thirteen of those months. One stinking year of my life."

Magruder's expression darkened. "Hey listen, I don't mean to pry."

I waved off his protest. "You've got a right to know who you're hiring. It's not something I advertise, but I'm not ashamed of it. I did time I shouldn't have for a conviction that shouldn't have happened, but it's been expunged. I have a letter from the Governor saying so."

"So that means you can carry a gun?"

"If I have to."

"I hope you don't have to. I don't like guns, myself. I'm representing Jean Pfeifer. Does that name mean anything to you?"

"Yes," I said. I knew that Jean and her ex-husband were locked in a bitter war over custody of their son. At issue was Jean's claim that her ex had abused the boy. She had stopped the court-ordered visitations and now faced contempt of court charges. The boy, Nathan, had disappeared.

There was probably not a woman in Honolulu who didn't know the story. I'd followed it in the media, more from a sense of duty to my sex than any other reason. Had I been a mother, I'd have had more interest in it.

Magruder said, "I was a Public Defender. I guess you know that. The people I represented didn't move the needle on the public interest meter. Most of the time, all I could do for them was plead them down. This case is different. There's a wrong to be righted, which is what I love about it. What I hate is that it is a cause célèbre. A lawyer's nightmare. My nightmare."

"Does this nightmare take a form?"

He nodded. "There's a rally for Jean tomorrow. I tried to discourage her from attending but she insists, or more precisely, the rally organizers insist and she feels indebted to them. I want you to protect her."

"You expect trouble?"

"Nothing I can put my finger on. A lot of people have taken up sides on this case and passions are running high. Where do you stand on it?"

"Why do you want to know?"

"I want to know if you're on our side."

"If you hire me, I'm on your side.

"Just like that?"

"No, not just like that. I have to live with myself. If I thought it was the wrong side, I wouldn't take it on."

Magruder beamed, "That's great! That makes two of us. Jean's doing what she believes is best for Nathan. I want to see that she can continue. I'd like to get her back together with her son so she can raise him the way a mother should."

"The ex-husband, what's his name?"

"Jason Pfeifer, goes by Jock." He reached into a desk drawer and brought out an accordion folder, which he passed across to me.

4

"This might help. It's a little background information I prepared for you. Tells you what I know about Jock Pfeifer."

"Do you expect Pfeifer to show up tomorrow?"

Magruder shook his head. A comma of hair fell across his forehead and he brushed it back. "We have a restraining order to keep him away from Jean."

"You think he'll obey it?"

"If Jock Pfeifer were the only problem, this would be easy. Once this broke, people began writing to the newspapers and calling in on talk shows. Jean received mail from every stripe of crazy. Had to change her number three times. It's the crazies, I'm afraid of."

"Look, Brian, I work alone because I like it that way. I have a tiny office because I can't afford better. But, as I understand it, the Magruder name and fortune goes a long way. If it's protection you want, you could buy a busload of Pinkertons."

"No," he said. "I don't want a lot of rent-a-cop footprints all over this. It's going to be big in the media as is. Let's not give them more to feed on. There will be mostly women at the rally. You can blend in and stay close to Jean."

"What happens afterwards?"

"Afterwards, she has to appear before the judge. If she produces Nathan and agrees to visitations she goes free. Otherwise she goes to jail. I expect her to choose jail."

"I can give her points on jailing,' I said.

Brian Magruder's face split into a big grin. "Jailing. That's good," he said.

I spent the next couple of hours reviewing the information Magruder had given me.

The folder contained photos of all three Pfeifers, Jean, Nathan, and Jason "Jock" Pfeifer. Nathan was thirteen, a skinny, gangly kid. If he took after his father, he had a lot of growing to do. Judging from a rather bad photo, Jock Pfeifer was a heavyweight. He had a barrel chest and a thick neck. The photo showed him at the tiller of a sailboat, shirtless and in shorts, mugging for the camera. The cocky, self-made man. The last picture showed Jean, a striking woman with strong, aristocratic features and honey-colored hair that belled around her face. The attached bio sheet gave her age as thirty-eight. I hoped I'd take a picture that good in five years.

Brian had written out a summary of the case on several sheets of yellow, legal paper. The Pfeifers had gotten married during Jock's last tour with the Navy. They'd settled in Honolulu even though neither of them had family here. The marriage was troubled from the start. Three years ago, Jean had filed for divorce after twelve years of marriage. Under Hawaii's no fault law, she kept the house that had been in her name and received half of the remaining property. Jock agreed to pay a thousand a month in child support and accepted responsibility for Nathan's education.

Jock was to have Nathan on alternate weekends and for one month during the summer. The arrangement worked well for two years. It fell apart in early September when Jean refused to allow Jock any more visits. Jock went to court. Jean accused Jock of abusing Nathan. She claimed the abuse had started before the divorce and had continued on the weekend visits. The court, however, ordered the visitations to resume. Jean continued to resist. Three weeks ago, Nathan had disappeared and Jean had hired Brian to defend her against a criminal contempt charge.

Jock Pfeifer was forty-two, the owner of a chain of video rental stores called Video Bazaar. At the time of the divorce, he'd owned two stores. Now, they could be found in strip malls on all sides of the Island. Recently, Pfeifer had been accused of promoting obscenity. A news clipping stapled to the sheet showed Pfeifer and a middle-aged woman in police custody. Another photo showed a pile of supposedly obscene videos seized in a raid by vice officers. The vice raid had occurred before Nathan's disappearance but after the court's order to resume visits. I couldn't help wondering if there was a connection.

2 THE LAW OF THE SPLINTERED PADDLE

At ten the next morning I was outside the YWCA on Richards Street. Jean Pfeifer's supporters began arriving about quarter after eleven. Jean showed up a half hour later, accompanied by another woman. They entered from the parking lot at the rear of the building. I caught up to them inside.

"Jean," I said, "I need to talk to you." Jean looked better in person than in her picture. She wore a gold blouse and an olive skirt with a broad leather belt. She looked at me with surprise and a little bit of fear. The other woman had on a tropical style fedora and a sleeveless top with a cat's face silk-screened on the front. She clutched Jean's arm reassuringly.

"Who are you?" said cat-face.

I introduced myself. "I work for Brian Magruder," I said. "I'm your protection, Jean."

"Oh," said Jean. "Yes, Brian told me you'd be here."

"A bodyguard?" said cat-face. "We didn't request a bodyguard."

"Who's we?" I asked.

"I'm sorry," said Jean. "This is Carol Fernandez. She's been helping me through this."

"We don't need a bodyguard," said Fernandez. "We're

capable of taking care of ourselves, thank you."

"Just in case…" The squeal of a microphone cut me off.

"We're starting," said Fernandez.

"I'll be over here if you need me, Jean."

"Humph," said Fernandez. She pulled Jean towards a podium that had been set up on the top step in front of the Y.

The crowd was two or three hundred strong, filling the thin strip of grass and the narrow sidewalk in front of the building and spilling out onto the street. I took up a position near the perimeter in the shade of a small street tree strung with Christmas lights. From there I could watch Jean and the people in front.

The city's elves had wrapped all of the trees from base to crown with lights, making downtown Honolulu into the mayor's vision of a winter wonderland. Bright sun, blue sky, and twinkly monkeypod trees. Where there was an absence of trees to wrap, the elves brought in Norfolk Island pines. A pair of Norfolks trimmed with leis and surrounded by poinsettias marked the entrance to the Y, but they were largely hidden behind a long banner held by two women. The banner said, in large block letters, "WOMEN TAKE BACK THE COURTS," and, in smaller letters, "Protect our children."

Jean, Carol Fernandez, and a third woman stood behind the banner. The shadow of the doorway partly concealed them. Fernandez stepped forward to speak, standing a step higher than the banner carriers. I took out my mini-tape recorder and switched it on. You never know when a recording of an event will come in handy.

Fernandez said, "We're going to fight not only for Nathan Pfeifer, but for all children raised in violent homes. Who speaks for the children? Fathers? No! The courts? No! Mothers speak for the children. It is our right and our duty, but the judicial system has taken that right away. Now we demand the return of our voice."

As she spoke, she raised her arms above her head, making throwing motions to emphasize her points. "We must take back the courts," she shouted, punctuating each word with a throw of her hands. The flesh under her arms rippled.

As a reflex, I extended my right arm and felt my triceps muscle. It seemed firm enough. Still, maybe I should add some dips to my morning sit-up and push-up routine.

The crowd had taken up the woman's chant, "Take back the courts." Now she held up her hands to silence them and said, "Here she is, the woman who is prepared to sacrifice her own freedom to take back the courts. Jean Pfeifer."

Jean stepped out from the shadow of the doorway. She and Fernandez hugged each other and Fernandez said, "Jean, we're all behind you." Then the two of them turned to face the crowd, holding hands and raising them high in a gesture of solidarity.

Jean said, in a clear, firm voice, "Your support gives me the courage to go forward. This fight is not just for me. Not just for Nathan. It is for all women and for all children. No laws have been made that can interfere with the duties of a mother to protect her children. No courts are strong enough. We will prevail. With your faith, we will prevail."

Not everybody was in sympathy with Jean's cause. Several men had appeared at the edge of the crowd. Clean cut, neatly dressed, they looked like other members of the downtown business establishment except that they carried signs with such messages as, "Fathers have rights, too," and "Paternity is Destiny." A man with a sign yelled, "What about a father's duty to protect his children?"

The crowd shouted him down. Jean and Carol Fernandez were joined by the third woman, who had remained in the shadows the whole time. The crowd let out a roar of approval.

"Who's that?" I asked a woman next to me.

"Sue Naito," she said. "She teaches American Studies at the University. She used to be a City Councilwoman."

Next to Jean, Naito was a frump. Her clothes had no style and her body had no shape. She wore her hair in a bowl cut with schoolgirl bangs. Her only concession to style was a pair of dangly, pewter-colored ball earrings that matched her hair color. I guessed her age at about sixty. Naito said, "The people of this state are with us. Let's show the politicians how strong we are."

Another roar of approval. At a signal from Fernandez, the banner carriers started down the steps. The crowd parted before them. Jean, Sue Naito, and Fernandez linked arms and followed. The crowd filled in behind them. They went single file between the parked cars and regrouped in the street. The procession crossed the street and went through the gate of Iolani Palace. TV news crews, tour buses, and clumps of visitors lined the palace driveway. I joined the group. We made a circuit of the ornate, gingerbread home of Hawaii's last monarchs, and headed out the palm-lined drive to King Street. The wind rattled the palm fronds like snare drums accompanying the chants of the marchers.

Nine years with the San Francisco Police Department had given me plenty of experience in crowd control. I've never been in a crowd that didn't leave my stomach tied in knots. The fact that most of the crowd were women made no difference. The knot forming in my stomach was as tight as a fist.

I had no problem spotting the troublemakers - not the men with signs, but a dozen men in two groups flanking the King Street gate. None of them looked older than twenty. Some sported buffed out physiques, the kind inmates, with time on their hands, develop. Maybe I was wrong. Maybe they were simply interested in current events, something they'd developed along with muscles.

Maybe we'll have a white Christmas.

As the first ranks went out the gate, the toughs spread out and moved closer to the marchers. They shouted, "Shut up," and "Go home," and, to every phrase, they added, "bitch." I looked around for police. Two officers were halting traffic down at Richards Street. Another was doing the same at Mililani Street where it intersected King across from the palace, but a pair of motorcycle cops were cruising up King from Richards. They parked their bikes near the gate just as I reached it.

I worked my way towards the front and Jean. If trouble broke out, I hoped I could get her away.

By the time we reached the statue of Kamehameha the Great in front of the judiciary there were only two people between me and

Jean Pfeifer. The banner was wrapped around the base of the bronze and gold statue and Naito stepped up on a makeshift stage to address the crowd. She began a speech, but I was too busy pushing closer to Pfeifer to catch anything but a few snippets. "It is Kamehameha's first law," said Naito, "the Law of the Splintered Paddle, which guarantees that the defenseless will not be harmed."

The Law of the Splintered Paddle sounded like my job description. Maybe I could put it on my business card. Camera crews from all three network affiliates were taping Naito's speech and one or two still photographers were shooting the scene. My own recorder was still turning in my hand.

I worked my way between a small woman who was standing on tiptoe and a photographer in a green and white cap that advertised a brand of snuff. In the press of bodies, I jostled his arm. He flashed me an angry scowl and moved away. The woman stepped aside, too, leaving me next to Pfeifer.

I said, "Jean, we have to get out of here."

Jean looked like a frightened animal. Eyes wide and darting from me to Carol and back.

"We'll be all right," said Fernandez. "Don't panic."

"Jean."

"No, Val. I have to stay with Carol."

The gang bangers were getting louder and more mobile with each minute. The crowd surged in response to the actions of the gang. With every surge my feeling of dread increased.

"There's safety in numbers," said Carol. "This is the kind of thing we need to get our message across."

I said, "We have to go, Jean. Now!"

"No," said Carol, "You can't abandon the cause. You said it yourself, this is bigger than you and Nathan."

I wanted to knock Carol down.

"This is not a time to argue causes," I said.

I pocketed my recorder and grabbed Jean by the arm. Together we pushed towards the edge of the mass of people, away from the bangers. At that moment, the situation exploded. A can of

Coke sailed over our heads and ruptured on the ground, spurting foam over my ankles. Rocks and other objects followed. Some women screamed and ran. Naito broke off her speech and tried to calm the crowd. The two cops had their hands full going after the rock-throwers. More police cars were coming, but they were still a block away and a lot of the troublemakers were still around.

Carol caught up to us. A woman panicked, stumbled and went down in my path, causing me to lose my grip on Jean's arm. Carol took the lead.

"My car's there," I said, pointing to the parking lot behind and left of the statue. Just then a young punk collided with Carol, knocking her down.

"Hey, look out," he said. He turned to Jean and a grin split his face. "Oh, man! You're her." He raised his arm and I saw the rock in his hand. I covered the distance between us in two steps.

"You're her," he repeated.

"And you're shit," I yelled. He checked his motion just long enough for me to grab his wrist with both hands. I stepped towards him, forcing his arm back, and kneed him in the stomach. His legs buckled under him and he twisted in my grasp. I kneed him again, this time under the chin, straightening him up. He made a sound like gargling razor blades and fell to the pavement.

Carol got to her feet, apparently unhurt. "Hurry, Jean," she said.

One of the motorcycle cops raced up to us.

"He just learned the Law of the Splintered Paddle," I said.

"From the school of hard knocks, yeah? You better go with your friends."

I caught up with Jean and Carol at the car. Led them to my old Nissan. Jean was pale and shaking. She leaned against the car making sobbing noises while Carol urged her to get in.

"Jean," I said, "do you still believe there's safety in numbers?"

"This is awful." She put her forehead against the car. "But they can't get me in jail," she said to the car.

I took her shoulder and turned her around. "And Nathan? You'll be safe, but who's protecting Nathan?"

"That look on his face," she said. "He wanted to hurt me."

"Answer me, Jean. What about Nathan?"

Jean's shoulders shook. She said, "Harriet -"

"Get in the car, Jean," said Carol.

"Who's Harriet?" I asked.

"Nobody! Just go, Jean."

At that moment, someone thrust a microphone past my shoulder. "Lehua Lopes, Channel 5 News. Jean, what's your reaction to this?"

"Ms. Pfeifer has no comment," I said.

"Who are you?" asked Lopes.

"My name's Lyon. I'm part of her defense team."

"Some defense," said the reporter. "Did you beat up that kid?"

"That kid attacked her."

"What about it, Jean? Did you feel you were in danger?"

"She's not answering questions," I said. "Get in the car, Jean," I put myself between the reporter and Jean who ducked into the back seat. Carol scurried in after her. I got behind the wheel, praying the old beater would start.

"Who is Harriet?" asked Lopes.

"Nobody," I said.

The engine fired. We swung through the parking lot and out onto Richards Street. Behind us, in the mirror, Lehua Lopes stamped her foot in frustration..

3 HARRIET

Jean and I found Brian back in his office. He looked like a mainland businessman in dress slacks, white shirt and tie. I prefer the casual look, but, even in Hawaii, attorneys have to dress for court.

"The rally's over so soon?" he asked.

"It broke up early," I said.

It was just after twelve-thirty. The whole thing - speaking, marching, and fleeing - had taken place in about a quarter of an hour. The gang had attacked early. The attack had ended quickly - much quicker than it seemed at the time. We had taken Carol back to the Y where she had left her car. Carol had been reluctant to leave Jean, but I insisted. With Carol out of the car, Jean recovered enough of her composure to freshen her makeup. Now a nervous hand-wringing was her only sign of distress.

"You didn't warn me there would be a gang at the rally," I said.

"What do you mean a gang?"

"A street gang. A bunch of punks. They charged us with rocks."

"Jeez," he said, and "Jeez," he repeated after I'd told him all about it. "I had no idea things would get so out of hand. I'm glad you were there." He looked at Jean. Worry lines creased his face. "Are you all right?"

Jean's hands moved in time to the music from the reception area. "Yes," she said. "Carol got me away from there."

I bit back a response. Magruder would get my report later. I rubbed my jeans over the part of my knee that was still tender from contacting the punk's chin. It had probably started to bruise. Maybe next time I should wear a skirt so the damage would show.

"Brian, things didn't just get out of hand," I said. "Something more than an interest in current events brought the gang bangers."

"Like what?"

"I think someone recruited them." Brian's face registered shock. I went on, "Look, I'd like to know what we're up against. What haven't you told me?"

"You'd better listen to this," he said. "It was on my answering machine this morning."

He pushed the machine to the center of his desk and played the message. A male voice said, "Listen to this, fat ass. Ka-boom! That's you if the Pfeifer bitch doesn't let go the kid."

"Oh, God!" said Jean. Her face had lost some of its color.

"Do you recognize the voice?"

Magruder played the tape again. The voice was not muffled but it had an odd quality as though the speaker was trying to disguise himself. He spoke slowly and carefully, with a slight rhythmic cadence typical of Hawaiian English, but with none of the other characteristics.

Magruder said, "'Ka-boom,' he says. Would you say that's a bomb threat?"

"Uh huh. The bangers called us 'bitch.' Same high class crowd. Could it be your ex, Jean?"

She gave a small shake of her head. "No. It's not Jock. I'd know his voice."

"Even if he tried to disguise it? What about the words? He ever call you, 'bitch'?"

"Yes, maybe, but it's not him. It's not anybody I know. Oh,

God!"

Brian came over to Jean and took her hand. "Jean, listen to me. The threat was directed at me. Ninety-eight percent of death threats are hoaxes. In custody cases, they are like fruit flies on mangoes."

I didn't share his confidence. "Screw the statistics, Brian. We have to take it seriously."

"You'll be safe in jail. I'll ask the judge to order special treatment for you."

"While you're in jail, where is Nathan?" I asked.

"I don't know," she said. "But he's safe."

"How do you know he's safe, if you don't know where he is?"

"I know that he's safe. He is in good hands."

"Whose hands? Harriet's?"

"Val," said Jean, "I'm no Joan of Arc. The thought of going to jail scares me. If I knew where Nathan was, I might feel compelled to tell, out of fear or weakness. So I arranged with some other people to hide Nathan. They don't tell me where he is being hidden, nor who is hiding him. That way I can't be forced to tell. He's safe as long as nobody knows where he is."

Magruder said, "Who is this Harriet person?"

"She's the person Jean gave Nathan to."

"I did not say that," said Jean.

"At the car -"

"She's nobody. There is nobody named Harriet. At the car I was upset. Couldn't you see that? I wasn't thinking. I don't know what I said."

"It's time to go," said Brian. "We can't keep the judge waiting."

"Let me have the tape," I said. "I'll take it to somebody for analysis."

"Okay. That's a deal." He popped it out of the machine and gave it to me.

The hearing lasted only a few minutes. Jean refused to

produce Nathan and the judge ordered her to jail. Brian asked that she be accorded special treatment. The judge agreed.

When we were outside the courtroom, I said, "I'll have to bring in some help if I'm going to protect you."

"Protect me? Why?"

"The threat was directed at you. If she didn't produce Nathan -"

"Hey, don't worry about me. Threats come with the territory. Tell you what. I'll lock my doors, check under the car before I get in, and look before I cross the street. Better yet, I'll run with you. I heard you're a runner. If I get some of this fat off my ass, they won't have anything to blow up. My doc's been telling me this weight's taking years off my life."

"Brian, be serious."

"Val, I am serious. Do you think you can find Nathan?"

"If I can find Harriet."

"Good! It's Nathan we have to protect."

Dr. Pamela Wright was the shrink at the Women's Community Correctional Center. She was my source of strength for thirteen of the lowest months of my life, when all my clothes were prison issued, and my moods swung between rage and self-pity. You don't expect to make lasting friendships in prison, but ours is the exception. I would drive over a cliff with Pam Wright.

In addition to her prison work, Pam had her own clinical practice on Union Mall, not far from the site of the rally. She specialized in treating victims of sexual abuse. I called her office from a pay phone.

"Talk quick, girlfriend," she said, "Got an evaluation and referral conference this afternoon. Can this wait?"

"Do you know someone named Harriet? I don't have a last name, but I think she's active in women's groups. I need to find her."

Her tone became guarded. "Harriet? Maybe you ought to come in."

I was in her waiting room in ten minutes and inside her office a minute later. The office's previous tenant had been an optometrist. Pam had moved in and got right down to work without bothering with such niceties as redecorating. The fitting table, which she used as a desk, and the eyeglass decal on the window told of the office's original purpose.

Pam was a strikingly attractive woman. On that particular day she wore a purple suit over a blouse that shimmered in peacock colors. Her hair was high on top, but pulled tight on the sides to reveal her ears, which were outlined with small gold studs. They shone like glimmering question marks against her coffee-colored skin. Below the question marks were big gold loops. Pam collected men like I collect running shoes. The gold studs, she'd once told me, were souvenirs of relationships. "One for each," she'd said. I didn't know if she was kidding.

Now she faced me across the table. I said, "Thanks for seeing me. I know you're busy."

Her dark eyes strayed down to my waist and back to my face. "Cut to the chase, sugar. You pregnant? You thinking of an abortion?"

"No, I'm doing an investigation."

"Your detective business?"

I nodded.

"Hoo-boy!" she said. "Why does that sound like trouble? I think I'd rather see you pregnant. That, I can handle."

"Trouble? How about congratulations on getting a client? Now I can keep the landlord off my ass without getting into you for loans."

"You'll get a thank you from my accountant, girl. Why do you want Harriet?"

"I'm looking for Nathan Pfeifer."

Pam, I knew, would be thoroughly familiar with the Pfeifer case. She asked, "Are you developing a political conscience or did you pick the right side by accident?"

"My client chose the side. His name's Brian Magruder. Do you know him?"

Pam moved some papers around on her desk, a mannerism

which signaled that her response would be cautious. "The Magruders, as in Magruder Estate, are an old Island family," she said. "I know the family by reputation only and Brian not at all. They represent a side of state politics I don't happen to agree with."

"This isn't political, Pam. My concern is for Nathan. I have to know where he is so I can determine that he's safe. Jean said to call Harriet, but that's all she said. She wouldn't have told me that much if she hadn't just been through an attack on her life. What does Harriet have to do with abortions?"

Pam leaned back in her chair and removed her half reading glasses. She placed them on top of her head, pushing the temple pieces deep into her dark hair. "In graduate school, back in the early 70s, I joined a consciousness raising group."

I nodded my understanding. Pam said, "Don't act like you know what I'm talking about, 'cause you don't. You're too damn young to know about consciousness raising."

"My grandmother told me about it."

"Humph! I won't even comment on that. Two of the women in our group were nurses. You have to understand that this was three years before Roe and abortion was illegal, even here. Too many women were dying from botched abortions. Most of those deaths could've been prevented. But with knowledge, training and the right equipment you could make abortions safer. These nurses put together a kit from stuff you could get over the counter at any pharmacy, plus a few items from the housewares department at Holiday Mart. They mimeoed some instructions and gave us all some training. Voila! We were an underground army of illegal abortionists. I tell you, it was exciting. I felt like a cross between Pancho Villa and Margaret Sanger."

"Pam Wright doing abortions?"

"I don't see why you find that hard to believe."

"It's just a side of you I've never seen. How many did you do?"

"Two was all. The first one was fine, but the second one was bad. Don't ask me what exactly went wrong, because I couldn't tell

19

you. Two of us were doing it. The patient started hemorrhaging and we freaked. We finally called one of our nurse friends and she got the patient to a hospital. I was walking on edge for days, afraid the woman would die, afraid we'd all be found out and I'd go to jail, or, at the very least, get kicked out of graduate school, but nothing came of it. The nurse was able to keep it quiet. However, I didn't do any more abortions after that. I did make referrals, though."

"So who was Harriet?" I asked. "The nurse?"

"Sugar, there was no Harriet. You could say it was the network, if you want, but that's not quite right. Here's how it worked: if you wanted an abortion, you called a number and asked for Harriet. You might get another number and another. Eventually, a time and place would be set up for a meeting. At the meeting you'd get counseling from someone to make sure you really wanted it. We didn't do anything without making sure you, the patient, thoroughly and completely understood all of the implications. It was your choice all the way."

"How would I get the number to start with?"

"You just dialed the letters, H-A-R-R-I-E-T. The women's groups spread the word pretty well. There were a few ob-gyn's who made referrals because they were reluctant to perform abortions themselves. But," Pam shrugged, "like all things, it came to an end. Roe v. Wade removed the need for a home abortion kit."

"What happened to the two nurses who made the kit?"

"One of them moved to another island a few years later. The other quit nursing and got involved in other things."

I was confused and disappointed. A secret network of women intrigued me, but I was looking for babysitters, not abortionists. Besides, the abortion network had disbanded two decades earlier.

"Pam, why would Jean tell me to call Harriet when they're no longer operating?"

Pam pulled her glasses out of her hair and set them on her nose. She went to a file cabinet and rifled through some folders. "Harriet is back in operation, sort of. The way things are going with the new-look Supreme Court and the Webster case, some of the sisters think we may be going back to home abortions. Here! This arrived in the mail six or eight weeks ago."

She sat down and gave me a three by five card. It said simply, "Pregnancy counseling. Call HARRIET."

"Now, I know you, sugar, you're not going to be satisfied with this. So, to answer your next question, no, I don't know who sent it. I could tell you who else was in the consciousness raising group with me, but since abortions were illegal then, and home abortions still are, I won't. I hope you understand, Val."

"Of course." I changed the subject to Jean Pfeifer. "What do you think of her charge that her ex abused Nathan?"

Pam leaned across the fitting table towards me. "I don't know if this will help you or not, sugar. I know Jean grew up as a Navy brat, moving around the world with her mother and stepfather. Jean's ex-husband, I believe, was also in the Navy. That's how they ended up here.

"The military doesn't like to publicize this, but family violence and abuse are problems for them. The incidence is probably far greater than they report. The moving around that military families go through shakes the normal support systems so much that little problems get to be big ones and they get handled inappropriately. All the separation, too. That isn't good. Couples don't have the time they need together. The same goes for parents and children. Everybody's growing, but the relationships remain frozen. On top of that, there's the male culture of violence that the military encourages."

"So you think it's probable that Jock Pfeifer abused Nathan?"

"I'm saying it's possible. Abuse is like a snake. You see the tail, but it goes back a long way. It's possible that Jean, herself, came from an abusive situation. We can't know for sure."

"Jean was with someone today - a woman named Carol Fernandez who seemed to have a lot of influence over her." I described Carol to Pam.

"I know her. If you were more active in women's groups,

you would, too. She works as an aide to one of the legislators. She's known as someone who gets her way. She can be a real bitch. In other words, girlfriend, watch out for her."

"I'll do that," I said.

Pam said, "Good. Let's get down to the important stuff. It's Friday night. You got a date?"

"No."

"Prospects?"

"I thought I'd cruise some bars to see what I could pick up."

"Humph. Something you can't shake is what you'd pick up, Sugar."

"It's a joke, Pam."

"What about your new client? Could he shake your tree?"

"Magruder? Strictly business. Besides, he's not my type."

Pam sat back and hooted. "Hoo! In that case, he's probably good for you. I know the type you're attracted to."

"Just what kind of guy is that, Dr. Know-all-about-love?"

"Your kind of guy," said Pam, "has the taste of raw tequila in his kiss and no more than five bucks in his jeans."

"Raw tequila's just fine when it comes with a kiss," I said, hating the defensive tone I heard in my voice.

Pam shook her head. "Girlfriend, we need to talk about this, but right now I have to do some work."

We made a date for Sunday evening and I left.

The Hawaiian Tel building was close to Pam's office. I searched the reverse phone directories but the number that HARRIET translated into wasn't listed. The only thing left to do was to call it.

I got a recording. The voice, a woman's, said, "This is the Choice Action Line. Preserve your right to choose. Our counseling services are not active at this time. Our next training seminar will be Monday. If you would like to take part in the training, leave only your first name and a telephone number when you hear the tone." I listened for the tone and left my name and number.

I knew the voice on the phone, had heard it not too long

before, in fact. I got out my tape recorder, rewound it to the start and played it, now listening, now skipping ahead, until I found it. Just to make sure, I called Harriet's number again and listened to the two tapes simultaneously. There was no doubt in my mind. Sue Naito was Harriet.

4 A PROMISE TO PROTECT

Leo Laskowitz had one eye and one lung. He'd lost the eye to a shell fragment on Omaha Beach; he'd lost the lung to cancer. His trademark was a black eye patch, which coupled with his hawk's beak nose, gave him a rakish appearance. In his prime, Leo had been the dean of private investigators in three states and a relentless pursuer of Las Vegas showgirls. Then the cancer had struck, leaving him desk bound. He pared down his business to insurance investigations in the San Francisco Bay Area and an occasional foray to the Islands. As for the showgirls, he never gave up chasing the rhinestones.

Our paths had crossed from time to time when I was with the SFPD. A stand up guy, I thought. Someone I could trust. After a stint in jail, the list of men I could trust had become very short, but Leo was on it. I'd been out a day when I called him.

"I'm looking for a license to work behind," I said. "I'll do the leg work and give you a percentage of what I bring in."

"And I give you my license."

"Trust me, Leo. I'm no cowgirl."

"Yeah," he said. There was a long pause on his end. "Yeah, I could use fresh legs in Hawaii. You got the legs for it. Good looking, too." He laughed a dry, thin chuckle. "My license, your legs. That's a knockout combination, kiddo." Another long pause and he said, "I still know people there. Now and then I turn down work. Maybe I can throw some your way."

"I won't let you down, Leo."

The promise to Leo was going through my mind as I drove up to the Hotel Halekulani where he was staying. It was Leo who had connected me with Magruder. After leaving my message with Harriet, I had called him; said I had to see him.

The parking valet shot my Nissan a look filled with contempt as he reached for the door handle.

"Your tetanus shots not up to date?" I asked.

He opened the door. Disappointment chased the contempt when he saw he wouldn't even get a leg show.

"Take good care of her," I said.

He mumbled something and peeled up the ramp.

"Cafone!" Asshole! I shouted after him, Italian being my favorite language for cursing.

I made my way through an elegant open lobby, admiring the tropical plants and the soothing cascades of water. Give Leo points for style and taste. I found him, as expected, in the House Without a Key, the oldest part of the hotel, rebuilt in the style of a 1930s Waikiki beach house. Leo was sipping a martini on the open lanai when I arrived. The martini had a pepper instead of an olive. I ordered a beer.

The lanai was sunny, almost hot. My jeans felt oppressive and confining. I had an urge to peal off a layer of clothes and offer my flesh to the Waikiki sun. After a week of steady rain, the tradewinds had returned, clearing the clouds and lifting the spirits of tourists and locals alike. A dozen or more triangular sails drifted out on the water where the sun haze erased the horizon. The beach, which stretched almost to Diamond Head, was thick with people, their bodies shiny with oil. I could smell the cocoa butter up on the lanai. There was probably a slick on the water.

Leo's eye was on a pair of women walking past the seawall. Their bikinis were minimal, their slender bodies tanned and flawless. He raised his glass in a grateful salute. The pepper sloshed in the clear liquid. He winked at me. "Great invention, the Halekulani martini," he said. "My age, the senses start to go. Takes extra stimuli to wake them up. Peppers for the tongue, young women for the eye."

"So that's why you sit out here Leo?"

When Leo puts his attention on you, you feel like a curtain has dropped, cutting out the rest of the world. You feel prettier, smarter, more capable. At least I do, and I'm sure others have, too. How else to explain four ex-wives who remain loyal to him? He gave me his whole attention, the full clip.

"It's why I sit here with you. You're extra stimuli yourself, kiddo. You look good."

"Yeah? So when do you make a pass?"

"At you? What would I do if you tumbled?" His eye sparkled with humor and keen intelligence. "Haven't got the stamina for someone like you. What'd you think of him?"

"Brian Magruder? He seems like a decent guy. Committed to his profession. I'd say he doesn't have a lot of personal ambition."

Leo made a wheezing laugh. "Not for someone with the Magruder name. What he lacks is avarice."

"So tell me about the Magruders, Leo."

Leo took a big swallow of his martini. "The first Magruder was a whaler. From the East. The whaling fleet was several hundred ships in those days. Gets here and sees his chance outfitting the fleet. He borrows, barters and steals until he has enough to open a ship's chandlers." Leo took another swallow and signaled the waitress for a refill. "Eight years later, prosperous, he goes to the mainland. Gets himself a bride, brings her back and founds the clan. The children continue the business the old man started. Some branch out into ranching and planting. Have some tough times. They're Catholics and the Protestant families don't take to them. But they hold on."

"Kept the land holdings?"

"Yep. Compared to the other estates, they rank maybe seventh or eighth in size. Lot of residential leaseholds. Some of the lessees want to buy out their leases and convert to fee simple - get title to the land their houses sit on."

"Who runs the family now?"

The furrows on Leo's brow deepened and grew closer together. I sensed some strong feeling for the Magruder family. He said, "Ed Magruder, Brian's father, owns Magruder Marine. The real estate's run mostly by Kenneth, one of the twins. He's been trying to get the family out of residential land and into commercial. More money in commercial ventures."

"Kenneth, is he older than Brian?"

"Yeah. Brian's the youngest. The other twin is Frank. He's a priest. Diocesan, not an order. Didn't have to take a vow of poverty. Typical Magruder. Between the twins and Brian is Molly. She went to Vassar, married a hotshot ad exec, got the church to annul it and moved back here with a big settlement.

"I did some work for the Magruder Estate back about fifteen years ago. Can't say I care much for the Magruders, most of 'em anyway. Except for Brian. He's a good kid. Didn't take the business courses like his old man wanted, went off to New York to study drama instead. Pissed off the old man."

"And now he's an attorney."

Leo nodded. "Acting didn't work out. Want you to do something for me, kiddo. I'm counting on you. Look after him. I'd like to see him get a break."

"I won't let you down, Leo."

If ever there was a statement I meant with all my heart, it was that one.

The parking valet trotted off to get my car. He returned a few minutes later on foot.

"Won't start," he said.

"*Merda*," I said. "Just tell me where it is."

He told me the level, his face a study in smugness.

I was damp under the arms and hot under the collar when I reached the car. She gave only a hum at the turn of the key. "*Brutta befana*," I said. The Nissan didn't say anything. Obviously a language barrier. A Japanese car, she should be sworn at in Japanese, not Italian. Was it my fault I didn't know Japanese? I ran the gear shift through all five gears, an action based more on superstition than mechanical knowledge, and tried again. This time it kicked over. A new starter was at the top of my list of ways to spend the fee from Brian Magruder.

The University of Hawaii is situated at the head of Manoa Valley - "Rainbow Valley" - named for the rainbows that form in the mists that spill over the mountains. Island ecologies can produce big weather changes over short distances. It was misting in Manoa when I got there and parked, two blocks from campus.

I found the American Studies Department in a building in the middle of campus. My hair was a wreck by the time I reached it. I stopped in a ground floor restroom to squeeze out the ends and dry my face with a paper towel before seeking out the office. Mink brown is how I describe my hair color. Wet rat is how it looked in the mirror. Normally it has a lot of curls. As a teen-ager, I would despair of ever getting it under control. I've learned to live with it, however, as I have learned to live with my face - the twice-broken nose that's slightly crooked and the ever-deepening lines, like parentheses, around my mouth.

The American Studies receptionist directed me to Sue Naito's office. The nameplate said Professor Suchiko Naito. She wasn't there but a schedule on her door told me she had a class at that time. Lucky for my hair, it was in the same building.

The classroom had a hundred or more seats, about seventy-five of which were taken. I was able to slip into a back row without attracting attention. Most of the students were female.

Naito was already into her lecture. A podium in front held an open notebook, but she seldom referred to it. Instead, she roamed the areas on both sides and in front, occasionally venturing among the students, working them like a talk-show host. Her manner was lively and her face was animated. To look at her, you'd never guess the tension and fear that must have been there a few hours earlier.

The topic of the lesson seemed to be language. "Okay," she said, "so now we've made language gender-neutral. We have chairpersons instead of chairmen, police officers instead of policemen, and mail carriers instead of mailmen. See how easy it is to get rid of men?" The class enjoyed it. "We use awkward constructions like 'he/she' or 'they' where we used to use 'he'. What does that do for women?"

"It empowers us," said one student.

"How?" asked Naito.

"Well -" began the student.

"Babyshit!" said Naito. "For language to empower women we have to do more than make babyshit changes in pronouns and affixes. Language is a male construction. What does it describe? The male experience, that's what. What about the female experience? What does it mean to be female? Can anyone tell me?"

One of the handful of males in the room spoke up. "It means you get paid less for doing the same work as a man."

"The same work as a man," echoed Naito. "Why do you use the male as a reference point?" The student mumbled something. Naito said, "Because the female experience can't be described at all except where it's the same as the male's, that's why. That which is uniquely female cannot be discussed in our modern linguistic systems; as a result, men can't be made to understand what women experience and we, women, can't share the experiences among ourselves. We need a new language for women."

There was a lot of head turning and some puzzled looks on the few faces I could see. One student raised her hand timidly. "What female experiences?" she asked.

Naito said, "Example: What does a woman do in intercourse?" Silence from the class. "There's no word for it. Oh, we have lots of words for the act, but they only tell what a male does, not what a woman does. Of course, some men would say that's because women don't do anything in intercourse."

That brought a laugh from the class. I found myself liking Sue Naito. If I'd had teachers like her, I might have finished college.

Naito continued, "Take the all-time favorite, the f-word." She paused; the class waited. "Break down its meaning and you have 'penetration' plus the male organ or something similar. The other words for the act have the same meaning." Heads were nodding throughout the room. She checked her watch and said, "Think about it this weekend. We'll finish on Monday and then review for the final. If any of you can come up with a word for what women do in intercourse, I'd like to hear it."

Some students made for the doors and some for the front of the class. I waited a few minutes and then joined the small knot of students surrounding Sue Naito. When she'd finally dispensed with the last one, I said, "Professor Naito, how about protect?"

She was busy gathering papers into a notebook, but she stopped and looked up at me with curiosity. "What's that?"

"You asked for a word to describe our experience. I'd say the word is protect. That's what I do, and I believe that's what you do."

"Ah. I was referring specifically to the sex act, Ms…you're not in this class, are you?"

I gave her my card. "My name is Val Lyon. I'm working for Brian Magruder. No, I'm not in your class and I'm not here to talk about sex. My job is to make sure that Nathan Pfeifer is receiving the protection he needs. I have reason to think you know something about that."

"And what reason would that be?" Sue Naito's smile was bright and friendly, but her eyes were two dark pinpoints scanning my face.

"I've been told that someone named Harriet is looking after him. I called a certain Harriet and heard a recorded message. Your message."

"I'm afraid you're very confused. What you reached was the pregnancy counseling line, I suppose. If that's the case, I won't deny you heard my voice. We provide help for women with unwanted pregnancies. I don't know how you imagine that would have anything to do with Nathan Pfeifer."

"Professor Naito, I know that Harriet was actually a code name of sorts for an underground, radical group of women about twenty years ago. I know that many of those same women have rallied around Jean Pfeifer. Obviously, Harriet isn't defunct, though you call it pregnancy counseling. The network of contacts in the group is probably still intact. My theory is that someone in the group is hiding Nathan."

"A conspiracy of radical women. That's a novel theory," said Sue Naito. "Who did you say you work for?"

"Brian Magruder. He's representing Jean Pfeifer."

"Are you an attorney?"

"No, I'm a private investigator. I also do personal security."

She looked at me intently and what friendliness there was in her expression seemed to wither. "I have seen you. You were at the Judiciary this afternoon. In fact, weren't you in an altercation with one of the troublemakers?"

"Jean was in immediate danger and I -"

"You reacted with violence." Her tone was sharp. "I'm a feminist. Feminists oppose patriarchal systems, Ms. Lyon, and the patriarchy is maintained by violence. A feminist eschews violence and the people who use it."

Her lecture made me flush hotly. "Professor, I don't like violence and I don't seek it, but the world is full of brutal people like those punks today. Sometimes you have to use violence to protect yourself or someone else."

"You may have to, Ms. Lyon, but I don't."

"Yes, I may have to and I can do it if I have to. That's why I've been hired to protect Nathan. We're on the same side, you and I."

Sue Naito stuffed her notes and books into a large tote bag and started for the door. She said, "Ms. Lyon, we are not on the same side. You will never find me on the side of violence.".

5 HOOPS

Naito's scolding put me in a lousy frame of mind. The hell with her. I'd once called myself a feminist, too, but after I became a cop, it didn't matter to me. The people on the street didn't care about your philosophy - they'd hurt you just the same. They'd hurt you more than Sue Naito could.

It was about a quarter to five when I reached the Waikiki studio I call home. The layout from back to front is bathroom, kitchen, main room, and lanai. A high counter separates the kitchen from the main room. From the lanai, I get a partial view, between the high rises, of Ala Wai Canal. The apartment comes furnished with a sofabed, one end table and lamp, a bar stool, and a chest of drawers. A bargain at $650 a month. I supplied my own deck chairs and hammock for the lanai. In the narrow hall that runs past my bathroom and kitchen, I keep my athletic shoes - thirteen pairs in all. Ask me what parts of my body are most important and I'll tell you my feet.

I deposited Magruder's folder on the end table and changed into cut-off sweat pants and a loose T-shirt, strapped a soft brace around my knee and laced on a pair of high tops. A rolled bandana headband and sunscreen completed the outfit. The warrior woman girds for battle. Basketball under my arm, I headed for Paki Park.

Outside the building were a couple of kids who lived on my floor. One of them said, "Chee, lady, ain' you kinda old fo' play li' dat?"

"Not on your life," I said.

I discovered basketball in tenth grade. While the other girls had ambitions of leading cheers, I had ambitions of drawing them. I also hoped it would please my mother. I did a lot to please her in those days. Little good it did. Like me, mother believed that erasing the inequity between men's and women's athletics was important. Her tactic was marching and demonstrating; mine was playing. I don't think she ever saw me play. Playing my best (and some help from Title IX) earned me a part scholarship to junior college and, later, to a four-year college. My dream shot came when I signed on to play pro basketball in Italy. The dream lasted just one season, but at least I had it. A lot of women don't. The fact that a lot of talented women could not play in their own country for so many years pisses me off.

The only person on the court was a firefighter named Kalani Daggett. Kalani was stationed at the firehouse next to the park and was always good for a game if he wasn't on a call. He'd had a run at the pros after making all-WAC two years in a row at BYU. He'd been picked up by the Knicks, but gave it up after three seasons because he found New York winters not to his liking. Kalani was built like an NBA power forward, but his face and his heart were all Hawaiian. He played playground ball in his bare feet.

Kalani gave me the kind of workout I enjoy. I like the feel of tired muscles after a match. I like the smell of my sweat. We played make it and take it and I had a good day. I burned him with a couple of twenty-footers and then worked it down low.

He said, "What you think you're doin'? You know you can't jump. You can't shoot. Those Air Jordan's you wear, they cost you what? A hundred dollars? I can jump higher'n you an' I ain't got any."

He toyed with my psyche for the umpteenth time while I backed cautiously towards the basket. It was then that I saw

Magruder jogging down the street. He waved and turned into the park.

Showtime!

"You're a chump," said Kalani. "C'mon, let's see you put a move on me. Let's just see it."

I spun around, made a quick crossover dribble from my right hand to my left, slipped my foot past him and floated towards the basket with the ball on my fingertips, cocked behind my ear. He lunged for the ball. At the last possible moment, I brought the ball down to my waist and flipped it upward, two-handed. It skidded in.

"In your face," I said.

"It's your tits that was in my face. You look like a wet T-shirt champ."

"And you played like your jockstrap was wrapped around your ankles."

"Hey, bravo, nice move," called Magruder. He came over and I made the introductions. "I used to watch you play," he said to Kalani. "What was it, ten years ago?" To me he said, "You put a move like that on a pro!"

"Takes a pro to play a pro," said Kalani. "Nex' time, tida, I beat you. Laters." He slapped my hand and shook Magruder's before heading off.

Magruder whistled. "You played pro? Where?"

"A place called Schio, in Italy. What brings you here?"

"I was jogging by and saw you. Isn't that a coincidence?"

I took the ball to a bench near the court. Magruder joined me. I said, "You just happened to be jogging by. Your normal route?"

"Well, actually, some kids at your building told me you were here. Want a beer? Say yes."

"Yes, but I'm all sweaty and I reek. Anyplace that would let me in, the way I look, would be below my standards." Anyplace that would let either of us in, for that matter. Magruder had on baggy walking shorts, a faded polo shirt and a terry cloth golf hat. He had headphones around his neck.

He said, "Not to worry. I've got the beer." He pulled two cans out of the pockets of his shorts and opened one. I shielded my face against an eruption but there was just a little ooze of foam.

"You didn't run very fast," I said.

"Hell, you saw me run. Would that shake anything? Here," he said. He opened the other one for himself.

"You didn't run far, either. It's still cold."

"Jeez, I confess, I didn't run far; I didn't run fast. I took the Lindbergh baby, too. You think I'd try to put something over on a detective?"

"You always run with a beer?"

"Two beers. One in each pocket for balance."

I made an adjustment to my knee brace. Magruder noticed and said, "Want some aspirin?" He pulled a small bottle out of his back pocket. "How about ice?" He lifted his hat to reveal a plastic ice bag, dripping with perspiration.

"My God, Magruder! You carry all that when you run?"

"Yes, ma'am. I also have bus money."

"You're crazy," I said. "You know, you shouldn't wear headphones. You lose awareness of your surroundings with them. You're the one who got a death threat. If you don't want me looking after you, at least look after yourself."

"Good safety tip," he said. "Drive you home? My car's just down the block. We can finish the beers on the way."

"Sure. Why do I get the feeling you weren't really interested in exercise?"

"Okay, truth time. I just wanted to see you. How about dinner? We can get some takeout and find a beach park. You won't have to change."

I didn't have to think long before agreeing. Maybe he was my client, but it wasn't a date. It wasn't like I had to dress or anything. It was important, I reasoned, to get to know my client.

Magruder's car was a late-model Lexus - just what you'd expect for a young attorney, but it seemed wrong for him, like a tuxedo on a bear. I looked through the window at the leather interior and demurred because of my damp clothes, but he insisted.

Before getting in, I checked underneath for bombs or other evidence of tampering. "Any more death threats?" I asked.

"Tell me what you think of this." He handed me a manila folder. Inside was a letter addressed to Jean in care of Brian Magruder. No return address. "It came by courier. The guard in the building signed for it."

The letter said, "From a concerned friend. The situation could become explosive if you keep hiding the kid."

I gave the letter back to Brian. "Explosive, huh? The guy's got a hard-on for bombs."

"That's one interpretation," said Brian. "There's no explicit reference to a bomb. This could be nothing more than paranoia."

"A little paranoia might keep you alive, Brian. First a creep with a rock tries to hurt Jean. Now we've got two death threats. You and Jean need someone watching your back."

"You, right? Val, Jean's safe for now and I can look after myself."

I decided to drop that argument, as I sensed that Magruder was digging in his heels. I said, "Jock Pfeifer's the one who wants Nathan. Even if that wasn't him on the phone, I have to believe he's involved. I'd like to meet him."

"We could both go," said Brian. "I'll arrange it. What'd you find out today?"

I told him what I'd learned from Pam and explained my theory that a group of women, sympathetic to Jean's cause, were hiding Nathan.

"How organized are these women?"

"I don't know. I'm going to find out more about Sue Naito and who she associates with. Then there's Carol Fernandez. I should talk to her again."

I had no more information to report. We were silent a moment and then Brian said, "Schio. That's near Vicenza, right?" He went on to tell me about the summer he'd spent in Italy. You'd think we'd have had a lot in common, but, in truth, our experiences couldn't have been less alike. He'd gone for his brother's ordination in Rome. I'd gotten to Italy on the strength of my *tiro in sospensione* - my jump shot. An enthusiastic traveler, he'd seen as many churches, palaces and Roman ruins as one person could see in a few months. I'd seen mostly the insides of arenas and locker rooms. Where Brian had absorbed the culture from well-placed Italians, I'd absorbed some of the language from the fans and players. I managed to avoid embarrassing myself by letting him do the talking.

Brian knew a Korean restaurant that specialized in takeout. We'd just pulled into the lot when the car phone beeped. He picked it up. I waited.

One of my nosy qualities is that I listen to people on the phone. It's almost an instinct with me. Although it has gotten me in trouble on more than one occasion, it's also gotten me a lot of information. I couldn't make out the words, but the caller's voice was in the female registers.

Brian said, "Molly! How are you?"

Molly would be the sister Leo had mentioned. I seized that conclusion with a feeling of relief and then wondered why I should feel that way. Brian said, "Now? Sure. Why not?" He hung up. "My sister," he said. "She's found some lamps she thinks will look good in my office and wants my opinion. Want to come along?"

"I should change first. I wouldn't want anyone to see me like this."

"Aw, come on. It's just Molly and it's after hours. Molly practically lives in gym clothes. I'm not changing. We can eat afterwards."

"Okay," I said, knowing I'd regret it.

6 FULL COURT PRESS

The elevator doors opened onto a hallway crowded with people. Men in dress shirts, a few in suits. Women in dresses and elegant muumuus. Someone said, "Here he is, now." And someone else said, "It's about time, Brian. They won't open the champagne without you."

"Jesus," said Brian.

"I wouldn't be surprised," I said. "Elvis, too, I'll bet."

We stepped off the elevator and a woman draped a flower lei around his neck. "Surprise, Brian," she said. "A toast, everybody, to Brian Magruder, up-and-coming attorney at law."

I looked at Brian's face. He smiled gamely through the toasts and applause but his eyes searched for a place to hide.

"Molly!" he said. "This is your doing isn't it? You shouldn't."

"Oh Brian, we just want to help you celebrate your new office." She stuck her chin at me. "Who's this?"

Brian's eyes lost their hunted look. "Val, meet my sister, Molly Gallagher."

Molly was half of Brian's size. She had the gaunt, hollowed look some women get from too much fasting and exercise. Probably a full-time job to stay a size six, and the size six she was wearing would have taken two full-time jobs to afford. I held out my hand, conscious of my own playground attire. She took it gingerly after a moment's hesitation. "Nice to meet you," she said. "Brian, don't neglect your guests. Dan's here." She grabbed his arm and dragged him away.

"Make yourself at home, Val," he said over his shoulder. "I'll be right back."

Not likely, I thought. From the reverential tone in Molly's voice, I guessed that "Dan" meant the senator.

A buffet table and a bar occupied the space half way down the hall. I loaded up a plate with chicken wings, wontons and some little sausages. I skipped the vegetables, the sashimi, too. Sharks can eat their fish raw, but not me. At the bar, I poured myself some Scotch and went into Brian's office.

I noticed, as I went in, that someone had replaced the five-by-eight card with a heavy brass plaque. I felt sure Brian hadn't done it. Inside, the receptionist's office and the middle conference room were jammed with people. The few chairs were taken and most of the other surfaces were covered with gifts. Brian was in the outer office surrounded by a throng of people. He spotted me and waved. I raised my glass to him and continued to his inner office.

The door was about three-quarters closed. I pushed it open and went in. Two men were having a conversation - one stood by the window looking out over downtown and the other sat in the big chair behind the desk. The one by the window seemed to be doing the talking while the other one swiveled back and forth in the chair. They turned their heads in my direction.

"Sorry," I said. "Didn't mean to interrupt. If this is private, I'll find someplace else."

"No, no. Stay," said the man by the window. He had a trim, youthful figure. A few streaks of gray at his temples put him in his forties. Something about his features seemed familiar.

The man in the chair also seemed familiar. The way he looked me up and down reminded me of the creeps who always managed to get seats on the floor of women's games, or who would wait near the locker rooms to grab a feel from an athlete. He confirmed it when he opened his mouth. He said, "Hoo, I like sweaty girls." He flashed the other man a sly grin.

I have a standard response to creeps like him. "*Coglione, vaffanculo!*" It came out of my mouth without thought. One of my favorite Italian expressions, usually accompanied by a raised forearm and fist. I'd have thrown the forearm if I hadn't been holding a plate of hors d'oeuvres. Anything to save a wonton.

The guy in the chair stared blankly, but the man by the window laughed. "Ah, the language of Puccini. She wants you to go fuck yourself, prick," he translated. To me he said, "*Un coglionaccio di prima classe. Un testa di merda.*"

"A first class prick. A shit head," I translated. Puccini scholar, me too.

Shit head scowled, knitting his thick eyebrows together. I'd seen that scowl before. It had been under a cap this afternoon.

I said, "You were downtown at the rally, today, taking pictures."

He shot an angry look at the man by the window, opened his mouth to say something and thought better of it. He stood up and went to he door. "Fuck it!" he said over his shoulder. "I goin' grind."

"It's my curse," I said. "People just fall in love with me."

"Don't worry about Art. His comment was crude and uncalled for. He had it coming but he'll get over it."

I wasn't at all worried about Art, but I nodded agreeably and took the chair he'd vacated. The guy at the window had a peculiar way of smiling that crinkled the corners of his eyes. Brian smiled the same way. But the similarity didn't end there. He was leaner than Brian, but with the same bone structure. The realization came to me in a rush that I was talking to Brian's brother and that he understood my off-color Italian. This had to be the brother who'd studied in Rome. I nearly choked on my wonton.

"You must be Monsignor Magruder," I said between coughs.

"Call me Frank. And you are?"

"Call me Val."

"Well, Val, would you like to continue in Italian?"

"I'll pass. I've already shown you half of my vocabulary."

"What about the other half?"

"The other half makes me blush."

"Really?" Frank Magruder had on dark dress slacks, black loafers and a muted Hawaiian shirt. Formal wear, island style. "So how do you know Brian, Val?"

"He hired me for consultation."

"Legal consultation?"

"No, security consultation, investigative work, stuff like that."

His eyes widened in interest. "Stuff like that." he echoed. "You're an investigator?" I could only nod, my mouth being full of chicken wing. "A private investigator?" I nodded again. "Interesting. What do you investigate for Brian?"

"Whatever he asks me to."

Frank Magruder hitched up his pants leg and hoisted his hip onto the window sill. "I suppose it has to do with the Pfeifer case."

As it wasn't a question, I chose not to respond to it. I sipped the Scotch and offered my plate to him. "I'm forgetting my manners, Frank. Would you like some? Try the chicken wings. They're good."

He looked at me curiously and smiled, "Are all detectives as cagey as you?"

"Some are," I said.

"And some aren't. You're harder to pin down than a Thomistic scholar."

"I don't like being pinned down at all. What's your connection to ...to that *testa di merda* who just left?"

"Art Spinoza? Don't judge him too harshly. He's crude, but he's not really a shithead. He had a rough tour in Nam, got himself into trouble when he came home, but now he's straightening himself out. Ken, my other brother, hires him for marina construction and maintenance."

"I take it your ministry is saving people like Spinoza?"

"Why not? The apostles were a rather crude sort, themselves."

"Apostles, my ass! Don't let the Monsignor snow you, Val." I turned to see Brian standing in the doorway. He crossed the room with his hand outstretched. They shook hands warmly. "Frank hasn't saved a soul in years. His mission field is church politics."

"And a very dangerous one it is, little brother."

"What kind of church politics?" I asked.

"Frank's chief secretary of the American Bishop's Commission on the Status of Women," said Brian with obvious pride. "Be careful what you say around Frank. He's going to be a bishop someday, maybe soon, and then he'll have even more influence to throw around."

A prudent person would have kept her mouth shut, but I was still smarting from Sue Naito's remarks and felt combative. I said, "Don't you find it ironic that women have no influence in the church, but a man can gain a lot of influence from a commission on the status of women?"

Frank responded quickly, "You're wrong in thinking women have no influence in the church. Quite the opposite. The bishops see women as having a unique and special role."

"Special role! That just shows they still don't get it."

"Oh, we get it. The American bishops are sympathetic to the condition of women in this country. What would you have us do to convince you we get it, Val?"

"How about birth control?" I said. "Drop the opposition to it."

"That's not so easily done. The church's opposition didn't arise out of nothing. It's based on centuries of inquiry into natural law."

"By men who never had to worry about the consequences of pregnancy. Get a bishop knocked up and see what they say."

"The word of God is eternal, but it's interpreted by men. Excuse me, persons." He made a wan smile. "Who's to say? Perhaps if the Pope were a woman we'd have a different interpretation. A ms-interpretation, if you will."

"Then ordain some women so we can find out."

Frank spread his hands helplessly. "It may happen someday," he said. "But the church has gotten along fine for twenty centuries without ordaining women. All I can do is counsel patience and assure you that I do take this commission seriously. In the meantime, Val, you're a worthy adversary. I hope we can go a few more rounds someday."

Three more people came into the room. One was an oriental man, about sixty. He was followed by Molly Gallagher. Last came Frank Magruder's double. They had different clothes but everything else about them was the same, down to the gray on the temples. Kenneth Magruder, I assumed. It was confirmed for me a second later when Brian introduced us.

We shook hands. Even up close it would be hard to tell the two older Magruder brothers apart. The one difference was a little mush of scar tissue on Ken's chin that was absent from Frank's.

Ken Magruder introduced the other man as Newton Yoshiki. I seemed to be the only one who didn't know Yoshiki. There was no mention of Yoshiki's connection to the Magruders.

Molly Gallagher said, "Val, you don't mind if I take you away from these men, do you? Is that okay with you, Brian? I'll bring her back, I promise."

She didn't wait for Brian's assent. Nor mine. I followed her, curious as to this sudden friendliness. Outside she said, "I hope you didn't think me rude earlier. I'm sure you do and I don't blame you, but Dan…" She used that reverential tone again as though he were a rock star. ". . . could only stay a few minutes and I know Brian wanted to talk to him. And then the way Brian looked when he came - like a slob. I'm sorry, I hope I'm not hurting your feelings. I don't mean anything about the way you're dressed. Brian needs to pay attention to appearance in his profession. Yours, I guess, you don't. Did that sound awful? I didn't mean it that way. You could wear almost anything and you'd look good. You like to work out don't you?"

"Now and then."

We were working our way through the throng of people in

the hallway. Molly leading and hanging onto my arm. I was finding her friendliness oppressive.

She said, "I knew you did. I should get you into my aerobics class. We have the best time and the instructor's great, just great. You come out completely exhausted. I mean completely. I know you'd just love her. We could do lunch afterwards."

I stopped and pulled back my arm. "Mrs. Gallagher, what's this all about? We don't even know each other but you're acting like I'm marrying into the family."

A mix of emotions, hurt and anger, took control of her face for an instant. They were replaced by a look of sheepishness. She said, "Val, I'm sorry. You're right, I'm going on and on like we're sisters. Call me Molly, please. What's this about you asked? Brian, of course. He's finally settling down and making something of himself, but he still needs someone to guide him. Do you know he could have been a clerk for the Chief Justice of the Hawaii Supreme Court? He turned it down." She grabbed my arm again and said, close to my face, "He turned down the Chief Justice. Can you imagine?"

I was getting a better appreciation of Brian. I didn't need to listen to Molly going on about the awful creatures he associated with in the P.D.'s office to understand what the family felt about that.

Molly cut into my thoughts. "Val, I want you to do all of us a favor. Look after him, will you?"

"Brian's a grown man, Molly. He doesn't need looking after." We were near the bar and I felt I needed another drink. I stopped and filled a glass with Scotch, reclaiming my arm from Molly. "He's got himself an important case. I'm sure he'll be famous when he wins this one."

Molly Gallagher's expression became solemn. She said, "It's a lurid, tabloid case. Why, there were a thousand people downtown today demonstrating about it."

More like three hundred, I thought. I almost told her I was one of them - the words were in my mouth. Instead, I did the wise thing and sipped my drink.

"It will bring him notoriety, not fame," she said. "But I

suppose it's too late to do anything about it." She sighed. "Listen, Val, we can't let this case run away with him. Just help us keep an eye on him. I know you're just starting your own investigation business."

Uh oh, here it comes, I thought, the big pitch.

The pitch was a suggestion that some of the security services at Magruder Marine could be thrown my way. "It's a perfect arrangement, Val. Brian spoke highly of you, and I thought, well, it can't be easy for you, a woman starting out by yourself, and there's no reason why we can't cooperate with each other. What are girlfriends for?"

"I didn't know we were girlfriends. Did we get pinned or something?"

Molly chewed at the inside of her cheek, trying to decide if I was being witty, then gave me a tight smile. "That's funny. Oh look, here's Brian. I meant it about lunch."

On the way back to Waikiki after the open house, I said, "The pow-wow with your brothers, is that something I should know about?"

"Oh that. They're not sure I can handle the Pfeifer case or that I should. They'd like me to bring in old Newt Yoshiki, the family attorney, as a consultant. The trouble is, Jock Pfeifer's involved in other legal battles with the estate and Newt's handling the estate's interest in those suits. It might confuse the issues to get Yoshiki involved."

"What sort of legal battles?"

"Oh, it gets rather complicated, but it goes something like this - Jock has a store in a strip mall built by the estate, on estate land. It's the Windward Cove Center. His lease is coming up for renewal and, like most other leases, it's being raised to market value. He's been getting a bargain in a lease for several years now because land prices have gone up so fast but the estate's been locked into a fixed lease. Jock doesn't see it that way. He claims the estate is trying to force him out because of the porno bust. In retaliation, he's organized the other tenants of the mall and has initiated condemnation proceedings to get the land in fee."

"So they want to unite the front against Pfeifer by working with you on Jean's case?"

"Right."

"What'd you say?"

"I'm not out to burn Jock Pfeifer. I just want justice for Jean and Nathan. So I said no. It was tough, though. My brothers worked me pretty hard."

"It was a full court press, Brian. While they were triple teaming you, Molly was covering me in the backcourt. She offered to throw some security work my way."

"Really?" said Brian.

"Really," I said. "Curious, isn't it?"

7 *AD FEMINAM* ATTACKS

Brian wanted to continue the evening, but I declined. What I wanted, I said, was the long soak in the tub I should have had hours before. It was a few minutes after nine when he dropped me off. Before getting out of the car, I reminded him of the threat and made him promise to look out for himself. I said, "I'll call you tomorrow when I know something about Nathan."

Once inside my apartment, I peeled out of my clothes and ran a hot bath. I slid in up to my chin and let the water do its work on my tired muscles. Some anthropologists think that humankind is descended from water apes and that the female ape was the most at home in the water. According to the people who know these things, the water ape theory explains why we don't have body hair and why we make love on our backs. They have degrees so they should know. As for me, I attribute my preferences in lovemaking to sixteen years of experience, but I'll accept their explanation for why I like the water. Showers are great for massaging sore muscles, but real relaxation requires a tub.

My relaxed thoughts turned to Brian. Poor Brian! How did he survive in a family like that? The look on his face as we got off the elevator said it all. I thought of that look on his face and then I thought of his soft brown eyes, the kind of eyes my mother associated with honesty. "Brown eyes don't lie," she'd say. Usually she'd follow that statement with a regret that mine were blue.

Brian Magruder was getting to me. He was a nice guy, funny and intelligent. Something about his little boy nature, his lack of concern for his own safety aroused a protective instinct in me. Was that the only instinct he aroused, or was there a more basic one? Since going to prison, there hadn't been many opportunities to be with men except for the guys on the basketball court. A couple of beers in the pocket isn't the same as tequila-flavored kisses, but it's a start.

It was a dangerous idea. He was, after all, my client. I covered my face with a wet washcloth and tried to drive the idea out of my mind. The ringing of my phone was more successful at it than my own efforts. Thinking it was Leo or Pam, or even Brian, I went to answer it, trailing water through my hall and kitchen.

It was Sue Naito and she was angry. She said, "I find myself being harassed, Ms. Lyon, and I hold you to blame."

I shucked off my annoyance at having been called out of my bath. "What harassment?" I asked.

"I've spoken to Carol Fernandez and she told me about your part in that attack by the hooligans this afternoon."

"My only part was to protect my client. You weren't there so don't try to tell me what to do. I've had nine years of experience on the streets as a police officer. I believe I handled the problem correctly."

"When all you have is a hammer, all your problems look like nails. There are other ways to deal with people like that. I told you in my class that violence is not an acceptable solution. In the long run it just leads to more violence."

I was dripping wet and my bath water was getting cool. My stock of patience, never in plentiful supply to begin with, was nearly depleted. I said, "What's your point, Professor?"

"Someone has left a threatening message on my answering machine. It proves my point about violence leading to more violence. You beat up a young man at the rally and now his group threatens me. They must think we're associated."

"It could be coincidence," I said without conviction.

"It is not coincidence," she said. Her tone was sharp. "The two messages - yours and this other one - were back to back."

"Professor, was this call to your personal number or to Harriet?"

"It was to Harriet."

"Well, I don't think it was those hooligans, as you call them. They didn't seem bright enough to make the connection between you and the organization. What was the message?"

"The message was, 'If it's choice you want, here's one: Turn over the kid or you'll be sorry.' It was a man. If not the hooligans, then who could it be? Until now we've never had any threats directed at us."

"Professor Naito, I don't know who's behind this, but it is more than a few punks. Brian Magruder got a death threat yesterday, before the rally and before I called you. Jean Pfeifer also received a threat."

There was a long pause and then she said, "My caller didn't say anything about death." She sounded frightened.

"I'd like to hear the tape."

"When?" she asked.

"I'll come now."

"Yes. Before Harry gets home. I don't want him to worry."

I hadn't finished my bath and my hair felt grungy. I hate dirty hair. If Naito hadn't sounded frightened at the mention of the death threat, I might have shampooed before leaving. Instead, I dried off and dressed quickly in shorts and a knit top. Pulled my hair back into a ponytail and grabbed my bag with the recorder and Brian's tape for comparison. To my relief, the Nissan started on the first try.

Sue Naito lived on Maunaloa Street in Kaimuki. Getting out of Waikiki by car on a Friday night was a bitch. Once out, it wasn't much better. Traffic on Kapahulu ground slowly, and, since I wasn't very familiar with Kaimuki, I did a lot of backtracking and circling before I found Maunaloa. To top it off, Maunaloa didn't go through between 12th and 15th streets and I had to do more circling. It was a few minutes after ten when I reached her house.

Kaimuki is a neighborhood of old homes and mature trees. You can tell the older neighborhoods by the abundance of trees - especially avocado and mango. The yuppies in the newer neighborhoods don't care for the mess from fruit trees. Sue Naito had two big ones flanking her front walk. I couldn't be sure what kind they were unless the fruit dropped on me. The trees cast a heavy shadow over broad concrete steps leading up to a large front porch which ran the width of the house. Naito's house was a two-story made of wood and lava rock. Lights were visible behind some of the windows.

The echoes of my footsteps as I mounted the steps resonated off the wall and ceiling. I rang the doorbell and heard it chime far back in the house. No one answered, so I rang again. Still no answer. I rapped on the door. It moved. Instinctively, I jumped back a step. Nothing worse than a door that's open when it shouldn't be. I stretched out my arm and pushed cautiously on the door. It opened farther. "Professor Naito," I called. "Sue, are you there?" No answer.

I opened the door wider and looked in. I could see into the entrance hall, the living room on one side and part of the dining room on the other. Empty. I took two steps into the hall and looked around. A shadow in the living room startled me and I nearly screamed. Nothing but an unadorned Christmas tree. I called Sue's name and this time I heard a noise from somewhere in the back of the house. Just a brief, indistinct sound like a gasp or a groan. Once again I called for Sue Naito but received no answer.

The house had it's own olfactory signature as old homes always do. I caught the pine tang from the tree, the fresh smell of cleaning fluids and furniture polish, and a myriad other inviting smells.

There was nothing inviting about the sound I'd heard.

Straight ahead was a short, narrow hallway. Beyond that was the kitchen. I could see kitchen cabinets and another doorway. The noise seemed to have come from that area. Maybe it came from outside the house. The windows were open. The sound could've been an animal. There was only one way to find out. I could feel the little hairs on the back of my neck standing up under my collar. I wished for a weapon but the gun fairy failed to appear.

The kitchen was clean, spacious and empty. I called again and my voice sounded too loud. As if in answer, the refrigerator motor kicked in behind me. My heart nearly burst through my chest. Three doors led out of the kitchen. One to the outside, one to the dining room. The third door was open. From where I stood in the middle of the kitchen, I could see books neatly arranged on tall shelves and a closed filing cabinet. I went to the door and peeked cautiously through, my heart beating uncomfortably fast. Sue Naito was prostrate on the floor. No one else was in the room.

I dropped down on my knees beside her. Sue's head was turned towards me. Her lips were blue. Likewise her fingernails. She didn't have a pulse. I'd seen enough heart attacks to recognize yet another one. I turned her over and began CPR. The procedure came back to me automatically as if a tape were being played in my head: compress the sternum, release, count out loud. One and two and three and four. I did fifteen compression cycles and followed with two rescue breaths, checking her pulse at the same time. Behind me on the desk was a phone. I pulled it to the floor and dialed 911.

The dispatcher's voice came through the receiver on the floor and I shouted, "I have a cardiac arrest. Send an ambulance. The location is -" Suddenly I blanked. "Maunaloa Street," I said, "between 16th and 17th. I don't remember the number."

"We have the number," he said. "Can you administer CPR?"

"Yes, but I'm not getting anything."

"Someone will be there soon."

I continued the chest compression. My arms ached from the effort. My face was oiled with sweat. Several ribs cracked in her chest. It happens sometimes. If she lived they'd heal. But she still wasn't breathing. A mouse was forming over her right eye. Probably where she hit the floor when she fainted.

"Breathe, Sue, please," I said.

I felt for her pulse again and thought I detected one - a faint one. At the same time I heard someone come into the room behind me. They're here, I thought. My second thought was that it hadn't taken them long to get here. They must've been close by. Fatigue, relief, and other pent up emotions surged through me. I almost cried.

"You'll make it, Sue," I said. "Thank God you guys got here. I don't think I could've held out much longer."

I felt a rush of air by my ear and saw an explosion of light behind my eyes. Then the lights went out.

8 DEATH OF A FEMINIST

God, what a hangover! What the hell had I been drinking? Whose party was it? There were people around me but they didn't sound like they were having fun. I opened my eyes. A bad thing to do. The light in the room was too bright. I seemed to be looking right into its source. I turned my head away. Another bad thing to do. The movement let loose a wrecking ball inside my head.

I eased myself up, getting help from somebody with strong arms. All I could see was his white jacket since I dared not move my head. He guided me backwards until I felt something solid behind my shoulders.

I knew that sooner or later I would throw up. It happened sooner and I felt better when it was over.

The guy who'd helped me handed me some water. He wore a white jacket with a patch on the sleeve, but its outline was blurry. So was the man in the jacket. He peered into my face, lifting first one eyelid and then the other. He asked me my name, the date, and the name of the President of the United States. Tough questions, but I passed.

"My name's Greg," he said. "Relax, but don't go to sleep on us. You've probably got yourself a concussion."

A rush of memories came back to me - finding Sue,

performing CPR and calling 911. After that, nothing. "How's Sue? Will she live?"

Several people were huddled over Sue Naito's form, a few feet from me. They seemed to be working furiously, but she showed no sign of movement.

Greg said, "We're doing our best."

I felt compelled to tell what happened, to be doing something. Afraid of slipping into unconsciousness. Talking required all the effort I could summon, but it helped me hang on to reality. "I found her on the floor like that. She wasn't breathing. Tried CPR. Working on her when you guys came in. Who hit me? One of you guys?"

My vision was improving. Greg turned to another man in a similar jacket and gave him a quizzical look. The other man shrugged in response. Greg said to me, "You were out cold when we arrived. Mrs. Davison was under you. Are you the one who called?"

I nodded carefully - very carefully. "Her name is Ms. Naito."

"Okay, how long was it between the time you found Ms. Naito and the time you called?"

"A few minutes. I think I had a pulse."

"She didn't have one when we got here. Lower your head a bit." Greg pulled back my hair from behind my ear and examined the injury. "Could be worse," he said. "Blood, but no clear fluid. That's what we worry about." He placed a dressing over the wound working quickly and efficiently, but not gently.

"Ouch! Your bedside manner sucks."

That brought a smile from him. "Good," he said. "The ones who bitch get better."

Two cops came into the room, looking around and conferring with one of the other EMTs. One of the cops - young, with a round face and glasses - came over to Greg. He said, "This the woman who called in?"

"My name's Lyon. I found Ms. Naito."

"You got some whack on the head. How'd you get it?"

"I don't know. Someone hit me from behind."

"You live around here? A neighbor?"

"No."

"You feel like answering some questions, Miss Lyon?"

"No, but that hasn't kept you from asking."

Just then another man came into the room. He was tall and thin with stooped shoulders and a prominent adam's apple. His hair was unruly and dark. He looked to be in his sixties.

"Sue!" he said. "Somebody tell me what happened."

He turned out to be Harold Davison, Sue Naito's husband. He tried to force his way into the group working on his wife, but the cop held him back. One of the paramedics questioned him about her medical history. Davison said she had a heart condition. At the medic's request, he went to get her medicine.

It was too crowded in the room and I decided to leave, but a wave of nausea and dizziness swept over me when I stood up. I had to support myself on Sue's desk. It was her desk I'd been leaning against. Judging from the clutter of papers and folders, she was very disorganized. Somewhat like me. Besides the papers, the desk held three photographs in frames, a calculator, a pen and pencil set, a phone and an answering machine. The lid was up. I stared at the spindles and heads, trying to focus my thoughts.

Greg interrupted me. "What are you doing?" he asked.

"Going home," I said.

"No, you're not. You're going to the hospital with us. The doctors will decide if you can go home."

I looked over at Sue's form. The EMTs had lifted her onto a stretcher and were wheeling her out of the room. The cop who'd questioned me came and took my elbow.

"C'mon," he said. "They'll take care of you at the emergency room." He started to lead me out.

"My bag." I looked around for it but didn't see it. The effort caused my head to ache more. I thought I'd dropped it by the desk when I found Sue. It wasn't there now. Maybe by the file cabinet. Some of the drawers were open.

The cop wanted me to leave. He said, "I'll find it and bring it to you."

I went reluctantly.

I sat with Harold Davison in the ambulance while the medics continued to work on Sue. There was an air of desperation about their efforts. Davison didn't say much. He sat hunched over with his head in his hands. I put my arm around his shoulder to comfort him.

"You have grandchildren?" I asked, thinking of the photos on the desk.

"Yes. Sue was…is devoted to them."

His shoulders shook and he sobbed quietly. So much for comfort. The ride to the hospital seemed long. The medics continued to work, but I sensed it was over for Sue before we arrived. Davison sensed it, too.

At the hospital, a doctor examined my head wound and a nurse cleaned and dressed it. Only the skin was broken. My vision was still a little blurry so he ordered me kept for observation. Now and then someone came to check on me to make sure I hadn't passed into unconsciousness. I guess they had ways of telling.

The cop came to ask me a few more questions. Was she unconscious when I found her? How'd I get in? Was she expecting me and why?

I told him she'd received a threatening message on her answering machine. "The tape's gone," I said, recalling what it was that had seemed odd to me back at her house.

"You have any idea where it might be?"

"I'd say the guy who hit me has it. He's probably the one who left the message. Maybe he killed her, took the tape, and was still in the house when I showed up."

"You suggesting she was the victim of foul play and not a heart attack?"

"Look," I pointed to the bandage on my head. "This is foul play. Doesn't that suggest foul play for her, too?"

"Does anybody else know about the message?" he asked.

"No, but my client received a similar one. That tape was in my purse."

"We didn't find your purse," he said.

"Then the guy took that, too."

He had me describe the purse and its contents. Besides the tape, I'd lost my wallet, keys, ID, my recorder and about thirty dollars in cash.

"No credit cards?"

"No," I said. As an ex-felon, my credit rating was zilch. I didn't see a need to burden him with my credit problems.

The cop had me sign the report and left. Shortly after that, the doctor came to look in my eyes again. He pronounced me fit to leave. I went out to the waiting room and sat for awhile, unable to shake the thought that I'd had something to do with Sue Naito's death. I watched for Davison to come through because I wanted to tell him that I really had done my best to save her. I doubted that would give him much comfort, but it might diminish my own sense of guilt. After half an hour of waiting, however, a profound weariness took control of me and I gave up hope. I called Pam. She came to get me around ten minutes to three

9 BREAK-IN

Pam said, "I hope that bandage is on good and tight because you can't afford to lose any more brains. What possessed you to go in that house anyway?"

"Curiosity," I said. "The door was open and I heard a noise inside. Besides, she had asked me over and she did sound frightened on the phone. And don't give me any shit about it because you knew she was Harriet and you wouldn't tell me. Now where the hell do you keep your wine?" I was rampaging through Pam's kitchen, yanking open cabinet doors and slamming them shut.

"Val, alcohol isn't such a good idea after a head injury. You can't tell how -"

"Don't tell me," I yelled, "what's a good idea and what's not. You didn't get your head bashed in. You didn't lose somebody in CPR. You didn't…you didn't…" I felt myself starting to shake all over. Yelling made my head hurt more.

Pam put her arms on my shoulders. She said, "I don't want to find you in a coma come morning, girl, that's all."

"The way I feel, a coma would be nice."

"I know." She held me close.

The thought of a head injury was enough to fill me with dread. What if the headache never goes away? Or the blurred vision?

What if there's a delayed effect? A loss of control of muscles or functions? What if?

"Pam, if you do find me in a coma, take a plastic bag and finish me."

"Can't do, sugar. You're gonna be okay. You still want that wine?" I told her "no." She got out linens and made up the couch for me. "I'll get you a nightgown," she said.

"I'll be fine without it."

"I'll get you one anyway. I've got a guest."

"Oh."

The gown was flannel. It had a high collar and little pink and blue flowers. I said, "Pam, this isn't your style."

"Damn right!" she said. "The only woman with any style sleeping in this house is gonna be me."

Obediently, I put on the gown and curled up on the couch. I hadn't worn a nightgown since junior high when I began to wrest control of my life from my mother. In my dream, she wore a smile of victory and looked remarkably like Pam.

Kitchen sounds and the smell of coffee. I rolled over, not sure where I was. The movement brought the tender spot behind my ear into contact with the pillow, causing a sharp jolt of pain. I sat up recognizing Pam's apartment. According to my watch, it was mid-morning. My head felt heavy. I knew I was going to have a bitch of a headache; it had already started. I smoothed down the nightgown and made my way to the kitchen.

The sounds I'd heard came not from Pam, but from a guy with pleasant Hawaiian features. I'd seen his face on album covers and TV. He was a regular headliner at the lounges in Waikiki. "Howzit?" he asked. "Heard you had a rough night. Pam's in the shower. Coffee?"

I said yes and took the cup he offered. They'd given me a small bottle of Tylenol at the hospital. I shook out four tablets, swallowed them with water and chased it with a slug of coffee.

The guy looked at me with sympathy. He said, "Looks like you're expecting an even rougher day. Pam'll be glad to see you awake. She must've gotten up about six times to check on you."

"It's nice to have friends," I said.

He said, "Say that again."

"It's nice to have friends?"

"Man, you ever been on radio? That's a radio voice if I ever heard one. Get yourself a late-night show, taking calls and spinning a few records. Who wouldn't want to spend the night with you?"

Pam came in just then. "Look at you," she said. "Leave you alone a minute and you're making a move on my man. See you've met Wayne. How're you?"

"Fine. Thanks for taking care of me. I'm sorry I put you through all that trouble."

"No trouble. I hardly knew you were here."

Wayne made a face behind her and shook his head.

I said, "Thanks just the same. Okay if I use your shower?" The least I could do was give her a few minutes alone with Wayne. With a rolled up washcloth over the knot behind my ear, I applied shampoo to a few strands of hair. I worked it in as gently as I could, barely touching my scalp, repeating it with a few more strands. When it came to rinsing, I cupped the water in my hand and poured it on, a handful at a time, so as to keep my head out of the spray. It was slow and tedious, but it gave Pam extra time with Wayne. He was gone by the time I finished.

On my second cup of coffee in Pam's kitchen, I reviewed the preceding night's events. "Somebody else is looking for Nathan Pfeifer. They found out about Harriet and made the connection with Sue. They threatened her and she had a heart attack."

"Was it stress-induced?"

"Probably. She had a mouse over her eye that could have come from a beating."

"Do you think she told him where to find Nathan?"

"No. He searched the room after he whacked me."

"What did he hope to find by searching the room?"

"Either a clue to the hiding place or a list of names of the other women in the group."

"Oh God," said Pam.

"Look, suppose the guy did find the names. He'll go after each of them until he gets the kid. Look what he did to Sue and to me. He beat her. He frightened her. He left her for dead. And me, too. You're not protecting them by keeping them secret."

"All right," said Pam.

Pam could only come up with eight names besides herself - Sue Naito, Carol Fernandez, and six others. There might be more, she said, but not too many. Harriet had been a small group twenty years ago, its influence greater than its numbers. Today, with only an anticipated need for an abortion kit, that number would be even smaller. Sue, she admitted, had been one of the two nurses who invented the kit.

"Val, these are good women. They are doing what they believe is right. They are taking a risk and their children and husbands may not even know what they are doing. I'm telling you their names to protect them. If I thought otherwise, you would not learn their names from me. Do you understand?"

I said I did.

It was close to noon and Pam offered to drive me to my car with a stop first at my apartment for a spare set of car keys. She double parked out front on Pau Street and waited, engine running, while I went looking for the building manager. I found him in back near the dumpster, sweeping loose trash into a squarish metal scoop.

"I've got a problem," I said.

He looked at me sourly. "Me, too. Your neighbor down below bitched me out this morning for the noise you made last night."

"Last night?"

"Yeah. Late. One, one-thirty. He said it sounded like you were moving."

Suddenly my headache became a throbbing pain. "Oh, hell." I headed to the stairs. "C'mon," I yelled at him.

"Where you goin'?"

"My purse was stolen last night. My keys were in it."

"So?"

"So I wasn't here last night."

"Oh." He dropped the broom and the scoop and caught up with me on the stairs.

"This is a safe building. We haven't had any robberies since I been here." He opened the door with his passkey. "Chee, what a mess," he said.

My things were scattered everywhere - drawers opened and emptied; clothes, books, tapes dumped in the middle of the big room in a sloppy mound. The sofabed had been pulled out and stripped of mattress and linens. The pillows had been slashed and stuffing strewn about.

I instructed the manager not to touch anything and called down to Pam from the lanai. She went off in search of a parking space. Meanwhile I called the police.

When Pam arrived she said, "You didn't do this without help."

"The guy who took my purse paid me a visit."

"Lucky you weren't here."

Three police cars arrived from different directions. They pulled up in front of the building. Two officers came up while one stayed in the car working the radio.

I met them at the top of the stairs. "I'm Val Lyon. It was my place that was broken into." They followed me to the apartment. One of them, an older man with a pocked face, started the questioning as we walked. What time had I gotten home? Where had I spent the night? What was missing?

In response to the last question, I said, "I don't know. I just got here. The manager let me in." He wrote it all down laboriously. I introduced Pam and the manager.

The other officer was a blonde woman whose equipment belt made her wide hips look even wider. The flak vest under her uniform blouse didn't flatter her either. That's the trouble with being a female officer in uniform: unless you look like a boy to start with, you end up looking like Daisy Duck. She said, "No sign of a forced entry. How'd they get in?"

"With my key."

That brought raised eyebrows, questioning glances and a whole new set of questions. I said I'd been hit on the head and had my purse stolen.

"Where'd this happen?" the older one wanted to know.

"It was at a house in Kaimuki." Then I had to tell them the whole story about Sue and her heart attack. Daisy Duck radioed her partner in the car, asking him to call for detectives. The older cop started questioning Pam and the manager.

I wandered around my apartment surveying the damage. There was hardly a place to walk without stepping on or over my things. My things! Not a great deal, nothing very expensive, a few items I treasured, mostly the everyday stuff of a single woman's life. Some of it once private and personal but no longer. I kicked at the mound of my possessions.

The manager picked up one of my athletic shoes. "All these yours?"

"Put it down," I yelled. "Do something useful. Change the goddamn locks." My voice quavered. I struggled to get it under control. First Sue Naito, then the hit on the head, and now this. I looked around at the destruction of the only part of the world that was all mine. "Damn," I said.

"That's a good idea, change the locks," the older cop said to the manager. To me, he said, "What do you think they were looking for, Miss Lyon?"

"I don't fucking know," I said.

10 NAKASHITA INVESTIGATES

The thief had taken the folder Magruder had given me on the Pfeifer case. Its loss would not greatly affect Brian's case or my investigation as it contained mainly background information. The fact that it was taken, however, was one more bit of confirmation that the break-in and the Pfeifer case were connected. The break-in was confirmation of something else, too - the guy hadn't found a Harriet membership list at Sue's. Else why look for one in my place? That thought was a minor comfort.

I took a few more Tylenols under the watchful eyes of the police. Just when I thought things couldn't get worse, Detective Sergeant Wally Nakashita, homicide, arrived with an evidence team.

I'd cleared a spot on the end of the sofa bed and Pam had joined me there. Nakashita took the reports from the officers and dismissed them. He gave instructions to the evidence team and they moved into the bathroom and kitchen. Finally, he came over to me.

Nakashita is solidly built without any fat to speak of. He has flat features and a plain face accentuated by a plum-colored birthmark over most of the left side. His eyes are hooded and sleepy. They could easily fool the unwary. Me, I've dealt with him before and I'm not fooled.

He said, "Well, Ms. L., how does an associate of Leo

Laskowitz's get into this predicament? You hiding something here?"

"Nice to see you, too," I said. "How'd you know I work for Leo?"

"Word gets around. Laskowitz has a lot of friends. Heard he's petitioning the licensing board to make you an associate. I don't expect them to object."

"But you do."

He shrugged and gave me an enigmatic smile. "Nobody asked me. I find it peculiar that one needs a police permit for a handgun but not for a loose cannon."

"Loose cannon? Me? I'm just a woman trying to earn an honest living."

"I'll tell Diogenes. I'm relieved that you're taking up a profession. I'd worry if you were a housekeeper." He walked around the room, carefully avoiding the mess. Nakashita is impeccably neat as if to make up for the blemish nature left on him. His trouser creases looked sharp enough to cut bread and his shirt, a short-sleeved broadcloth, looked as fresh as if he'd just taken it from the box. He is one of the few men in Hawaii who wears a tie on a regular basis. The stripes formed a neat chevron where they met at the knot.

He hiked his pants up at the knees to keep the crease and bent down to pick up a book. "Pride and Prejudice," he said, straightening. "Yours?"

"Yes," I said. Actually it was my mother's - the hardcover volume she'd used when she wrote her thesis in literature. It still had marginal notes and inserts in her handwriting. I'd probably read it half a dozen times since taking it from her bedside table after her death. I'd read every single note and examined every underlined passage, hoping to understand the woman I'd never understood in life, looking for some message she might have left me.

"I'd never have guessed Pride and Prejudice was your type, Ms. Lyon."

"We all have our guilty secrets, Sergeant." I got up and took the book from him before he could drop it back onto the pile. "If you don't mind," I said. I put it on the bookcase where it belonged.

Nakashita gave me a hard look and said, "You haven't answered my question. Are you hiding something here?"

"Not any more. Except for the stuff at the bottom of that pile there, everything's out in the open."

"So what were they looking for?"

"I haven't any idea. I'd like to ask the guy that, myself."

"Is anything missing?"

"Look, Sergeant, my lips hurt from all this kissing. Let's get right to the big event. Last night a guy threatened and killed Sue Naito. He attacked me, searched her place and then searched mine."

"What makes you think it's the same person?"

"I know it's the same. You do, too, or you wouldn't be here. Homicide detectives don't answer lousy breaking and entering calls."

One of the evidence techs said, "Sergeant, there's prints everywhere you look - one on top of the other. Old, new, you name it. Been a long time since the counters seen a cleaner. No telling how many different sets we could pick up. Take weeks to sort 'em all out. You got any specific thing you want dusted?"

Nakashita considered that a moment and said, "No, I guess not. We don't want to spend a couple weeks on a lousy breaking and entering." He sent them away.

He said, "Nobody has established that Sue Naito was murdered. So far, it looks like a heart attack. She might have suffered it while a robbery was in progress, but that doesn't make it murder."

"She might have suffered it while she was being beaten."

"Did you see anybody hit her?"

"No."

"The message tape was taken from her answering machine. Why would anyone want that?"

"The message tape contained a threat. Probably from the guy who hit her. He threatened my client in the same way."

"You listened to both tapes?"

"No."

"What was the threat to your client, Ms. Lyon?"

"I can't tell you. It involves his client so it's privileged."

"Why were you at her house? Don't tell me that's privileged, too."

"No. It was about pregnancy counseling. She was expecting me."

"Pregnancy counseling. You're pregnant?"

"Don't be an idiot, Sergeant. I wanted to take the training to be a counselor."

Nakashita stood looking at me while he considered that. He said, "God help us. I don't know which worries me more - you as detective or you as pregnancy counselor. Maybe you shouldn't be too quick to give up on housekeeping. If the tape should turn up in your cleaning, I'd better be the first to know."

"You will," I said.

"Well, sugar," said Pam, when he'd left, "I'm glad I still have my job at the prison because it'll make it easy for us to meet when he nails your white ass."

11 CATS

Pam stayed to help me clean. I gathered up every article of clothing, whether on the floor, in the closet, or still in drawers and took them to the laundromat. In my mind everything had been pawed over and sullied. We spent the better part of the afternoon straightening up. The manager came and installed a new lock on the door. It wasn't adequate and I told him so, but he insisted it would have to do. Figlio di puttana! Son of a bitch! Pam drove me out to Kaimuki to get my car. I had a few questions to ask Harold Davison, but nobody was there. On the way back to Waikiki, I stopped at a hardware store and bought a power drill and a good deadbolt lock, which I installed myself when I got home.

My efforts so far had gotten me a new lock, a knot on my head, and a ripped up apartment. Some detective! My only leads to the kid were the names Pam had given me.

It was about 4:30 and I'd had nothing to eat except for some slices of toast at Pam's. I heated up a can of chili and poured it into a bowl with a handful of Fritos. I washed it down with a Coke. While I ate, I took out my list of names, found their addresses and phone numbers in the book, and marked off the locations on a street map. All the remaining Harriets were on Oahu: four in the Honolulu area, one in Kaneohe, one in Hawaii Kai, and one way out in Wai'anae.

Carol Fernandez was the Hawaii Kai one. She sounded like a good one to start with.

Hawaii Kai is about ten miles from Waikiki. It was already dark when I found Carol's house - a cozy, one-story on a quiet cul-de-sac. Neat lawn, well-tended flower bed, the whole suburban bit. I'd bet she didn't serve Fritos and chili for dinner. The house was well-lit from both street lights and yard lights. I parked on the street and walked up the driveway to the front walk.

A woman with a cat in her arms and another draped over her shoulders opened the door to my knock. A third cat came and took up a station at her feet, eyeing me with unblinking eyes. "Yes?" the woman asked. She was late twenties, petite, with a delicate mouth and chin.

"I'm looking for Carol Fernandez. My name's Val Lyon. She knows me."

From somewhere in the house I heard Carol's voice. "Who is it, Annie?" she called.

"Someone named Lyon. Said you know her."

"Oh, it's that damned bodyguard. Send her away. I don't care what she wants."

I pushed my way past Annie, who made a weak protest, and found myself in a living room with three or four more cats. "Carol," I called, "If you won't talk to me, I'll just sit here in your living room. Sooner or later Sue Naito's murderer is bound to show up."

She came into the living room wearing a flowing caftan. I couldn't help noticing that her makeup was fresh and her hair soft and shiny. "What are you talking about, Sue's murderer?" she demanded. "Sue had a heart attack. Who said she was murdered?"

"Nobody's admitted it was murder, but it was certainly a suspicious death. The police are still investigating."

"Oh my God," said Annie.

"Hush," snapped Carol. To me she said, "I think you'd better explain yourself."

"Of course." I sat down on a rattan armchair. Annie and Carol sat together on a sofa, also rattan. Annie continued stroking the cat in her arms. Carol rested her hand on Annie's thigh. There were two wine glasses, a wedge of Brie and a basket of French bread on the coffee table. I appeared to have interrupted something. All of a sudden I felt movement at my feet and a sharp nip on my ankle. I gave a yelp and looked down. A small black and white cat had curled around my foot and was about to sink its teeth into my flesh again. I gave a swift kick and it flew through the air, turning and twisting as it went. Annie gasped. I smiled at her and said, "I hate cats. I'll wring its neck if it comes at me again." Annie moved quickly to scoop it up before it could make another attack. "That goes for the others," I said.

"She's just a baby," said Annie. "You're not nice."

"Never said I was. I sat on my hands for Tinkerbell."

"Say what you came here for and leave," said Carol. "The cats won't bother you."

In fact they did bother me, even if they didn't attack. My eyes felt puffy and watery and my nose had started to run. I fished some tissues out of my pocket and wiped my nose before going on. "Someone else was in Sue's house at the time of the attack. He hit her. That caused her heart attack." Even coming from a runny-nosed detective, the statement made an impact. I had their full attention. "I showed up and he attacked me, searched Sue's office, stole my purse and searched my apartment. My guess is that he's the same one who threatened Sue earlier in the day. She called to tell me about it, to accuse me of it, actually. The caller wanted Nathan Pfeifer. He knows about Harriet. He knows someone in the group is hiding the kid. He tossed Sue's place and mine hoping to find a list of names of the Harriets." I dabbed at my eyes and wiped my nose again. Carol Fernandez stared intently at me. Annie had resumed her seat and was stroking the cat nervously. The cat meowed and jumped off her lap. I said, "That's where you come in. You belonged to the group back in the seventies."

Carol said, "Big fucking deal!"

Annie said, "Carol, dear, please don't use that language. You know it sounds ugly coming from you."

"Annie, I'm sure Val isn't shocked by that word, or much else for that matter."

"Yes, but it's so harsh and you've such a gentle nature."

Carol patted Annie's hand reassuringly. "I won't use it again." To me she said, "Who didn't belong to something in the seventies? Yes, I was in a group and we called ourselves Harriet. Compared to the Weatherpeople or the Symbionese Liberation Army we were nobody's threat. You've got no business hassling us now."

"I'm not hassling you. Someone else is. I'm trying to get to Nathan before that guy does. In the process, I might just save the remaining Harriets from Sue's fate."

"Even if I believed Sue was murdered, I wouldn't trust someone who works for the Magruders. You know what our purpose is - to give women a choice. The Magruder family's philosophy is antithetical to that. They are the state's largest contributors, outside of the Catholic Church itself, to the anti-choice movement. I advised Jean against retaining Brian Magruder, but she had her own reasons and wouldn't be swayed. Now there's nothing you can do for me and nothing I'll do for you."

"Carol," I said, "I'm not working for the Magruder family and I don't give a damn about their causes any more than I give a damn about yours. But I might be able to save your life. This guy will surely come after you and each of the other Harriets until he gets the boy."

"Carol," said Annie, "what if she's right?"

"I think Val is just being melodramatic. Even if someone was in Sue's house when she died, for which we have only Val's word, there's nothing to indicate he was looking for Nathan, or former Harriets. There's not a shred of evidence that you or I are in any danger. Is there, Val?"

"It's a hunch."

"A hunch. Was it something you felt in your big toe?"

I shrugged off the sarcasm. "It hit me over the head. I can usually tell I'm on the right track when that happens."

"I told you yesterday that I don't know where Nathan Pfeifer is. That's still the truth. But, if I did, I wouldn't be frightened or bullied into revealing it."

"How do you know Jean Pfeifer?" I asked.

Annie stiffened. She and Carol exchanged quick glances and Carol said, "Annie and I have known Jean socially for several years."

"I see. Just socially?"

"How else do you mean?" asked Annie.

"I don't know. Why don't you tell me?"

"We have nothing to hide here," said Carol. "It started off as a professional relationship between Annie and Jean that, well, blossomed into a friendship for the three of us."

"What sort of professional relationship?"

"If you must know," said Annie, "as part of my internship in counseling, I led a support group for women in transition. Jean was in it. She was going through a difficult time and needed a lot of emotional support."

"When was this?"

"Almost five years ago."

"That was before her divorce." I wiped my eyes again.

"The marriage was already over," said Carol. "It was nothing but a sham, really, from day one. It just took Jean time to recognize it."

"But you helped her recognize it?" I asked Annie.

"She was confused about her needs. I think I helped her get rid of some of the confusion."

"Isn't that what psychiatrists call transference?"

Annie blushed deeply. Carol said, "We don't have to put up with any more of your snide insinuations. Why don't you go do your snooping somewhere else?"

There wasn't anything more that I could get from either of them. No point in further arguing and pleading. Besides, the longer I stayed in the house with those cats, the more miserable I felt. I was happy to get out into the warm night air. I had a swimsuit in my car so I drove a few blocks to Maunalua Bay, parked at the beach park and changed in the back seat. The beach was lightly populated, a few couples, some fishermen, and a group in wetsuits preparing for a night dive. It was well-lit from the moon and the street lights. The surf line - an irregular seam of iridescent foam - was in sight of the road. I waded out till I felt the waves break - about waist deep - and stood there until I felt cleansed of cat dander.

12 THE WAY TO A DETECTIVE'S HEART

I showered off the sand and salt at the beach park, toweled off and drove back to town wearing just my shirt over my swimsuit. When I reached my apartment, I found a paper bag outside my door. A note on the bag read, "Found in dumpster. - The Mgmt." Inside was my purse. I'd agonized for a week over its purchase. Now the soft leather had acquired an ugly stain and a nauseating smell. Inside was my wallet and driver's license. No cash, no recorder, no tape.

I tossed the purse and the rest of my things into a pile in the bathroom. Then I went into the kitchen and poured myself a glass of red wine from a big jug of Carlo Rossi. It was a few minutes past seven. I thought of calling Pam, but knew she had a date. Pam had a date every Saturday night. She had an unbroken string going back more than five years. Prison had interrupted my string and I hadn't gotten back on track. I wandered into the living room and put a K.T. Oslin tape in my stereo, flipped the sofa cushions to the unslashed side and settled down with my wine.

Carol and Annie had a date, too.

K.T. asked where a woman should go when she's feeling low.

I thought about making the rounds of Waikiki watering holes, pick up a tourist and bring him back. I'd done it before, but

74

considering the other things you could pick up, I decided to stick with Carlo Rossi.

K.T. sang about 'round the clock lovin'.

Round the clock, Carlo. Would that be twelve hours or twenty-four? Maybe we're talking about the minute hand. In that case, it had better be quality lovin'.

Carlo went dry. As I went to the kitchen for a refill, I heard a knock on the door. Magruder was on the other side of the peephole. I opened the door to him. He carried two paper bags in one arm. In the other hand he held a bouquet of chrysanthemums and baby's breath.

"Scotch whiskey, Chinese carry-out, and flowers," he said. "I didn't know the way to a detective's heart, so I chose all three."

"That's a switch. Everybody else tries to go through my skull."

"Uh oh. There's a fourth way?"

"No. Flowers are better." I took them from him. He followed me to the kitchen. "Glasses are above the sink on the left."

He opened the Scotch and poured two glasses while I found an empty peanut butter jar for the flowers. He said, "Hey, country and western, huh? You listen to country and western?"

"When I'm in a shitty mood."

"Oh," he said, "why the lousy mood?"

"Sue Naito died."

"So you heard?"

"Yeah, I was there when it happened." We took the drinks to the couch. I gave him the blow by blow from the time he dropped me off to my visit with Carol Fernandez. I finished up with my suspicions about Harriet and Sue's part in hiding Nathan.

Brian said, "Sue could've been killed for another reason. She was a powerful figure - city councilwoman, feminist activist, prochoicer. Lots of people had reason to hate her. Any number of people and groups could've wanted information from her."

"The only connection between Sue and me was your case. They took your file, by the way."

He thought about that for awhile. "I've got a duplicate. We might be able to use that in court to show that Nathan really would be in danger. Are you hungry yet?"

"Famished."

I spread a cloth on the foot locker I use as a coffee table and took some cushions off the couch for us to sit on. Brian arranged the cardboard cartons on the locker. There were noodles, Mongolian beef, garlic eggplant, and lemon chicken. I dimmed the light and turned the stereo down.

What bothered me was how Sue's attacker had known of my connection in the case. I'd been working on it less than a day to that point and had told only a few people of my interest in it. Brian, Leo, Pam, Jean, Carol, and Sue. I trusted the first three. That left Jean and Carol. Jean would've had to find a way to do it from jail. And Carol? I could think of no reason why she'd attack Sue, but I had to admit that I didn't know her well enough to rule her out.

What about the Magruders? Brian had told his family about the case and they'd known of my involvement. And, if Carol was to be believed, the Magruder family and Sue were at odds on the abortion issue. Was there enough heat there to lead to murder?

"Penny for your thoughts," said Brian.

I joined him on the floor. "Huh uh. It's your turn. I told you about my fun last night. What'd you do?"

"Nothing very exciting, I'm afraid. I got cleaned out in the card room at the King Kamehameha Club by no less a personage than my own brother the priest."

"You at the King Kamehameha Club?"

"Oh yeah. Pop's been a member for years. Frank goes there whenever he's in town. As for me, I'm uncomfortable there, but I need to get out and network. So I've been told."

We turned our attention to dinner. The best thing about Chinese food is the chopsticks, the only true utensils that don't discriminate against left-handers.

"Just you and Frank last night?" I asked.

"Nope. Dan Kamalu was there. He's a captain with HPD."

"That would cut down on cheating."

"Yeah, and anybody who did could confess to the bishop. He was there. So was some hot shot real estate dealer. Kept trying to interest me in some property out near Temple Valley. Ken showed up later."

"The bishop was Frank's guest?"

Magruder shrugged his big shoulders. "Yeah. What're you implying, that Frank was sucking up to the bishop?"

"You said it, not me."

"Actually, it was the bishop who was doing the sucking."

"To a monsignor?"

"A fast-track monsignor. The bishop's got about as high as he's going to go, but not Frank. I hope I don't sound like I'm bragging on him, but Frank's going far in the Catholic Church unless he gets involved in some serious scandal."

"How about his brother defending a lesbian?"

Magruder paused with a piece of lemon chicken halfway to his mouth between the ends of his chopsticks. "Jean's a lesbian? How do you know?"

"Carol and her companion, Annie, made some references to it. I had the impression that Annie brought Jean out and then introduced her to Carol."

"Well that's interesting. I don't think that would bother Frank much, though. He's pretty tolerant and liberal-minded."

"He sounded pretty conservative to me."

"That was just for effect. Frank likes to argue. When he gets serious, though, he can fight pretty hard. Frank's ambitious and he's got some ruthless enemies. He can be ruthless himself. If you want to fault Frank for anything, it's too much ambition. You can't fault him for lack of compassion, though. Ken's the same way. He makes a lot of money, but contributes a lot to charity."

"Any more efforts to get you to drop Jean's case?"

"Nope. The subject never came up. I had to suffer through a lot of gossip about who's doing what to whom in the church hierarchy. To tell you the truth, church matters bore the hell out of me."

"The rest of your family's very religious, aren't they?" I asked.

"Some more than others. Frank had no interest in religion before going to Vietnam. Sometimes I wonder about his religious commitment now. He's more a churchman than a holyman."

"But your family's active in the anti-abortion movement."

"Right to life," he said. "That's mainly Pop and Mom. And Molly."

"If Frank's such a churchman, he'd be anti-abortion."

"Sure, but he's also pragmatic and ready to make compromises. You have to be to rise in the Church hierarchy. That's how he got pegged for this commission on women."

"Pragmatism and ambition. Personally, I prefer people with conviction."

"Give him a chance, Val. I think you might like his convictions. He'll be a good advocate for the cause of women."

"The best advocate would be a woman bishop."

I cleaned up the remains of dinner and put the leftovers in the refrigerator. Magruder poured more drinks. We took them back to the couch.

"You know," I said, "I'm feeling a little guilty. In twenty-four hours, I haven't called you at all."

"Considering all that's happened to you, I'd be surprised if you had called."

"I should have checked on you. You did get a threat, after all."

He laughed. "You were worried about me? You're the one who was hurt. Hey, can I see your injury?"

I peeled back the tape holding the gauze pad, scooted closer and bent my head down to his chest. He pulled back my hair and touched the wound lightly.

"Does that hurt?" he asked.

"A little."

"It's still swollen. What'd he hit you with?"

"I don't know. A piece of pipe, a gun, maybe a sap."

"A sap?"

"A blackjack."

"People carry blackjacks?"

"Yeah. Some professional muscle aren't above it." I straightened up. Magruder's face was twisted in concern.

"You think a professional hit man attacked you?"

"I didn't say that, but look, you can sap somebody at the base of the skull and, if you're real good or they're real lucky, you'll put them out for awhile and they'll wake up with a massive headache and maybe a concussion. Otherwise…" My body shuddered involuntarily. "Otherwise you can put them out for good or turn them into vegetables."

"So he was good or you were lucky. That's what you're saying?" I nodded. Magruder seemed to go pale. He chewed on his mustache and was silent. Then he said, "This is getting scary. If you want to drop it, I'll understand. You can keep the retainer. It's the least I can do."

"No, Brian. I'm not giving this up. I don't like people abusing kids or attacking women. I don't like to quit a job I've started. I'm a little bit scared and whole lot bitchy because I may be up against somebody bigger than me. But, I've been up against bigger guys before and I've been hurt worse. So, I'm not going to drop this. You can fire me if you don't like my work, but not because I might get hurt."

Magruder threw up his hands in mock submission. "Okay, okay. Leo said you were obstinate." He took a long pull of his drink. "You've been hurt worse?" he asked.

"Yep. Got a scar here to prove it." I pointed to the spot above my eye where the tracks of stitches had all but faded away. "See it?"

He had to move close. "Yes. Did somebody hit you?" He traced the scar with his finger.

"Uh huh. Long time ago. Split my lip, too. Right here." I raised my face to him and he leaned closer. "See it?"

"No."

His mouth was very close. I kissed him. It was a light, almost casual kiss, but it turned on a switch somewhere deep inside me. I hadn't realized until then how much I wanted him. Gone were my earlier concerns of getting invoved with a client. This was need, this was lust. Caution warnings didn't have a chance. I flicked my tongue across his lips. It sparked something inside him, too. He growled into my open mouth and pulled me to him with such force I spilled my Scotch into my lap. I yelped.

"God, I'm sorry," he said.

"No, it's okay."

"I'll clean you up."

I felt his head go down to my lap, felt his tongue licking the spilled liquor off my skin. He slid to the floor between my knees. His mustache scraped my thigh and his hands tugged at the waistband of my swimsuit bottom. With a groan, I lifted my butt so he could pull it off. He tossed it aside and reached under my shirt, fumbling with the clasp of my top.

"Damn! I ripped it."

"It's okay, Brian." I slid to the floor on top of him and lifted my shirt over my head. "Slow down. We have a long night."

"If I live that long. I've got a case of terminal tumescence."

"Hold on to it, then. I'll be right back."

"Where are you going?"

"For protection. It's my business."

When I got back, Brian had pushed back the trunk and pulled out the sofabed.

13 MOTHER'S DAY AT THE JAIL

Our lovin' didn't go 'round the clock, but it did last a few hours. I woke up in a tangle of sheets and a pool of sunlight. Brian's outflung arm lay heavily across my chest. I tried unsuccessfully to extricate myself without waking him. He raised his sleep-heavy eyelids and said, "Well, here we are."

"Here we are," I said. "You do remember me, don't you?"

"How could I forget? The lady whose business is protection."

"Well, I'm out of business now. We used them all up."

"Not to worry. I brought some myself." He noted the look on my face and said, "Sex burns calories. I had hoped to get skinny."

I made a tent over us with the sheet and pulled him to me. "We'd better get busy then. We've got a lot of work to do."

Afterwards we had coffee and the leftover Chinese food while we watched a football game. My little black and white TV was between us on the bed. The one plus to Hawaii's time difference is that you can watch football and still have the rest of the day free. We caught the last quarter of the first game and the first half of the second one. Forty-niners and Eagles. Steve Young - a left-hander - was having a great game.

Magruder said, "I'm going to visit Jean this afternoon. Do

you want to come along?"

"Yes. I'm sure she's heard about Sue. Maybe she'll give us something on Nathan."

He left for a change of clothes after promising to pick me up in an hour and a half. I padded after him to the door and locked the deadbolts behind him. Then I went back to bed to catch more of Steve Young. Maybe it was the glow of sex, but it felt like love. I'd have to retire my Joe Montana jersey with the number sixteen for one with a number eight. Sorry, Joe.

Leo wasn't in his room when I called so I left a message. He returned my call about twenty minutes later. He'd read the papers, but Sue's death had meant nothing to him. Once again I went into an account of all that had happened between Friday afternoon and Saturday evening.

When I'd finished, he said, "So what's your plan now, kid?"

Count on Leo not to patronize me. I said, "You know, Leo, you could've asked if I was okay. You could've said it was getting dangerous and maybe I should drop it. You could've blamed yourself for getting me into this."

"Anybody but you, I would've. You're too hard-headed."

"Thanks Leo. How good are your contacts here?"

"I keep in touch. Any species in particular?"

"I'm interested in the muscle boys. I'm working on a hunch that the guy that sapped me is somebody's soldier. He had enough presence of mind not to leave the instrument at the scene. Maybe he brought it to the house with him."

"You want me to ask around? Maybe somebody's been talking."

"Right. Or maybe we could get a lead on who hired the muscle. Somebody had to advertise for it."

"Unless the guy was already on a payroll. I could find that out."

"If I knew who was working and who they worked for, I could look for a connection between the employer and Sue or Jean."

"I'll do what I can," he said.

A guard examined Brian's briefcase and my handbag - an inadequate beaded number that had once complemented an evening dress I no longer own. He ushered us into a small room. The room was done in a light pastel shade of blue with patio carpeting on the floor. The only furnishings were a small conference table and four chairs, two on each side. The table and chairs were bolted to the floor. We sat in the chairs on the same side as the door through which we'd entered. A door in the opposite wall opened and Jean Pfeifer entered, followed by another guard. Jean took a seat across from us. The guard remained by the door.

Jean was wearing a plain prison smock and the kind of plastic sandals kids call 'jellies,' but known to inmates as 'jailies.' She had no makeup or jewelry, of course, but it was evident that she paid attention to her appearance. That was a good sign. Apparently she was adjusting to prison life. She looked rested and relaxed.

Magruder briefed Jean on his next steps to get her out of jail. It didn't look good, though. There was no limit to her sentence. Until she relinquished Nathan, she was to be held on contempt.

"I called Harriet," I said. "The number belonged to Sue Naito. Did she hide Nathan?

"I don't know," Jean said. "She might have. Carol arranged it."

I said, "Sue's dead, Jean. Possibly murdered because she was trying to protect him. You're not alone in this. Other women are in danger from this man as long as Nathan's in hiding. Nathan could be in danger, too."

Jean's lips quavered and her hands betrayed her emotions. She knotted a tissue into a tight ball and tore small pieces off it. "Carol said she knew people who could be trusted. That's all I know."

"You don't know anything about the person who's looking after your own son?"

"I talked to a woman on the phone. It wasn't Sue. Carol set up the call."

"Did you talk to Nathan?"

"That first week that he was gone and again about two weeks later. After that, Carol started to worry that the calls could be traced through phone records, so we quit. Maybe it's better this way."

Magruder said, "Jean, it would help our case if we could have him examined by specialists and document the abuse. We might be able to get the court to order protection for Nathan and have the contempt citation lifted."

"And what if they don't find evidence of abuse?" she asked.

Magruder said. "You've been telling me all along that he's been badly abused. Surely there'd be evidence of it."

"I know that most of the evidence in abuse cases is ambiguous. Besides, Jock's abuse was less physical and more psychological."

"How?" asked Magruder.

"He tried to turn Nathan against me. He told him lies about me. For awhile I tried to ignore it, but Nathan was starting to believe it. And he was reaching that age where young men are very impressionable. I didn't like the influence Jock had on him."

"Influence and abuse are two different things," said Magruder.

Jean glared at him. "I know what abuse is. I lived with it from the time my mother married my stepfather when I was three. Hardly a week passed that he didn't hit her at least once. He beat her so bad sometimes she wouldn't leave the house for days."

"Did he hurt you?" I asked.

"Nothing like what he did to mother. He decided early on that I was stupid and not worth much of anything."

I said, "Brian, could I talk to Jean alone?"

He shrugged. "Sure, why not?" He went to the door and knocked for the guard to open it.

When we were alone, I said, "Jean, I talked to Carol and Annie so I know something about your relationship."

"They told you?"

"Not directly, but enough that I could guess. Is that what you meant about the lies Jock told Nathan?"

"Miss Lyon -"

"Val."

"Val, I married Jock to get away from my stepfather. I didn't recognize, then, that what he was doing was abuse. I thought it was just the way men treated women and fathers treated children. I only knew that I hated it. Jock was my escape and, yes, I thought I loved him. Jock didn't hit me, but in other ways he was not much different from my stepfather. Annie and Carol helped me see that he, too, was abusive. They also made me see that I was allowing myself to be a victim."

"Was this before the divorce?"

"Yes, but I'd already decided to leave him. Jock says they turned me against men and against him in particular, but he's wrong. I think I knew all along, at least after that first year, that I had to get away from Jock. Nobody turned me against men. I didn't start seeing women until after the divorce."

"Why did you stay with Jock so long?"

"I thought Nathan needed a father. I didn't always like his way of raising Nathan, but I thought it was better that he have Jock as a role model than that he have no model at all."

"And now?"

"Now I know how wrong that is. Carol and Annie made me realize that the pattern of abuse was being continued in Nathan. He was becoming just like Jock. He was learning to use violence to solve his problems. Then there was the matter of music. Nathan plays the piano beautifully. His hands are made for a keyboard, so long and slender. God gave him such wonderful hands and extraordinary talent. Jock detests that. He wanted Nathan to give it up and concentrate on sports. I understand that sports can build character, but Jock pushed him harder and harder. Nathan wasn't good at sports. You could see the frustration in him whenever he tried. Jock had him convinced he was spending too much time on music. He had him ready to give it up."

"You wanted Nathan to be a musician. Jock wanted him to be an athlete. What did Nathan want?"

"Nathan isn't old enough to decide for himself. Don't make this out to be a battle between selfish, uncaring parents with a child caught in the middle. There is much more at stake here than you'll ever know."

"What's at stake, Jean? Are you afraid of losing custody if it becomes known that you're a lesbian?"

"What difference does it make to anybody who I sleep with? It makes no difference to Nathan. He doesn't know and he won't know until I tell him. Yes, I'm afraid of what would happen in court. I am a fit mother but no judge will agree with me. How many women have lost their children because they've had female lovers? How many times have the courts taken the father's side in cases of child abuse? When it's a boy, society is even more biased towards the father. I wouldn't stand a chance. My only recourse to protect my child is what I'm doing now. As long as I'm here and as long as Nathan's location is unknown, we're both safe."

"Safe from what, Jean?"

"Safe from death."

I felt that I'd made a breakthrough with Jean, that she wanted my help. I said, "Brian told me about the message you received. Did the writer threaten Nathan, too?"

Jean shook her head. "The letter was a warning to me only, but I know Nathan's in danger."

"From whom?"

"From his father. Val, in spite of what I said earlier, I want you to find him and look after him."

"Okay, but I have to know what I'm up against. Would Jock do physical harm to Nathan?"

She thought about that a minute looking off to a point over my shoulder. When her eyes returned to mine, I knew she was hiding something. She said, "Jock? I don't know. He would do anything to get Nathan back." She got up from her chair. "I'm sorry I can't be any more help, Val."

"What aren't you telling me, Jean? Why can't you trust me?"

She paused before she reached the door. "I know you'll find

him and keep him safe. I do wish I could tell you more, but there's nobody I can trust."

We'd been so close. I could've thrown the table over in my frustration. Maybe that's why they're bolted in place.

14 A GLUT OF TESTOSTERONE

Jock Pfeifer lived in Kahala, about two blocks from the beach and the same distance from Wai'alae Country Club. The area had seen an invasion of Japanese investors in the past few years. In more settled real estate markets, Pfeifer's house might have brought two hundred to two hundred-fifty thousand. In the volatile Kahala market, I'd guess it to bring one and a half million, give or take a quarter mil. It was a long, low house with wide, double front doors flanked by white pillars. A wide driveway on the right led to a two-car garage. Atop the garage was a backboard and hoop. A narrower driveway branched off and made a horseshoe past the front door and back to the street.

Magruder parked on the horseshoe drive by the front door. I rang the bell and a plump woman opened it. She wore white pants and a white top, like a nurse's uniform. Her round face was framed by dark, finger-waved hair. She blinked up at us through saucer-size glasses.

I asked to see Pfeifer.

"He is busy," she said in a sing-song Filipino accent. "You must wait." She closed the door on us.

"Guess we wait," said Brian.

"Not me." I crossed the lawn to the side yard. The front of the house was laid out with flower beds filled with ti plants and elephant ears in white and green. At the side of the house was a wooden privacy fence running from the corner to the end of the lot. I grabbed the top of the fence with both hands and pulled myself up. I could see a small side garden and, beyond that, partially hidden by the house, a lanai and swimming pool. Sunlight glinted off the surface of the pool. It seemed to be a narrow, lap pool, though most of it was out of sight. The woman who'd answered the door was down on one knee, her back to me, apparently talking to someone in the water.

I pulled myself up a little higher for a better view and almost got a face full of dog. I heard a low growl and looked down just as it sprang for the top of the fence. Its front paws caught the same top board that my hands gripped and its momentum brought its gnashing teeth inches from my nose. I yelled my surprise and let go of my hold, landing hard on my ass. The dog's hind paws scrabbled at the boards on the other side and for an instant I thought it might make it over. I brought my knees up and covered my face with my arms, but the dog didn't make it. It disappeared briefly and tried another leap, not as high this time. A man yelled out, "Genghis! Down!" The name fit. Genghis obeyed but continued to snarl his disapproval from the other side of the fence.

I brushed myself off and returned, red-faced and sheepish, to the front door where Magruder was waiting. Impress the boss.

"I'd prefer that this meeting be non-confrontational," he said.

"Me, too. Somebody should tell Genghis."

"Did you get hurt?"

"Just my pride."

"Your pride? I want to see that bruise."

The door opened and the Filipino housekeeper said, "You can come in now. This way."

She led us through a living room, dining room and family room that flowed into one another and out onto the lanai. She gestured towards the pool and then turned and left. Magruder and I crossed the lanai to the pool. It was, as I'd guessed, a lap pool, about

twenty-five meters long and two lanes wide. A man I figured to be
Pfeifer was plowing the water with more power than grace. Genghis
spotted me first. He was in a dog run in the far corner of the back
yard, but when he saw me, he rose up on his hind legs against the
fence and barked furiously. Stretched out his full length, he looked
like seven feet of black hatred topped with a head the size of an NFL
helmet.

"A rottweiler," said Magruder. "I hope the chain link can
hold him."

Pfeifer swam his lap, did a kick-turn and glided back to
where we waited by the side. He heaved himself out of the pool.
"With you in a minute," he said. Rivulets of water made flow patterns
through the hair on his shoulders and chest. His photograph hadn't
let me judge his height. Now, I put him at five-eight with over two
hundred twenty pounds. He had wide shoulders and muscular arms,
an ample, protruding gut, and short, thick legs. Fingers like sausages.
My gaze went to his Speedo trunks and the tight knot in front.
Magruder caught me looking and jabbed me in the ribs.

Pfeifer's hair was fine and sparse like the hair on my arms.
When dry, it would probably be reddish-blonde. It went with his
complexion. He had regular features but they were blurred by his
extra weight. Without it he might have been handsome. He put two
fingers in his mouth and gave a shrill whistle. To my amazement, the
housekeeper emerged from the house carrying a terry cloth robe and
a towel. Pfeifer slipped his arms into the robe, leaving it open, and
toweled off his face and head. He tossed his housekeeper the towel
and dismissed her with an imperious wave.

"Jock Pfeifer," he said to Magruder. Brian introduced
himself and shook hands. Pfeifer turned to me.

"Val Lyon," I said ignoring his outstretched hand.

Pfeifer's smile disappeared. He thrust his hands in the
pockets of his robe and looked me up and down with such
thoroughness I felt naked. Genghis, who had quieted down when
Pfeifer got out of the pool, started another racket. Pfeifer said,
"You've already met Genghis."

"Just briefly," I said. "I was trying to get a look at your pool, but Genghis must've thought I was trespassing."

"Genghis ain't stupid." He turned to Brian. "Brian, right? Sorry to keep you waiting, but I make it a rule not to let anyone disturb my lap time. I do a hundred laps twice a day, rain or shine. I also do a hundred sit ups and a hundred push ups, morning and evening. You believe that?" He looked at me and patted his bare gut. "You probably think this is all fat, don't you? Well let me tell you, it ain't. It's muscle. I worked hard to get this." He grinned again, winked at Magruder, and said, "When you got a great tool like mine, you wanta build a shed over it. I guess you got a great one, too. Keep it oiled and working for the little woman?" He patted himself again. "Show you this ain't fat. Brian-buddy, you're what? Two sixty, two seventy-five?"

"He's two hundred thirty," I said.

"Close enough. It's still a lotta beef. Hit me. Go ahead, take your best shot. Show you how tough it is."

"Pfeifer," I said, "this is stupid. We came to talk, not play some schoolyard games."

Pfeifer said, "You keep outta this, babe. Don't listen to her Brian-buddy. Go ahead and do it."

Brian said, "I think Ms. Lyon's right, why don't we sit down and talk."

"Hey, Brian-buddy, you can't let the little woman lead you around by the joint."

"She's my associate," said Brian.

"Gentlemen," I said, "I'm on the clock. You want to go at it, join a Sumo club. I'm here for business."

Brian said, "Jock, I don't want to hit you. I'll take your word that you're fit."

Pfeifer wouldn't let Brian get out gracefully. "Fit? I do two hundred laps a day, fourteen hundred a week, fifty-six hundred a month - "

"You're getting into higher math," I said. "You'll give yourself a brain aneurysm."

Pfeifer glared at me. I'd violated some law of the forest, I guess. The doe should keep quiet while the stags butt heads. There was a glut of testosterone. You could almost smell it.

"Brian-buddy, you oughta take a lesson in handling women. Yours has got quite a mouth on her."

Magruder's face darkened. I said, "Let it go, Brian." It seemed to have an effect. He said, "Pfeifer, can we have a friendly, civil discussion?"

"Sure. Don't get me wrong, we're all friends here. Look, Brian-buddy, I'm tryin' to make a point. Just humor me, okay? I want you to hit me. I'm gonna show you even a big guy like yourself, a Magruder to boot, can't hurt me. Now, c'mon, gimme your best shot. You don't wanta look like a wuss in front of the little woman." He patted his gut again and then gave Brian's stomach a backhand pat. "Hit me!"

Uncertainty and anger showed on Magruder's face. It occurred to me that if I weren't there, he'd probably do the sensible thing and tell Pfeifer to fuck off. But with women around, men have trouble doing the sensible thing. Brian's resolve was clearly waning. He clenched his right hand.

"Brian," I warned.

"Okay," he said, not to me, but to Pfeifer. He drew his arm back. Pfeifer put his hands on his hips, pulling his robe back and exposing more of his gut.

"Guys," I said, "this is stupid." I took a half step forward and drove the heel of my left hand into Pfeifer's belly about a hand's width below the sternum where the flesh belled out.

15 THE WORLD ACCORDING TO JOCK

Pfeifer was muscled all right, but he'd been watching Brian, not me, and my punch caught him before he could harden-up. His eyes went wide and his breath escaped in a loud, "poof." He doubled over, clutching his abdomen. I took him by the elbow and guided him backwards to a patio chair.

Magruder looked at me in amazement. "What the hell'd you do that for?"

"You were about to put on some dumb, macho show and hit him with your fist - like he was trying to get you to do - and all you'd get out of it would be a handful of busted metacarpals. I don't know how many times I've seen it: you want to find a guy that hit another guy, you just check the emergency rooms for a busted hand. Too many guys don't know how to hit."

Pfeifer struggled for breath. He went, "Unhh…unhh…unhh." I pushed his head down to his knees and held it there.

"Unhh…Jesus," he said, "you hit me…unhh…I wasn't ready."

"You looked plenty ready to me."

"You hit me."

"You asked for it. You want to try whistling for your

housekeeper?"

"Unhh…very funny. Got no breath."

"Keep your head down. You'll get it back."

Pfeifer took a few more breaths and then sat back in the chair. His complexion had turned from ruddy to ashen. "You're lucky you're standing. Anybody else does that to me, they don't remain standing long."

"Is that a threat, Pfeifer?"

"Statement of fact. It's because you're a guest and because I don't hurt women."

"But your scruples don't keep you from threatening Mr. Magruder's client."

"Jean? Don't know what the fuck you're talkin' about."

Brian said, "Jean got a letter telling her she was creating, quote, explosive conditions, end of quote, by hiding Nathan. It was anonymous of course, but she believes it came from you."

"That's it? The letter didn't say I was gonna cut her throat or anything? That ain't no threat."

"Did you send it?" I asked.

"No. 'Course not. If she says I did, she's lying."

Brian pulled a chair up for me and one for himself. I sat down and leaned close to Pfeifer. "Jean says she thinks you'd harm her. Would you?"

Pfeifer studied me with narrowed eyes. He crossed his arms self-consciously over his middle and said, "You got kids?"

"No."

"Then you don't know what it's like when someone takes your kid and says you're not a fit parent. If I tell the both of you, her shylock and a witness, I'd hurt her, that'd ruin my chances of gettin' Nathan back. And that's all I'm after. I haven't threatened her with anything but gettin' the kid back. I'll tell you, though, she oughta watch herself 'cause the slander she's spreadin' could push anybody to the edge. You see what I'm sayin'?"

"As for who's fit, she's the one not fit to raise a boy. She's got him doing recitals and going to art shows. Dressing in clothes he's not allowed to mess up. Listen to this, he gets picked on at school, so he goes to her, right? What does she tell him? She tells him don't associate with boys like that."

"What do you tell him?"

"Nothing. I teach him to fight. Then, she says I'm too rough on him because he has a black eye."

"You hit him?" I asked.

"Of course, I hit him. I'm teaching him to fight. You don't learn how to fight from a book."

"What else do you do, you and Nathan?"

"We go to games, we go fishing. Things she won't do for him. On one visit, I take him hunting. We go to Wyoming where he gets his first elk. On the way back we stop in Las Vegas. I let him try his hand at blackjack and he gets a kick out of it. Jean hears about the trip and has a fit. Her son shouldn't be shooting animals and gambling, she says. She doesn't allow any more visits. Then this abuse shit starts."

Brian said, "Gambling? He wouldn't be allowed in a casino."

"That's what you know, Brian-buddy. You show the right kind a money and you can find a game for anybody. Hey, what's the big deal? It was just a few hands. Look, I'm just a guy who loves his kid, who wants to show him a good time."

"Old-fashioned father-son bonding, is that it?" I asked.

Pfeifer leaned forward in his chair and leveled a stubby finger at my face. "Let me tell you something," he said. "The kid needs a father. He's thirteen, he's startin' to wonder about women. He wakes up with a hard-on, who can he go to? You think that lipstick lesbian can tell him what to do with it? If I don't teach him how to handle women, he won't ever learn right."

I said, "If you don't teach him, there's a chance he will learn right. Do you have him whistle for a woman's attention? If you ask me, I'd say your teaching him is a case of serious child abuse, itself."

Pfeifer rose out of his chair. Brian did, too. I stayed where I was. Pfeifer said, "What right have you got to criticize the way I treat women?"

"I think it should be obvious," I said. "Of course, you've probably never listened to a woman in your life."

Brian imposed his bulk between me and Pfeifer. "Val," he warned.

"Let her talk," said Pfeifer, "just to show you I do listen to women, Brian-buddy." He sat down again leaving Brian standing uncertainly. Brian looked at me and I shrugged. He sat down, too. Pfeifer said, "I'm forgetting my manners. I should offer you something to drink. Of course, you think I don't have manners, do you, Ms. Lyon? You want to join me in some lemonade?"

I declined and so did Brian. Pfeifer whistled again and, when the housekeeper appeared, said somewhat loudly, "Lydia, explain to Ms. Lyon why I whistle."

Lydia said, "I do not hear so good. I ask him to whistle so I can hear him."

"I see," I said. "It's your idea, Lydia?"

"Precisely," said Pfeifer. "Now, Lydia, would you please bring us some lemonade? Three glasses. Our guests may change their minds about having some."

We waited while Lydia went off to get it. Pfeifer made small talk about how much his pool cost and Nathan's swimming ability. Lydia returned carrying a tray with a pitcher and glasses. She filled all three and offered each of us one. Brian accepted, but I didn't. If we were in the middle of the Sahara and Pfeifer were offering us the only available water, I still wouldn't take it. Principles are terrible things to be saddled with.

"Lydia," I said, "tell us what happens when Nathan is here with his father. Have you ever seen Mr. Pfeifer hit him?"

Lydia looked anxiously at Pfeifer. He nodded. "Go ahead," he said.

"No. I didn't see anything like that."

"What about other forms of physical abuse?"

She shook her head. "No," she said.

"What do they do together when they're here?"

"They play games. They watch the movies."

"What kind of movies? Does Mr. Pfeifer show him dirty movies? Movies about sex?"

Pfeifer had been listening impassively, but the last question caused him to knit his brows together. He said, "Thank you, Lydia. You don't have to answer that. You may go back to the house."

Lydia looked uncertainly at me for an instant and then turned and headed across the lanai.

Pfeifer said, "I know where this line of questioning is going. You're trying to make it like I'm morally unfit. Well it won't wash."

"I understand you've got a morals charge hanging over your head," said Brian.

"A shoddy setup attempt. A person's an adult, they can watch whatever they want, right? Who's gonna say I can't watch this or you can't watch that? At each of my shops I got a special room where I keep the sex stuff. All kinds of people go in there and come out with movies they want to rent. Professors, ministers, judges, even mothers and grandmothers. But nobody goes in without being eighteen or older. Any doubt at all, we check your ID."

"What makes you think you were setup?" I asked.

"What makes you think I wasn't? Look at the facts. Two men come in the store and go to the back room. We got a big sign over the door says you must be eighteen. My clerk sees where they're going and stops them. She doesn't think they're of age. About that time another guy comes in, obviously younger. She doesn't pay him any mind 'cause he stays in the regular section. She checks the IDs of the first two guys and they look okay to her. My clerk, you understand, pays attention to this. She's got grandkids, teaches Sunday school, used to be a librarian. These two spend some time in the room and come out with some videos they want. My clerk starts to ring it up. Meanwhile, the young guy tells one of the two that he wants a video, too. Up to this time, my clerk doesn't know they're together. The young guy picks out a video. Die Hard. Doesn't have a single tit, but it has language nobody should listen to. One of the older guys gives it to my clerk to ring up. Nothing wrong with that, right? She's renting the videos to two guys who are of age. Who sees it at home, ain't her business. She puts them in the same bag and gives it to one of the older guys. She don't pay attention after that 'cause she's got a customer. All of a sudden there're cops comin' in sayin' she rented pornography to a minor and there's the kid holdin' the bag of videos. The two older guys turn out to be rookie cops. You think that wasn't a setup?"

"So who set it up?" asked Brian.

Pfeifer looked at me and then gave Brian a harder look. "This is a joke, right? You can't be that dumb, Brian-buddy. It was your brother who set it up."

I glanced over at Brian. Other than a reflective look on his face, I found little reaction. The accusation seemed not to have affected him much. I said, "Ken Magruder? What makes you think he could do something like that?"

"The Magruders have got influence," said Pfeifer. "They've got enough room in their pockets for some cops and the City Prosecutor. Besides, I cause them trouble." He sat back in his chair and beamed at us.

Brian said, "Pfeifer, the Windward Cove Center doesn't mean that much to Ken that he'd stoop to corrupting police and city officials to keep it."

"I can cause a lot more trouble than Windward Cove," Pfeifer said. "Your brother knows it, too. Once I settle this thing with Jean and get Nathan back, the Magruder family will find out how much trouble I can cause." He rose out of his chair. "Listen, it was fun talking to you, but I got lots of stuff to attend to and Genghis needs to be let out so he can run. You don't wanna stay around for that." He said the last sentence while looking straight at me.

"We've learned what we came for," said Brian. He got to his feet, too, and I followed.

"Tell us about Sue Naito," I said.

Pfeifer frowned. "Who the fuck's Sue Naito? A friend of Jean's?"

"Yes."

"Wouldn't know her. I never paid much attention to Jean's friends. Is she a les, too?"

"She's dead. She died Friday night of a heart attack, but someone threatened her before she died. The person may, in fact, have caused her death. You don't know anything about that?"

"I told you, I wouldn't know Sue Naito from Sue Burrito."

"What about that gang of punks that disrupted the rally for Jean on Friday?"

We were walking towards the house, Pfeifer in the lead. He said, "Now wasn't that a shame? Seems like a lot of people have some strong feelings about father's rights."

"Did you have anything to do with it, Pfeifer?"

He paused in his tracks and said, "Me? No, but I've got an idea who did. I'd say Brian-buddy's got a good idea, too. Anybody that could get the services of the police, they would certainly be able to line up a handful of protesters."

I was getting in the car when Pfeifer called to me. "I just thought a somethin'," he said. "You know what's brown and black and looks great on a gumshoe? A rottweiler."

16 A DISH ON THE LANAI

We headed up Kahala towards Diamond Head. The street teemed with the usual Sunday afternoon crowd: golfers on their way to the club, joggers on their way to their personal nirvanas and tourists hoping to glimpse the rich and famous.

"Tell me what you think, Brian. Could your brother be involved?"

"No, but I want to ask him about it. For my own satisfaction."

"Want me to come along?"

"I think I'd better do this alone."

I agreed. My presence might put Ken on his guard if he were hiding something. The dashboard clock said it was five after four. I remembered my four o'clock date with Pam at the beach. Brian dropped me off there.

Kaimana Beach is listed as Sans Souci on the maps, but most people call it Kaimana because it fronts the New Otani Kaimana Hotel. Being at the very end of Waikiki near Diamond Head, not many tourists find their way to it, but the ones that do tend to be upscale.

My swimsuit was back in my apartment so I stopped in one of the hotel shops before heading to the beach. Since I was willing to pay a premium price for a functional one piece, the saleswoman let me change in the shop's dressing room. I don't look bad in a swimsuit and could probably wear most styles, but my idea of functionality is something that gives me both freedom of movement and freedom from worrying that I might expose myself, unintentionally.

Pam had a different idea about the functionality of sportswear. She was face down on a beach towel wearing one of those Brazilian-style bikinis that make my crotch hurt at just the thought. I mean I don't even like thongs between my toes. The suit was red, a color that looks stunning on her but cheap on me. Judging by the density of males in the area around her blanket, her suit was fully functional.

"You know," I said, spreading out my towel next to hers, "that suit practically disappears up your ass."

Pam turned to look up at me, a move which displayed her magnificent cleavage and caused one guy on a nearby towel to jerk bolt upright. "When you got it, you flaunt it," said Pam. "At my age I don't know how much longer I'll have it, so I'm flaunting it now."

"I'll say." I flopped down beside her.

"Speaking of flaunting, I saw a chick who looked an awful lot like you smooching some guy out on the street a few minutes ago."

"You can't have seen that far," I protested. Once as a teenager, my mother had caught me necking in front of the house and my defense had been similar, "You can't have seen anything that far away." When the facts are against you, discredit the witness.

"I saw it all," she said. "I happened to be parking my car and waved at you, but you were so caught up in the moment, you didn't see me. Now, are you going to tell me about your man, or do I have to drag it out of you?"

"What's there to tell?"

"Is this the guy who, in my office on Friday, you proclaimed was not the kind of man you were attracted to?"

"Yes."

"It looks like you worked out your doubts about him."

"Maybe." Pam gave me the look shrinks give you when you're holding back. "Okay. He came over last night."

Her eyes got wide. She sat up expectantly. "And?"

"And he left this morning."

"Wahoo, sugar," she screamed, beating her fists on her knees. "This calls for a celebration. I'm buying."

"Uh, Pam," I said, looking at her brief suit.

"Oh don't worry, I got a cover-up. C'mon."

Pam's cover-up was ankle-length, white, and about ninety percent see-through. Quite a few heads turned in our direction as we walked across the beach. One Japanese tourist made a pretense of taking a sweeping panorama of the beach with his camcorder, but mostly he swept Pam's backside.

"So," she said, when we'd found a beach side table at the Hau Tree Lanai restaurant, "was he good?"

"Pam, I'm not answering a question like that."

"Well, was he gentle? Considerate? How about exciting?"

I turned my chair to face out to sea. "I'm not answering."

"Okay. Be that way, sugar. You gonna see him again? Outside of work, I mean. Surely you can tell me that."

"Yes," I said, turning back to face her.

"Aha! I knew it. That plus the smug look on your face tells me the answer to my previous question is, 'all of the above.'"

"Aren't you the one who warned me about entangling relationships with a client?"

"Girlfriend, there will be plenty of time to worry about that when the sex stops being good."

A waitress came for our order. Pam ordered a strawberry daiquiri. Since Pam was treating, I ordered Glenlivet with a splash.

"You're going to Sue Naito's funeral, aren't you?" Pam asked.

"I haven't given it much thought. When is it?"

"Tomorrow afternoon. Lot's of people will be there."

Mention of Sue Naito brought with it a whole host of

feelings, among them a profound sadness. Though I'd only met her once and talked to her twice - both times being confrontational - I respected her. I would have liked to have known her and I wanted her to know me. Acceptance by a woman like Sue would have meant a lot. She was an intelligent, principled woman. She had enjoyed the love of a husband and children plus the admiration of a lot of women. It was fucking unfair that she should die. "Fucking unfair," I said.

"Yes," said Pam. "And you want to do something about it."

"Damn right."

"Just what do you think you could do?"

"As things stand, not much," I admitted. "If I could find the kid, though, I might have a better chance of finding the killer."

"Like how?" Pam's expression was doubtful.

"I could make him come to me, assuming what he wants is the boy."

"In other words, you're gonna be out there on a street going 'Yoo hoo, Mr. Killer. I got the kid. Come and get me.' Is that right? Remind me to stay away from you. You ever think you could wind up dead?"

"What else am I going to do? I'm not a cop. I can't grind out a murder investigation. The police have got all the resources, but they aren't treating it as murder."

"Well, I'm sure, sugar, you'll think of something. And I oughta be worried."

Our drinks arrived. We sipped them in silence and watched a lousy sunset. The sky to the north and west was a uniform gray and a north breeze ruffled the trees. The sun was nothing but a pale disk whose outline was blurred by high level clouds. As sunsets go, it wasn't up to Hawaii Visitors Bureau standards.

Pam and I have formed our own rituals around our excursions to beach side bars. One such ritual is spotting the HITs - hunks-in-trunks. The first one to spot an HIT calls it out and, if the other agrees that the target is indeed a hunk, earns a point. Whichever one of us has the fewest points when it's time for another round, buys the drinks. It never bothered us that we were engaging in a behavior we detest in men.

I was still thinking about Sue Naito when Pam started the game. "A gen-you-wine HIT at two o'clock coming this way," she said.

I saw him then. He was about six-feet tall with wide shoulders and good hips. He wore lime-green trunks and a loose, sleeveless top. When he saw us looking at him, he waved and broke into a run.

"Looks like you're going to have company," I said. "Maybe I should leave."

"Hunh uh! He's looking at you, sugar."

The hunk came onto the lanai, hardly breaking stride. When he was near our table, he said, "Val! Good to see you. How's the head? All right I hope."

I recognized the voice of the EMT named Greg. "The head's fine," I said and invited him to sit with us. He took a chair from another table and placed it between me and Pam. Closer to me than to Pam. She caught my eye and flicked her tongue over her lips. Yum yum.

Yum yum was right. Greg had sun-streaked brown hair, longish but well-cut, a broad unlined face, and pale blue eyes. He wore a dangly silver earring in one ear. The best part, though, was the muscle definition in his arms and shoulders. From the ease with which he'd lifted me on Friday, I knew he was strong, but it was somehow gratifying to be able to confirm it with my eyes. I said, "I didn't recognize you. My vision was pretty blurry when we met before."

"Not surprising with a hit like you took."

"I don't remember your last name, either," I said, suppressing a fear that my memory had suffered from the injury. His response was reassuring.

"Bauer. It was hardly the place for formal introductions. The wound healing okay? Let me take a look."

He felt around the base of my skull with gentle fingers. I was acutely aware of the heat from his body and the tangy, murky smell it gave off.

"Your technique has improved a lot," I said.

"Oh I can be gentle when I want to be. The wound's closed up nice. Guess I can stop worrying about you." He pushed an errant strand of hair over my ear.

"You worried about me?"

"I worry about all my patients. Understand you're a detective. You investigating the case?"

"Not officially. The police would like to close it up as a death by natural causes. They're not much convinced by the evidence of foul play."

Greg's face registered surprise. "What about the bruise below her eye?" he asked.

"The official explanation is that it could've happened in the fall."

"No way! The skin was broken. She had an uneven laceration like she'd been hit by somebody wearing a ring. It was plain as day. Rap, my partner, he said the same thing."

"Suppose she fell against something sharp?"

Greg shook his head. "We always look around for what might've caused the injury because it could give a clue as to how to treat it. No sharp corners on the desk, no jagged hardware. Nothing sharp or broken on the floor, either. Then, of course, there's your wound. You didn't get that by falling on your head unless you kind of twisted your neck around and scrunched up your shoulder a bit, like so."

He dropped one shoulder, raised the other and ducked his chin down on his chest. It was an amateurish version of Dick Van Dyke's headless man, but I got the point and laughed politely at him. He was too well put together for comedy. I glanced at Pam. I could tell she agreed with me.

"Tell me your version of Friday," I said. "Who was first in the house, you or Rap?"

"Me."

"What'd you see?"

"The front door was open, about three-quarters."

"I opened it," I said. "Go on. What'd you do?"

"I called. Got no answer. Rap joined me. We went in together."

"Nobody else inside?"

"Didn't look like it, not 'til we found you and the other victim."

Victim! I hate that word. I didn't think of myself as a victim, and didn't want Greg to think of me as one, either.

"Oh, and the back door…the one from the kitchen to the yard…it was open. Did you open that one, too?"

"No. That was closed when I saw it. The guy must've gone out that way. Did you hear anything?"

"Some dogs were barking in the yard next door when we drove up. It could've been our lights. We came up with lights, but no siren. The lights sometimes set dogs off."

"Or they could've been barking at a stranger running through the yard. Could you tell which side it was?"

"Sounded like it came from the house on the Koko Head side."

"Greg," said Pam, "Miss Nancy Drew here is gonna continue to pry you with questions about the case until somebody puts a stop to it. So, I'm stopping it. Can we buy you a drink or a beer?"

"A Coke would be great," he said. "I go on duty this evening."

Pam ordered a Coke for Greg and another round for her and me. Then she managed to get from him all his vital stats. Stud number one is twenty-eight and single. He has recently broken up with his girlfriend of three years. His favorite activities are sailing and diving.

The drinks came and Greg said to me, "Do you have any theories about who caused Ms. Naito's death?"

Pam snorted. "Greg, honey," she said, "this girl doesn't work with theories. You won't see any clever deductions or great insights into the criminal mind coming from her."

"You've never seen me work," I said, wishing I didn't sound so petulant.

"But, you've told me plenty about your methods."

"So how does she work?" asked Greg. He seemed truly interested, which only added to my discomfort.

"Val favors the roller derby approach. She slams into the pack, knocks people down, and then goes after whoever is left standing. No slick traps, no brilliant solutions from our gal Val."

"I'm glad somebody recognizes my abilities."

"So what's your next step?" Greg asked.

"Nothing," I said ruefully. "Much as I'd like to find out who was in the house that night, I don't have any standing in the case. I've got my hands full as it is trying to find Nathan."

"Whose disappearance is connected to Sue," said Pam.

"I suppose I could break into her house and try to find a clue to his location."

"Break in!" Pam exploded. "See, Greg? That's how Val works. It doesn't matter that it might be against the law."

"All right! It's a lousy idea. For the time being, I'm just going to plod along and hope I get lucky."

Greg took a long pull on his Coke and said, "As your healer, I think you need a break from plodding. I'm taking care of a friend's boat. He's got some new sails coming this week and I was planning to try them out. How about coming with me? We could go out Saturday."

"I don't know," I said. I was thinking of Brian.

"You're invited too, of course, Pam. It's a thirty-six footer. There's plenty of room."

"That sounds nice, but I've got a crisis management seminar on Saturday. You two go ahead and have fun."

"I think I'd better leave Saturday open in case I find Nathan," I said.

"Sure, I understand," he said. "Can't fault a guy for trying, right? Let me give you my number in case you decide you'd like a boat ride. The offer'll still be good. No strings attached." Pam produced a pen from her beach bag. Rather quickly, to my mind. He wrote the number on a napkin which he folded and placed in my palm, closing my fingers around it. "It's a cellular number. I wouldn't want to miss your call." He leaned towards me. "I've got to run, but I hope you change your mind. Meantime, take care of yourself. Don't let anything else happen to your head." He brushed his fingertips lightly across my cheek, stood up and left.

I watched him go. My cheek was still tingling when I turned back to Pam. The urge to brush the spot with my hand was strong, but I resisted it.

Pam was beaming. She said, "Now that is a real dish. And, girlfriend, is he hot for you!"

"Why would you say something like that?"

"Because it's obvious in the way he looked at you."

I groaned. "*Merda*! That's just what I need."

17 BREAK-IN NUMBER TWO

The breeze picked up a notch and the temperature dropped a few degrees once the sun had set. We felt chilled in our swimsuits on the open lanai. We downed our drinks and left. Pam gave me a lift home.

"Greg is gorgeous, sugar. Don't you agree?"

"Yes."

"And Brian sounds sweet."

"Uh huh."

"I'd say your life is beginning to turn around."

"I'd say it's beginning to get complicated."

"Well, girlfriend, I didn't see you throw away his number."

"Waste not, want not," I said.

Pam dropped me off at an ABC store near my apartment. I bought their last Star-Bulletin/Advertiser, some Mexican dinners and a six-pack of Coke. Back in my apartment, I opened the Coke and put one of the dinners in the microwave. While it cooked, I put on a long-sleeved indigo body suit, jeans and a pair of black Reebok Triple Threats. By that time my dinner was ready. I poured picante sauce over the whole thing - enchiladas, rice and beans - then opened the paper to the vital statistics section and spread it out on the counter, eating as I read.

Funeral services for Sue Naito were to be held on Monday,

one o'clock, at Kaimuki United Methodist Church. Burial would be at Diamond Head Memorial Park. Friends could call at the mortuary from six to nine tonight.

It was six thirty-seven.

I finished dinner and fished my Swiss Army knife and driver's license out of my purse. I put the license and a twenty dollar bill in a plastic card holder and stuck the holder in my back pocket.

The Nissan's starter hummed when I turned the key. I ran the gear shift through all five gears and tried again. Another hum. The damn thing was getting worse. I slammed the gears harder. On the third try it started and I headed towards Kaimuki. Breaking into Sue Naito's house still seemed like a lousy idea, but it beat sitting around thinking how men were complicating my life.

Heavy gusts whipped the fronds of palm trees. There had been a moon last night, but tonight it was hidden by clouds. I'd probably have a couple of hours at most before it rained.

I drove past Sue's house. One light burned on the front porch and another one on the detached garage. Otherwise the house and yard were dark. I parked down the hill at the end of the block.

Two things I always have with me are a pocket knife and a flashlight. I keep a four cell flashlight under the front seat and a mini light with a headband in the glove compartment. I took the mini and the headband and went back up the hill.

At Sue's I walked casually to the door and knocked, just in case someone was there. After the second knock, I peered through the windows on the porch and shone my light in. Nobody. The front of the house was too visible for a break-in. The same with the side of the house along the driveway. The other side of the house was concealed by a tall oleander hedge but the windows were too high even for a peek.

My luck was better in the back where three steps led up to a narrow porch. Two low jalousie windows with frosted panes flanked the back door. They were locked. The back door, too. Few Hawaiians close their homes completely, however. I played my light around the porch until I spotted a set of wooden jalousies above the door -

open, but out of my reach. Using my light sparingly, I searched the porch and the yard for something to stand on. Near the garage was a galvanized garbage can without a lid. More searching turned up a ceramic rainwater jar with a wooden cover for keeping out mosquitoes. The lid was thick enough to hold me and its diameter was wider than the mouth of the garbage can. I carried both lid and can to the porch.

Breaking in is not something I'm accustomed to. My heart pounded rapidly and my pulse raced. Despite the cool breezes and occasional gusts, my body suit was damp under the arms and sweat-streaked in front and back. I could feel moisture pooling in my lower back and streaming between my breasts. Wearing the headband and light, I climbed onto my makeshift platform. The can was not very stable, but by standing spread-legged, I could steady myself against the top of the door frame until I was shoulder-level with the lowest window slat.

The window was about a foot and a half high and as wide as the door. I removed the aluminum screen. It slipped out of my sweaty hands and clattered to the porch. No yard lights came on at the neighbors. I counted to thirty slowly, got my breathing under control, and went back to work.

The slats wouldn't yield when I tried to pull them out. I shone my light along them. They were screwed into the side brackets. More bother. I attacked the screws with the screwdriver blade of my knife. It was slow work. The first two slats were below eye level where I could see the screws but the other two required me to work by feel. I took out three, eased them to the porch, and pocketed the screws.

With three slats gone, I had about fifteen inches to squeeze through. I levered my shoulders and torso through the space and twisted around until I was balanced on the window frame in the small of my back. I grabbed the top of the frame, pulled myself through and hung there like Charles Barkley grabbing iron before dropping awkwardly to the floor.

My watch said seven thirty-three. The visitation went until

nine. The family might stay around the mortuary for awhile, but I couldn't count on that. Any one of them might choose to come back early.

The stiletto beam from my light picked out kitchen cabinets, appliances and the door to Sue's office. I unlocked the back door for an escape route. Just like the guy who'd whacked me. My skin prickled at the thought.

Someone had tidied the office since Friday. The desk had been straightened and the file cabinet closed. The first rule of burgling: go for the locked drawers. Just my luck, they were all unlocked. I'd have to go through everything.

The center desk drawer had the usual supplies and notepads, all neatly arranged. I held the notepads at an angle to my light, looking for indentations of writing, but found none. I did find a claim check from a computer repair shop which explained why there was no computer.

One side drawer contained the Davison family's financial records, paid bills and tax returns. I read just enough to learn that Harold's business was real-estate development and that he was successful at it.

The file cabinet was a four-drawer file organized alphabetically. It contained files belonging to both Sue and Harold. The second drawer, G to L, was the obvious place to look, but there were no files labeled "Harriet." Everything under 'H' had to do with real estate. In contrast, a lot of files under 'A' concerned abortion. I went through them as quickly as I could, aware that time was running out on me. They were mostly articles, reports, and opinions by Sue and others. My mini light made reading difficult but I wasn't interested in reading, anyway. I was looking for a list. No luck. I put the last file back and shut the drawer. I'd been in the house about forty-five minutes and had found nothing. I was hot and sticky from being in the airless room, my mind was warning me to get out, but there were two more drawers to go. I pawed through them quickly, leaving drops of sweat on manila folders. More real estate stuff. I was becoming so accustomed to seeing real estate files that I almost missed an important one. It was under 'W.' It was labeled "Windward Cove."

Why would Sue be interested in Windward Cove I wondered? But the file turned out to be Harold's. It contained letters, contracts and other legal documents. I couldn't understand most of it, but two documents were revealing. One was an agreement of partnership, dated ten years earlier, between Harold Davison and the Magruders represented by Ken and Molly. The partnership was to develop the Windward Cove Center. Davison had a five percent interest for $100,000. I didn't know what real estate was like ten years ago, but it seemed that Davison was getting in cheap. The other letter explained it for me. It was a memo to Ken in which Davison promised Sue's help, as a member of the City Council, in getting the Windward Cove property rezoned from residential to commercial. He also said that Sue would try to get the council to reimburse the partnership for the costs of street lights on the perimeter of the development.

I hoped Sue hadn't gone along with what to me was an obvious conflict of interest. The rest of the documents gave no indication of her role in the project. The final document, dated three years later, was an agreement to terminate the partnership. The Magruder family would buy out Davison's share for $250,000.

In Hawaiian politics, land is as good as money, and money, everywhere, alters ideology. That is as sophisticated as my political thinking gets. Even so, I had a hard time believing that two families from opposite political camps could work out such a tidy arrangement. The partnership had ended, apparently amicably, with Davison making a handsome profit.

I closed the folder and refiled it neatly. Time was running out and I still hadn't found what I came for. When you're looking for something, you try to put yourself in the place of the person who hid it. In desperation and frustration, I sat in Sue's chair behind her desk. Friday night's disorder was gone. All that remained on the polished surface was a calculator, a pen and pencil set, family photos, the answering machine, and the phone.

The phone. The same one I'd pulled to the floor. The one I'd used to call for help. I needn't have punched 911 that night because it had three emergency memory buttons. Above the buttons was a LCD display and a name index card with twenty memory codes. The name index card listed the Davison children, Harold's office, Sue's office and Carol Fernandez, but five codes had no names. Oh, Sue, I thought, how simple. I punched the memory button, the asterisk button, and the first unnamed code. A number appeared in the LCD display. I wrote it down on Sue's notepad and tried the next one. Another number. The same with all the other unnamed codes. I wrote all of them down in a hasty scrawl. Lastly, I tried the emergency buttons. The police and fire were 911, but the medical was a seven-digit number. I copied it down, too.

You gotta know when to hold 'em and know when to fold 'em. It was time to fold. I tore the paper off the pad and stuffed it in the card holder between my license and the twenty. Then I headed out the back door, making sure it locked behind me. It was ten to nine, but I couldn't leave the evidence of my entry. I replaced the jalousie slats and carried the garbage can back where it belonged.

Headlights came halfway up the driveway and stopped just as I reached the shadow of the garage. The driver cut the engine and got out, clearly visible in the light above the garage - one of the Davison children. He walked back towards the front of the house. I moved around the garage until I was on the other side from where I had a clear view all the way down the driveway. Davison was talking to a cop. In front of the house was a blue and white patrol car and a plain car with a blue light on top. Davison and the cop went to the front door and, shortly after, lights went on inside the house. A few minutes later, the blue and white left. Several more minutes passed and the other cop left. It was now after nine and the rest of the Davison family would be returning soon.

Even as the thought went through my head, a car turned into the driveway and Harold Davison emerged with more members of the family. Everybody went into the house. I'd taken enough chances for one night. The wind gusts increased and big drops of rain started falling.

Between the driveway and the neighbor's house was a low hedge, its outline clear in the light from the garage. The yard on the other side was dark. I sprinted away from the garage and hurdled the hedge. The drop was farther than I expected and my ankle twisted under me. Shit! I thought. But when I stood up and tested it, it was okay. I'd not only jumped a hedge, but a low stone wall into a yard that was two feet lower than Davison's. Lucky to get away without a sprain or a break.

From somewhere near the back of the yard, a dog barked furiously. I hoped he was penned or chained. I moved across the yard as quickly as I could, carefully avoiding obstacles. The rain came harder in thick sheets, soaking through my cotton top, but quieting the dog. I went over the next hedge with more care, but I bumped my hip on some lawn furniture and slipped on the wet grass. Now the rain had reduced visibility enough that I decided to chance going down a driveway to the street. I made it out to Maunaloa Street and ran the rest of the block to my car, flung open the door and threw myself into the driver's seat. I tore off the headband, put it into the glove compartment and reached in my pocket for the keys. My hand closed around keys and something else - wood screws. I'd forgotten to screw the slats back in place. Well, that couldn't be helped.

My clothes were soaked completely. I shivered violently and turned the key in the ignition. All I got was a hum. I slammed the gears angrily and tried again. Another hum, followed by a knock on the window. I cracked the window enough to see the man standing next to the car.

"Having engine trouble, Ms. L?" asked Detective Nakashita.

18 BOOK HER, DANA

Nakashita wore a triumphal grin as though he'd just stolen the ball from my hands and jammed it in the hole with seconds on the clock. He said, "Please step out of the car, Ms. Lyon."

"In the rain? Are you kidding, Sergeant? You can't imagine what it will do to my hair, not to mention -"

The grin disappeared. "Knock it off! The rain or a magistrate."

I chose the rain. Nakashita stepped away from the car when I opened the door. He carried a large golf umbrella for his own protection, but made no effort to protect me with it. Where the hell has chivalry gone?

Nakashita was accompanied by a uniformed officer. She stood near the rear bumper, feet apart and baton in hand, wearing a rain slicker.

"What's this all about?" I asked.

"Turn around, Ms. L. Face the car, hands on the roof," said Nakashita.

I had to lean forward and brace myself with my arms while the rain pounded the Nissan's roof and splattered back at me. My hair fell around my face and lay heavily on the back of my neck. My clothes were plastered to my skin like one more epidermal layer.

"Oh, golly! I must be in a no parking zone, right? How could I have missed the sign? You know, I might have paid more attention to it if I knew it would bring a homicide detective. Maybe you should have signs, like, 'Parking enforced by -"

"Why don't you can it, Lyon? Officer, would you check her for weapons, please?"

"Oh hell, Sergeant, you can see I'm not carrying anything."

The female officer patted me down smoothly and thoroughly. "What's that in your back pocket?"

"My license."

"Take it out please."

I reached behind me with one hand, removed the ID holder and offered it to her. "It's really a lousy picture, don't you think? They use head-on lighting so it looks like you have no bone structure. I mean my face looks like it's all puffed out. Does yours look that bad?"

"Tell me about it."

"Don't encourage her, just get on with it," said Nakashita.

The officer gave the ID holder back to me without inspecting it. She continued the search. It didn't take her long to find my pocket knife and the screws, all of which she handed to Nakashita.

"Screws, Ms. Lyon?"

"I'm taking up carpentry. Look, I don't mean to be forward, but do you think I could share your umbrella?"

"You're not going to get any wetter than you are. What were you doing back there at Davison's house?"

"How long are you going to continue with this Japanese version of the water torture, Sergeant?"

"Answer the question Ms. Lyon."

"Hunh uh. If you're going to charge me, I want to call my lawyer. If not, well…no charge, no questions."

"You can call from Beretania Street," he said.

I pleaded with them to let me get a T-shirt and towel out of my car. Nakashita relented after the officer intervened on my side.

Her blue and white was parked around the corner behind Nakashita's. I rode in the back. On the way to the station, I slid down in the seat and peeled out of my sodden body suit. I had to keep the jeans on, but the dry towel and T-shirt stopped my shivering.

The woman officer walked me into the station, towel around my shoulders and my wet garment in my hand, dripping water behind us. We were buzzed through a heavy door and ushered to a small room with a folding table and six stacking chairs.

"When do I get to make my call?"

"When the sergeant says you do. He'll be in soon. You want some advice? Don't fuck with him. Coffee?"

I said, "yes," and she left.

Nakashita's arrival caught me with the towel draped over my head in a desperate effort to dry my hair. He came in carrying a blank tablet and a plastic bag containing my knife and the screws. The officer followed right behind him with a steaming cup of coffee. I draped the towel around my neck and accepted the coffee gratefully. It was warm and strong - the closest I might get to comfort for a long while.

Looking at Nakashita, you'd never guess he'd been out in the same rain that had drenched me. Except for an irregular wet line around the cuffs, his trousers were as clean and neatly pressed as if he'd taken them off the hanger moments before. My jeans, on the other hand, squished every time I moved on the plastic seat.

The cop left and a minute later we were joined by a woman detective named Dana…"DANa Hannigan," she said. In spite of her name, Hannigan was clearly Polynesian. She had broad, flat features, dark eyes, and clear, luminous skin. I'd give anything for skin like that. Nakashita took the chair across from me and Hannigan sat at the end.

Nakashita said, "Let's talk, Ms. Lyon. I want the complete truth for a change. No half-truths, no lies, no smartass remarks."

"Are you going to charge me?"

"If it comes to that. Disturbing the peace, trespass, obstructing justice."

"Those are a little vague, don't you think?"

"So it'll take a while to write them up tight enough to stick. I might have to sleep on it. Get the point?"

I got the point. He'd sleep at home and I'd sleep in a cell. The main thing was that I wasn't under arrest - not yet, anyway.

Nakashita waited for me to speak. He took a ballpoint from his shirt pocket and tapped it against his front teeth. I found it unnerving, but I wasn't about to let him know that. I squeaked a damp strand of hair between my fingers. He tapped his teeth again. I squeaked another strand. Hannigan rolled her eyes.

I said, "You didn't just happen to be driving by at the very moment my car wouldn't start."

"One of Ms. Naito's conscientious neighbors reported seeing a strange vehicle. An unexpected death makes folks vigilant for awhile."

"They send homicide to check them out? On a Sunday? I don't believe that. You're putting in your own time on this one." Nakashita just looked at me, giving nothing away. I resolved never to play poker with him. "So somebody reported a strange car in the neighborhood the night of Sue's death. Right?"

Nakashita went back to tapping his teeth. I pulled at another strand of hair. "That would be the killer's car," I said brightly. "Did anybody get the license?"

Nakashita said, "If you're done, then let me tell you something. I can yank your PI's license for interfering with an investigation or for concealing evidence of a crime."

"What investigation am I supposed to have interfered with Sergeant? I told you everything about the break-in at my apartment."

"You haven't told me what the guy might have been looking for that he missed in Ms. Naito's office. You didn't tell me why you went to see her in the first place."

"Pregnancy -"

"Can it, Lyon." Nakashita's whole face darkened, his birthmark turned the color of an eggplant. "Don't think I believed that line about pregnancy counseling for a second. You're looking for the Pfeifer kid. You hounded Carol Fernandez about it yesterday. She said you threatened her."

"You talked to Carol Fernandez? What'd you think about all those cats?"

"Don't dance around with me, Lyon. Did you threaten her or not?"

"No. I told her she was in danger from the same person who killed Sue. Know what I think? You're convinced Sue was murdered but somebody higher up wants you to see it differently. The murder of a former city councilwoman would make some people uncomfortable. Better to leave it death by natural causes. So you're working weekends because you don't have much time to make the case."

Nakashita's eyes were dark, round holes like the bores of two guns. I wondered how far I could push him.

"Who's pulling you off, Sergeant? What's your deadline?"

"Val," said Hannigan, "the medical examiner has determined that Ms. Naito's death resulted from a heart attack. The announcement will be tomorrow after the funeral. Help us on this. There's no way it was murder. But if the heart attack were stress-induced, we're looking at the possibility of involuntary manslaughter. We think you know who might have stressed her."

"Me? How would I know?"

"Did you, yourself, stress her?" asked Nakashita.

I could only look at him, stunned and speechless. Finally, I managed, "I admired Sue. I had no reason to kill her."

"Maybe you didn't have a reason, but your client could have. There's a lot of bad feeling between the Magruders and Ms. Naito."

"Look, my client is Brian Magruder, not the Magruder family. He hired me to find Nathan Pfeifer, nothing more. As for his own leanings, I don't know if he's pro-choice, pro-life or pro football."

Hannigan asked, "What about your leanings, Ms. Lyon? Are you anti-abortion?"

"No."

"Are you sure?"

"I'm sure. Look, suppose it was me. How would it work? I kill her and then hit myself on the back of the head? C'mon, you can do better than that."

Nakashita went back to tapping his teeth. Hannigan said, "You're holding something back, Val."

"I've already given a statement that she was unconscious when I arrived. She said she'd been threatened and she believed the threat came from the punks at the rally." I gave them the whole story, the rally, the fight with the tough who tried to harm Jean, and Sue's phone call.

When I was finished Nakashita said, "You beat up somebody and I didn't hear about it?"

"I was protecting my client,"

"Is that why Sue Naito called you?" asked Hannigan.

"More or less."

"Give us the more or less," said Nakashita.

"We disagreed about my methods. She thought the threat she'd received might have been in retaliation for what I did to the guy."

"She didn't think she was being threatened for her pro-choice stance?" asked Hannigan.

"No."

Nakashita said, "Lyon, the Magruders and Davison and Naito have been going at each other for years over abortion and over land. Now I find you in the middle of this case, working for the Magruders and I want to know why. Were you at Davison's house tonight?"

"You haven't charged me with anything," I said.

Nakashita was frustrated. It wasn't readily apparent - a flick of the eye, a tightness of the mouth - but it was there. He said, "Level with me, Lyon. What were you doing there? What are the wood screws for?"

I rubbed my head vigorously with the towel and kept my mouth shut.

"Let her call her lawyer," said Nakashita. "Then book her, Dana."

19 SLAMMER

Brian wasn't home. I left a desperate message on his answering machine. "Get me the hell out of here, Brian. Please," I added. It was quarter to eleven.

I was fingerprinted, photographed, charged with concealing evidence, and put in a holding cell with two ladies of the night. One wore tiger-striped capri leggings and a bandeau top. The other wore a tight tube dress cinched with a snakeskin belt. Both had impossibly high heels.

"So what're you in here for, honey?" asked tiger stripes.

"Robbin' dumpsters?" asked snakeskin.

"Bestiality," I said.

That seemed to deflate their curiosity and they left me alone. I took over a corner of the cell and did some wall squats until my thighs burned. I followed up with crunches, leg lifts and calf raises. It didn't do much to dull the edge, but it was something. My cell mates gave me plenty of space. About midnight, their pimps came to collect them. Half an hour later, Brian arrived.

Brian said, "I came as soon as I got your message. I love it when you beg, Val."

"Well? Am I going to have to stay here all night?"

"I'm afraid so. You have to appear before a judge in the

morning. You're charged with concealing evidence of a crime. What've they got on you?"

"Nothing. Nakashita's frustrated because he's not getting anywhere. I think he's being pressured to dispose of Sue's case."

"C'mon, Val. There's more than that. How'd they pick you up?"

"My car betrayed me. If the starter worked right, I'd have gotten away from there."

"Jesus!" he said. And "Jesus!" he repeated after I told him the story.

"Don't worry, Brian. Nakashita doesn't know about it."

"He will when Davison's window slats fall out and he figures out what the screws were for. You better get some sleep. I want us in court early and out of there before they find something else to charge you with."

After Brian left, they took me to another cell. I got maybe three hours of uneasy sleep, what with the woman in the cell next to me going through withdrawal from something and another woman crying hysterically the whole night. As if that weren't enough, the single cup of coffee had me up peeing twice. When breakfast came around seven, I felt like hell and couldn't eat.

Brian returned not long after. He'd never looked better. He wore a navy blue suit, rep tie, and white shirt. He'd combed his hair and shaved.

"Geez, you look awful," he said. "Your hair looks like Medusa's. You want a comb?" He produced one from his jacket pocket. "How about a mirror?"

"Good morning to you, too."

Brian reviewed my case while I made myself as presentable as possible. Then we went to court. Before going in, he made me promise three times that I would not say a word. It was a brief hearing. Brian used all of his skills to convince the judge I was not a threat to anyone despite my Medusa-hair. The judge let me go on my own recognizance.

Outside, the morning air was clean and fresh. There was

little evidence of the previous night's rain, except, perhaps, a greener tint to Diamond Head. The sky was the kind of clear blue that would make a Kodak exec weep with joy. Cresting Maunaloa Street on the way to my car, we could see a shimmer of Maui's Mount Haleakela way off across the channel beyond Molokai.

Though too early for the funeral, there was already a row of cars in front of Sue's house. Brian drove past without slowing. I pointed out the houses whose yards I'd run through the night before. "The guy that was in Sue's house must've run that way, too."

"Sounds like a favorite route of fugitives," said Brian. He threw me a quick grin and stopped alongside my Nissan. "He called last night after I left you at the jail. Another threat."

It was the same voice with the same message for Brian but with a new one for me. Sue Naito's death, he said, was an accident, but the girlfriend's (his words) headache was not. The next time I could expect a permanent headache. Girlfriend! The guy knew, or thought he knew, something about Brian and me.

My Nissan refused to start at all this time. I called a mechanic friend on Brian's phone and arranged for him to tow the car. Brian and I went back to my apartment. He opened the trunk and got out a bag of groceries.

"Breakfast," he said. "You're pantry is a disgrace."

The phone was ringing as I put my key in the lock. I reached it on the fifth ring.

It was Leo. He said, "Figured you'd be out by now, kiddo."

"How'd you know I was in?"

"Good contacts."

"It wouldn't happen to be Wally Nakashita would it?"

Leo made a dry chuckle. "My contacts are well-placed." After a pause, he said, "Got a name for you on that punk kid you beat up. Alex Miller. Ex-juvenile offender. No sheet as an adult."

"He's not hired muscle?"

"No. Word is, he's been tryin' to stay clean. He's in a program, Work Straight, that takes kids like him, gets them jobs cleanin' schools, playin' soccer, and keepin' outta trouble."

"Is this a government program?"

"No. It's part of the St. Don Bosco Youth Apprenticeship Foundation. A Catholic lay organization. Respected group. Anything else you need?"

"Yes. Who can give me background on the Magruder's land dealings?"

"Pete Hagen, editor of Pacific Economic News. You want I should introduce you?"

"Please."

Brian was getting out pans and utensils as I hung up. "This is going to be the best breakfast you ever had," he said. "Then we need to talk."

"The shower comes first," I said.

It took extra conditioner to tame my Medusa head and extra scrubbing to erase the memory of jail. I could smell coffee and something cooking when I emerged from the shower. I toweled off, put on a terry cloth romper and wrapped a towel into a turban around my head.

Leo called back. Hagen would meet us at eleven.

Brian had removed his jacket and loosened his tie. He'd set the table on the lanai for two. While I sipped coffee he went to the kitchen, returning with a big plate stacked with pancakes and bacon. Suddenly I realized how hungry I was. I had two large helpings while Brian had a small one. At last I was full and satisfied. I undid my turban and shook my hair free.

"That was a wonderful feast," I said.

"Stick with me, kid, and you'll feast like this everyday."

"I'll get fat."

"I'd still be crazy about you."

"And the check's in the mail."

"Hey, we could get fat together. You, me, a fat little cottage with fat little roses in the garden."

"Fat little kids, too?"

"Sure. Fat little kids. You'll come home from a hard day of detecting and the kids -"

"Little Brian and Little Val."

"Little Brian and Little Val will massage your tired feet and I'll bind your gunshot wounds. We'll live happily ever after."

"I know all about happily ever after. That was what I was supposed to get from my first marriage."

"You were married? When? You didn't tell me."

I hadn't told many people. Who likes to dwell on failures? But I was feeling comfortable with Brian, basking in the warmth of the sun on the lanai. I took a big swallow of coffee.

"It was in Italy. He had looks, money, and an American education, but his attitudes towards women were strictly old world. No intentions of being faithful. Me, I was the American basketball star, a thing to show his buddies, like the Ferrari and the Arabian stallion."

"How long did it last?"

"Too long. No more than a couple months, actually. We got married at the end of my rookie season. I knew it was a mistake even before the beginning of the next season. They don't like divorces in Italy. Honor and all that. I had to get out of Italy fast. Flew back to California and filed there. Who knows? I might still be married in Italy."

Magruder's eyes were wide in amazement. "Wow, there goes the honeymoon in Rome."

I laughed. "Honeymoons just aren't in my future, Brian." Brian didn't find it funny. Something was eating at him. "This isn't what we needed to talk about, though, is it?"

"No. I went straight to Ken's after I dropped you at the beach. I told him about Jock's allegations. He denied them, of course. When I mentioned Sue Naito, though, he went into a tirade. I'll be honest with you, Val. He's bitterly opposed to abortion. He hated Sue Naito, probably as much as he hates Jock Pfeifer. It wouldn't be hard for anyone to believe that he could do some of those things."

"Do you believe it?"

"No. The thing is…" He looked out to the street and then back at me. "Val, Friday night when Sue died, I'm not sure where

Ken was. He didn't meet us at the club until later. It was after eleven when he showed up."

"So his whereabouts at the time of the attack on Sue and me are unknown."

Brian sighed. "No. The reason for the card games is to give Ken an alibi for something else. He's seeing another woman. He was with her Friday night so he's got an alibi for Sue's death, but how the hell can he use it? Helen suspects, but everyone there will swear that Ken was with us, which he was, but not all evening."

"Even the bishop would go along with that?"

"Sure. Ken's always been good to the church."

"What about you? Would you go along with it?"

"Val, I can't countenance what he's doing. I went along with it up until now because I thought it would never come up. I mean, if Ken wants to cheat on Helen, that's his business. She's already put him on notice that she'll divorce him if he strays again."

"I take it he's been unfaithful before."

"Yeah, often."

"You know, that's almost a perfect alibi," I said. "How do you know he was with this woman? He could have been at Sue's, but you guys will swear he was with you. Men of honor, protecting one of your own in a transgression of the heart. I'm sure none of you would think of covering for him in murder, but cheating? All that rates is a wink."

I could tell by Brian's face that he'd thought of that, too. Once the lies start, there's no end to them.

He said, "Val, I'm telling you because I don't know what to do about it. I'm not going to lie for him if it comes out, but -"

"You'd like me to look into it and see what kind of damage control I can do."

Brian's face showed relief. "Yes. I have to know."

"Do you know her name?"

The woman's name was Myra Akuna. She was the Associate Director of the Honolulu Arts League. The situation was rife with possibilities for gossip and scandal. You could just hear the whispers circulating wherever the chosen gathered. I told Brian I'd look into it, but I couldn't promise to contain it if rumors got out. He understood. We turned the conversation to the search for Nathan Pfeifer.

"I'm hoping the numbers I found at Sue's will lead me to him. First, though, I need to get a dependable car. It's going to take some running around."

"Hey, use mine. I insist. You'll look good in a Lexus."

"What'll you do?"

"I can walk or take the bus. It'll do me good."

"No way, Brian. Not after this second death threat. I'll drive you. I don't care what you say, I'm looking after you until we settle this."

"You won't get any objection from me," he said.

I stretched my legs out in front of me and pointed my toes. It made my calves nice and round. Brian noticed. His eyes made a slow glide past my calves, ankles, feet and back up the length of me.

"You must be exhausted," he said.

"Actually, I'm kind of wired."

He nodded. "I know a proven relaxation technique." He smiled shyly. "I had my secretary clear my calendar this morning."

"I have a lot of work to do today. Three places to go before lunch."

"Tension robs you of effectiveness."

"That's true," I said. My voice sounded unusually tight. I wondered if he noticed.

I got up and carried some of the plates into the kitchen. Magruder followed with the rest. I took them from him and stacked them in the sink. He put his hands on my waist and nuzzled my neck. "Your hair smells good," he said.

I turned in his arms and offered him my mouth. Brian slipped his hands behind me. I pressed against him. He pulled down the top of my romper. It slid past my hips and piled at my feet. I put my arms around his neck. His tie felt cool, his shirt crisp, the buttons hard.

"Couch," I said. I wrapped my legs around his waist.

"Yes, the couch," he said. He made it without stumbling. No mean trick with a hundred forty-five pounds of detective hugging him like a jellyfish.

20 WEALTH, ART, AND ADULTERY

Brian was right, I did look good in a Lexus. I had on a cream-colored, drapery-front blouse, a light blue suit, and matching pumps. The suit jacket was long and the skirt was not - three inches showed beneath the hem of the jacket. The Lexus was the perfect accessory to the outfit. I was calling on wealth, art, and adultery. I had to look the part.

I drove. Brian was next to me with his eyes closed. He said, "Hey, did I tell you about my work on television? Maybe you saw some of it? Miami Vice, the one where the Colombian general gets assassinated in the hotel spa? That was me. One line, 'Maria, the champagne's flat.' Bang! She shoots me. It was a great moment. I did three Simon and Simons. Spoke four lines but I got to punch Gerald McRaney once and fire six shots at him. Helluva guy. He sent me a Christmas card."

"Missed them all. I must have had headaches those nights."

"Yeah, you didn't miss much. I'd have been better at directing. I'm great at picturing a scene in my mind."

"Let me guess. You're picturing one now."

"You bet. Every slick crime show has this kind of scene. I see a stylish car - a Lexus, of course - smooth and sleek like a panther, pulling into a parking space. I start with a long shot of it and then move in close - the cowl, the trim, the wheels, the door."

"Sounds like a car ad."

131

"It's setting the viewers up. Now they're expecting something. The door opens - low camera angle here - and a terrific pair of legs slides out. The camera does a long, slow pan: well-turned ankles, smooth thighs, short, blue skirt. The driver stands, shoulders her bag. Nice hips, good chest, and finally, the killer blue eyes. Where'd you get those killer eyes?"

"Dream on, Magruder. My nose would need a stand-in."

"Naw," he said, "your nose is part of the charm, like Ellen Barkin's. That was the prime time version. Now for the director's cut."

I glanced over at him. His eyes were still closed and he had a broad smile on his face. I elbowed him under the ribs.

"Hey!"

"You were having too much fun without me. Besides, we're almost there and you can't go into your office with a hard-on."

"You could do something about it," he said.

"Here in traffic? That's not what you're paying me for, Magruder. But hang onto that thought. Tonight's my own time."

He sighed. "It'll be a long day."

I let Brian out on Bethel Street, gave him a quick kiss and watched him enter the building. It was going to be a long day for me, too. The night couldn't come quickly enough. Once he was inside, I put the Lexus into gear and headed for Kaka'ako and my appointment with Leo.

Earlier, I'd matched the numbers from Sue's phone with the names on Pam's list. One number didn't match. I dialed it from Brian's car phone. The pleasant, male voice on the other end told me I'd reached Friendly Isle Air Tours. I frowned. What could be the connection between an air tour and an abortion network? Probably nothing, but you have to play out all your leads. I asked to speak to Harriet.

"Ma'am, I'm the only one who works here. I'm pilot, mechanic and baggage handler."

"Do you know anyone named Harriet?"

"I get it. This is a joke, right? This is about the picture? I

don't want to sound rude, ma'am, but I'm on a tight schedule here. I
don't -"

"What picture?" I demanded.

"The picture of Harriet Quimby in our waiting room. If you
want to see it, drop by. If you want a tour, call Hideaway Travel.
They handle our bookings. I've got a tour leaving right now. Bye."

At a red light I jotted "Hideaway Travel" into my notebook.
Beneath that I wrote "Harriet Quimby" and two question marks. She
was not on my list of "Harriets," but she was the first real Harriet I'd
come across.

Kaka'ako is an area of medium and light industry near
downtown. The streets are narrow, the buildings are featureless, and
the open areas are paved over. Pacific Economic News occupied a
low building between a foundry and a truck body repair shop on
Cooke Street.

Leo and another man were waiting on the sidewalk in the
shadow of an overhang in front of the building. I pulled into one of
two vacant spots and got out under the gaze of both men, self-
consciously following Magruder's script. Killer eyes.

Leo said, "Val, this is Pete Hagen. The politics he doesn't
know about hasn't happened."

Hagen had unkempt red hair and wire rimmed glasses. I
figured him to be around fifty. His face brightened when he looked
at me. He said, "Pleased to meet you. Leo here's running true to
form."

"How's that?" I asked.

"He told me his associate had good legs. I should've known
the rest would be good, too."

"It's the eyes you have to worry about."

"Huh?"

"Never mind. Mr. Hagen, Leo said you might know
something about the Magruder Estate's land dealings."

"Call me Pete. Please. Listen, if I get outta line, just tell me.
Leo said you're savvy and you don't take shit. I like that kind of
gumption. Don't often get to see it packaged like this. Yeah, I know

about the Magruder Estate. Let's go back to my office." He turned and went into the building.

I looked at Leo. He said, "Sensitivity ain't his long suit, Val. Information is." It better be a lot longer, I thought, because he's void in sensitivity.

The interior of Pacific Economic News was a warren of tiny, partitioned spaces around two large work rooms. People were hunched over computers or congregated around work tables. The air was pungent with vapors from solvents and rubber cement and noisy with the whir of office machines and the buzz of voices. Hagen's office looked like the collection point of a recycling drive. There was not a surface that wasn't under several inches of paper. Even the usual office photos and mementos had no space of their own, but sat on top of piles of paper.

Hagen moved a stack of pasteups from a wooden office chair and motioned Leo into it. From the workroom, he wheeled in a scuffed typists chair for me. He dropped his own frame into an executive chair whose vinyl upholstery had been repaired in places with cellophane tape.

"We don't print the paper here," he said as if in answer to a question neither of us asked. "That's done at Hawaii Newspaper Association. Drink?" He produced a bottle of Jim Beam and three paper cups.

Leo said, "Sure," and Hagen took it to mean both of us. He gave each of us a cup with about two inches of whiskey. "Water's outside the door," he said.

I went out to the water cooler and dumped about an inch and a half of bourbon into the spill grate. I refilled the cup with water and went back in. Leo and Hagen were content to sip theirs neat. Hagen watched me sit down and tug the hem of my skirt.

"Magruder Estate," said Hagen. "What do you want to know?"

"Tell me about the Windward Cove Center."

"Windward Cove. Ken's folly. It was supposed to rival Ala Moana Center when it was finished. The plan called for it to be built in three stages. Ambitious project, right? It was Magruder Estate's first foray into commercial real estate development."

"The Magruders were the primary backers?" I asked.

"Yeah. See, the estate was flush with money at that time. For years it had a lot of residential holdings with residents under long-term leases. Land-poor, you know? The income from the leases, though steady, didn't amount to much because some of the leases were twenty-five, thirty years old. Then the state stepped in and allowed residents to sue for condemnation and buy the land at fair value. Well, suddenly, the Magruders have a large cash flow, because they're selling off their property in a boom market. Ken had these visions of himself as Donald Trump. His plan was to put all this cash into commercial real estate. The windward side was growing fast and he saw a need for one of these super malls over there. It just so happened the estate had a large parcel of undeveloped land on the windward side."

"But it was zoned residential," I said.

"Right," said Hagen. He took a long pull on his bourbon and stared at my knees.

"I had surgery."

"What?" he asked.

"You're staring so hard at my knees I thought you might be wondering about this little scar here."

Hagen flushed almost to the color of his hair and coughed up some of his whiskey. I waited while he wiped his mouth with a handkerchief before getting back to the topic.

"Since it was zoned residential," I said, "Ken brought Harold Davison into the deal. Davison was supposed to influence Sue Naito into getting it rezoned."

"Which one of us is asking and which one is telling?"

"I know a little bit, but not all."

"Well you're right up to that point." Hagen was looking at my eyes now. Killer eyes, killer knees.

"Naito got it rezoned?" asked Leo.

"Yeah. She swung some clout on the city council."

"Davison seemed to be in the deal for pocket change," I said.

"You know a lot," said Hagen. "The Magruders didn't need Davison's money. They needed Naito. Davison's name didn't even show on the Windward Cove Development Prospectus."

"So nobody knew he was involved, leaving Sue free to swing her clout without any apparent conflict of interest. That sucks," I said. All my professional life has been on the streets or inside city hall, so corruption, like violent death, shouldn't surprise me. It still saddens me, though, and in this case it did both. Didn't we hope that electing women to politics would somehow bring an end to corruption? Why force our way into the boy's club if it was going to be run by the same rules? "That really sucks," I repeated.

Hagen said, "Naito would later claim Davison never told her about the deal." He poured himself another shot and raised the bottle questioningly. Leo and I shook our heads. He went on, "If you believe that, how about whales swimming backwards? Our paper got wind of it and did a nice little piece of investigative journalism. We couldn't find any hard evidence of wrong doing. Basically everybody clammed up on it. But it put the scare into Davison and he quit the partnership."

"For a quarter million dollars," I said.

"Helluva return," said Leo.

"The Magruders thought so. Davison thought it should be more. He filed a civil suit. According to him, the Magruders were spreading their costs over the first three years of the project instead of five or more, so revenues for those three years appeared lower than they really were."

"What happened in court?" asked Leo.

"The Magruders won. They owned the judge."

"So the Magruders were satisfied?" I asked.

"Yeah, but it was short-lived. Naito had the last word. See, the Windward Cove was a three-phase project. Phases two and three also required rezoning, but this time it was blocked in city council."

"Sue swung her clout?"

"Swung it like a transvestite with a purse-load of bricks. No rezoning meant there was no place for your Sears and your Penney's. The big stores went elsewhere and Windward Cove shriveled. There you have it, Ken's folly."

"Pete," I said, "would you say Ken Magruder had reason to hate Sue Naito?"

"Like a dolphin hates a shark."

"So whattya think?" asked Leo when we were once again out on the street.

"You know the Magruders better than I do, Leo. Would Ken kill over Windward Cove?"

"Two things the Magruders want. Have always wanted. Money and respect. Ken took a beating in both departments with Windward Cove."

"It doesn't add up. The death threats, Brian's and Sue's, were about Nathan Pfeifer. The tape recording and her address book were the only things taken from Sue's. And what about the trashing of my apartment? What did that have to do with Windward Cove? Is it just a coincidence?"

"I don't believe in coincidence, kiddo. So what's your next step?"

"I'm going to visit Ken's alibi," I said.

The Honolulu Art League occupied all of a stately frame house in Nu'uanu Valley above downtown. The receptionist made it clear that Myra Akuna couldn't see me but perhaps there was someone else who could help.

"Oh, I'm afraid not. My client, who's interested in making a major donation to the arts, has a lot of confidence in Ms. Akuna. A few minutes is all I would need to make some preliminary arrangements." Two minutes later, I was in.

Myra Akuna's office looked out through French doors onto a lanai bordered by a bed of torch ginger. The doors were open and a light breeze ruffled the pages of the calendar on her desk. It also ruffled the ends of her black hair and the folds of her silk blouse. Silk described her. She reminded me of a silk flower, fragile yet indestructible, and perfect down to the last detail. We shook hands across the desk. Her movements were nervous and quick.

"Miss Lyon is it? I'm afraid I can give you only a few minutes."

I took a quick look at her calendar before releasing her hand. It was one of those leather-bound time management systems that come with to-do lists, goal statements and inspirational thoughts to get you through the day. Akuna's day was organized in fifteen minute segments. Each line had an entry in a clear, rounded hand. Some of the entries had picture comments beside them. The twelve o'clock entry read, "Board luncheon," beside a drawing of a lit dynamite stick. No wonder she seemed nervous. It was ten to twelve.

"How do you manage to look so fresh with a calendar that's about to explode on you?"

Myra dismissed it with a quick wave of her hand. "Most days aren't as bad as this one. Now, I understand you want to talk about a major donation. Please." She gestured towards a chair.

When we were both sitting I said, "I think there's been a misunderstanding. I want to talk about a major donor, not a donation."

"A misunderstanding? It isn't like Jennifer to get confused. Should I call her in?" Her voice held enough ice to freeze a margarita.

"That won't be necessary. I probably didn't make myself clear."

"I see. So you're not representing a client?"

"Oh, I am, but the donor is not my client. I'm a private investigator. I'm looking into the whereabouts of the donor in question on the night that a crime may have been committed. I think you may be able to help me."

"I don't see how. The private lives of our supporters are none of my business."

"The donor in question is named Ken Magruder. Do you know him?"

She said, "Of course, I know him." Akuna's face was unreadable. "Mr. Magruder is a member of our Golden Circle, our biggest contributors."

"Do you see him often?"

Akuna steepled her slender fingers and regarded me narrowly. "He is a frequent guest at Arts League functions," she said. "I find it incredible that anyone would think him a criminal."

"I didn't say I thought him a criminal. Have you seen him recently?"

"He could have attended our last opening. Jennifer can get the guest book for you."

"What does it cost Ken Magruder to get into the Golden Circle? Ten K? Twenty?"

"I don't see that as being any of your business."

"Contributions to the Arts League are public records, are they not?"

"Miss Lyon, I've been patient with you up to now. I really don't see any point in this discussion. If they're public records then you can certainly find the answers to your questions yourself."

"What does he get for his contribution, you?"

Color burned in Akuna's cheeks. She said, "I won't respond to that. This interview is over, Miss Lyon."

"Do you know where Ken Magruder was on Friday night?"

"Miss Lyon -"

"Was he with you?"

"I insist that you leave." We stood up together.

"Thank you, Ms. Akuna. I won't take any more of your time. I hope you understand I'm just doing my job."

I held out my hand across the desk and put my sincerest smile on my face. She extended her own hand uncertainly. I grasped it before she could change her mind. With my free hand, I flipped her calendar back three pages to Friday. The nine p.m. entry read, "Kenneth." It was followed by a hand-drawn pair of intertwined smiley hearts.

"The smiley hearts are a nice touch," I said.

"Get out!" she said.

21 RHYMES WITH . . .

The Lexus's dashboard clock and my stomach agreed that it was noon. I stopped at a drive-through for a couple of cheeseburgers, some fries and a Coke on my way to the offices of Magruder Estate. The offices were located at Kewalo Basin above Magruder Marine, close to the source of the original family fortune. I approached the receptionist and asked to see Ken Magruder.

"Is he expecting you?" She looked from me to the bag with the golden arches and the drink cup dripping sweat. "Mr. Magruder is very busy. If he's not expecting you, I don't think you can see him."

"Why don't we let him decide?" I put my bag and cup on her desk and wrote on the back of one of my cards, "Myra," and two smiley hearts. She'd had plenty of time to call him after I left, so there was no need to try to bluff my way in. "Give him this."

She looked at it dubiously. I settled into one of the plush chairs in the reception area and unwrapped a cheeseburger. That seemed to decide her and she went down a hallway towards what I guessed was the Magruder Estate inner sanctum. I'd finished off a burger and most of the fries when she returned with the message that Ken would see me.

"So what kind of a mood is he in?" I asked as she led the way.

She gave me a sidelong glance and said, "I don't know what this is about, but I've never heard him use the words he used about you."

"Like what?"

We paused before a door with no nameplate. "Rhymes with runt," she whispered as she pushed it open.

I entered an executive office that was larger than my entire apartment. It was furnished expensively: desk the size of a dining room table, visitors chairs in front of the desk, an armchair and sofa group at one end of the room, and pictures on the wall. In a little alcove of its own, was a valet stand displaying the satin-lined cape, plumed hat, and sword of a high-ranking Knight of Columbus.

Ken stood in the middle of the room, rocking back and forth on his heels. His handsome face was composed but unsmiling. The receptionist pulled the door closed behind me, leaving just the two of us in the room. He held my card between his index and middle fingers and strummed it against the palm of his other hand. His agitation was unmistakable when he spoke. "Miss Lyon, what the hell is this? Is it supposed to mean something to me?" He sailed the card at me. It fluttered to the floor between us.

"That's a new card. I wish you'd treat it with some respect."

"That asinine message on the back. What the hell's that supposed to mean?"

"Blood pressure Ken," I said calmly. "You had a date with Myra Akuna on Friday when you were supposed to be playing cards with your brothers."

"I get it. You think you can shake me down? How much will this cost me?"

"It's not a shakedown. I'm trying to find Nathan Pfeifer for your brother and I need some answers."

"Getting nowhere? Well I'm not surprised. I told Brian to hire himself a real detective and not some skirt."

"Don't let the skirt fool you, Ken. I don't always wear it. Did I say I'm getting nowhere? What I'm getting is your name at every turn. The good news is I can't pin Sue Naito's death on you. You've got an alibi within an alibi. If your poker buddies crack, the worst that can happen is that your affair with Myra will be exposed."

"In other words the good news is a messy scandal and a nasty divorce. What's the bad?" Magruder ceased his agitated rocking. He took a bottle of Perrier from a wet bar in a corner of the office. "I'd offer you something, but I don't think you're staying long." He twisted off the cap and took a swig from the bottle.

"Don't mind if I sit, do you Ken?" I plopped down on his sofa without waiting for a reply. "The bad news is that I'm not giving up. I know you hated Sue."

"Big effing deal. You're going to make some kind of case on that? Of course I hated her. She was a baby killer, a law-breaker who encouraged abortions. That's anathema to me."

"Pardon me, but the right to an abortion is the law of the land isn't it?"

"There is a higher law, Miss Lyon, but I don't expect you to know about that. Be that as it may, I'm not the agent of retribution. That's a divine prerogative."

"She messed you up on Windward Cove. You hated her for that, didn't you?"

"Listen. Do you know how much her actions cost the estate? Tens of millions in future revenues, that's how much. But if you think I went and killed her, you're crazy."

"What did you do, slap her around? Threaten her?"

"I didn't do anything. I wasn't there. Can't you understand that?" His voice had suddenly increased in loudness and shrillness, like a knife touching a grinding wheel.

"Maybe you weren't there yourself, but you could have hired someone to do it."

"Miss Lyon, you're flirting with libel. Those accusations are actionable."

The door opened and Molly Gallagher entered, a big multi-pocketed exercise bag slung from one shoulder. Molly was wearing shiny pink tights under a violet leotard. She had nails and lips that matched the tights and earrings and eye shadow that matched the leotard.

She said, "Ken, you can be heard all the way out in the hall." She regarded me coolly. "Oh hello, Val. I almost didn't recognize you in drag."

"On your way to a workout, Molly? Or to Marvel Comics?"

"Ooh Ken, she bites. Val, I can't imagine that wicked tongue would have made you very popular in the slammer. I'm surprised someone didn't rip it out."

I laughed. "For all you know they may have tried, Molly."

Ken said, "Miss Lyon has been making some wild accusations, Mol. She fancies herself quite the detective. For one thing, she's found out about Myra and me."

Molly dropped her bag on the floor and took the other end of the sofa. "And now you're trying to blackmail Ken? I knew you couldn't be trusted."

"Blackmail, shakedown. It seems to be a big issue with the two of you. Is someone trying to use this affair against you, Ken?"

"Nobody knows about me and Myra."

"Oh, come on," I said. "Your whole family, with the possible exception of your wife, knows about you and Myra. Even the bishop knows, though I suppose that's under the seal of confession. So tell me, is this what Jock Pfeifer has on you?"

Molly and Ken exchanged looks. Ken sat down behind his desk and put his feet on its shiny surface. He sighed heavily. "Yes, that's what he's got. I don't know how he got it or what his evidence consists of."

Molly picked up on the theme. "Oh, he doesn't have anything you need to worry about, Ken. It's probably just some pictures from one of the Art League functions. Vicious-minded people can take perfectly innocent pictures and twist them to suit their own vicious ends. Don't you agree, Val?"

"Did you ever see Jock Pfeifer at these functions?" I asked.

"Of course not, Pfeifer is a clod and a boor."

"With some boorish pictures."

"Molly was engaging in speculation about the nature of the

pictures. I don't know for certain that he even has pictures," Ken said in irritation.

"Have you tried to find out?" I asked.

"I wouldn't give that man the satisfaction of taking his allegations seriously."

"No? Did you make arrangements with your police captain friend for the porno raid on his shop?"

Ken swung his feet off the desk so suddenly he knocked the telephone to the floor. Molly went pale beneath her eye shadow and her blush. She said, "That is truly vicious."

"And actionable," said Ken.

I shrugged. "I'm just repeating what Jock told me. Brian heard him say it."

"My brother," said Ken, "would neither believe nor repeat a charge like that, especially when it comes from a liar like Pfeifer."

"And you work for Brian," said Molly. "You should be ashamed for believing that man's lie."

"I didn't say I believed it. It has occurred to me, though, that a porno raid would be a good cover for finding out what he has on you."

Ken said, "You're clutching at straws, Miss Lyon."

"I suppose so, " I said irritably. "You see, everybody I talk to is trying to stonewall me. When people keep secrets from me I have to clutch at something - a straw here, a twig there. Sooner or later, I'll latch onto something substantial."

"I hope I live long enough to see it, Miss Lyon."

"I think you will, Ken." I stood up and headed to the door, but a framed certificate on the wall caught my attention. It had been presented to Kenneth Magruder in recognition of his sponsorship of several youth apprenticeships through the St. Don Bosco Foundation. "Does this foundation sponsor field trips, Ken?"

"What do you mean?"

"Just that the gang that broke up the rally on Friday were a part of this organization."

"That's ridiculous. You can't prove anything like that."

"I put one of them in the hospital, Ken. You know, Molly, we should get to know each other better. Maybe you could join me for a workout at my gym sometime. But first we'll have to find something to replace that little number you're wearing. We sweat where I go."

Out in the car with what was left of my burger and Coke, I gave some thought to the encounter. Scratch the theory that Pfeifer was blackmailing Ken with knowledge of his affair. The look that had passed between Ken and Molly when I suggested it had been one of relief. It meant I was on the wrong track as far as what Jock had over Ken. On the other hand, their reaction when I'd suggested that they'd been behind the raid made me think I was close to the truth on that one.

Was there any connection between Ken Magruder and the gang at the rally? Like Leo, I don't believe in coincidence.

22 A GRAVE INVITATION

Even in death, Sue Naito attracted a big following. By the time I reached Diamond Head Memorial Park, every foot of curb along the long drive had a car parked beside it. I finally found a spot near the top of 18th Street at Diamond Head Road across from the National Guard Armory. When I opened the door, the Hawaiian air hit me like a blast from a hair dryer. Driving around in the Lexus with the windows up and the AC on had spoiled me. I could get used to the luxury of arriving at a place fresh, with my clothes and hair in order instead of their usual windblown disarray. The midday sun beat down relentlessly on the walk down the hill to the cemetery. Sweat formed beads along my hair line and ran in long rivers from my armpits to my waistband. I carried my jacket over one arm, but put it back on inside the cemetery. Better to be too warm than to let the damp crescents under my arms gross people out.

The service was already in progress as I made my way past the low markers to the outskirts of the crowd of mourners. Members of the Davison family were seated in folding chairs two rows deep on both sides of Sue's flower-covered casket. The minister stood at the head intoning prayers while the rest of the mourners formed a dense, ragged horseshoe around the site. I spotted Pam and joined her, trying to slip in among the crowd as unobtrusively as possible, but not entirely successful at it: Carol Fernandez, standing close behind Davison, noticed me and glared. Beside her, Annie made a point of not looking at me. Carol whispered something to Davison who looked my way briefly and scowled before giving his attention back to the minister.

"Looks like you're not very welcome here, sugar," whispered Pam.

"Seems to be the way my day's running. Do you see any of the other Harriets here?"

"A few," she said. In fact, there were five besides Carol, leaving one unaccounted for. None of them looked like wild-eyed baby killers and law breakers. They all gave the appearance of being solid middle-class citizens.

I dragged Pam away from the crowd in the direction of the mausoleum. When we were out of earshot, I asked what she knew of Harriet Quimby.

"Nothing. Should I?"

"You called yourselves Harriet. The name doesn't belong to any of your members, but it must have some significance." I explained about my call to Friendly Isle Air Tours and the picture of Harriet Quimby.

"And now you think you're getting warm."

"Right. The name means something. This is the first clue. If I counted right, all but one of the group are here. Who's the missing woman?"

"Aileen Burch. She and Sue organized the group."

Odd, I thought, that Aileen Burch, of all people, would miss the funeral. There had been no number coded into Sue's phone for Aileen. That too was odd.

"Was Aileen the other nurse in the group?"

"Yes."

"It was Aileen who saved your butt in that botched abortion, wasn't it?"

"Yes again. Sugar, that woman is Wonder Woman. She nurses, she flies, she does things for other people."

"Did she fly for an airline?"

"No. The Public Health Service. She flew patients between Kalaupapa and Honolulu when they needed treatment."

"Kalaupapa? They had leprosy?"

"Hansen's disease," she corrected me.

The minister finished his part of the service and now the mourners began a slow procession past the grave. Suddenly, I spotted, among the mourners, an all too familiar figure - the man I'd just left. "What the hell's Ken Magruder doing here?" I asked loud enough for Pam and nobody else to hear. At that moment, he turned and I saw the Roman collar. It wasn't Ken, but Frank. Same question.

Frank was getting a cool reception from Harold Davison. They exchanged some words, though it seemed Frank was doing most of the talking. Davison remained stony faced throughout the brief meeting. While other people continued to hang around the site, Frank set off across the lawn alone.

"Pam, you better pay your respects to Sue. I gotta go."

"Hey! That's all you dragged me over here for?"

"You've been a big help. I'll call you later."

Frank had reached his car when I caught up to him. I was slightly out of breath from running across the soft earth in the damn pumps. Why they call them pumps, I'll never understand. A pump should get you moving, not hold you back.

He paused with his hand on the door when I called to him and his face brightened. "Val Lyon, the lady detective. Buon giorno, Signorina. I thought I might see you here. Tragic about Sue, isn't it? I understand you were hurt in the incident. You're recovered, I hope."

"I don't know," I said. "Running across this lawn took a lot more out of me than I expected." I leaned my hip against the front fender of his car, a late model Buick Century. The Magruders seemed to have a stable of fine cars. "I'm surprised to find you here, considering everything I've heard the last few days about your family and Sue's. In fact, I just had a chat with Ken. His hatred for Sue seems to be matched only by his disgust with me."

Frank's eyebrows shot up. "Did he try to snap your garters?

I hope you put him in his place."

"He didn't like some of the questions I asked."

"He might've thought you were prying into his business. He's sensitive about that."

"Most people are, but prying is my business. Do you feel the same way about Sue as Ken does?"

"No. I've never fully understood the depth of his feelings towards her. I won't say I haven't been guilty of hate, but I don't feel it towards her. Nor you."

He let his hand fall lightly on my shoulder. I've never been comfortable around priests and I stiffened involuntarily. Frank took his hand away.

"You and Ken look so much alike," I said, folding my arms across my chest, "I'd expect the two of you to have similar likes and dislikes."

"Ah," he laughed. "People have the wrong idea about twins. There's so much pressure to be alike, so many expectations, that we devote a lot of our energies to being different."

Other people were now leaving. Cars were pulling away from the curb and passing us closely on the narrow lane. We moved onto the grass and out of the way. I caught a few hostile looks from behind some of the rolled up windows. They were directed more at Frank than at me, I assumed, since I was unknown to most of the people there. Frank ignored them.

He continued, "I think psychologists who study twins place too much emphasis on the genetics and not enough on the individual's struggles. In my opinion, it's what men…and women…struggle against that builds their character. Ken and I may have the same genes but we were shaped in different struggles. After Vietnam, Ken went to Harvard Business School and I went to Rome." He gave a conspiratorial laugh. "Ken thinks he had it tougher, but we know better."

"Yet both of you have gotten pretty high up in the church. Besides Knights of Columbus, Ken's involved in something else, I believe. Don Bosco something."

"The St. Don Bosco Youth Apprenticeship Foundation. They provide a lot of services for needy youth - jobs, training, scholarships. Ken's been very active with them. He does good works, but I wear the collar. There's a bit of irony there."

"Even more irony if there should be a connection between the Don Bosco group and the thugs that broke up the rally for Jean Pfeifer."

Frank frowned. "You think the foundation was involved in that?"

"Oh, I'm just speculating. One of the gang had taken part in some of the foundation's programs. That doesn't mean the foundation was involved."

"Of course not. What are you getting at, Val?"

"Well, Ken was active in the foundation, he was at odds with the things Sue stood for, if the gang members belonged to the foundation -"

"That's quite a big 'if.' I have to believe that if any of the Bosco kids were involved, they did so on their own. You have to be careful of tarnishing Ken with guilt by association."

"Absolutely, Frank. I tarnish people with nothing but the truth."

He grinned as though he actually enjoyed the joke. He said, "You don't give up do you? I admire that. I admired Sue, too. That's the truth, Val. She stuck to her principles and didn't give up. I like a good fight and she could always give one. The fact is she and I weren't too far apart on many issues."

"Except abortion."

His face darkened. For just a second I saw the same passion I'd seen in Brian's face when he'd explained why he'd taken Jean's cause. Other people's beliefs don't interest me, but the people who hold them do. Especially men with strong beliefs.

"Except abortion," he echoed. "Abortion is murder. That's what the church teaches. I can't alter that."

"That's what a male-centered church teaches. Those teachings have denied women the right to sexual pleasure, to good protection in sex, and to self-determination. Plus," I was warming to the subject, "the church denies us any say in its policies."

"I agree," he said, nodding vigorously. "But we musn't let the issues become divisive. Listen, I'm not unsympathetic to most of the changes that women such as Sue, and yourself, want in the church."

"To be honest, Frank, I gave up on the church long ago."

"So did Sue. That's the point. We're losing too many good Catholic women."

"Sue was Catholic?"

"She was baptized in the church but she abandoned her faith over the slow pace of change. She and I had many discussions about it. I counseled patience but she wouldn't have it. Women have to understand that changes will come but they'll be gradual. The church has been getting along fine for 2000 years. It will not be moved over night."

I'd heard that line too many times before. Take out the word "church" and put in whatever institution you want. It's always the same thing.

"That's a load of crap," I said. "You know how you can spot an oppressor? He's the one asking for patience."

"Amazing! You sound just like Sue. That's a compliment, Val. I told you I admired her. You know Brian's quite taken with you. I can see why."

"Are you changing the subject?"

"Mea Culpa. A postponement, actually. I'd like to continue this discussion later. How about dinner tomorrow night? I'm out at the Diocesan Retreat House in Kailua. It'll be just you and me. We can explore these issues in depth. I think we'll have enough to talk about that we can fill up an evening. If all else fails we can trade experiences of Italy."

"Brian must have talked a lot about me."

"That's how I know he likes you. Maybe we can dust off our Italian. I'd like to find out what expressions make someone like you blush. What do you say?"

"I'd like that," I said.

"I'd be honored. Eight o'clock."

I accepted a lift up the hill from him. "Arrivederci," he said when he left me off at Brian's car.

One thing I was not getting from the Magruder brothers was indifference: passion from Brian, anger from Ken, and a dinner invitation from Frank. There was something flirtatious behind Frank's suggestion that we exclude Brian. I was more and more curious about these brothers. The Cartwrights, they weren't.

23 WORK STRAIGHT

I had an idea that Harriet Quimby was an historical figure and a visit to the library confirmed it. From a book on notable women I learned that Harriet Quimby had been an adventurer - a San Francisco reporter who took up flying in its infancy. She was the first woman to have a pilot's license and the first to fly the English Channel. She died in an air show in 1921.

To me, and probably to most women, Harriet Quimby was obscure, but, to a woman pilot and activist, she would have been a heroic figure. I could imagine twenty-something years ago, Sue and Ailene setting up their network of home abortionists, trying to decide on the code name and Aileen, the pilot, drawing inspiration from her heroine, Harriet Quimby. That would account for Friendly Isle Air Tours' number being on Sue's phone. Friendly Isle was the means of contact between Sue and Aileen.

From the library phone, I called the Friendly Isle number and got a recorded message, "This is Captain Phil. The Friendly Bird is on the wing right now. We'll be back on the ground at five. Our next tour leaves at eleven tomorrow."

With about two hours left in the afternoon, I decided to find out what I could about the Don Bosco Youth Apprenticeship Foundation. The phone book had an address for it which turned out to be a Diocesan Community Center in Kalihi.

Kalihi is a working-class neighborhood of mostly Hawaiian and other Pacific Islanders. Except for the ethnic composition, it reminds me of the neighborhood in San Francisco where my mother and I lived after my father left us. Close enough to the edge of poverty that you can see into its depths anytime you choose to look.

The Diocesan Center was a new building between two rows of public housing. A narrow strip of grass and some low shrubs in front of the Center softened the hard edge of the neighborhood. Alongside the building was a paved area marked off for basketball and hockey, but when I drove up it was being used as a stage for hip-hop routines by a group of kids with a boombox. They watched hungrily as I parked the car and got out. Whether the hunger was for me or the Lexus, I couldn't tell.

The Apprenticeship Foundation occupied two small offices on the ground floor. Desk, file cabinets, personal computer, and bulletin board with announcements. The guy behind the desk was early twenties and clean cut.

"Are you in charge?" I asked.

He smiled brightly. "More or less. I'm doing a practical ministry. They gave me a key and a place to sit. So, what can I do for you?"

I gave him my card and introduced myself as a private investigator. He seemed impressed. He was a seminarian, he said. When I asked about the foundation, he was only too happy to tell me about it. It was named in honor of St. John Bosco, known as Don Bosco, a priest who worked with needy and troubled youths, providing them with jobs and education. The foundation's work continued his legacy. It was run by a board of Catholic businessmen and community leaders. They solicited jobs and scholarships from local businessmen for young men and women. The foundation also provided job skills training, leadership training, and recreational programs. Youths were enrolled in the program on the basis of need or by referral from juvenile authorities and social services agencies. Work Straight was a special program for juvenile offenders.

"Who are the board members?"

"They're all lay members of the community," he said. He shuffled through some folders on the desk and came up with a three-page list of names and addresses. The first eleven names were listed under the heading, Executive Board Members. Ken Magruder was one of the eleven.

"I'll make you a copy," he said. He took the papers and stepped out of the office.

I took the opportunity to look through the papers on the desk, not really sure what I was looking for. Most of them seemed to be schedules of training sessions and lists of participants in various activities. One, in particular, caught my attention. The session was called "Work Straight: Ethics and Honesty on the Job." Alex Miller's name was on the list of participants with a line through it. Please excuse Alex. Some woman beat him up and put him in the hospital.

I heard voices just outside the door. The first voice belonged to the seminarian. ". . . Yeah, she said she was a private detective. I didn't ask why she wants this." The other person said something in low tones I couldn't hear and the seminarian said, "Dark hair, kind of tall." More words I didn't catch followed by an embarrassed laugh from the seminarian. "That's, uh, outside my realm of experience," he said. "You'll have to ask her that yourself."

He came in and said, "I was wondering what a detective needs with this information."

I saw no reason to lie. I said, "A few days ago, a woman I was protecting was attacked by a gang of young guys. I'd like to find out who was behind the attack. One of the attackers is in the Work Straight program."

His forehead creased in concern. "Gee, I'd hate to think our guys were involved, but I have to be honest, we can't change all of them. Some of them are pretty tough."

"Were you talking to someone in the hall just now?"

"Yes." He reddened slightly. "Wait," he said as if the thought just occurred to him, "he could tell you about some of the guys, if he's still there." He went out the door and I followed.

The man was still there, heading away from us down the hall. He moved with a noticeable limp but stopped and turned when the seminarian called to him. It was Art Spinoza, the man I'd blasted with Italian obscenities. Spinoza looked me up and down the way he had before but this time I held my tongue. Ms. Restraint.

The seminarian started the introductions, but I cut him off. "We've met. How did you hurt yourself?" I asked. An elastic bandage was visible beneath the cuff of his right trouser leg.

"Eh. I got nuttin' fo' say wit' you." Spinoza's pidgin accent was so thick I had to look right at him to understand him. He turned to the young man and unloaded a string of complaints about me, saying that I'd called him an asshole, that I was a frigid bitch who thought I was better than men, and that I slept around. The last didn't seem logically consistent with the frigid bitch part, but I've been called things many times worse. It's one of the joys of the profession. You try and let it blow past you.

The seminarian didn't have my experience, however, and Spinoza's tirade clearly shook him. He looked like he wanted to be any place but here. Nevertheless he tried manfully to restore order. "Miss Lyon wanted to know about the Work Straight program and about some of the men. She thinks one of them -"

"Eh, dem good boys." Once again he favored us with an angry harangue that was even more difficult to understand through the pidgin and the emotion. The gist of it was that they were all trying to turn their lives around and that they'd be successful if people would just leave them alone. The poor fellow I'd beaten up hadn't done anything wrong. I was the one who should be in jail with the other whores. He nearly spat the last word at me before turning and heading away from us.

"Spinoza," I called, "how did you hurt your ankle?"

"Playin' soccer. What you think?"

The seminarian shrugged helplessly. "Mr. Spinoza works with some of our youth athletic programs. I've never seen him so angry or heard him speak like that. Usually he's well-spoken and articulate."

"Guess I caught him on a bad day," I said. "What was it he asked you in the hall that was outside your experience?"

The seminarian turned several shades of red. "He…uh…he wondered if you engage in oral sex."

24 MAKING OUT IN PUBLIC

Back in my apartment, I opened a can of Coke and let it defizz while I undressed and hung up my suit. The lack of sleep in jail was catching up to me. I thought of just climbing into my hammock on the lanai, but rejected it. You have to meet fatigue head on or it takes you out. I put on shorts and a singlet, did a pre-run stretching routine and slipped on a pair of New Balance trainers. I drank the Coke on the way down to the street.

5:30. I had half an hour of daylight left. It was still light when I headed up the Ala Wai Canal, crossed Kapahulu to the rose garden and turned up Monsarrat. Behind Diamond Head the light seemed to be going fast. Shadows lengthened, blurred and merged with other shadows, creating extended pools of gloom. The street light at 18th Street, where I'd parked earlier in the day, emitted a faint warm-up glow.

Ordinarily I'd go around the crater to Diamond Head Avenue, but this time I turned down 18th towards the cemetery. A mix of curiosity and the feeling that I didn't yet have closure on Sue's death drew me to her resting place.

The gate was still open as I approached, but the cemetery seemed deserted. Who would be visiting graves at dusk anyway? Something about a cemetery in the twilight gives me the creeps. I stopped by the gate to retie my shoes and stretch my calves. All my senses were alert. Suddenly movement way off to my right made my skin prickle. A lone figure was in the area near Sue's grave. I couldn't make out any features, couldn't even tell if it was a man or a woman. All I could determine was that he or she was tall and slender. I gave a violent shiver and jogged through the gate.

As I got nearer, I determined that the visitor was a woman. I was still about fifty yards away when she bent over, placed something on the grave, and straightened up. She looked over in my direction as I quickened my pace. I don't know if she saw me or not, but she turned immediately and made straight for a dark van waiting in the shadows. I'd have missed it if the lights hadn't come on. It was one of those Pontiac minivans with the high tail lights. Knowing she was leaving spurred me into a desperate sprint. The woman got in the passenger side and the van sped away, leaving me with a vague kerosene taste from my anaerobic burst.

I went over to the grave to see what she'd left. On the fresh sod lay a bouquet of white anthuriums. Their stems were wrapped, not in florist's tissue, but in a banana leaf tied with a rough, homemade twine.

I went back the way I had come, my mind working furiously. Who was the woman? One name kept popping into my head - Aileen Burch. Why hadn't she made the funeral? Maybe she'd come from off-island and had been delayed. Or maybe she didn't want to be seen.

It was not until I was at the bottom of Monsarrat near the rose garden that I realized my body had been keeping pace with my thoughts. I leaned against a light standard to catch my breath. The more I thought about it, the more certain I was that if I could find Aileen Burch, I'd find Nathan Pfeifer. I jogged slowly back to my apartment.

While I showered, I went over what to report to Brian. I'd let him know that I'd checked out Ken's alibi and that it had held up. He'd hear from Ken about it anyway, if he hadn't already. As to my theory about Aileen Burch, I decided to wait until I had something more substantial than a shadow in a graveyard.

I left the shower invigorated. The run had chased away my fatigue, at least for the time being, and the certainty that I was close to finding Nathan Pfeifer lifted my spirits. I'd thought of wearing jeans and a shirt for the evening, but in my elated mood, I decided on a denim halter dress and jacket - one of several outfits I'd gotten before prison but hadn't had a chance to wear.

Brian was putting files away when I arrived. He'd removed his jacket and was in his shirt sleeves, the cuffs turned back on his forearms and the shirt opened at the neck. His tie was loose. I liked the look. I hoped he liked mine. I'd removed my jacket, too.

He gave me a lingering appraisal and followed it with a hello kiss. "You look great," he said. "I'm ready to eat. Let's go somewhere close."

"Make it somewhere with valet parking so you won't be exposed in the parking lot."

He gave me a questioning look and I said, "You and Sue received death threats. Sue was buried today. Understood?"

"Understood." He went to button his shirt.

"Don't," I said. "I like it loose. You look kind of sexy."

"You, too."

Brian locked up his office and took my hand as we went to the elevator. Inside the car, he pressed all the buttons between our floor and the ground. "Elevator roulette," he explained. "What we do is we kiss until we reach the bottom or until someone sees us."

"That sounds like a juvenile game, Brian."

"Absolutely." He beamed.

"Well then," I said, "let the games begin."

We made it to the bottom without being seen, still in a clinch when the doors slid open at ground level. Brian muttered his disappointment and I echoed it. We were both breathing hard.

"Next time," I said, "we'll start at the top floor."

I drove us to a restaurant near Kewalo Basin, not far from Magruder Estate's office. We made small talk until our drinks came. Then I said, "I visited Ken today."

160

"I know. He wasn't happy. He called and demanded that I fire you. I told him to go to hell. I said I needed you."

I thanked him for the vote of confidence. "Brian, I had to check out his alibi. Assuming Sue's death wasn't due to natural causes, Ken is a prime suspect. He hated her as much as anyone. She cost him a lot of money. Now the alibi checks out. What's he got to complain about?"

Brian drank some of his beer before answering. "He doesn't think you're going to let it drop at that."

I set down my Scotch and met his eyes across the table. "I'm not, Brian. I told him so. Do you want me to drop it?"

"I don't know, Val. I don't care that much about Sue Naito. As far as I'm concerned it's not been shown yet that there's any culpability in her death. That's Ken's feeling, too. I tried explaining to him that you're looking for the Pfeifer kid, but he doesn't see the connection. He feels you're on a crusade over Sue that's going to drag him into scandal. That's what he's afraid of."

"Not afraid enough to keep him away from Myra."

"Val, this is about love. What if Ken feels about Myra the way I feel about you?"

I felt the pressure of his hand on my thigh. "I'd say the Magruder brothers are ruled by their gonads. Don't you ever think about the consequences?"

"Do you always think about the consequences?"

I took hold of his fingers and lifted his hand off my thigh. "I'm thinking about them now," I said.

The waiter returned for our dinner orders. Brian ordered a second drink for both of us. I ordered their special, lobster, and Brian ordered opakapaka, a white fish.

A serious look creased Brian's face when we were alone again. He said, "Val, if the only one to suffer consequences from a scandal were Ken, it wouldn't be such an issue. Ken feels the real threat is to Frank's career."

"How?" I asked.

"Think about it. Frank's on his way to becoming a bishop. A

scandal in the family could derail that.”

“And Ken thinks I’m the one who’ll do it? Look, I’m sorry Brian, but I’m not taking the blame.”

“I’m not blaming you. I’m just letting you in on Ken’s thinking.”

“Well, you can tell Ken to relax. I’ve got a hunch about Nathan’s whereabouts. I’m this close to finding him.” I held up my thumb and index finger. “This close. Reassure your brother that all I want is the kid.”

Those were the words he’d wanted to hear. His eyes lit up and relief flooded his face. “How do you know you’re so close?”

“I’m not ready to tell you, but you’ll be the first to know.”

“Great,” he said. He kissed me lightly on the cheek.

Our dinners arrived. I could tell from the size of my lobster that I was going to have trouble finishing it. Brian had ordered a wine to go with the meal, a bottle of Haut Brion.

“Good old Irish wine,” he said, pronouncing the name “O’ Brian.”

I went right at the job of cracking the shell and digging out the meat between big swallows of Haut Brion. The conversation slid to childhood and then to sports. Generally, I have a lot of enthusiasm for the topic, but not this time. Somehow my energy began to flag, taking with it my interest in the subject and the food.

It had to be the Haut Brion and the Scotch. They’d wiped out the boost I’d gotten from my run. I knew Brian had a yearning for some bed activity, but all I yearned for was bed. Period. Unless we moved quickly, he was going to be stuck with one comatose date.

Brian paid the check and we waited for the car. The night air and the sound of the surf pounding on the rocks near us revived me somewhat. When we were in the car, I turned up the AC and put a Doors disk in the CD player, cranking up the volume. I hoped the noise and cold air would keep me alert, but even Jim Morrison seemed to call me to bed.

Brian’s condo was on Judd Street, not far from downtown. I pulled into the lot and we walked to the front door.

"Brian, I'm sorry," I said. "It was a lovely dinner, but I've had a long day, not much sleep, and I'm fading fast. I'm not going to be good company tonight."

I hated to look at the disappointment in his face. He framed my face with his hands and kissed me sweetly on the lips. "There's nothing I can do to make you change your mind?"

I put my arms around his neck and opened my mouth to him. He took my offering. His hands moved around my waist. I pressed against him.

We were in a corner near the front door, hidden from the street by hedges and from the lobby by a concrete column. The light above the entryway failed to penetrate our area. In daylight we'd be clearly visible from the parking lot, but at night it was as private as a hotel room. Lousy security, I thought. But what I said came out something like, "Mmmmm." He teased me with his tongue, and I responded with a lot of body work. He knew where to put his hands. The call of my bed dwindled to a distant whisper.

From somewhere nearby, an engine cranked to life and a pair of spot lights pinned us against the entry. "What the hell?" said Brian. My heart pounded against my chest wall. We separated quickly. I had to shield my eyes against the glare in order to see the truck with the spots on top. It roared out of the parking lot taking the lights with it and leaving us once again in darkness. The afterimage of the spots, tinged red from the blood pounding into my head, danced in front of my face.

"God," said Brian. "I've never been caught making out, before. This was my first time. Was it your first, too?"

"Yeah," I lied. "So how was it?"

"Good. How about you?"

"My heart's still pounding."

I readjusted my dress. "Brian, I have to go," I said. We both knew we'd lost the mood for the night.

"Yeah," he said. "Tomorrow night. It'll be better the second time."

I got in the car, turned Jim Morrison up high and headed

home. Nu'uanu to King Street. Didn't trust myself on the highway. I'd had a sudden rush of adrenaline when the spots hit us, but that wore off quickly. By the time I reached Kalakaua, I was racing fatigue. I found an open parking spot near my building, next to a sign saying no parking from six to eight a.m. on Tuesdays. Hell with it. Set the alarm. I parked the Lexus at a crazy angle and stumbled to my apartment. Inside, I fumbled the deadbolts shut and peeled out of my clothes, letting them lay where they fell in the hall. I didn't bother to pull the bed out from the couch, but wrapped myself in a blanket. My last conscious thought was that I had to be up at six.

25 NIGHT TERROR

Dinner with Brian in a strange restaurant. The waiters and Brian
wore tuxes while I wore nothing. They brought dish after dish and I
ate ravenously while Brian's hands roamed over me. He kept insisting
we leave. Finally I gave in. Once we got outside, he began kissing me
passionately. His mouth was everywhere. My legs felt like jelly. If I
weren't sandwiched between Brian and the wall, I'd fall down. All of
a sudden a light caught us in its glare, burning into my face. Brian
seemed not to notice. He continued his ministrations. I wanted to
scream at him to stop, to get away, but the scream died in my throat.
I tried to push away and succeeded only in falling backwards as a hail
of bullets drilled the wall and ripped into Brian. Even then I couldn't
scream. The light came closer. Beyond it I could see the muzzle of
the gun pointed at my face.

I sat bolt upright and looked around. No gun, no light, just
the comforting familiarity of my couch in my apartment. My face was
hot from sunlight streaming in through the lanai doors. I exhaled in
relief and lay back down. The sunlight, though, was too intense and I
gave it up after a few minutes. The digital clock radio said it was a
quarter past nine. My body was stiff from the contortions into which
it had been forced on my love-seat sofa. I stretched out the kinks and
followed the trail of my clothes to the hall - underwear, dress, jacket,

purse, shoes. Must be the maid's day off.

I started the coffee maker and called Brian. I hoped he didn't have an appointment this morning. Hoped he wasn't sitting in his apartment waiting for me to show. If he'd needed me to drive him, he'd have called, I reasoned. Perhaps he'd tried and I'd been sleeping too soundly to hear the phone.

His phone seemed to ring a long time. Perhaps he was sleeping soundly, too. I started counting the rings. At twelve I gave up. Now what? I thought. The memory of the truck with the spotlights was all too vivid. I fought back a rising tide of panic. Had he been waiting for Brian? I'd screwed up leaving Brian alone last night. Calm down, I told myself. How could the guy have known we'd show up when we did? It was just a coincidence. If you're going to get passionate in public, you have to expect such things. It's part of the thrill. Brian was probably in the shower, or doing his laundry. I decided to try again in fifteen minutes.

I poured myself some coffee and held the cup under my nose to steam the sleep out of my face. The phone rang and I lunged for it causing coffee to slosh out of the cup onto my bare skin. I yelped into the phone and put the cup down.

Brian, on the other end, said, "Hey, are you all right?"

"No, I am not all right. I just burned myself with coffee." It was a relief to hear his voice. I yanked five or six sheets off the paper towel roll, stuck them under the faucet and ran cold water over them.

"Where did you get burned?" he asked.

"In my apartment," I said, patting myself down with the cold wad.

"I know that. What I meant was -"

"What you meant is none of your business. Where the hell are you, Brian? Where have you been?"

"I'm at the office. I didn't want to wake you, you were so tired last night."

It took a couple of seconds for his words to sink in. "How the hell did you get to the office?"

"I walked. It's a gorgeous day. I'm not that far from

downtown. If I'm going to keep up with you I need to get in shape."

"Walked?" I yelled. "Dammit Brian, you've got no business being out in the open in daylight. What about that truck last night? It could've been waiting for you."

"Oh, c'mon. We saw it leave and it wasn't there this morning. I looked for it. Give me some credit. Listen, I've seen that truck in the visitor's spot before. It probably belongs to the guest of a tenant who just got lucky and caught a little show on his way out. He'll be telling his friends on the golf course all about it."

While Brian talked, I stretched the phone cord through my living room so I could look out on the street, keeping well back from the window. I didn't see any truck either, but that didn't do much to calm me. Why couldn't Brian just accept my judgment in this?

"Listen," he said, "take care of that burn, wherever it is, and you can show it to me this evening. If it makes you happy, I won't leave the building. Bye." He hung up.

I slammed the phone down. The coffee burn was all but forgotten in my annoyance at Brian. First there was his cavalier attitude towards his own safety. On top of that there was his cavalier attitude towards me. What the hell made him so sure I'd see him tonight? Was he taking me for granted? What if I had other plans? Dammit, I did have plans and if he'd asked me about them instead of assuming, I'd have told him.

The boy/girl issues were distracting me from my job. It was time Val Lyon earned her pay. I scrubbed my face and pulled on jeans and a sleeveless Hawaiian shirt. For breakfast, I fried a strip of bacon, spread some toast with peanut butter and put the bacon on top. I washed it down with another cup of coffee, careful not to spill any on me this time. Before leaving the apartment, I looked up the address of Friendly Isle Air Tours.

It was close on ten when I went looking for Brian's car, but it wasn't where I thought I'd left it. Where exactly had I left it? I walked up and down the street without any luck. Could I have been that tired? At last I flagged down a cop in a three-wheel traffic scooter.

"If you parked here," he said, "you got towed. This side's a tow away on Tuesday morning. So the street cleaner can go by, that's why. There's the sign."

An hour and ten minutes later, I'd paid the fine and towing charge after taking the bus to the A-1 Towing Company's yard on Nimitz. The Lexus had a few scratches on the door near the window. The owner shrugged it off when I pointed out the damage.

"We ain't responsible for damage," he said. "You the one parked illegally." He pronounced it, "ee-lee-gol-lee." "Anyway, it ain't us. The scratches they was there already."

"Those scratches were not there. They look to me like they were made by a jimmy."

"We don't use a jimmy 'les there's no other way. Anyway, the car still locked. Could be somebody tried to steal it."

Or tried to break in. Given the threat to Brian, I couldn't ignore that possibility. After a few more minutes of arguing with the guy, I got him to find me a convex mirror. He watched contemptuously while I used it to look under the car. Nothing was out of place. Nothing that didn't belong there. Next I opened the hood cautiously. Again, nothing. Finally, I looked for signs of tampering around the column and ignition. Negative all the way around. I gave the mirror back to the owner. He accepted it with a smirk and a shake of his head. I spun the wheels on the gravel and peeled out of the lot.

I'd hoped to arrive at Friendly Isle before their tour, but I'd burned up most of the morning retrieving the car. It was past eleven when I turned onto Nimitz. The tour had already left if they were on schedule, but maybe I could learn something snooping around the office. I headed to the airport.

Friendly Isle's address was actually on Lagoon Drive, before the entrance to the terminal. Many of the smaller air companies have their offices on Lagoon. I left the Lexus in a parking lot in front of a row of low buildings. On the other side of the buildings was a tarmac where planes of various size and design were parked. Farther out was the reef runway where big jets, their size magnified by the heat lens rising from the pavement, lined up for takeoff.

The tour company shared one of the low buildings with a flight school. "Friendly Isle Air Tours," was painted on the side above a picture of the island of Molokai. A Pontiac minivan, just like the one at the cemetery, was parked next to the building.

I went in the single front door. The building was a strand steel shell divided into offices by temporary walls and partitions. A large area on the left had a counter and a row of stack chairs. The counter bore the Friendly Isle logo but no one was behind it. The wall was lined with photos of people. On closer look they turned out to be aviators - Wily Post, Charles Lindbergh and others. Among them was Harriet Quimby. She was a young woman in post-World War I clothing. I was amazed at how attractive she was. She'd probably been considered a beauty in her time. She'd be over a hundred if she were alive today.

"Looking for someone?" asked a voice behind me.

I turned quickly. The speaker was a middle-aged man with a shirt pocket full of pens and a clipboard in his hand.

"Are you the pilot?" I asked.

"Of Friendly Isle? Nope. I'm with the flight school." He gestured behind him with his thumb. "They took off about twenty minutes ago."

"Figures," I said. "That's how my luck's been running. I tried to get here before they took off, but my car was towed and I had to get it back."

"That's rough." His sympathy sounded genuine. "How about a cup of coffee? Maybe your luck will turn."

I said okay and followed him to the flight school part of the building. He filled two foam cups from a restaurant-style coffee maker and dropped some coins into a coffee can.

"Cream or sugar?"

"Black, please. Is it a good tour?"

He put cream in one and handed the other one to me. "Yeah," he said. "They all give you the basics, of course - Napali coast, Waimea Canyon - but Phil Burch is the only one gives you

Kalaupapa."

At the mention of the two names, Burch and Kalaupapa, I almost spilled my coffee for the second time in the morning. I recovered myself quickly and said, "Why do you suppose that is? That he's the only one?"

"Oh, the residents gave him a monopoly. The Burch family's been associated with the community for a long time. His mother lives there."

"You mean she has lep - Hansen's disease?"

He laughed. "No. If you ever get to take the tour, you'll find that not all of the residents have the disease. Aileen's about as healthy as they come. Quite a pilot, herself."

"Do you ever see her?"

"All the time. In fact, she was at the controls last evening when the tour got back. She does that sometimes when there's an extra space."

"She sounds like a remarkable lady," I said. "Is she around today?"

"I doubt it. She probably went back with Phil this morning. He has a regular newspaper and supply run - Kalaupapa, Molokai and then some of the Leeward Islands." He looked at his watch and drained his coffee. "Gotta earn my pay. Have to check out a plane before my student gets here."

I thanked him for the coffee and left.

So, Aileen had arrived at five yesterday. Allowing forty minutes for driving to the cemetery in traffic, she could've reached it just ahead of me. I paused by the Lexus and watched a big jet lumber down the runway and lift off with all engines straining. There must be a moment of elation inside the cockpit when that happens. Kalaupapa, I thought. What better place to hide Nathan Pfeifer?

26 THE ROAD LESS TRAVELED

The agent at Hideaway Travel, a friendly guy with a nice smile and two small rings in one ear, explained that the package included a ground tour at the Kalaupapa settlement.

"Could you get me on the flight tomorrow?" I asked.

"I think it's all full up tomorrow. How about next week?"

"I won't be here next week. Can't you do anything for me? I really want to take the tour." I chewed on my lip, going for the pathetic look.

"Well, let me see. Honestly, though, I don't see the hurry. The island will be there for a long time." He turned to a terminal and continued his chatter. "See the plane is a six-seater Beachcraft and I know he has six people going, but sometimes he lets a seventh passenger sit in the co-pilot's seat. It all depends on their weight."

"What does weight have to do with it?"

"Well, it's a small plane and he does a lot of maneuvers. If there's too much weight, he won't be able to maneuver. He might even crash. Now wouldn't that be awful?" He pulled up a list of names on his screen. "Well, there aren't any fatties," he said. "Would you say you weigh under a hundred fifty pounds?"

"Yes. You want me to step on a scale?"

"No, but Captain Phil might. I'll put you on the list, but

don't blame me if he won't take you."

"Fine," I said.

"The tour leaves at eleven. Don't be late because -"

"I know. He won't wait."

"Well it's not my fault. That's Captain Phil's rule. You don't have to get huffy about it."

From the car phone, I called the mechanic who had my Nissan. It needed a new starter but he thought the part was on the island. He'd call me when it was ready. Probably tomorrow or the next day. Since I wasn't sure where I'd be tomorrow, I gave him Brian's number.

As it was the noon hour, I checked in with Brian. He'd sent out for lunch.

"See? I'm doing what I'm told," he said. "I'll see you this evening."

I hung up and drove to Ala Moana Shopping Center. Once again I hadn't told Brian about my plans this evening. You're not managing this well at all, I told myself.

For the next hour, I searched through one store after another looking for a leather bag to replace the one that had been ruined in the break-in. I finally found one that was both stylish and roomy. Best of all, it was marked down fifty dollars. In the flush of triumph, I was an easy mark for the sale at Foot Locker. I barely escaped with nothing more than a pair of Saucony Grid running shoes. When the salesman mentioned mediolateral control, it was like talking dirty.

I spent the rest of the afternoon with a bestseller at the beach. About five I packed up, pulled nylon shorts and an over-sized T-shirt over my swimsuit and jogged to Iron World Gym. No way was I going to let my weight go and be responsible for the deaths of my fellow passengers, not to mention my own.

Iron World is your basic no-frills gym. Two stationery bikes and a stair stepper are all they have for aerobics. No bright rooms with picture windows so the guys in the juice bar can scope out the girls. No juice bar. The place smells of talcum and sweat. There are lat machines, leg curl machines, and tons of free weights. There are also lots of guys with wide shoulders and six-pack abs who don't hassle you. It's a great place for women as a few of us have discovered, but we keep it our secret.

I did an insanity workout - low weights and high reps on the first set with higher weights and fewer reps on the second and third sets. I started out with calf raises and worked up through curls and presses. By the time I finished my set of shoulder presses I had a nice sheen of sweat over my body. The scale went up to 146 when I stepped on it. Not bad! Allowing for two pounds for clothing, I'd dropped a pound. Maybe that would translate into extra lift on the flight tomorrow. I hoped my fellow passengers were as considerate.

Night had fallen during my workout. I jogged back to my apartment keeping to the well-lit, well-trafficked areas. A good workout with weights can leave you feeling invincible. At such times I have to remind myself of the dangers around me. I recited my personal litany of all the women and a few men I knew who'd been raped or assaulted in the streets. By the time I reached my apartment, I no longer felt like Superman, but like Jimmy Olsen. I was thankful for the new deadbolt I'd installed.

It was time to get ready for dinner with Frank and I still hadn't told Brian. What to wear to dinner with a priest? It was for just these occasions that muumuus were invented, but I wasn't the muumuu type. I settled on a simple tan skirt - knee-length - and a forest green blouse.

Brian called as I emerged from the shower. Tell him now, I thought. But no, "I'll pick you up at seven-thirty," I said.

I dressed with a vague sense of irritation. Why not just tell him you've got an important engagement? Why string him along when you know he's expecting you this evening? It was business, after all. Nothing underhanded about it.

I spent a little extra time on makeup and used some gel to style my hair. I'd chosen a stylish, conservative outfit, but just so the signals would be completely scrambled, I applied perfume.

My irritation lingered on the drive downtown. I worried it

like a sore tooth. This was the first test of our relationship. I was asserting my need to be independent, to be free to do my job as I saw fit without answering to Brian or anyone else. Pam would probably describe it as a passive-aggressive response to relationship pressure from him. Or maybe she'd say it was childish bullshit. Whatever one might call it, the outlines of my own needs had never been clearer. Privacy was paramount, something to be jealously guarded. After a stint in prison, the value I placed on privacy had risen considerably. Somehow, I'd have to reconcile that with my need for intimacy.

Brian was waiting in his office.

I said, "Something's come up and I feel terrible about it. It means I'm not free tonight after all. Do you mind if I just drop you off at your place?"

"Uh oh! I was afraid of this," he said. "You're tired of me already. There's someone else isn't there?"

"Only your brother. Frank asked me to dinner."

To my relief, he wasn't upset. "And I wasn't invited?" was all he asked.

"No, you weren't and I don't have any idea why."

"Which of course, Ms. Shamus, fueled your curiosity so you couldn't turn him down."

I had to admit the truth of that. "So why did he invite me and not you?"

"If I had to guess, I'd say he's sizing you up to see if you're good family material. You'd better bone up on your Apostle's Creed before you get there."

"Seriously, Brian."

"Seriously, I don't know, but I'm anxious to find out what the good monsignor wants. How about stopping by afterwards?"

"It might be late," I said.

"I'll count the hours, Val."

In spite of his agreeable tone, I knew he didn't like me going off without him. For my part, I wasn't happy leaving him alone. The memory of the truck and the vividness of my dream were all too strong. I made a show of circling the parking lot before pulling up to his door.

"All clear?" he asked.

"All clear," I said, ignoring the sarcasm in his voice.

I watched through the glass doors until he was on the elevator, before heading to the highway. Knowing that the building was secure didn't make me feel much better. I'd made a mistake in getting involved with my client and we were both paying for it.

Traffic on the Pali Highway never ceases, but at quarter to eight it had thinned out enough that I could go the speed limit. Moonrise was late and the sky was a shade lighter than the mountains. Their jagged peaks were a vague outline on either side of me as I headed towards the notch opening to the Windward side. I passed the turnoff to the Pali lookout near the spot where Kamehameha, the first monarch, had forced his enemies over the cliff. A marker at the lookout commemorates the event. There is no marker on the highway - just a sign urging trucks to use a lower gear.

The highway dropped down into the tunnels and came out, hugging the cliff face high above Windward Oahu. I pulled into the left lane to pass a driver who'd slowed down, probably daunted by the line of highway lights snaking down the mountain. In the mirror, I saw another vehicle coming out of the tunnels. It was going much too fast for a road that dropped so steeply. I moved back to the right lane where a sign advised me of a runaway truck ramp up ahead.

The highway at that spot is two lanes in each direction. A concrete barrier topped with light baffles separates the Kailua-bound traffic from the Honolulu-bound. A narrow shoulder and a guard rail separates the motorists from oblivion. I passed a warning sign indicating hairpin turns.

When the other vehicle didn't pass me, I checked my mirror and saw its headlights slide into the right lane. It was still bearing down on me. My internal alarm went off about the same time that the car phone beeped. I took the phone from the cradle, expecting it to be Brian, but it wasn't.

The caller said, "Lyon, did you ditch the boyfriend?" The voice sounded like the one on the tape threatening Brian.

"Where are you?" I demanded.

"Right behind you," he said.

I glanced in the mirror and tensed. The vehicle on my tail resembled the truck that had been outside of Brian's apartment last night. It had a bar of spotlights on top. My eyes were still on the mirror when he hit his brights and spotlights.

"*Merda*," I yelled and slapped away the mirror with the phone.

He said, "You should watch the hairpins, Lyon. They're killers."

The Lexus's front wheels bumped across the raised lane markers as I blinked away the afterimage of the brights. My vision cleared in time to see the highway dividers looming ahead. I spun the wheel to the right, losing the phone but holding the car into the first turn. It was a broad turn, almost ninety degrees. He stayed on my inside, moving up beside me. I was thankful I didn't have the lights to contend with, but I didn't want him alongside where he could force me into the barriers.

We shot out of the turn and I floored the Lexus. It responded well. I pulled ahead of him, passed the emergency ramp and cut back into the right lane. He was behind me again. His lights washed out the car's instrument panel and threw my silhouette onto the dashboard. The guy was enjoying himself. His laughter came up from the floor where the phone had fallen.

The second turn was tighter and steeper than the first and I had to back off on the gas, but I was still well above the speed limit. The Lexus held onto the road through almost a full one-eighty degrees. Its styling gave it an edge over the truck. He dropped back.

Another runaway ramp sign. I floored it again coming out of the turn and found my lane blocked by a city bus.

"Move, damn you," I screamed at him. I laid on the horn and moved into the left lane. The damn bus moved with me. I flashed my brights and rode up on its tail, braking hard to keep from ending up inside it. Behind me the truck was closing again.

"Tough shit, Lyon," I heard from the floor.

The wheel felt sweaty under my palms. I wrenched it hard to go around the bus on the right. The sudden maneuver caused the Lexus's rear end to shimmy slightly, but once again it held the road. Suddenly my headlights picked up a child's face and the bottom fell out of my stomach. The kid was twisted around in the back seat of a family sedan about a car length ahead of me. His eyes went wide and his mouth dropped open. I braked again and braced for the impact, but at the last second I saw room between the sedan and the guardrail. Just beyond, I saw the light standard marking the runaway truck ramp. I made for it.

The truck ramp is eight hundred feet of loose gravel raked into a tall central ridge to stop heavy trucks. Deep furrows on both sides of the ridge are meant to receive and guide the wheels.

One furrow caught the left wheels and wrested control from me while the right wheels rode up on the ridge causing the Lexus to list at a sickening angle. I thought it might roll over, but the right side dropped and it snowplowed into the gravel. The sounds, rocks hailing on the car, metal tearing, overwhelmed my senses. The sudden deceleration threw me forward against the shoulder harness as the air bag popped.

The bag inflates and deflates in about the same time it takes a Nolan Ryan fast ball to travel from the mound to the plate. Even a pillow hurts at that speed. It stung my face and knocked me back into the seat. After that, silence.

For all I knew, the truck had followed me onto the ramp. I pushed open the door as far as it would go, undid my seat belt and dropped to the gravel where I rolled into a stand of weeds. No one had followed me, though some vehicles seemed to slow down in passing. I must have whetted the curiosity of a lot of morbid thrill seekers.

The car's path through the gravel was clearly visible in the light from the highway. Despite its speed, the Lexus had neither the clearance nor the weight to travel far. Its nose was buried in gravel almost to the windshield which was spider-webbed with cracks. Behind the car was a Hansel-and-Gretel trail of parts stripped from the underside.

I hauled myself to my feet and took stock of my own damage. I'd lost a little skin from my palms when I dove into the gravel and my nose hurt terribly from the air bag. It was bleeding profusely. The last thing I needed was another broken nose. How much abuse can one schnozz take? I went back to the car and found my handbag on the floor, tangled up with the phone. I hauled both of them up, settled back in the seat and dug out a wad of tissues for my nose.

The phone line was still open. I broke the connection, but before I could dial for help, it beeped.

"Yes," I said, knowing who it would be.

"Lyon," he said. "The boyfriend won't like what you did to his paint job. Maybe you'll wish you had died. Think about it." He hung up.

My hands were shaking so badly I could hardly punch the three emergency numbers.

27 THE LEAST REVEREND

A lot of tissues and a little compression stopped the bleeding. Several cars did finally stop and shortly after, the police arrived. First, they satisfied themselves that I wasn't dying and then they satisfied themselves that I wasn't drunk. By the time I'd finished the field sobriety test, my frustration was at the spillover level.

"So, how'd you end up on the truck ramp?" asked an officer.

"I was looking for a goddamn shortcut."

He didn't like that answer. Insisted on a different one.

"A guy tried to run me off the road. How's that?"

He liked that a little better. We went through the drill - make, model, color, tag number of the truck - but because of the brights, I couldn't give him anything definite.

"Okay. So what'd he do?"

"He rode up on my tail and flashed his brights to blind me." It sounded pretty lame, and the officer didn't buy it.

"Then what? He cut you off? Impact you?"

"No."

Another officer joined us. "No sign of any damage that mighta come from another vehicle," he said.

"Look, I got away from him. It was good driving."

"From the marks on the road back there and the distance

179

you traveled, you had to be moving pretty fast. How fast were you going?"

"I don't know my speed. I was trying to get away."

"I'm gonna cite you for failure to control your speed and unauthorized use of an emergency route. If you want, you can file a report at the station and talk to the detectives."

"I don't believe this," I said. "Doesn't anybody fucking care that someone tried to kill me?" I kicked at the gravel, sending a few rocks flying and lodging one painfully between the pad of my foot and the sole of my open-toed shoe. To my horror, a drop of moisture leaked out of my eye. I turned away as a photographer arrived, followed by a tow truck.

More reporters and photographers showed up. It was the kind of scene that makes a newshound's nipples hard. The sight of a luxury car half-buried in gravel had them thinking Pulitzer. I hid out in one of the patrol cars away from the crowd and managed to calm down enough to accept a ride, semi-graciously, from one of the cops. He dropped me off at the retreat house, an hour late.

Frank, himself, opened the door when I rang the bell. He was dressed casually in brown slacks and an open-neck sport shirt. he said, "Val, we were starting to worry. Did something happen? Is that blood on your blouse?"

I looked down at myself. In the lighted hallway where we stood, my blouse looked an awful mess. It was, indeed, splotched with reddish brown patches of blood.

Frank put a protective arm around my shoulders. "Are you all right?"

"I'll live, in spite of somebody's best efforts. A guy in a truck tried to force me off the road."

Frank's face twisted in more pain and sympathy than I felt a bloody nose deserved. I reassured him that he didn't have to worry about me. "Brian's car is totaled. He's going to need some sympathy."

"Cars can be replaced. We'd about given up on you."

"We?"

"Bishop Connor's here. I thought you might enjoy meeting him. We've been waiting dinner for you, but if you want to freshen up first, go ahead. I'll have a drink ready for you. Scotch, right?"

"Right. Double."

I borrowed a golf shirt from Frank and had him direct me to the bathroom. Inside, I rinsed my blouse in the sink, splashed water on my face and dragged a comb through my hair. Why would Frank think I'd enjoy meeting the bishop? Maybe the bishop wanted to meet me, but I couldn't think of a reason for that either. I touched up my makeup and went in search of a phone to call Brian.

Frank met me in the hallway. He pushed a rocks glass into my hand and showed me to a study with a phone. I took a big swallow of the Scotch for courage before dialing Brian's number. I needn't have worried. He took the news of his car with the same equanimity as Frank. His main concern was for me, he said. He interrupted my account so often to ask if I was all right that I finally despaired of getting my story told over the phone.

"Later, Brian. I'll come by and tell you all about it."

I left the study and went looking for Frank and the bishop. I found them engaged in quiet conversation at one end of a large living room. Frank was seated in a wing chair covered in a muted gold brocade. The bishop sat on a brown, crushed velvet sofa at a right angle to Frank's chair. A wine glass holding a small amount of red wine and a rocks glass with a pale amber whiskey stood on the end table between them. The table was a dark walnut as were the rest of the tables and wood furnishings. The room itself was paneled in light oak. On the walls were framed oil paintings depicting mountain and forest scenes. The lighting came from table lamps, mostly brass. Except for the large crucifix on one wall, I could have been in a downtown men's club. All-in-all, the room reminded me of a high-class funeral parlor - warm and comfortable but lacking a personal stamp.

Both men rose to their feet when I entered. In contrast to Frank's casual attire, the bishop wore a dark suit with a Roman collar. He was slightly built, about three inches shorter than me, with a pink scalp showing through his white hair. His eyes, behind bifocals, were a steel gray. Frank made the introductions, referring to the bishop as the most reverend and me as the lady detective.

"The least reverend," I appended.

Bishop Connor's mouth formed in a quick smile. "Marvelous," he said. "It's nice to meet a girl with a sense of humor for a change. Young ladies today - these so-called feminists - could use a little more of that."

"Oh, I think you'd be surprised at the humor among feminists," I said, "but you might not get the jokes."

"Probably not," he said. His smile faded and he offered me his hand. It was about the same size as mine only pink and soft. I gave it a moderate squeeze to let him know he wasn't dealing with a girl, sense of humor or not.

"So where's your beau?" asked Connor. "I expected to see him tonight."

Before I could answer, Frank jumped in with a response. "A third party always dilutes the occasion. I thought you two should have a chance to get acquainted on your own terms. Let me refill your glasses." He didn't wait for a response but took my glass and the bishop's wine glass before disappearing into the hall.

"You ought to sit down, Val," said the bishop. "It sounds like you had a harrowing brush with death. Providence was certainly on your side."

"I like to think my driving skills had a lot to do with it," I said. I sat on the sofa at the end opposite from where the bishop had been sitting. He remained standing. I smoothed my blood-dappled skirt over my knees and waited. The audience had begun.

"You weren't hurt, that's the important thing. Private detective seems like a very dangerous occupation for a young lady."

"The danger's the same for a young man," I said.

If my irritation at this second reference to young lady showed, Connor ignored it. He clasped his hands behind his back and said, "In an absolute sense, I suppose that's true. No matter how long I live, though, I think I shall never get used to that idea. The conviction that women are destined to bear different burdens and sorrows than men is second nature with me. Ah, but forgive me, Val. I know modern women don't share those convictions, and that's probably good. I just wanted you to have some understanding of our older generation before we disappear."

"I think I do."

"Do you?" He pushed his glasses up his nose. "I hope so, because it will help you appreciate all the more the ones who are taking our places. I'm referring to men like Frank, of course. I've known Frank and Ken ever since they were altar boys. Frank never had any trouble with the idea of women sharing the workplace with men or shouldering some of their burdens. You know, in my first parish, I worked hard to build a strong ladies sodality. The ladies prepared meals after funerals, they repaired vestments, they arranged flowers for the altar, and they kept the sacristy scrubbed as only a woman can. Then along came Frank, a young assistant just back from Rome, and he told me that was wrong. Can you imagine that? Oh, we had some marvelous rows in the rectory. Frank maintained the church was patronizing women, making them second-class citizens, and depriving them of their rightful participation in the liturgy. I'm sure you've heard all those words. I can't believe he learned them in Rome, but he was bright, inquisitive and at the forefront of current thought."

"Why are you telling me this, Bishop Connor?"

"One thing I've learned in my years, Val, is that you don't change ideas: you change generations. Frank is a part of the new generation of priest. He has a tremendous future in the church, a future that belongs to good Catholic girls like yourself."

"For your information, your most reverend, I'm not a girl; I'm not very Catholic; and a lot of people think I'm not very good."

"That humor, again," he said, though it was absent from his expression. "I understand from Frank that you're a woman with strong opinions, often critical of the church, but backed by reason. The church is by no means a democracy, but we do allow and encourage reasoned discussion."

"Is that why Galileo's finally getting his due?" I'd hoped to get a rise out of the bishop, but he ignored the gambit.

"Val, the church needs new men with new ideas like Frank's. And Frank needs the support of women - not sodality ladies, but intelligent young women as yourself."

"I'm waiting for the day when the church needs new women supported by intelligent young men."

"That day may be sooner than you think, but in order for that to happen Frank needs our support for his positions."

"I can't support positions I don't agree with, but I'll agree to listen."

Bishop Connor bowed slightly in my direction. "That's certainly reasonable. But I'm hoping for more from you."

"Like what?"

"You're in a very unique position. I understand you are currently employed by Brian Magruder, another fine man. I take it you have his interests at heart?"

"In a manner of speaking."

"Yes, well." He pushed his glasses up again. "I'll come to the point. The Magruder family is going through trying times. There are rumors flying everywhere about what this or that member of the family has done. I don't have to tell you that rumors needn't have any validity to taint someone irrevocably. These wild imaginings could even taint Frank with disastrous consequences. He could lose his position on the Bishop's Commission on Women. Indeed he could be deemed unworthy for the bishopric. The conservatives on the commission would have the upper hand for sure. You seem like someone who would take a case you believe in. What would it take to employ your services?"

"I couldn't take on another client."

"Then that's a no?"

"Look, Bishop Connor, I know about Ken's affair if that's what you're referring to. I don't care who Ken sleeps with and I'm not one to spread the news about it. On the other hand, I won't cover for him, either." Connor flinched and his eyes clouded with emotion - anger or embarrassment, I couldn't tell. The soft flesh under his chin quivered but he said nothing. I went on, "What I do in my job is ask questions and follow leads while trying to keep an open mind. Sometimes I dig up answers that embarrass people. If that bothers Ken, maybe he should examine his relationship with Myra and quit cheating on his wife."

"I certainly concur with that analysis."

"I'm sure you've counseled him on it. Believe me, I'm not out to get Ken, and I would not intentionally wreck Frank's career."

"Then we are in agreement after all?"

"Maybe. I -"

"Wonderful. It's refreshing to find a young person of integrity.

Frank chose that moment to enter with our drinks. "I hope you haven't gotten too thirsty. I apologize for taking so long, but I decided I'd better do something about our dinner."

"Think nothing of it, boyo. This attractive young lady and I have been having a delightful conversation. I believe we've come to a mutual understanding."

Frank suggested we eat while everything was hot. Connor agreed, saying he was famished. I wasn't at all hungry, but I didn't let that be known. In truth, my stomach was still churned up from my encounter on the road. It wasn't helped any by the bishop's attempt to put some heat on me. The only thing that helped was the Scotch, but I knew I'd have to eat something or I'd be drunk on my ass. Bishop Connor offered me his arm and I accepted. We followed Frank to the dining room.

In other circumstances, the dinner would have been great. Frank served a beef Wellington that he claimed was his best recipe. He'd worked all day on it and I believed him. The meat was deliciously tender and the dough was light and flaky. It came close to awakening my appetite. The two men quizzed me at length about the incident on the highway. The bishop, in particular, seemed dismayed that such a thing could happen, especially to a "fine young lady like yourself." If given the choice of plowing into a pile of gravel again, or hearing the words, "fine young lady" one more time, I'd take the gravel. Instead, I sought refuge in the Scotch.

Connor said, "If I understand you correctly, this person waited for you at Brian's apartment and followed you up the Pali."

I thought back to the drive on the highway. It was possible that I'd been followed. Past Nu'uanu there are few places to get on and off the highway so a tail could hang way back and not be spotted.

"Possibly. I looked for suspicious vehicles - that truck in particular - around Brian's. I also checked for a tail on the Pali."

"Yet, somehow you missed him," said Frank.

"That happens. But maybe he didn't tail me. He could have been waiting near the lookout. Someone might've told him to expect me." I caught Frank's eye and held it. I could tell that he caught the implication and I went on, "The funny thing about it is that I was having a little conflict with myself about how to tell Brian that I was coming here. I didn't tell him until about the time I dropped him off. So he couldn't have set it up and I didn't mention it to anyone else."

"I haven't told anyone but Pat," said Frank. "That includes the retreat house staff. There are no retreats here this week, so there's hardly anyone around."

Bishop Connor coughed and both of us looked at him. He had a sheepish expression on his face. "If it's loose lips you're seeking, it's mine that have been leaking."

"Who did you talk to?" I asked.

"Before you go jumping to wild conclusions, young lady, I want you to know that Kenneth Magruder is a fine man from a fine family and I do not believe he's done any of the awful things of which you've accused him. Nor this, for that matter."

"You talked to Ken."

"Yes, it was Ken."

"God help us, Pat, how could you?" demanded Frank. His face had turned a bright red. Angry purple veins stood out on his forehead.

"Now you listen here, boyo," countered the bishop.

"Nobody said this was a matter of national security. Ken called me this morning in a very agitated state over this woman's suspicions. I told him I would see her tonight and I would try to allay them."

"Instead you've added to them," said Frank.

28 RIDING IN GOOD COMPANY

Frank was adamant that Ken could not and would not try to kill me. The bishop was equally adamant, but he was also stung by Frank's accusation that he was to blame for any suspicions I might have of Ken. He seemed to me to be draining and refilling his wine glass too quickly. His face had taken on an alcoholic flush and his eyes were glazed. I had a little buzz myself, but the bishop's condition was enough to warn me to go slow.

"Bishop Connor," I said. "You asked where my beau was, did you tell Ken you expected to see Brian tonight?"

It was a complicated question for someone in Connor's condition. He puzzled over it. "Did I tell Ken I expected to see Brian tonight? I probably did."

"You're sure you did?"

"Yes, I'm sure I did." He gulped some wine. "But I don't see –"

"I do," said Frank. "Whatever Val's suspicions about Ken, they don't extend to an attempt on Brian's life. The bond of brotherhood is too strong." To me, he said, "Isn't that what you're getting at?"

"I'm not ready to give up on Ken, yet. The bond of brotherhood didn't keep Cain from doing Abel." I pushed away from

188

the table. "Look, this has been such a crazy evening, I need to get back to Brian. He's probably worried sick about me. To tell the truth, I'm worried about him."

"With good reason," said Frank. "I'd better not keep you."

I offered an apology for leaving early, but he dismissed it graciously. "When duty calls you have to respond. I'm afraid duty calls for me, too. I'll be leaving for DC in the morning. Perhaps we can have dinner again when I get back. Only under better circumstances."

As Connor was in no shape to drive and I had no vehicle, Frank said he'd take both of us back. "You'll be safe with Pat in the car," said Frank. "Nobody would dare try to run the bishop off the road. Sorry, bad joke."

"God takes care of His own," said Bishop Connor.

That didn't give me a lot of comfort. As I retrieved my still-sodden blouse from the bathroom, I recalled one of my more-cynical professors back in college gloating over nineteenth century research showing that the ships of missionaries sank just as often as the ships of slavers. He took it to mean that there was no Divine Providence; I took it to mean there was no way to know when you were in good company.

When I returned, Connor was already in the back seat of Frank's Buick. I climbed in the front seat and looked back at him. His eyes were closed and his glasses were pushed up on top of his head, but he wasn't sleeping.

"A little tired, young lady," he said. "A little tired. What I'd give for your energy."

I hoped for a good view of the runaway truck ramp on the way back, but we were on the wrong side of the highway and went by it too quickly. Frank and I made light conversation up the Pali and down the other side. From the backseat came the measured sounds of the bishop's breathing. As Frank exited the highway at Nu'uanu Ave, I said, "I saw Art Spinoza yesterday. He seemed to be carrying a grudge about Friday. Do you think he could carry it all the way to running me off the road?"

Frank thought it over. "I don't know him well enough to answer that."

"I had the impression you knew each other pretty well."

"No. We were attached to the same unit in Nam for about three months. You develop a bond under those conditions, but when the conditions change, the bond becomes frozen in time. He was brutish then, but you can't judge a man on what he does in combat. We lost contact until a couple of years ago when he did some work at my parents' farm. Ken's the one to talk to about Art. He knows him better. Did it sound like Art on the phone?"

"No. Nor the threats."

"Where did you see Art?"

"At the Don Bosco Foundation. I was curious about Ken's involvement so I paid them a visit." Frank didn't respond. His face, in the passing illumination from street lamps, seemed set on the task of driving, although the traffic was light and I was sure he'd driven it many times before. I continued, "Art Spinoza, it turns out, takes on Work Straight people. I confirmed for myself that the punk I put in the hospital is in the program."

"Really?" asked Frank. "What about the others?"

"I don't know."

"I wouldn't be surprised. These men are violent when they come into the program and violent when they leave. The only difference we make in their lives is giving them something to believe in." He glanced at me. "Violence and belief," he said, "have resulted in a lot of suffering. A lot of wars. I don't really believe women could change the equation much, do you?"

"No." But they won't change the subject, either. "These men with their strong beliefs could easily be swayed by a pillar of the community with similarly strong beliefs, couldn't they?"

"Ah," laughed Frank, "I knew it was coming. Ken the demagogue. It's perfectly clear - Ken hates abortion, has connections to the Don Bosco foundation, and he knows Art Spinoza. Art is angry at Val Lyon and he hires Work Straight men, one of whom threw rocks at an advocate of abortion. Ergo, Ken threw rocks at the abortionist. Or did Ken run Val Lyon off the road?"

Frank's mockery pissed me off and I felt myself getting hot. But before I could say anything, Connor said, "I thought we had an understanding about Ken Magruder, young lady."

I turned around to face him. "Our understanding is that Ken can screw anyone and anything he wants as long as it isn't me and I won't tell on him. But we don't have an understanding on murder."

We had reached Brian's condominium. Frank pulled up to the front and stopped. He said, "Honestly, Val, Ken wouldn't do anything like that any more than I would, but I doubt you'll be swayed by what I say. I'd be disappointed if you were."

I got out of the car and leaned into the open window. "I won't disappoint you, Frank. Count on it. Good night, bishop."

Frank said, "I can see why Brian's taken by you. I hope for his sake, and yours, that your spunk doesn't get you into something over your head. Ciao!"

I watched him drive away with the bishop. Spunk, hell. Spunk is for puppies. As for the connection between Ken, Spinoza, and Work Straight, Frank could mock it all he wanted, but it made sense to me.

I punched the numbers for Brian's apartment and he buzzed me in. I stabbed at the elevator button, but, too impatient to wait for it, ducked around the corner to the stairs. Took them two at a time. Seven floors. Brian was standing in his doorway. His face had accumulated a century of worry. I hustled him inside before allowing him to kiss me.

"So go ahead, say it," he said.

"Say what?"

"Say, 'I told you so.'"

"All right. I told you so."

"Does that make you feel better?"

"No. Nothing will make me feel better until we have this guy put away. Brian, who has your cellular phone number?"

"Ken. Frank. Molly. Mom and Dad. Agnes, my secretary. Most of the P.D.'s office. I'm also listed with an attorney's referral service."

"Except for the referral service, these are people you know and trust?"

"Implicitly."

"Well, one of them betrayed your trust. One of them tried to kill you tonight or knows who did."

Brian chewed on the ends of his mustache before speaking. "So now what?" he asked.

Now what, indeed? I needed to protect Brian and find Nathan at the same time. Time to bring in some muscle. I said, "I'm going to put a guard on you round the clock."

"Does that mean you're moving in with me? Hey, pinch me, I'm dreaming."

"Keep dreaming. I'm getting someone else to watch you."

He threw up his hands in protest. "Do I have any say in this?"

"None. You can make the coffee."

The muscle I had in mind was Moon Ito, another one of the guys who frequent the basketball court at Paki Playground. Moon is compact and powerful, like an Asian pony. He doesn't talk much and never calls a foul, but if you foul him you can expect it coming back right at you. I've come away from matches with Moon bruised in more places than I care to think about. When he isn't playing basketball he does freelance bodyguarding for celebrity visitors. That much he admits to.

Moon doesn't have a permanent residence that I know of. He can be reached through a noodle shop on King Street. I called and left a message: Urgent! Call Val. I hoped my name and Brian's number weren't ending up on a restroom wall. Hoped he'd call me back soon.

Brian poured coffee for both of us and gave me a tour of his apartment. The living room, dining room and master bedroom opened onto a lanai, which looked out towards the mountains. A few homes up there had an unobstructed view of the apartment and the closer ones were within range of a high-powered rifle. I closed the drapes on all of the lanai windows.

The apartment had two other bedrooms, one of which he'd made into an office and the other he'd furnished as a guest bedroom with a Nordic Track in one corner. The Nordic appeared to have very few miles on it.

"The only thing that contraption's lightened so far is my wallet," he said. "Maybe you'll inspire me to get busy."

"I like you the way you are," I said. "Alive."

We took our coffee into the living room and settled down in front of the TV. It was after eleven and Brian fell asleep in a short time. Concern for me had taken its toll. I was touched. Wired, too. I watched an endless series of infomercials and CNN reports. Around one, Brian woke up enough to lumber off to the bedroom. Sometime around three I began to nod off myself. About three-thirty the ringing of the cordless phone on the end table by my head jarred me back from the edge of sleep.

"This Moon," he said.

I explained what I wanted.

"How much?"

"Two-fifty a day. It's half of what I'm getting."

He thought it over. "Gun?"

"Yes."

"Three," he said.

I agreed to three hundred. Moon said he'd be there at seven. I hung up and drifted back into an uneasy sleep.

29 RETURN OF A FORMER ADVERSARY

I woke up to a sound like a toy car being run back and forth on my head. My head, itself, felt like someone had poured cement into it. It took me a minute to orient myself on the couch and to locate the source of the sound. It came from somewhere down the hall. My watch said a quarter to seven. I stumbled to the bathroom and splashed cold water in my face. It did little to wake me up and was totally useless at washing away the circles under my eyes.

"Here's lookin' at you, kiddo," I said to the haggard face in the mirror.

The sound came from Brian's spare bedroom. He was on the Nordic Track. The hair on his bare chest was matted with sweat and his face was flushed with exertion.

"Do you have to do that?" I asked.

He flashed me a grin. "I intend to make it tough for someone to kill me. But if they succeed anyway, I shall leave a good looking corpse."

I knew he was kidding, but was in no mood for dark humor. "Don't talk like that, Brian." My head and shoulders ached from tension and lack of sleep. My mouth felt cottony. "Your babysitter oughta be here soon."

He showed up right at seven, carrying a paper bag and three

paper plates covered with foil. He greeted me with one word, "Breakfast." He put the plates on Brian's table and pushed one in my direction. I peeled back the foil. Underneath was a high cholesterol, Hawaiian workingman's special - rice topped with a meat patty, gravy and a fried egg, three pancakes on the side. Normally, I would have attacked it with gusto, but this time my stomach churned at the sight.

"What's in the bag?" I asked.

In answer, he reached in and withdrew a Colt King Cobra, .357, with a six-inch barrel.

"Going whale hunting?"

He grinned and returned it to the bag just as Brian walked in.

"This the guy?" asked Moon.

"Yes." I introduced the two of them.

"What makes you think you can protect me?" asked Brian.

"Need the money," said Moon. "Dead men don't pay."

"Moon brought us breakfast," I said.

"Thank you, but no. That stuff's as deadly as a bullet."

"How you gonna kill a man with this?" asked Moon. "Without you make it into a ball and throw it?"

Brian excused himself to get dressed. I could tell he wasn't happy with the situation. Tough shit, I thought. It's better than dead.

I choked down the pancakes and about half of the egg. No telling what might lie ahead on the flight to Molokai, or how much of my strength I'd need. While I ate I explained to Moon what I wanted done. He didn't ask where I was going and I didn't volunteer the information. I did say I expected to be back that evening. Brian reappeared just as I was leaving.

"Trust me," I said. "And do what Moon tells you."

As I was still feeling nauseous, I had the cab driver take me to a pharmacy near my street so I could buy some Dramamine for the flight. The morning paper on the rack caught my eye. Brian's Lexus was front page news. The accompanying story said that the driver, Val Lyon of Pau Street in Waikiki, escaped without injury. I paid for the paper and the Dramamine and fled the store. The article, and my name in it, put me into a near panic. My attacker knew where

I lived, had broken in once, knew my movements.

I crossed Kalakaua against the signal to the accompaniment of angry horn blasts and covered the half-block to Pau Street in a near sprint. Pau Street is one block long. I could see the whole length of it from the corner. No pickup trucks sat at the curb. I made for my building, in the middle of the block, at a fast walk, scanning the cars at the curb for signs of movement inside.

Jock Pfeifer came around the corner of the building next to mine and blocked my way on the sidewalk. He had his rottweiler on a leash. The dog bared its teeth at me and emitted a low growl.

My heart jumped into my throat and I backed away.

"You won't get far if I release the dog, Lyon."

"Don't release him." I hated the note of pleading I heard in my voice.

"Genghis, down!" he commanded.

To my relief, the dog obeyed. It settled down at its master's feet and put its massive head on its front paws, looking at me with more curiosity than hatred.

Pfeifer said, "Lyon, I gotta talk to you."

"What do you want, Jock?" The words came out in a hoarse whisper.

"We've got a mutual problem." He moved a half step closer and I moved a half step back. The dog lifted its head and tensed its shoulders. I stood stock still.

"I read the papers. That's how I found you. Somebody run you off the road?"

"The paper didn't say that, Jock"

"No trick to figurin' it out. You ain't Miss Congeniality. You probably think it was me that ran you off for poppin' me like you did."

"Your name made the short list."

"That ain't my style, babe. I might wanta get back at you, but I'd do it man to man."

"You mean dog to woman, don't you, Jock?"

"You're a wit, Lyon, but I ain't after you now. You an' me,

we're on the same side."

"Blow it out your ass. You and me will never be on the same side."

"Listen to what I got to say before you make your mind up. Someone tried to break into my place last night. I even thought it coulda been you until I read the papers this morning. Then I thought it over an' decided it was probably the same guy did both."

"What time? Who?"

"Knew you'd be interested. Okay. Midnight, thereabouts. I don't know who, but I got suspicions. You think hard enough you'll come up with a short list, too. But Genghis knows. He got a piece of him. That's why I brought him along - to see if he recognized you. If you'd been the one, you'd find his teeth fittin' your throat tighter than a choker of pearls."

I'm not a strong believer in animal intelligence, so the fact that I wasn't yet wearing a dog-tooth necklace wasn't at all reassuring. At any moment, I figured he could go for me. At least I resisted the impulse to put my hand to my throat. I asked, "What makes you think he was the one who ran me off the road?"

"You've been thinkin' you're smart, babe, but you ain't. I can see you ain't got a clue on this. You're stumblin' around in the dark."

"So enlighten me, Jock."

"We both got somethin' the guy wants."

"What've I got?"

"You know where Nathan is."

I sucked in my lip and stared at him without saying anything.

He rolled his shoulders. "Okay, I don't expect you to tell me. You'd only lie anyway."

"What've you got?"

"What I got's just as good. Better, maybe, to the right people. But I'm willing to deal. I'll give you what I got, you give me Nathan."

"Assuming I have Nathan, why should I?"

"'Cause your boss get's somethin' just as valuable as the boy. And you get somethin' you want."

"What might that be?"

"The name of the guy that killed Sue Naito. The guy who tried to kill you."

"No deal, Jock. You said you didn't know who it was."

"Hunh uh. I said I wasn't for sure. But I got the pieces and if you're such a smart girl, you can put them together."

"No deal."

Pfeifer said, "Didn't figure you for an easy lay. Think you might be too stubborn for your own good, though. Change your mind, you know where to reach me." He tugged on the dog's leash and it sprang to its feet. I jumped back a half step. My reaction brought a smile to Pfeifer's face. He turned and headed to a late model Beamer at the curb. The dog marched smartly at his side. Pfeifer and the dog climbed inside. He started the engine and said, "Remember, Lyon, Genghis knows the guy." As he pulled away, he shouted, "Don't let yourself be outsmarted by a dog."

30 IN THIS PLACE THERE IS NO LAW

It was not long after nine. I'd have to leave no later than ten if I was to make the flight. The phone was ringing even as I let myself into my apartment. It was Pam, wanting to know if I was all right. I stuck the phone in the crook of my neck and undressed while reassuring her that I was, indeed, alive. It was fifteen minutes before I was able to break away and get into the shower. Leo called as I was getting out. My watch said twenty to ten; I cut him off shortly. It's nice to have people who care about you, but sometimes you can trip over their concern.

I dressed hurriedly in camp shorts with big pockets, a yellow tank top, and a loose cotton shirt. There wasn't time to do anything about my hair or makeup, so I put on a broad-brimmed straw hat and big sunglasses. I couldn't remember where I'd put my ticket and my panic level almost reached meltdown. It turned up at the bottom of my beach bag under yesterday's gym clothes along with a Friendly Isle Tours brochure. I put the ticket in my purse and swore on the pile of clothes under the phone to be a better housekeeper in the future.

The phone rang a third time on my way out the door. Cursing to myself, I picked it up. I don't like to leave calls unanswered because I only give my number to people who are important to me. This time I didn't recognize the voice.

"Hi," he said, "I read about your accident in the paper and I called to see if you're all right."

"Who is this?" I asked. A lot of irritation and a little fear filled my voice. It didn't sound like my attacker but you never know.

"It's Greg. You don't remember me? Your personal healer?" He sounded hurt.

"The hunk," I blurted with relief. *Merda!* Why did I say that? Relief gave way to embarrassment, which gave way to suspicion. "How did you get my number?"

"I have ways. You're not the only detective." He sounded pleased with himself. "Actually, I'm on good terms with the intake nurse at the hospital and she gave me your number."

Now I began to get angry. Wasn't that supposed to be confidential information?

"I know," he went on, "I shouldn't have done that, but I really am concerned about you. When I read about the accident I had to take the chance. I couldn't get your number any other way."

Just as quickly as it rose, my anger subsided. After all, I wasn't above breaking and entering to get information, myself. Any other time, I might have been flattered at the effort he'd made. Now, though, I was anxious to make the flight. I told him I was in a hurry.

"Okay, I guess this is a bad time. That invitation for sailing is still good. You don't have to tell me now. You can just show up. No strings."

If only life could be that simple; if only all hunks came with no strings. With my new Sauconys under my arms, I ran barefoot to Ala Wai and hailed a cab.

The cab dropped me in front of Friendly Isle Air Tours at six minutes before eleven. A twin engine Beachcraft with Friendly Isle's logo on its tail sat on the tarmac. Beside it, a man in dark trousers and a white shirt was folding the steps into the plane. I sprinted across the parking area, wearing shoes this time.

"I'm here," I panted when I reached the plane. "On time and under a hundred fifty."

"Glad you made it," he said. "You almost missed us." His tone was friendly, but his eyes betrayed his irritation. His shirt had double flap pockets with gold wings over one flap and the name, "Captain Burch," over the other. "Get aboard so we can get off before we lose our place in the line. You get the copilot's seat."

I made my way up the narrow aisle between two rows of seats. Every seat was occupied, two by men and the rest by women. The two men appeared to be around Leo's age. Some of the women looked younger, but none looked younger than fifty. I squeezed under the half-steering wheel and buckled the lap belt. Burch followed right behind. Some chatter with the tower, a run through the checklist, and soon we'd joined the line of planes taxiing out to the reef runway, a jumbo jet in front and another behind us.

Burch said, "You're not with the church group are you?" indicating the people in the cabin with a shake of his head. I told him no.

"Listen," he said, "I apologize for being short with you out there."

"I busted my ass to make it on time. What's so sacred about a minute or two on the schedule?"

"Schedules are sacred. This group's got to catch a mainland flight at eighteen thirty hours so I want to avoid all delays. If you're not with the group, what got you here?"

"Adventure," I said.

"Well I can make sure you get some."

We were airborne after a short wait. Burch switched on the intercom and launched into his sightseeing patter as we flew along the southern shore of Oahu. Past Koko Head, he turned the plane south and we headed over open water to the Island of Lanai. Burch banked the plane over vast expanses of pineapple fields, lifted up over the central ridge and dropped down low along the shoreline on the other side. We swooped above the surf line along a flat stretch of beach, past the hulks of two ships grounded in the shallows and then across the channel to Maui. A short time later we were on the ground at Kahului airport. "Thirteen seconds late. Always room for improvement." The tour included a buffet lunch - heavy on the carbos - and a ground tour of Iao Valley. The sightseeing failed to stir my interest. I was anxious to get on to Kalaupapa to prove my theory about Nathan.

Once we got back in the air, however, I dozed off. I'm not sure for how long, but I was jolted awake as the plane dropped suddenly. From the back came a chorus of gasps and cries of wonder. We were flying parallel to a line of truly magnificent sea cliffs. Although we were well above the breakers, the tops of the cliffs were still higher.

"After that little surprise," Burch said to the passengers, "it's time for our second ground tour, Kalaupapa." To me he said, "For someone who's along for the adventure, you're missing most of it."

"I'm sure there will plenty soon enough."

Ahead, the Kalaupapa peninsula jutted out from the base of the cliffs like an overturned fla n. Heavy waves pounding against large boulders marked the shoreline. Burch turned out to sea, made a wide banking turn and approached the peninsula head on. From this direction, the geography that made Kalaupapa a prison was abundantly clear: on two sides was ocean, while the third was a sheer cliff forming a green curtain backdrop.

The airstrip occupied a narrow section of the rocky point between a lighthouse and the water. Burch brought the plane down and taxied over to a small pavilion.

"Your tour guide should be along any minute," he said.

The pavilion had bathrooms, shade, and a sign welcoming us to Kalawao County. Beneath the words of welcome was a list of rules. Official visitors and guests of patient-residents are allowed limited stays with a permit. Trespassers are subject to arrest. Children under sixteen are not allowed.

Our tour guide arrived in a Ford Econoline van. He got out and introduced himself as Zeke. "I'm a patient," he said, "but my leprosy is inactive, as it is with most of our patients."

Zeke was a heavyset Polynesian, in his early sixties. The disease had left him with puffy features and disfigured hands. His first and second digits were nearly gone from both hands while his ring and little fingers were complete to the top knuckle.

"We have one hundred thirty residents on Kalaupapa. Ninety of us are patients and the rest are either staff of the treatment center or members of the Park Service. Kalaupapa is a national park. Leprosy is now controllable by sulfone drugs and is no longer contagious. All of us patients could leave at any time. We stay because this is our home. The median age of the patients is 69 years. Most of us have lived here forty years or more. When the last patient dies the Park Service will take over Kalaupapa completely. Our first destination is St. Philomena's Church built by Father Damien De Voerster."

We climbed into the van. I managed to get the seat behind Zeke. Despite his disease-ravaged hands, he had no trouble handling the controls.

"The sign said no children. Don't the residents have kids?" I asked.

"All the kids are grown. Some of us have grandchildren but they live with their parents on the other islands. Some on the mainland."

"Do you get to see them?"

"From time to time we go to Honolulu for a visit."

"It's not the same as having kids around, is it?"

"No," he admitted. "We have everything else, though."

The road to the settlement followed the shoreline for about a mile and a half through an area of low vegetation. We didn't encounter any traffic on the road, but Zeke pointed out several fishermen down on the shore. He chose not to stop at the settlement but turned, instead onto another road that cut across the peninsula.

"We're going to the historic part, first," said Zeke. He launched into a narrative about the history of the colony, beginning with the first boatload in 1866. "The Hawaiian government gave lepers no help. People who got here had to fend for themselves. You had every kind of crime and sin and immoral acts imaginable. When lepers got off the boats, the first words they heard were, '*A 'ole kanawai ma keia wahi.'* That means, 'In this place there is no law.'"

He brought the van to a stop in front of a wooden church next to a cemetery that sloped gently to the ocean. The church of St. Philomena was clearly the high point for my fellow passengers. They couldn't wait to get inside. I'd had to accompany my mother's aunts on enough Good Friday church tours that one more church, historical or not, held no interest for me. I tagged along for the sake of appearance. Thankfully, the church was small and the tour was brief. In a short time we were heading back to the settlement.

The settlement, itself, was a collection of residences, small commercial buildings, and a few other support structures clustered in an area of about six square blocks. The community had an aura of timelessness about it, created in part by the number of residents tending gardens or chatting outside the post office.

There were two more churches on the tour, but I pretended a greater interest in the external architecture of the buildings. After assuring Zeke that I'd stay close, I wandered around the outside of the first church, pondering my next move. So far, there'd been no sign of Nathan, or any juvenile. If he were here, where would he be? My best guess was that Aileen Burch had him hidden away, but there was no sign of her, either.

My father used to say that you could tell a player from a gambler by what they do when nothing's happening in the game. The player tallies his winnings; the gambler looks for an opening to influence the action. I found my opening outside the second church while the others toured the inside.

The front and side yards were well-tended - neat flower beds and carefully trimmed lawn. Behind the church was a different story. At one side of an area about ten feet square was a pole supporting a backboard and hoop. The grass under the hoop was completely gone, while around the periphery it was heavily trampled. On the backboard, in shiny red and blue letters, were the words, "Slam 'n Jam Powerglass." A new red, white and blue net hung from the hoop. I could imagine a group of local kids hanging out here, except that there were no local kids. I ran a couple of steps, jumped and touched the rim. Not regulation. Nine feet at most. What use would people whose median age was 69 have of a basketball hoop, regulation or not?

My thoughts were interrupted by Zeke.

"It's time to get back to the plane," he said.

"The church has a basketball team, Zeke?"

"Captain Burch hates to be late taking off."

"Zeke, you didn't answer my question. Who does the slammin' and jammin' here?"

He paused uncertainly. "Don't know. Some of the young men from the religious orders, maybe. Now everybody's waiting in the van. We'd better go."

By the time we reached the van, I'd decided how I could influence the action. On the way back to the airfield, I said loudly, "I hope we can have a minute to go to the bathroom before we get back in the plane." Several people echoed the sentiment.

At the airfield pavilion, most of the passengers made straight for the bathrooms. The lines were already formed when I caught up to them. Burch urged everyone to hurry. As always, the women's line was unfairly long. When the second of the male passengers emerged from the men's bathroom, I saw my chance to buy myself some time.

"Guard the door for me, Zeke," I said and went into the men's room, locking the door behind me.

The bathroom had a sink, a toilet and a wastebasket. High in the wall next to the toilet was a narrow window. To my relief, it was the kind with two panes, one of which slid open. It would be a tight squeeze. I'd have to abandon my purse and hat. Turning the wastebasket upside down, I mounted it and opened the window. It faced the beach and ocean on the opposite side of the building from the plane. The beach itself dropped steeply out of sight. To the left were rocky outcroppings and, beyond, was a cluster of beach houses. I had a few minutes until my absence would be discovered. Enough time to reach the cover of the rocks.

As soon as I tried to push my shoulders through the window, I knew it would be exceedingly tight. I pulled back and removed my loose shirt which I tossed on the sink. Then, dressed in my tank top and shorts, I tried again. My shoulders went through with little difficulty. My shorts, however, caught on something sharp sticking out from the aluminum frame. I tugged until a ripping sound told me I was free.

I dropped to the ground and ran straight for the beach. It was white sand littered with coral rubble. I rolled down the slope to the tide pool at the bottom and ran along the shore to the rocks. Aside from my back pocket, which was flapping loose, I'd made it without any trouble. Hidden by the rocks, I could see the rest of the passengers boarding the plane. Burch paced impatiently, said something to Zeke and pointed to his watch. Schedules are sacred. Zeke went into the pavilion and emerged shaking his head. He and Burch conferred and Zeke went back to the pavilion. I figured he was too much of a gentleman to break into the restroom. He came out once again shaking his head and waving his hands. Burch gestured with finality and climbed into the plane, shutting the door behind him. A few minutes later it was airborne. Soon after, Zeke got into the van and drove away.

I waited a while longer and then headed back toward the settlement, following the shoreline. The rocky shore made the going hard and avoiding fishermen made it slow. Another van - Zeke's or one like it - heading to the airfield to meet a private plane, forced me to take cover until it had returned to the settlement. After nearly an hour of walking, I reached the long stretch of white sand fronting the settlement proper. A line of trees and a few unoccupied structures afforded me enough cover to reach the area of the church unchallenged.

The church seemed to be unoccupied. Not so the basketball court. The thump of the ball against the backboard reached me before the player came into view. I hurried over. The shooter was a lone kid, wearing long shorts and a ball cap turned backwards. He was about five and half feet tall, skinny and awkward. He looked like his picture: Nathan Pfeifer.

"Hi," I said.

He turned with a startled expression on his face that quickly turned to distrust. "Who are you?"

On the way from the airport, I'd given some thought to how to introduce myself to Nathan. If he'd been coached at all, he should be suspicious of strangers, especially strangers claiming to be friends of his mother. I decided to stick close to the truth of my circumstances. "I'm a tourist. My plane left without me. I guess I'm stuck here for awhile."

That explanation seemed to dispel some of his suspicion. "Too bad," he said. He turned back to the hoop and shot a disinterested jumper.

I tried another tack. "My name's Val. What's yours?"

No response.

"Want to play some one-on-one?"

"Girls can't play basketball," he said, over his shoulder.

"Is that what your father told you?"

"You don't know my father."

Nathan head-faked an imaginary opponent and dribbled towards the basket. He went up for a lay up and I went up with him to reject the shot. Beating a kid wasn't something I was proud of, but it got his attention.

"Hey, I said I don't want to play. Why don't you leave me alone?" He retrieved the ball and clutched it tightly, his back to me.

"Look, Nathan, I came to talk to you."

"You'd better talk to us first, Miss Lyon."

The voice came from behind me. I turned to find myself facing Zeke and another man - younger and trimmer than Zeke. Zeke cradled a shotgun in the crook of his arm. The other man wore a badge over his breast pocket and a sidearm on his belt.

"I'd like you to meet Sheriff Kent," said Zeke.

Kent said, "If you don't have a permit, you're trespassing."

31 GET THEE TO A NUNNERY

Try as I might, I couldn't keep my eyes from straying to Zeke's finger on the trigger - his ring finger. Zeke noticed.

"You don't have to point straight to shoot straight," he said.

"You said there was no law here, Zeke."

"That was the old days."

"You'd better come with us," said Kent. "Nathan, bring your ball and come along, too."

"No cuffs, Sheriff?" I asked.

"Don't think you'll try to get away, Miss Lyon. No place for you to go. The two ways out are the way you got in and the mule trail. If you take the trail, we get somebody to wait for you up topside."

"We're not going far," said Zeke. "Just a short walk. Please don't make it inconvenient. You can't hide long on the peninsula."

"Look, I'm working for Jean Pfeifer's attorney. My job is to find and protect the boy."

"We have a lot to talk about." said Kent.

"Are you my mother's friend?" asked Nathan.

"You could say that."

"Figures," he said.

"What does that mean, Nathan?"

"Nothing." He was silent the rest of the way.

Our route took us through the center of the settlement. Zeke, good tour guide that he was, pointed out the sights as we went.

"Bay View House, where the patients stay who can't care for themselves. The gas station, open two hours a week. This is a bar owned by patients. It's open a lot more than two hours. Grocery store, meat market. This is the house of our sister Aileen."

We were in front of a frame bungalow with a small, neat yard - the kind of residence I'd begun to think of as typical of the Kalaupapa settlement. The yard was bordered with beds of white anthuriums.

"Aileen Burch?"

"Uh huh," said Kent. "That's who you come to see, yeah?"

"Is this where you've been staying, Nathan?"

"Yeah. It's boring."

We crossed a low concrete stoop and through a screen door into a comfortably furnished living room. Nathan made immediately for the TV in a corner while Kent made himself at home in an antimacassar covered armchair and Zeke excused himself from the room. Since no one had ordered me to sit, I moved about the room studying the pictures and momentos on the wall. There were photos of Kalaupapa and patients, family portraits including a recent one of Phil Burch, many photos of a tall woman with different models of airplanes, and a group of photos of Harriets, including Sue, of course, and a very young Pam sporting an Angela Davis afro. I stopped to examine a picture of Sue and the tall woman in nurse's white, taken in the days when even uniforms showed a lot of leg.

"Didn't we look like Mutt and Jeff?" asked a voice behind me.

I turned for my first close-up look at Aileen Burch. Gray hair and eyes, Katherine Hepburn cheekbones. Older than in the photos, but definitely the woman at the cemetery.

"Val Lyon, I presume. Somehow, I feel we've already met. That was you at the cemetery, wasn't it? Carol Fernandez told me a little about you. When Zeke informed me that a passenger had been left behind, I knew it would be you even before he told me your name."

"So where's the band and the welcoming party?"

"You may be in my house, Ms. Lyon, but that doesn't mean you're welcome here. Let's talk in the kitchen."

The three of us, Aileen, Kent and myself, went into the kitchen where Zeke was already waiting. We took seats at a round table. I found myself between Zeke and Kent facing Aileen.

Zeke said, "That was a pretty good trick having me guard the door while you went out the window. One of the Park Service people opened the lock and found your things. He'll bring 'em by."

"Now that we're all here," said Aileen, "you've been caught trespassing and snooping around. Maybe you'd like to explain yourself."

"I think you know why I'm here, Aileen. I'd like to know why Nathan's here."

"For protection," she snapped. "We rescued him from an abusive, dangerous situation. He's safe here, or he was until you showed up."

"Did you think you could hide him here indefinitely?"

"We don't intend it to be indefinite. Jean will be vindicated in time. Nor is hiding him here that great a problem. Since visitors must be escorted, all we have to do is keep him away from the scheduled tours. As for official visitors, they seldom stay over."

"But what about the other residents of Kalaupapa? Surely someone would see him."

"They all know he's here," said Zeke.

"Everybody's in on it?"

"Most everybody. Some of the folks in Bay View don't know about it. We had a meeting where Aileen explained Nathan's situation. Aileen has given a lot to this community over the years. We agreed this was our chance to give something back. Lepers have a lot of sympathy for people who've been treated badly by society because they've suffered it all. None of us wanted to come here. Nobody wanted to leave their home and families, but nobody stepped forward on our behalf. Now we have a chance to do for somebody what nobody would do for us."

"So what about Nathan? Did he want to come here?"

"He didn't have a safe home where he came from. Here he does among people who know something about what he's going through."

"Are you really thinking about him? Most of you are half a century older than he is. Many of you are disfigured. Don't you think that can be terribly frightening for him?"

Aileen's jaw hardened. "There is no disfigurement here. There's nothing but beauty. The disfigurement is in the souls of the outside world. It's the people who find the face of a leper horrifying, or comical, who are disfigured. What right have you to judge us on your ideas of beauty?"

"I don't see anything beautiful about kidnapping children."

"Perhaps if you understood what kind of life we've given him, you wouldn't be so judgmental. You see, Ms. Lyon, Nathan goes to school up topside during the day. It's a private school run by the same order of nuns who supply nurses for our clinic, so we don't have to face a lot of questions about where he's from. Phil picks him up in the mornings and takes him along on the newspaper run to Hilo and then drops him off at the school. I usually get him in the afternoons and bring him back."

"That plane I saw landing earlier?"

"That's the one. We try to give him the same outlets he'd have at home. Some of the residents erected that basketball goal for him. I suppose that was our undoing, wasn't it Zeke?"

"I forgot it was there or I wouldn't have let her wander around outside," said Zeke. "Some afternoons I take him fishing. He's a great fisherman."

Aileen continued. "Saturdays and Sundays we go topside, or one of the other islands where he can swim and surf with kids his own age."

"Not the way a kid should grow up," said Kent, "but it's far better than the situation he left."

"Do you mind if I ask him that, myself?"

"Then what?"

My plan hadn't gotten that far. All that Brian had specified was to find him and make sure he was safe. I shrugged. "If he agrees it's better than it was, I guess I'll go back alone and report that he's safe."

"We have a problem with that," said Kent. "You see, we can't let you leave."

"You can't keep me here."

"We have to. The kid's not supposed to be here. All of us are breaking the law."

"Besides," said Aileen, "we can't be sure you're on Jean's side just because you say you are."

"I'm working for her attorney. Isn't that enough?"

Aileen shook her head. "Ms. Lyon, nobody can know where Nathan is, least of all the attorney. As an officer of the court, he would be required to divulge the location, if asked." She turned away but not before her eyes filled with tears. "Sue," she said fiercely, "died protecting the secret. We can't do any less."

Aileen excused herself and went outside wiping her eyes. Zeke and Kent conferred in low tones about where they would put me.

"I do not intend to stay here," I said.

"No choice tonight," said Kent. "No lights at the landing field. No planes until morning. No lights on the mule trail either. You'd kill yourself on it."

"I suppose you've got some cozy little jail cell for me?"

"The convent is the best we can offer. The beds are comfortable and the doors have locks."

"What about the windows?"

"If you go out a window, we'll find you in the morning."

Zeke went to make the arrangements. He returned a short time later, bringing with him the things I'd left behind at the airport. Kent went through my purse and removed my pocketknife after offering an apology. The two of them then escorted me to a moderate-sized house near the hospital.

The sisters seemed unconcerned about my status as a prisoner. They showed me to the room of one of their members who was off the island and would not be returning for a few days. I'd always been curious about what went on in a convent, and somewhat apprehensive as well. As a girl, being sent to a convent was the solution to my misbehavior favored by my mother's aunt Julia. So I was a little disappointed by the ordinariness of the sisters' lives. After dinner, during which I had to satisfy their curiosity about a detective's work, two of the sisters returned to the hospital to look after patients and one went to her room to work on the community's finances. She unplugged the phone and took it with her. I wasn't to be allowed any calls - orders from Kent. The remaining sister pulled me into clean-up duty and, afterwards, a game of Scrabble. She beat me handily. By 10:30 the house was dark and everyone was in bed, myself included. My room was unlocked but the outside doors required a key, inside and out. All of the sisters had keys, but overpowering a nun to get one was not my style.

In the morning, all of the sisters were awake and going about their business when I woke up. Using a borrowed sewing kit, I repaired the pocket of my shorts before joining the group for breakfast.

"So," I said when I'd poured myself some coffee, "what's the prison routine?"

My Scrabble opponent giggled at the joke, but the sister who did the finances said sourly, "Zeke will tell you."

Zeke was outside, sitting in a lawn chair with his shotgun across his lap. He stood up when he saw me.

"We thought it best that the boy not go to school today," he said. "Since you came for him, you can look after him."

"And you'll look after me?"

"I don't like doing this, Miss Lyon. None of us do."

"You can tell me what you don't like all you want, but I'm still a prisoner."

"Let's go to Aileen's."

"You really don't need that gun, Zeke. I'm not all that dangerous."

"In this community, youth is dangerous," he said. "I want you to think twice about making trouble. This is loaded with birdshot. It'll hurt a lot. We've got one scheduled tour, today. While it's here, we have to lock you up. Sheriff's cleaning out a place."

When we got to Aileen's I began to wish for a lock up. Nathan was in a sullen teenage mood and the prospect of spending the day with me didn't please him. He sat with his arms folded and his chin on his chest staring at the television in Aileen's living room. Aileen was already at the hospital. Zeke went into the kitchen for coffee.

"Hi," I said. "How about some basketball?"

"No," he said.

"A hike, then?"

"Go away. Leave me alone."

I switched off the TV. "Nathan, I have to talk to you. When I see your mother, I want to be able to tell her how you are."

He curled up into a ball and turned his face into the back of the couch. "I don't want to talk to a damn lesbian."

I took his shoulders and turned him to face me. "What did you say?"

"I said I don't want to talk to a lesbian. Dad said all of mom's friends are lesbians. Leave me alone." His brown eyes burned with hurt and betrayal.

"Nathan, did your mother tell you that she's a lesbian?"

"No. Dad told me. And all her friends are. And you are." He hurled the last sentence at me and curled back into his ball on the couch.

I sat down beside him and put my hand on his shoulder. He shrank from my touch. "Nathan, does it bother you that your mother could be a lesbian?" He didn't answer. "Nathan."

This time I heard a reply, muffled by the fabric of the couch and punctuated by quiet sobs. "Why can't she be a normal mother? Why does she have to be queer?"

"Nathan, I can't answer that. But whatever she might be otherwise, she's still your mother and she still loves you."

"Go away," he said. He pressed a sofa pillow over his face.

"Okay," I said. I got up and went to the kitchen. At the door, I paused to look back at him. He still had the pillow over his face.

"That kid has a lot of anger," I said. "Do you think his father put it there?"

"Everybody contributed," said Zeke. "Even you."

"Me? How?"

"You don't even know the boy, but the first thing you do is beat him at his sport."

"I wasn't proud of it."

"What about his pride? Listen, I know what's going on in the world. You modern young women want to wear pants like men. You don't care what that does to a man's pride."

"The men I know take their pride from what they can do, not what's in their pants."

Zeke waved off my objection. "Women don't think for themselves any more. They're all brainwashed by Gloria Steinem. Do you know Nathan's father?"

"We've met."

"Everything the boy does, it's 'Dad says this, dad says that.' What do you think dad says about being beaten by a woman?"

"Let me guess. Men don't let that happen?"

Zeke nodded. "Now you understand. You kicked the chair right out from under him."

32 JOSE CUERVO WAS A FRIEND OF MINE

Kent showed up about noon and announced that lunch would be served in the bar. The four of us - Kent, Zeke, Nathan, and myself - walked the short distance.

"Had to take down the basketball contraption," Kent said. "Can't risk someone else seeing it and making the connection like you did. Zeke's got another tour this afternoon. You can wait it out here."

On the inside, the bar resembled a thousand other small town roadhouses - sturdy, Formica-topped tables and padded chairs, a short counter, and a cooler with a noisy, erratic motor. For entertainment, there was television and shuffle-bowling. Kent moved around the room unshuttering the windows. Wrought iron grills covered each one on the inside.

"Most everybody in Kalaupapa keeps their windows and doors open," he explained. "The only thing anybody might want to steal is the beer and liquor in here. That's why the bars. Cooler and cabinets are locked, too. This is the most secure place in the settlement."

After a lunch of hot dogs and chips from the community dining hall, Kent and Zeke took their leave of us.

"I'll be back to check on you from time to time, Miss Lyon," said Kent. "Son, you be good." He locked the door behind him.

"Well, this is cozy," I said. "Looks like we're going to be together for awhile, Nathan. We may as well try to be friends."

"Who cares?"

"Why are you mad at me? Is it because I blocked that one shot yesterday?"

Nathan shrugged. "I wasn't ready," he said.

Those were Jock's words. "That's no excuse," I said. "Did it make you mad? Ashamed?"

He looked up at me, his eyes large and brown and brimming with tears.

"Tell me the truth, Nathan. Brown eyes don't lie."

Large glistening tears formed on each of his lower eyelashes, hung on the edge and then slid down over his freckled cheeks.

"My dad…dad says sometimes…sometimes I play so bad a girl could beat me. He says I play like a…" Nathan's voice dropped to a whisper.

"He says you play like a what?"

"You don't want to know."

"Yes, I do. It's important. What word does your father use?"

"Pussy, all right? He calls me a pussy when I make bad plays. He says if I play like that I'm going to end up q…q…queer." The admission broke down what remained of his restraint and the tears streamed down his face.

I'm never good when people cry. Especially boys. I'd rather face a car wreck than an adolescent in tears. I watched helplessly as the sobs shook his frame. When they subsided, I said, "Nathan, I'm sorry. I didn't mean to shame you. Look, I've been playing basketball since before you were born. I've played against lots of guys and beaten many of them and they're all still men."

"My dad says there are three kinds of people in the world - winners, losers and queers - and you can't tell the difference between the last two." He wiped his face on his T-shirt collar and turned his back to me.

Jesus! What kind of man would bring his son's self esteem so low? What kind of man calls his kid names when the kid doesn't play up to the old man's inflated level of expectation?

"Listen to me, Nathan. It doesn't matter who beats you or who you beat." I bit off my little pep talk before I got to the part about playing your best. In the face of his despair, it was all crap. So, Ms. In-your-face Val Lyon, who's not afraid to drive the lane against the likes of Moon or Kalani, why does this kid's misery make you feel so inadequate? Where the hell is that maternal instinct when you need it?

Someone had neglected to lock up a case of orange pop. I opened two bottles and gave one to Nathan. He looked at it suspiciously and then at me with the same suspicion before taking a drink of it.

"Sit down, Nathan," I said gently. He sat down at a table and I took the seat across from him. "Does your father ever hurt you?"

"He's a man. He wants me to be a man, too."

"That's not what I asked. Does he hurt you?"

"He wants me to be strong. He says if it won't kill me, it'll make me tougher."

"How does he hurt you, Nathan?"

The question touched something inside him, because he responded fiercely, eyes shining like wet stones.

"I didn't say he hurt me. He makes me do things until it hurts. If I could do it better, it wouldn't hurt."

"Like what?"

"Like swimming. I have to swim laps and if he thinks I'm getting tired I have to swim more. One time I got a charley horse and he made me swim it out. Five laps."

"Don't you like swimming?"

"It's okay."

"But?"

"But I wish he'd let me do what I want to do."

Little by little Nathan's resistance wore down. Music was Nathan's real love, but Jock ridiculed his tastes in music and declared that playing it was sissy stuff. For his part, Nathan had no great interest in swimming or hunting, but went along with his father's ambitions for him. It didn't help that Jean encouraged him in music, but discouraged his other pursuits.

I said, "Tell me about your mother. Do you love her?"

"I hate her. She shouldn't have left dad. Besides, she doesn't care about me."

"She cares enough to want to see you safe. She's willing to go to jail to make sure you're safe."

The fire flashed in his eyes again. He said, "All she cares about are her stupid causes."

His statement caused a dull ache in the pit of my stomach. I'd said something similar to my mother once. I'd never taken it back when I had the chance to take it back. Now there were no more chances and the statement seemed to accumulate more and more regrets with each year since her death.

"Adults don't always do what's right, Nathan. We don't always act out of love, either. But sometimes we can do both and it still hurts. I don't know your mother that well, but I'm sure she loves you. Try to understand that."

I didn't know if I'd reached him or not. The mind of an adolescent male has always been a complete mystery to me. I give junior high teachers a lot of credit for what they do.

Nathan sipped his pop in silence for awhile. I turned on the shuffle-bowling machine and started a game. I could feel his eyes on me. At last he joined me and said, "Are you going to escape from here?"

"Well, I'm going to try to find a way to leave."

"Will you take me with you?"

"Nathan, I'd like to, but I don't think I can do that."

"Yeah, I didn't think so." He went back to his chair to sulk. "You're gonna leave me. Just like everybody else."

There wasn't much I could say to Nathan, nor anything I could do to get him out of his sulk. My luck was better with the shuffle-bowling machine. Maybe there's a pro circuit I could get into if detecting doesn't work out.

Zeke returned about 3:30 to let us out. I convinced him that I needed to run. He clucked his displeasure at the idea, but went with me to the convent so I could change. After rummaging through my host's drawers I found a violet sweatsuit that I could get into. It would be more clothes than I was accustomed to running in, but then the residents of Kalaupapa were not accustomed to having a woman half their age running around in skivvies. Youth is dangerous in this place. I convinced Nathan to run with me while Zeke followed behind in the van. Nathan dropped out after fifteen minutes and joined Zeke. I kept going. It was not a satisfactory run. My irritation at being kept prisoner, my worry about Brian, and the gnawing sense that there was more than fear of parental abuse behind Jean's hiding of Nathan combined to choke my own energies. I felt like I was driving a speedway with a four-wheel drive - lots of rpm's but little headway. At times my pace would fall to a walk and then I'd kick it up to a short sprint. After nearly an hour I called it quits, changed and showered at the convent and the three of us went back to Aileen's.

Aileen was conferring with some of the other residents when we arrived. They acknowledged Nathan with friendly hellos and me with quiet nods, but our arrival seemed to put an end to the meeting because shortly after everyone but Aileen and Zeke left. Aileen appeared worn. Deep lines creased her forehead.

"Well, you haven't ruined our coalition but you have managed to shake it some," she said.

"How so?"

"Some of our residents…" She nodded after her departing guests. ". . . are concerned that your being here means our secret has gotten out. What concerns them the most is that if the authorities decide that all of the residents conspired to break the law, they may choose to close the settlement and move everybody to Honolulu. This is our home and we'd be devastated to leave it."

"But you're willing to take that chance with everyone's livelihood to preserve your own cause. From a distance I suppose that sort of fanaticism is admirable, Aileen, but up close it's ugly."

Aileen's eyes flashed angrily, "You've got no business judging us. You're a trespasser. We are saving this child."

"Saving him from what? A father who expects a lot from him? According to Nathan, Jock hasn't hurt him. Nothing he says indicates that he's in physical danger."

"Jean believes he's in danger and Sue believed Jean. That's good enough for me."

"It's against the law. She'll stay in jail if she can't show there's a real danger to the boy."

"Then that's where she'll stay. Nathan will stay here and so will you."

"The hell I will." I turned and left the house. Aileen shouted to Zeke to stay with me and soon I heard him puffing behind me. I was moving at a fast walk, not trying to escape, but just needing to be moving.

"Where do you think you're going?" said Zeke.

"I don't care." I slowed my pace to allow him to catch up. "I'm just angry. Where can we eat that I won't have to talk to nuns?"

"The hospital has a dining hall. The food's good."

"Can we get a drink there?"

"No, but we can go to the bar after."

For prison fare, the food at the hospital was excellent. By any other standard it was merely good. Many of the residents suffered a disability of some kind, so most people took their meals in the dining hall. I was an object of friendly curiosity. It gave me an opportunity to quiz the residents about their lives on Kalaupapa. Aileen, I soon learned, was held in deepest affection by nearly everyone. For many years her plane service had been their lifeline to the rest of the world. Besides taking them and bringing them back, she'd ferried in needed supplies in the winter months when the seas around the peninsula were too rough for barge landings. As a result, they'd been more than willing to go along with her plans to hide Nathan. Kalaupapa was a sanctuary. If any of them were worried that I would rat on them to the authorities, they didn't show it.

As promised, we went to the bar after dinner. A small group

of people from the dining hall, the more able of them, joined us. They were mostly unmarried men. The rate of marriage on Kalaupapa, I learned, was considerably lower than in the general population. Zeke had grown accustomed to my presence and left his shotgun in the van. Not that it mattered - I'd have had difficulty breaking away from the crowd in the bar. Zeke bought my first drink. The bar's brands of Scotch were unremarkable, but their brand of tequila was Jose Cuervo. I had a shot of Jose and a beer. There was no shortage of men willing to pay for the second drink. Or the third. Or the fourth. The last call came around two in the morning. Somehow I made it back to the convent, clinging to Zeke for support after having to shake him awake. Sister Mary Sourpuss opened the door with the kind of look people reserve for a dog who's been rolling in the garbage.

I woke up with a throbbing headache. God, I thought, who hit me this time? Gingerly, I felt the back of my head. The skin was intact. No blood or bumps. It was when I tried to roll over that I was hit with a wave of nausea and the memory of the night before. Jose Cuervo, you were a friend of mine. My shaky legs propelled me to the bathroom just in time. I had no trouble remembering the night. Someone had put a tape in the bar's boombox. Someone else had pushed the tables to the side. One gent asked for a dance and then another. Drinking and dancing and slapping a few hands. Did I really dance on the tables? Getting back to the convent was a vague memory. Getting out of my clothes and into a nightgown was even vaguer.

"Jose can you see, how you fu-ucked up me," I said as I spread some sister's toothpaste on my finger. I gave my teeth a cursory brushing and swilled another nun's mouthwash around my mouth. Feeling pleased with myself, I said more loudly, "Jose can you see, how you fu-ucked up me."

A knock on the door. I opened it to find Sister Sourpuss with my clothes, cleaned and neatly folded.

"If that's poetry, your meter's lousy," she said, "Whatever you had last night must have killed it. I have coffee and aspirin in the kitchen. You look like you need it."

"I don't think I'm cut out for convent life, Sister. I'd better turn in my veil, but I forgot where I left it."

"According to the story making the rounds of the settlement, you peeled it like Salome, last night."

I groaned.

"Are you sure you wouldn't prefer some cloister time until your head clears…Salome?"

"I'll try the aspirin, first."

Back in my room, I noticed with a shock that it was a few minutes past noon. I dressed as quickly as my head would allow and went to the kitchen for the coffee and aspirin. Two aspirin, two cups of coffee, and a glass of orange juice had me feeling better. At least my head was back to its normal weight. This wasn't captivity, it was cruel and unusual punishment. Hangover or not, I had to break out.

Sheriff Kent's arrival interrupted my plans.

"Plane coming in," he said. "Zeke's gone to meet it. Gotta get you and the boy locked up."

Once again, I was back in the bar with Nathan. This time, it was me who was in the uncommunicative mood. My thoughts wouldn't stay focused on the problem of getting away. The only solution I could come up with was a desperate one. I'd disable Kent, get his gun and force him to take me to a phone from which to call Leo.

The sound of voices outside alerted me. One was Kent's. I couldn't make out the other one. They had returned sooner than I expected. I searched around for a weapon. The only object heavy enough to use was a puck from the shuffle-bowling game. I grabbed it and flattened myself against the wall alongside the door. I motioned to Nathan to get behind the bar. The lock clicked, the door opened and Kent entered. I had my arm raised to bring the heavy puck down on Kent.

"Don't do it, cookie." said Leo.

I checked my swing in its downward arc. Kent spun out of the way.

"Where's the boy?" asked Kent.

"Leo, what're you doing here?" I demanded.

"Came for you," said Leo.

Aileen was with them. "Where is Nathan?" she asked. Nathan emerged from behind the bar. She said quietly, "I have some bad news about your father."

I looked to Leo for confirmation.

"Jock Pfeifer," he whispered. "Somebody croaked him in his pool. Put a clip of bullets in him."

33 MURDER SCENE

Kent held out his hand and I dropped the puck in it. He let it swing casually at his side. "Guess your business here is over," he said to me in a low voice. "No reason to hide the kid if Pfeifer's dead."

Aileen had taken Nathan over to a corner of the bar and was talking quietly to him. He showed no emotion. Jock's death removed a great weight from him. No more name-calling, no more belittling remarks when he couldn't meet his dad's demanding standards. Now he had only his mother, whom he professed to hate.

"Brian wants the kid home so he can get the mother released," said Leo. "Got a judge's order for his return."

"How is Brian?"

Leo chuckled. "Doing okay, if he hasn't killed his babysitter."

"How'd you find me, Leo?"

"Got into your apartment." He caught the look I gave him and said, "Lockpicks, kiddo. Get you into more places than American Express. Never leave home without 'em. Found the travel brochure in your beach bag. Followed my nose to it." He chuckled again and laid a finger against his hawk's beak. "Not all the senses go at once."

"You looked through my gym clothes?"

"You're a creature of habit. The gym stuff's important to you. Tracked down the agent and the fly boy. That's all there was to it."

"I could kiss you, Leo," I said gratefully.

"That's why I shaved."

Aileen joined us. "Nathan would like to talk to you," she said.

I went over to where he was standing near the shuffle-bowling machine. "Nathan, I'm sorry about your father."

I put my arms around him and pulled him close. He responded stiffly, at first, trying to be tough, but after a brief moment he relaxed and hugged me back.

"I'm taking you back with me, after all," I said.

"I didn't mean what I said about mom. You won't tell her will you?"

"Of course not."

Leo had gotten Phil Burch to cancel a tour and fly him in. Phil was waiting at the airport to take us back. While Nathan packed, Kent told me how much they regretted forcing me to stay for two days. All Aileen said was, "Now you're responsible for his safety. I hope you know what you're doing." Zeke drove us to the airport. He invited me to return anytime I wanted to do more drinking and dancing. I think I blushed; I know my head throbbed.

Nathan rode in the copilot's seat while I sat in the cabin across the aisle from Leo, the barf bag open on my lap. Fortunately for my condition, Burch chose a direct route with none of the stomach-churning maneuvers of the first flight.

"You don't look too good," said Leo.

"I can't look worse than I feel. Jock was ready to deal something. That's why he was killed."

"Who do you think? The guy that ran you off the road?"

"Yes. The killer's still out there and we're bringing the boy home."

"It could be you next, kiddo. Or Brian."

I got through the flight without using the barf bag. We went straight to Brian's. He was relieved to see us. I suspected it was due as much to my safe return as to his freedom from Moon.

"Do you know what that guy does all day? He watches soap operas. And that's not all. The whole time he's watching he's doing pushups. Up, down, up, down. The only time he stops is to change channels. Where the hell'd you find the guy?"

"I take it you guys got along," I said.

"Like brothers," said Moon. "Us two guys, we're in love with Erica Kane."

"Shit," said Brian.

"Well you guys can bond a little more while I go talk to the police about Jock."

"No way," said Brian. "I've got a ton of work at the office and I've had it to here with this musclehead. What's the deal any more? You're back, the kid's back -"

"And there's still some creep who threatened your life running loose."

Leo said, "I'll stick with Brian. You talk to the police."

"Hot damn!" said Brian.

That still left Nathan. After Leo and Brian left, I called Kalani Daggett, explained the situation and told him we were on our way to Paki Park. He agreed to meet us. My Nissan, which had been delivered to Brian in my absence, was in the parking lot. Nathan made a face when he saw it.

"This old relic?" he asked.

"It's mine and it's paid for," I said. "Get in and shut up."

The new starter turned over without aggravation. One less thing to worry about.

I had no worries about putting Nathan's security in the hands of Moon and Kalani. A head of state wouldn't have been better protected. My concern was that Nathan would prove difficult for the two of them to manage. On that account, I needn't have worried. The prospect of playing with a former pro thrilled Nathan. He greeted Kalani with a touch of awe in his voice. I figured I went up a few notches in his estimation. Probably enough to overcome the deficit I'd suffered from driving an old beater.

My first destination, after dropping them off, was Jock Pfeifer's house in Kahala. I wanted to see the murder scene for myself although I didn't have much expectation of learning much from it. The police would have gone over it in detail and removed every bit of evidence by now.

In fact, they were still working on it. Jock's house was taped off with police tape and two plain cars were parked at the curb. I cruised past and parked on the street in front of Jock's neighbor's. As I got out and started back to the house, a Channel 5 news truck arrived on the scene. This late in the afternoon reporters were scrambling to update the murder story for the evening news.

I'd reached the police tape and was contemplating ducking under it when I heard my name being called.

"Ms. Lyon. It is Ms. Lyon, isn't it?"

The speaker was Lehua Lopes, the same Channel 5 reporter who'd covered the rally a week earlier. She got out of the truck and hurried over to me, leafing through a notebook as she walked.

"Val, right? Do you think Jean killed her ex-husband?"

I turned to face her. "Yeah," I said, "Elvis sprung her from jail and Buddy Holly drove the getaway car. But you're too late with the story because they're telling it on Geraldo."

Lopes' small mouth tightened into a knot in response to my sarcasm. "Are you still a part of her defense team?" she asked. "Or her offensive line?"

"What does that mean?"

"Did you pull the trigger for her?"

"Of course not."

"What about Nathan? Where is he?"

"No comment."

I turned and came face to face with Wally Nakashita.

"What about you, detective?" asked Lopes. "Do you have any new developments to report?"

"Ms. Lyon, come with me please," he said.

"If you insist," I said.

"I insist," he hissed in my ear.

"Casey!" Lopes shouted. "Get a shot of the detective and get the audio rolling. I want to go with this. Detective Nakashita, is Ms. Lyon a suspect? Are you questioning her about the murder?"

"We have nothing new to report," said Nakashita. He propelled me away from the reporter, his hand on my elbow.

Behind us we heard Lopes say, "Police are continuing to question witnesses in the Jock Pfeifer murder case. One of those witnesses is Val Lyon, a private detective. Ms. Lyon is known to be closely involved with Pfeifer's estranged wife and was involved in an altercation at last week's rally for Jean Pfeifer."

We reached the farthest unmarked car and Nakashita said, "This is far enough, Ms. Lyon." He spoke into his lapel mike and asked detective Hannigan to join us.

Nakashita had evidently put in a long day. His collar points had lost their starch and his trouser creases were dulled with wear. I noticed a smudge on the cuff of his left sleeve and my mouth pointed it out to him before my brain could intercept the message. He looked at it with distaste, produced a white, ironed handkerchief from his pocket and worked at the smudge. "Tell me what you know about this," he said as he continued to work at it.

"I don't know anything about it, Sergeant. For all I know, you were cleaning a barbecue grill and your sleeve got in the way."

Nakashita's birthmark darkened to the color of a thunderstorm. He refolded the handkerchief along its original creases and returned it to his pocket. "Hannigan," he called into his mike.

A moment later, Dana Hannigan, the detective who, along with Nakashita, had interrogated me after my break-in of Sue's, hurried across the lawn. She flashed me a quick smile, though it was clear from her face that her day had been as long as Nakashita's.

"Pat her down and put her in the car," said Nakashita.

"I'm fresh out of wood screws," I said.

"Shut up," Hannigan mouthed to my face. She announced that I was clean and put me in the back seat. I slid across and she got in beside me. Nakashita got in the driver's seat.

"Let's start with the basics," said Nakashita, turning to face me. "Where were you this morning between 6:00 and 8:00?"

"I was in a convent, Sergeant, paying for my excesses of the night before."

Nakashita regarded me coldly. He said, "Don't mess with me, Ms. Lyon."

Hannigan coughed a warning.

"It's the truth," I said. "Cross my heart and hope to die. I went out drinking and dancing with a bunch of old men last night and I got wasted. Totally, completely, shit-faced. The only extra bed happened to be at the convent, so that's where I stayed. I got in about two or three in the morning and didn't get up 'til around noon."

Nakashita and Hannigan exchanged glances and Nakashita said, "What convent would have you, Ms. Lyon?"

I shrugged. "I never did get the name. It was on Kalaupapa."

"What were you doing on Kalaupapa?" he asked.

"I went there to find Nathan Pfeifer. Look, Sergeant, I'm telling the truth about this. I came back this afternoon. The kid is no longer there and there's no reason to involve the patients. They did what they thought was right. The sheriff will verify what I told you. He or a deputy kept me under guard the whole time"

"We'll check. Did you have an argument with Pfeifer on Sunday?"

"We talked."

"The housekeeper saw you punch him."

"Pfeifer dared Brian to hit him. It was a stupid male trick. Pfeifer was showing off and Brian was about to make a fool of himself, so I hit Pfeifer first. It took some of the wind out of his macho sails."

"Is that the feminine alternative to conflict resolution?" asked Nakashita. "God help us."

"Sarcasm doesn't become you, Sergeant," I said.

"I don't need a critique from you, Ms. L. What happened after you hit him?"

I told them about our meeting. Nakashita's face remained impassive when I mentioned Pfeifer's claim that Ken Magruder had used influence to set up the porno raid on Pfeifer's store.

Nakashita asked, "Was that the last contact you had with Pfeifer?"

"No. He came to see me Wednesday morning, right before I left for Kalaupapa."

"Why did he come to see you?"

"Pfeifer said somebody had tried to break into his house the night before, a few hours after they ran me off the road. He believed it was the same person in both cases."

"And what do you think?"

"I don't know who broke into Jock's. All I know is that the guy who ran me off the road was the same one who'd threatened Brian and Sue Naito and probably killed Sue."

"Did Pfeifer name anyone he suspected?" asked Hannigan.

"He didn't say. He said Genghis, the dog, got a piece of the guy and would recognize him."

Nakashita tapped his front teeth with his ball-point pen. He said, "What was the guy looking for, Ms. Lyon?"

"I don't know. Jock offered to deal for it. Whatever it was, he was willing to trade it for Nathan."

"He thought you had the boy?"

"He thought I knew his whereabouts."

"What made him think you'd trade?"

"Pfeifer said that what he had was as valuable as Nathan. Once I had it, he said, I could figure out who killed Sue."

"Whatever it was, it's probably gone now," said Hannigan.

"The killer searched the house?" I asked.

"They tore it apart," she said.

"Just like my apartment."

Nakashita put his pen back in the exact center of his shirt pocket. "The only difference is that Pfeifer was home."

"How'd he die?"

"Somebody shot him and dumped him in the pool. Anybody

else try to make any deals with you?"

"No. Who found the body? Lydia?"

Hannigan said, "Yes, Lydia."

"Are you finished with me, Sergeant?"

"Yes," said Nakashita. "Consider this, Ms. Lyon. If the boy's as important as whatever the killer was looking for, and if he didn't find it, he'll try to get the boy."

A uniformed officer, sunlight glinting off his shield, approached the car as we got out. I noticed the shine on his shoes. Sucking up to Nakashita, I thought. The officer said, "We're about done in there, Sergeant."

"Did you search the dog pen?"

"Nothing but shit," he said. "What about the dog? My men can't get near that animal."

"Can anybody control it?"

The officer checked his notes. "The housekeeper, Mrs. Pacaro. Seems she likes the dog. He's a beautiful animal. Be a shame for animal control to take him."

"Have Mrs. Pacaro look after it," said Nakashita.

34 SHOCK WAVE

It was after seven when I wheeled the Nissan into an open parking spot almost directly under Brian's lanai. Brian greeted us at the door. Leo was working on a martini in the living room. I told Brian I thought it best that Nathan and I stay with him until Jean's release. Brian agreed, but he objected to Moon's gun.

Leo came to my defense. "It's like life insurance. You won't miss it until you need it." He hung around for one more drink before heading back to Waikiki and the dancer he'd been seeing.

"How'd the car work?" asked Brian when Leo had gone.

"Great. It started right up. For two hundred fifty bucks, it'd better work."

As I was still wearing the same clothes I'd worn to Molokai two days before, I locked myself in Brian's bathroom for a long soak in his tub. I filled it as hot as I could stand it and added about half a bottle of the bath gel I'd brought from my apartment. Forty-five minutes later, the two day stay on Molokai was a dim memory. I put on a T-shirt dress and went in search of a glass of Scotch.

I found the Scotch and Brian in the kitchen. He poured me half a rocks glass of Glenlivet. "Hey you look great! And you smell great, too!"

"Careful, Brian. There's an impressionable adolescent

nearby."

"Nathan? He's asleep in the guest room. I'd say he's out for the night."

I cocked an eyebrow at him. "How'd you do that?"

"Simple, shweetheart," he said, in a passable Bogart voice, "I slipped a mickey into his gin."

"You're too good-hearted. I'd have gone with bribes and threats."

Back in his Magruder voice, he said, "I think the events of the day caught up to him. Can you cook?"

"Anything, as long as it's chicken."

"Good! I'll make the salad and you make the chicken."

While Brian stripped the leaves off a head of romaine, I washed two chicken breasts and rubbed olive oil onto them until all the flesh was coated. I put them side-by-side in a small baking pan. Next, I went through his spice rack - mostly green spices with a few reds and yellows - and took out all the ones that looked fresh.

"Smell," I said holding an open jar under his nose.

"Mmm," he said.

I shook some of it over the chicken and did the same for each of the other spices. It's a great dish to make in a boyfriend's kitchen. So it's not the art of Julia Childs; if there's an art to it, it's the art of love. A guy's spice rack is as individual as his medicine cabinet. The stale spices are the ones his mother gave him or his roommate left behind. The fresh ones are the ones he likes. Cooking with his spices is almost like tasting the guy himself. I get different results with different boyfriends

Brian coddled an egg and made a dressing for Caesar salad. He arranged the lettuce spears on a plate and unrolled an anchovy sliver onto each one. He poured the dressing over everything.

"So what's going on with Jean?" I asked.

"We're going to win this," he said. "The hearing's set for Monday. I'm ninety-nine percent certain the judge'll drop the contempt charges. As of 10 a.m. Monday, Jean Pfeifer will be free and she'll have Nathan back. Nice Christmas present."

He began setting the kitchen table with plates, silver and wine glasses.

"How did Jean take it when you told her?" I asked.

"I think she's still shocked by the whole turn of events. She wasn't as excited as I'd expected her to be, but come Monday she'll be different."

"Then what?"

"Jean has family on the East coast. I expect she'll take Nathan back there. As for you and me? I've drawn up a check for the balance of your fee through Monday. I'm looking forward to a totally non-professional relationship with you. What do you say?"

"That would be nice, but I don't think -"

He framed my face and kissed me. "What's there to think about?"

I drew back from him. "We've got a lot of work left. Two people are dead, Brian, and the killer is still at large."

"After Monday, that will be police business. We'll be out of it."

"I wish I could be as confident as you are."

"Don't be so serious all the time."

"It's my job to be serious. We'll see what happens Monday. In the meantime, I'm in charge of Nathan's safety. Yours, too."

"Hey, I love it when you take charge. You can take charge of my whole life."

"Your life is what we're talking about." Why the hell couldn't he take it seriously?

The chicken lay under a humid green blanket of spices. My fingers looked like mossy twigs. I put the dish in the oven, washed my hands and climbed up on a tall kitchen stool.

Brian sniffed the air. "Smells good. What do you call it?" he asked.

"Pollo di amore," I said. "Chicken of love."

"Chicken of love. I missed you, Val," he said. "I'd have gone nuts if I'd spent one more night with that samurai babysitter."

"And where was I, Club Med? No, I was a prisoner in a

convent on a leper colony."

He gestured to the table set for two. "Do we really want this now?" he asked.

"I think it can wait."

"Race you to the bedroom?"

"Okay," I said, "but it's the only point you'll get for speed."

The race to the bedroom ended in a draw. Brian moved surprisingly fast and I was handicapped by the weight of Moon's gun. The chicken, when we finally got back to it, was nothing but two lumps of dried incense. We ate the salad with our fingers and made another race for bed.

Brian's alarm went off at 6:30. I used some of my considerable charm to keep him in bed a while longer, but no amount of charm or threats of violence could keep Nathan from pounding on the door and demanding breakfast about seven.

While Brian got out cereal and milk for Nathan, I put on gray cotton shorts, a loose T-shirt and cross-trainers. The shorts had the letters, "WCCC," across the seat and the shirt had "Women's Community Correctional Center" stenciled in front. The shoes read, "Saucony." The elastic in my waistband wasn't up to the weight of a long-barreled Colt, nor was my flesh ready for the bruises such a weapon would leave. Before leaving the bedroom, I removed the cylinder from the gun and hid both cylinder and frame in separate closets.

"Going running?" asked Brian.

"No. I don't want to leave the building. I'll just do the stairs."

"There's a workout room on the top floor," he said.

"Too many people." I took a key to the apartment. "Back in about half an hour. Keep the door locked," I said as the door swung shut behind me.

The hallway was empty except for two women waiting for the elevator, obviously headed for the workout room. They had on coordinated outfits of shiny, flesh-packing Spandex. One carried a plastic squeeze bottle and the other had a disk player strapped to her waist. Neither of them had WCCC - or anything else - on their seat. How can you claim pride in your alma mater if you don't wear it on your butt? I had to pass them to get to the stairs.

As I approached, one woman said to the other, "They have to do something about these elevators. All I want is fifteen minutes on the Stairmaster. Can anybody tell me how to get a good workout when I spend all my workout time just trying to get there?"

"There are stairs around the corner," I said.

They looked at me with open disbelief and disgust.

"Oh, sorry," I said, as I went past. "What was I thinking? You might sweat up those cute outfits."

"Excuse me," the second woman called after me. "Do you live in this building?"

"No," I shouted back. "I'm visiting my pimp."

Nice going, Val, I thought. Next thing you know Brian will be getting a visit from the owners' morals committee.

I walked to the bottom of the stairwell and began my workout. Run up two flights and walk down one. Didn't want to risk a joint injury or, worse, a fall by running down the stairs. In twenty-five minutes I'd reached the twelfth floor. My quads and glutes burned and my pulse was so rapid the beats seemed to merge into one. I took it slow going back to the seventh floor, leaving a trail of sweat behind me on the stairs. As I entered the hallway the elevator doors sighed shut. The Spandex ladies, I thought self-righteously. All that time waiting, they could have at least stretched out.

Inside Brian's apartment, I made straight for the kitchen and poured myself a tumbler of water. My pulse had slowed to triple figures. Between gulps I called out, "I don't think your neighbors approve of me, Brian. I told them you're my pimp."

"He's not here," Nathan called from the living room.

My heart thudded to a halt. "What do you mean?" I demanded. "Where is he?"

"He left. You just missed him."

The elevator. "Why the hell did he leave?" I shouted. "Where did he go?"

Nathan seemed to cringe under my barrage. He said, "He went to the jail. Soon after you left he got a call. He said Mom hit a guard with a cafeteria tray and they were locking her up. He said to tell you he's taking your car and he'll be back as soon as he straightens it out."

"Why?" I asked. I set the glass down but missed the counter. It hit the floor and shattered. "Why couldn't he wait?"

"I don't know."

"Why did she hit a guard?"

"I don't know! Okay?" Nathan had sunk way back into the cushions of the couch.

If that was Brian on the elevator, maybe I could stop him. Surely Jean knew that hitting a guard would delay her release. I raced to the lanai. She had to know they'd lock her up.

From the lanai railing, I searched the lot below, saw my car off to the right and Brian approaching it. Cupping my hands around my mouth, I yelled, "Brian! Brian!" He turned and looked up. "Jean wants to stay in jail. Don't you see? She doesn't want to leave."

He put his hand to his ear and shook his head.

"Brian," I screamed, "Wait!"

He cupped his hands to his face and shouted back. All I could understand was, ". . . back soon." Then he waved and turned back to the car.

"Brian," I screamed one more time, but he didn't hear me.

He got in the car and shut the door. I couldn't see him, but I could imagine him turning the ignition. All at once the hood popped up.

Damn! I thought. The starter again. Two hundred fifty dollars. But even as the thought went through my head, I knew it wasn't the starter. The hood flew up on a pillow of black smoke and a skirt of orange flame shot out from the underside of the car. An orange-red ball appeared inside and grew like a rapidly expanding weather balloon until it burst out the hatchback and the doors.

I was still screaming his name long after the shock wave and the sound of the explosion had reached me.

35 MOLOKAI EXPRESS

I felt the heat as far away as the seventh floor. Flames consumed my Nissan. The car on its left exploded and the car on the right caught fire. No Brian.

The sound of the explosion brought Nathan out to the lanai. "Cool," he said.

"It is not cool," I yelled, my voice breaking. "Brian is in there."

Nathan backed away from my rage. "You mean that big guy? He got blown up?"

"Yes. Don't you understand? It could have been you." I pushed him into the apartment. "Go, dammit. Get your shoes on." I pushed him again. He fell backwards on the floor. "Now! Move!" I screamed at him.

"Why?" he demanded. "What's going on?"

I saw the fear in his face and heard the confusion in his voice, but there wasn't time to explain. Whoever planted the bomb could be on his way up now. I raced to the bedroom and grabbed the pieces of Moon's gun from their hiding places. From the bedroom phone, I called the number Moon had given me.

Let him be there, I thought. I took off my sodden T-shirt and pulled on a sweatshirt while I waited. As I was about to give up in despair, he answered. "I need a car right now at Judd and Nu'uanu Streets," I said. "Explain later."

Moon didn't ask questions. With the gun assembled, I went back to the living room. Nathan was struggling into his shoes.

"We're leaving," I said. "You do exactly as I say and you don't make a sound."

"Can't we stay here?"

"No, dammit, we can't." I tried to calm myself. "Nathan, listen to me. Your mother hid you away to keep you from harm. Now someone is trying to harm us both. They have killed Brian and they may be coming for you. I have to get you away."

"Can you…? I mean, you're a…"

Oh God! Not now. "Move! Do what I tell you!"

With my bag over my shoulder and the gun in my hand, I led Nathan out of the apartment. The elevator picked that moment to stop at the floor. I pushed Nathan against the wall and raised the gun. The door opened and the two Spandex ladies emerged. They stopped short at the sight of the gun and screamed.

"Shut up," I commanded. "Get in and close the door. Push the emergency stop between floors. Do it!" They nodded dumbly. If they did as they were told, it would tie up one elevator. Nathan and I headed for the stairs. I didn't want to have to shoot our way out of an elevator.

I let the fire door close behind us and paused on the landing. The stairwell was quiet, but I knew from my workout that sound carried well in there. The opening of a fire door on any floor would make enough noise to alert us. We would probably notice a pressure change, too. We stayed close to the wall going down, making sure nobody was waiting on the other side of the doors at each landing. To my relief, Nathan obeyed me.

The lobby was empty, but a crowd had gathered outside the front door to watch the police and fire vehicles arrive. For all I knew, the bomber could be among the bystanders. Our only exit, however, was through the crowd. I put the gun in my shoulder bag, grabbed Nathan's hand and skirted the throng. I didn't recognize any faces, but there was something oddly familiar about a man getting on the elevator. I had a fleeting glimpse before the door closed. I tugged Nathan's arm and together we made it to the street at a fast walk. Nobody followed us.

Moon met us at the corner in a rented limo. I shoved Nathan inside.

"Awesome," he said.

"Armored," said Moon. "This ride courtesy of Acid Rain. The rock group? Only they don't know it. They still sleepin'."

"Double Awesome," said Nathan.

"Moon, they killed Brian."

"Sorry," he said.

"I have to get Nathan someplace safe."

"Small island. Even smaller when somebody's lookin' for you."

"Then we have to get off," I said.

"Can't drive off."

I remembered Greg's invitation. It gave me a wild idea. "We can sail. Go to the yacht club. Make sure we're not followed."

"Can do," said Moon.

While Nathan played with the limo's sound system, I called the police department on the limo's phone. Nakashita wasn't there, but Hannigan was. I preferred to talk to her anyway. She hadn't heard about the explosion as it wasn't her division. I filled her in.

"It was my car," I said. "Brian Magruder was in it. He couldn't survive. No one could." The phone in my hand was shaking.

"Where are you, Val?"

"The boy's in my protection. I had to get him out of the building and I may have terrorized a couple of women. I'll contact you when I know he's safe. Do you understand?" My hand shook more.

"Yes," she answered. "Wally won't like it."

"Do me a favor and keep him off my ass."

"It would be easier if you came in."

"Not 'til Nathan's safe." I hung up and slumped back in the

seat. The car was chilly. My skin felt cold and clammy. I wished I'd put on jeans before leaving. Even the sweatshirt was inadequate. I asked Moon to turn down the air conditioner. He obliged but it didn't seem to help. If anything, I felt colder. I jammed my hands under my armpits to stop them from shaking.

"Moon, will you turn off the damn air? And hurry up."

"Almost there. You all right?"

"Just drive."

The Ala Wai Yacht Harbor sits at the mouth of the Ala Wai Canal where it empties into the ocean. Moon drove around behind the Ilikai Hotel and pulled into the Yacht Club entrance. The limo looked like it belonged among the expensive vehicles in the parking lot.

"I better take the gun," he said as we got out. "You're not in shape to shoot. You're in shock."

"I'll be okay. Gotta find Greg's boat."

"Know the name?"

I shook my head. I wasn't thinking clearly at all. Suddenly I remembered I had his phone number. I started fumbling with the catch on my purse, but my hands shook too badly.

"Give!" said Moon. He took my purse and pawed through it until he found the napkin. "This it?"

I nodded. Moon called Greg from the limo while I leaned against the car and shivered. Even in full sun, I was chilled. Moon got out of the limo.

"Honi. He's there."

He led the way through a forest of masts. Nathan followed and I stumbled after them. Greg was waiting in the cockpit.

"Val? What's going on?"

"We need your help. Can you get us out of here?"

"Where? Out of the harbor?"

"I don't care where, we just have to go." My voice sounded flat and my whole body shook. "We have to get the hell away."

"Are you all right?"

"Shock," said Moon.

Moon and Greg helped me aboard the Honi. Nathan clambered up behind.

"Can you get us away?" I asked.

"First we'll get you taken care of."

I protested, but Greg insisted that I get below. It took a threat of force from Moon before I gave in. The cabin was large enough to hold a table, a tiny galley, and berths for six people. Greg wrapped me in blankets and opened a can of juice from the boat's larder. He made me drink it while Moon did the explanations.

Greg said, "The sensible thing is to get you some medical treatment."

"Not until Nathan's safe," I said.

"She ain't sensible," said Moon. "She got her mind made up."

"All right. Where do you want to go?" he asked.

The only safe place for Nathan was Kalaupapa. Greg wasn't enthusiastic. With favorable winds, it would take about eight hours of sailing across the Molokai channel, known locally as the Molokai Express for its rough seas. Finally, however, he agreed to try it. Moon declined to go. Nathan stayed below with me while Greg piloted the Honi out of the harbor using the inboard engine. When we were out at sea, Nathan went on deck to help with the sails.

I don't remember much of the voyage. Greg checked on me often and plied me with liquids. Eventually, the chill left me. I grew accustomed enough to the rocking that I could lie down in one of the berths without fear of rolling off. As the effects of the shock wore off, however, I was left with the reality of Brian's murder. My shoulders started to shake, but not from the chill. I choked back the dull ache that filled my throat and spread through my upper body, but it wouldn't go away. With a groan, I gave in and let the flood come. Finally, exhaustion and sleep overtook me.

The rolling of the boat tossed me awake. It was going on four o'clock. I'd slept for about six hours. I emerged from the darkness of the cabin into the bright sunlight. Greg had the tiller and Nathan was pulling in the jib sheets. Nathan had on a life vest.

"How are you doing?" Greg asked.

"Better, now. I must've been a mess this morning."

"Who wouldn't be? We're on the windward side of Molokai. The sea's kind of rough here. You better hang on. You might want to put on a vest."

"How much longer?" I asked.

"An hour or an hour and a half. Do you think you'll be safe there?"

"Nathan will be safe. I'm not staying."

"I can take you back tomorrow. It's not fast but it's safe."

"You've done enough. I can't involve you any more."

"Look, maybe I'm just a big Boy Scout, but I want to be a part of your adventure, if only to see you in one piece."

"Greg," I said, "you're sweet. At one time, I could fall for a guy like you and maybe I'll be able to do it again someday. But don't you see? I just got Brian killed. I can't risk involving you that way."

We reached the Kalaupapa peninsula in an hour and a half. The seas got rougher as we approached the small harbor. Nathan and I lowered the sails in the fading light while Greg started the inboard engine to get us into the channel. Inside the breakwater, the seas were noticeably calmer, but not enough to trust docking the Honi at the wharf. Instead, we anchored in the harbor and inflated the boat's rubber dinghy. We landed under cover of darkness. Our arrival in the harbor had been noted and a small knot of residents had gathered at the wharf. Kent and Zeke were among them. The explosion had made the news.

"HPD is looking for you," said Kent.

The five us went to Aileen's. I expected some accusation from her, but all she said was, "We heard about Brian. I'm sorry, Val."

"I failed," I said. "I shouldn't have taken Nathan." Any other time, I would've gagged before eating crow, but when you're at your lowest you don't even taste it.

"You did what you could. Nobody could have foreseen this."

"Somebody should have. Somebody's not telling me the truth. I need to go back."

"You need rest," Aileen said. "You can't do anything for him in your state."

Kent spoke up. "They're lookin' for you there, but nobody's lookin' for you here. A day or three won't hurt."

Aileen had some jeans that fit me. During dinner, which I could only pick at, I recounted the events for Kent and Zeke's benefit. Nathan sat through it all in silence. I didn't think that unusual given what he'd been through.

Greg planned to sail back to Oahu in the morning with Zeke as crew. He turned down Zeke's offer of a bed for the night, saying he ought to stay with the boat. He wanted me to join him and I agreed. A part of me insisted on proving that I was strong enough to handle Brian's death, that I was not a hostage to grief.

We bought a bottle of wine at the bar on the way to the boat. We got some glasses and took the wine up to the bow where we sat holding hands and looking at the stars. The sky above Molokai held infinitely more stars than I had ever seen above San Francisco or Honolulu and Greg seemed to know all the constellations. Greg was gentle and understanding, but there was no fire between us. After awhile he just held me and I thanked him with a tentative kiss. I needed his quiet more than anything else. Sitting there beside him, listening to the waves lapping at the boat, I became aware of the thing inside me. It had mass and weight. It had a shape. I was certain that I'd feel its outline if I poked around with my fingers. I knew it was solid and smooth, that it had no cracks or seams. It was sucking in all my emotions and crushing them - a black hole from which no feeling could escape. Brian's death had left me changed forever. I knew that the black hole would stay with me as long as Brian's memory. It was Greg's misfortune to come along at the wrong time.

Eventually, we went below and crawled into separate berths. I didn't get to sleep immediately. Nakashita's warning kept coming back to me: if they didn't find what they were looking for, they'll try to get the boy. They'd tried and they got Brian. They'll try again for

Nathan. But that meant they hadn't found what they were looking for at Jock's and I thought I knew where it was. I resolved to go back in the morning, if I could get Aileen to fly me. The other thing that haunted me was the memory of the man getting in the elevator as we fled Brian's building. It wasn't the man, himself, that was familiar, it was the way he walked. Even so, I couldn't identify him. In frustration, I drifted off to sleep.

Zeke showed up at first light and the two of them made ready to sail. From the wharf, I watched the boat until it had cleared the breakwater. Then I headed to Aileen's.

She met me at the door. "Nathan's missing," she said. "I just went in to check on him and he's gone. His bed's empty."

36 IN THE DOG HOUSE

Two Park Service workers, hiking down from topside, found Nathan among rocks near the bottom of the mule trail. He had a compound fracture of his arm and a mass of scrapes and bruises. I paced the hospital corridor while Aileen waited with him in the recovery room. About quarter to twelve, almost four hours after he'd been found, Aileen beckoned me in.

"I think you'd better hear this," she said.

Nathan looked small and frail in the middle of the hospital bed. His arm was immobilized in a cast and propped up on pillows. His face looked like a boxer's after a rough fight. He seemed to be sleeping, but opened his eyes when Aileen spoke to him.

"Nathan," she said, "tell Val what you told me. Why did you run away?"

He looked at me with drug-dulled eyes. They reminded me so much of Brian's I almost cried out. Nathan said in a voice so soft I had to lean close to hear, "I don't want anybody…anybody else to get hurt. It's my fault."

"What's your fault, Nathan?"

"I…I killed your friend. And my dad. I killed my…my dad, too. It's my fault."

"You didn't kill anybody, Nathan. None of this is your

fault."

"Yes, it is. Something terrible was supposed to happen if I told anybody. The man said I mustn't tell or people would get hurt, but I did and it happened."

"Tell anybody what, Nathan? Was it something you did?"

Aileen motioned me away from the bed. "He was sexually molested," she whispered. "Now do you understand what we've been doing? I think trying to get more out of him right now will just hurt him more."

I had to agree with her. I doubted that I had the skills to bring out the details of the incident. But there were still some things I needed to know. I went back to his bedside and stroked his forehead.

"Nathan," I said, "who did you tell this to?"

"My dad. Now he's dead and it's my fault."

"It's not your fault. Don't beat yourself up about it."

Nathan was near exhaustion. The best thing I could do for him would be to leave him alone, but I had one more question I needed desperately to ask. "Who told you not to tell anyone?"

He turned his head away from me. "Go away," he said. "I can't tell you. I don't want anybody else to die."

Aileen took my arm. "We'd better leave him for awhile."

I shook myself out of her grasp. Out in the hall, I turned on her. "You knew all along, didn't you? Who told you? Jean?"

"Jean told Sue who told me."

"And you thought you could keep it secret? You weren't going to tell me?"

"Keep your voice down," she said. "We're in a hospital. What difference would it make if you knew?"

"Go to hell," I yelled. "Two people are dead, that's what difference it makes."

"Knowing couldn't have saved them."

"Who molested him? At least tell me that."

"Jean said it was his father," she said.

I stopped in my tracks. "That can't be. Nathan said he told his dad about it and that led to the killings. Why would he tell his dad if his dad molested him?"

Aileen frowned. "I'm only repeating what Sue told me. If it wasn't his father then who was it?"

"I don't know, but I think Jock knew."

With Kent guarding Nathan, Aileen flew me back to Honolulu. My cash reserves were too low to rent a car, so I called Leo from the airport to pick me up. He met me at Kelly's Coffee Shop on Lagoon Drive.

"Do the police have any leads on Brian or Jock?" I asked.

"No. They're looking for you."

The waiter brought the dinner I'd ordered while waiting for Leo - a New York strip steak, baked potato, and a beer. Leo ordered a martini for himself. When it arrived, he said, "You got somethin' in mind. Need some help?"

"I need a car and lockpicks from you," I said between bites of steak.

"You know what you're gonna do?"

"I'm going to see what I can find in Jock's house. After that…" I shrugged. "I only know I won't stop until I get this guy."

"It won't help Brian, kiddo."

"No, but it might help me. It's the only way to put an end to this anger. Leo, do I look different to you?"

He peered across the table at me. "You look fine, kiddo. You look good. I know what you're gettin' at. You've changed inside. You think you've changed outside."

"I have changed. I feel like the She-Hulk. I'm afraid to look in a mirror because I might see something ugly."

"Not ugly, hard. You've hardened up inside. But you're still a good person and you ain't ugly."

I managed to consume all but a few scraps of the steak. The waiter's offer of a doggie bag, however, gave me an idea. I had him wrap the meat. Leo paid the tab and we left. I drove his rental car to Waikiki and dropped him off a block from his hotel.

"Stay away from your apartment," he warned, handing me the lockpicks.

I had no intention of going near my apartment, though I badly wanted a change of clothes. Except for Aileen's jeans, I was still wearing the clothes I had on in my flight from Brian's. My sweatshirt, in particular, was beginning to reek. I rolled down the car windows and headed to a supermarket.

The parking lot was crowded. A much-reduced Christmas tree lot took up about a dozen spaces. Only a few pathetic trees remained. I was suddenly saddened to realize we were only three days from Christmas. I've been a good girl, Santa. Bring me a gun so I can blow somebody away.

The butcher gave me seven pounds of chuck steak for fifteen dollars. He cut it into cubes for free. I spent another four dollars on batteries for my mini-light. It was dark by the time I got back to the car.

I drove to Kahala and cruised past Jock's house. The street lights did a good job of illuminating the front yard, but the house itself was set back far enough that its features were barely discernible. All of the windows were dark. I parked several houses down and walked back, carrying my purchases. A light breeze stirred the night air and brought a slight chill with it. The sky was clear, but only the brightest stars were visible. I had a longing to be far away, to be stargazing with Greg on the boat. It was followed by a twinge of guilt as though even the thought was a betrayal of Brian's memory. Perhaps I hadn't lost all my emotions to the black hole. Where there's guilt, there's hope.

I felt completely exposed as I went up the driveway, but I made it to the shadows of Jock's front porch without attracting attention. After a few minutes spent listening for sounds inside the house and hearing nothing, I went to work with Leo's lockpicks, the minilight between my teeth. Pfeifer hadn't bothered with state of the art security devices. His two locks were standard home security models, resistant enough to forcing and jimmying, but no match for high-quality lockpicks. No match, that is, in the hands of an expert. My skills were a little rusty. I hadn't picked a lock in over two years. The first one took twenty minutes and most of my patience. My arms and shoulders ached from working hunched over and my jaw ached from holding the light. I stood up and stretched. Unbidden images ran through my mind - Sue Naito sprawled on the floor, Nathan in the hospital bed, Brian with a can of beer in each pocket, Brian arguing my case before the judge, Brian getting into my car. Brian, Brian, Brian. I picked up the light and went back to work. Ten minutes later the second lock yielded.

I made a quick tour of the house to make sure I was alone. The house showed signs of a search - slashed upholstery and emptied drawers - but the disorder was greatly reduced in the main living areas. Someone, probably Lydia had been at work. That meant the police were through with the place. Nakashita would've given the place a thorough search. Not much chance of my stumbling across something they'd overlooked. What I was counting on was that they'd missed the dog pen. What better place to keep something secure than right under the nose of a trained attack dog? Even a cop would think twice about searching it.

To get in that cage, I'd have to make friends with Genghis. I found a bowl in the kitchen and dumped the meat in it. I had only a faint hope that he'd go for it. I'd be lucky to get close to the pen. He'd smell me from several yards away and know I was a stranger.

I carried the bowl out to the enclosed part of the lanai. Suddenly, my light picked up something bulky and white and I almost lost the bowl. It was only a robe, probably Jock's, but it gave me a wild idea. I set the bowl on the table and put on the robe.

Genghis knew something was up the minute I stepped outside. I could hear his low growl and his restless movement inside the pen. The breeze, coming from behind me, must have carried a confusing olfactory image - Jock, raw meat, and unwashed detective. Genghis's restlessness increased. He punctuated his growl with a short snap. I kept the same, slow pace. He growled and snapped again. There was just enough light from the street and from neighboring houses that I could make out the outlines of the pen and, beside it, a structure about the size of a tool shed. Genghis's moving shadow seemed to merge with the shed and disappear completely, only to reappear after a short time. I'd gotten to within about six feet when Genghis made me. He stopped still and growled ominously. I took one more step and he launched himself at the gate. It bulged outward, but, to my relief, the chain and padlock kept it closed. He bounced off it and started barking.

"Genghis!" I commanded. "Shut up!"

The note of authority had some kind of effect on him. He ceased barking but continued to growl. Cautiously, I brought a hunk of meat close to the fence and shoved it through before he could snap at my fingers. Then another one. He snatched the second one up, barely ceasing his growling. "We're making progress, Genghis."

The tool shed beside the pen was a flat-roofed, cinder block structure, about eight feet wide and twelve long, maybe a foot taller than me. Entrance from the yard was through a padlocked wooden door. Beside it stood two garbage cans. A low, narrow opening in the wall allowed Genghis access from inside the pen. When I tested the door, Genghis sprang into the shed and hit it with a solid "whumpf." The padlock rattled, but the hasp held. With a choice of two locks to pick, I chose the one on the shed. That way I wouldn't risk losing a finger to Genghis's jaws.

I tossed a few chunks of meat into Genghis's pen and set to work on the lock. Genghis continued growling his threats. He would run into the pen, press against the fence to snap at me, pause to gobble the meat, and then run back to the shed. The lock was a standard padlock. It might resist a bullet, but it should have yielded easily to the lockpicks. Several times I nearly had it, only to lose it when he threw himself at the door. Finally, it opened. I left it in the staple while I stretched out the kinks.

Now to get Genghis out and me in. I carried a chair from beside the pool out to the yard and placed it about ten feet from the shed. I put the remains of the meat on the chair and draped Jock's robe over the back. With my weight against the door, I removed the lock. Genghis signaled his assaults on the door by scratching at it before attacking. I waited for the scratches before letting it swing open under his weight. His momentum carried him to the chair. He caught Jock's robe in his teeth and pulled the chair over. I ducked into the shed, shut the door, and slammed the inside bolt into place before he could get to me.

The pen was the first place to look. I had to stoop low to get through the opening. As I straightened up, Genghis charged the fence. Instinctively, I took a step backwards and my left foot, wearing a brand new Saucony, squished in a dog pile. "*Merda!*" I said, ever the observant detective.

Shit was about all I could see outside. I went back into the shed and played my light around. It was both tool shed and dog house. In one corner was a trough with a faucet dripping fresh water. Nearby was a pile of dog bedding. I used the bedding to wipe off my shoe. "You owe me this, Genghis." Except for the bedding, the shed was neat and orderly. Yard and pool implements hung on the walls along with coiled hoses and shelves holding dog care items. Along the back wall was a wooden bin, waist high, about five feet long. It had a hinged top with no lock. Inside were two lidded, galvanized cans of dry dog food. Nothing resembling an ammunition box. Next I searched the shelves, opened all the bottles and cans, even the ones that couldn't hold anything but a handful of pills. Outside, Genghis continued to snarl, interrupting it for an occasional bark. Nothing under the hoses or behind the tools. I shone my light in the water trough. Nothing there, either.

Finally, I went back to the food bin and took out the cans. They were heavy. One was half full, the other about three quarters. I rolled up my sleeve and plunged my arm into first one and then the other. It was in the second one at the bottom. I knelt down beside the can and started to scoop out the dog food with both hands. In my eagerness, I didn't realize that Genghis had been silent for a few minutes. I had both hands around the metal box when I heard him scrambling onto the garbage can outside. That was followed by a heavy thump above me. He was on the roof of the shed. An instant later, Genghis's dark shape dropped into the dog pen. I yanked the box out of the can, spilling dog food everywhere, and ran to the door. Behind me, Genghis sprang through the opening, knocking one of the cans over and tumbling with it. He regained his footing but I was already out the door. I slammed it shut and threw my weight against it to counter the force of his lunge, slipped the padlock into place, and sprinted across the yard. I hoped Jock had screwed the hasp in securely.

37 BASIC GENETICS

The box contained a video cassette and a thick folder of documents. A quick look through the folder was all I needed to tell me why Jock had considered it valuable. I carried it back to the car and headed to the Halekulani Hotel and Leo. On the way, I stopped at a Long's Drugstore to rent a VCR and to call him so he would expect me.

The marbled elegance of the Halekulani's lobby made me self-conscious of my state of dress. Although Jock's shed had been orderly by my own housekeeping standards, it was, after all, a dog house. My sweatshirt and jeans had acquired a little more grime and a faint but unmistakable odor of dog. If I needed confirmation of that, I had it in the sidelong looks and cautious behavior of the tony couple who shared my elevator. Trouble was, I dared not go to my apartment for fresh clothes for fear of being picked up by the police.

Getting in and out of Jock's had taken about two hours. It was now 9:30 and past the extended Christmas season hours of most stores. Leo, however, saw that as a challenge. "Leave it to me, kiddo," he said.

"I'm planning a visit to the Magruder clan in the morning, Leo."

"Trust me," he said. "A man learns a lot from four wives."

Leo was perhaps the only man I would trust to pick out the

256

right things. By the time I got out of the shower, wearing the robe that the hotel provided for its guests, he was back and the clothes were laid out on the bed. He'd bought a blue blouse, a brightly patterned wrap around skirt, and some flat shoes. There was even underwear and hose.

"I know the lady owns the boutique downstairs," he explained.

"She owe you a favor?"

"Yeah. Whattya think? The blouse go with your eyes?"

"Perfect."

While Leo hooked up the VCR, I took the documents from the folder and spread them out across a small table and the dresser. They included notes in what I took to be Jock's handwriting, diagrams, medical records, newspaper clippings, photographs, and correspondence. Judging from the dates on some of the documents, Jock had been at the project for a little more than a year.

"What've you got?" asked Leo over my shoulder.

"It's a paternity case. I know what it's supposed to prove, but I don't understand these things. I need you to translate."

"'Cause I know from paternity?"

"You've been down both sides of this street, Leo."

"There ain't any tykes runnin' around with this beak, though."

"For which their mothers thank you. Now what is this stuff?"

Leo picked out a set of diagrams and photographs. The photos were pictures of hands - Jock's, Nathan's, and Cecil Pfeifer's, according to the labels on the back. Cecil Pfeifer was Jock's father. His picture was a grainy enlargement of an old snapshot. The enlargement showed a hand with stubby fingers holding a fishing rod. The fingers resembled Jock's.

"Simple inheritance, kiddo. Those fingers are dominant. Father to son."

"Cecil to Jock, but not Jock to Nathan. He has normal, almost long hands."

"Like a musician."

"Yeah," I agreed. "But Jock would have had trouble with most instruments. That's probably why he was so dead set against Nathan's music."

Next was eye color, but I didn't need instruction. Mine are blue with flecks of green. The blue is from my father and the green from my mother. Both traits are recessive. Brown eye color, like stubby fingers, is a dominant trait. Nathan's eyes were brown; Jean and Jock's were blue. For Nathan to have brown eyes, one of his parents must have brown eyes.

Finally, there was the matter of blood type. Nathan was type A and both Jock and Jean were type B. Jean could have a child with that blood type, but not by Jock.

Leo summed up the evidence. "Jock can't be the father."

"And he figures Ken Magruder is, right?"

"Yeah," said Leo. He pulled a document out of a manila envelope. "Cost him something to get this."

The document was a photocopied serology report. It was accompanied by a cover letter from the lab that did the blood work and was addressed to a Honolulu physician. To my untrained eyes, the report was indecipherable. What I did get from it was that the patient's name was Kenneth Magruder.

"So what does it tell us?" I asked.

"Nothing without the same thing on the mother and the kid. That's what this is."

"This" was a handwritten spreadsheet with seven columns labelled "blood type system," "K. Magruder," "Jean," "Nathan," "required father genes," "gene freq," and "combined gene freq." The spreadsheet had eleven rows. The entries under "blood type system" had names such as "ABO," "Rh," "MNS," and so on. I knew about ABO and Rh, but after that I was lost. The other cells didn't help much either - mostly letters and symbols except for the frequency columns, which contained percentages. I appealed to Leo for an explanation.

"Blood type systems," he said. "You figure what genes of the kid came from the mother. The others come from the father. Here." He stabbed a finger at the column labeled "required father genes." In the ABO row, the entry under Nathan was A1 and under Jean it was B, so the required father gene was A1. K. Magruder's gene was also A1. The other entries followed a similar pattern: genes that Nathan could get only from his father were genes that Ken possessed.

"A lot of men could have those genes, Leo." The gene frequency of the A1 gene was 19.4% which I took to mean that 19.4% of people possessed it. The required Rh gene (CDe) had a frequency of 41.5%. "So we've narrowed the father down to twenty to forty percent of people."

"It's the combo. Go down this last column. Each number is the percent of men who have the combination of this gene and the ones above it. You have only 7.9% of people with both A1 and CDe. The numbers get smaller as you go down. The last number is for the whole combo."

"So only one out of one hundred thousand people have the right combination of genes to be Nathan's father," I said, reading the last entry.

"Half of them are women."

"And Ken Magruder happens to be one of them."

"Almost like catching him in the bed."

Having struggled for a 'C' in sophomore biology, I was impressed with what Jock had done. "But how did he suspect Ken?" I asked.

"Ken had a rep with women an' he knew Jean back then."

Hard evidence of that was in a snapshot of three people - Jean, Ken and Helen Magruder - at a table set with formal place settings. The three of them were staring directly at the camera and Ken had his arms around both women. From the youthful features of all three, I guessed it had been taken more than a dozen years ago.

"Pretty tight with both of 'em."

I shook my head. "The body language isn't right. Ken and Helen are clearly intimate, but Jean's only posing for the camera."

"Jock didn't see it that way." Leo popped the cassette into

the VCR. "Showtime," he said.

The video was nothing more than a blatant attempt at extortion. Jock's off-camera voice addressed Ken and took him though the collection of records and notes that Leo and I had viewed. He wanted a partnership in Windward Cove and a trust fund set up for Nathan. He wanted a million dollars in cash.

"Kinda steep, ain't it?" asked Leo.

"But he thinks he can get it. He hasn't told us everything, yet." Aileen had been close to the truth, but Jean had not told her the full, awful extent of it.

It came out, according to Jock, when Nathan saw a picture of Ken in the newspaper. Something in the boy's reaction to it had aroused Jock's suspicions. He questioned Nathan at length and over several weeks until the outlines of the incident emerged. Jean and Nathan had spent the weekend with a man whom Jean apparently knew well. The location, Jock later deduced, was in Waimanalo on the windward side. The Magruders, it so happens, have a farm there where they raise horses. The man had taught Nathan how to ride and had invited him back for another weekend. Two weeks later, Nathan took him up on it. This time, he went alone.

Jock had recorded Nathan's account on audio. So we heard, in Nathan's words, everything that transpired that weekend. I don't know which disgusted me more - Jock's interrogation of Nathan, or the incident itself. Nathan spoke softly and haltingly, evidently feeling great shame and confusion. As the enormity of the story came out, a new note crept into his voice - fear. He was clearly torn between obeying Jock's insistent demands that he tell everything and concealing it in order to prevent the terrible things he'd been led to believe would happen.

Leo stopped the tape and fixed us drinks from the mini-bar.

"The makings of a scandal," he said. "But it doesn't follow that Ken would kill people."

"He didn't set out to. Sue was an accident, but her death raised the stakes. This stuff," I gestured towards the documents and the tape, "is explosive enough, but you add a homicide to it -"

"Yeah. Jock's easy enough to figure after that. He keeps making demands, he has to be eliminated."

"And Brian?" I asked.

"Brian was a mistake. It was you they wanted."

38 CONDOLENCES

With a generous tip from Leo in his pocket, the bell captain was able
to find us another VCR and two blank tapes. While I made copies of
Jock's tape, Leo used the hotel's copier to make two complete
duplicates of the other material.

"So who gets these, kiddo?"

"Your buddy, Hagen, at Pacific Economic News, and Lehua
Lopes at Channel 5. Now, since I've got a big day tomorrow, I intend
to make use of your bed for a few hours."

"You trying to give me a heart attack? All these years I never
expected to hear that."

"I'm on duty, Leo. You're not, so you get the chair."

I was awake at six thirty and dressed by seven. I delivered
one set of Jock's material to the newsroom at Channel 5, and the
other set to the offices of Pacific Economic News. By eight o'clock I
was negotiating the tight switch backs on Roundtop Drive above the
city.

Ken Magruder lived about three-quarters of the way up the
mountain at the limits of the city water supply. The higher reaches
are occupied by people with some sense of independence, who are
willing to sacrifice the amenities of city life for a spectacular view and
the feeling of being above, literally and figuratively, the stresses of

urban living. The Magruder home was high enough to afford a view, which must have cost him plenty.

I pulled Leo's car into an elongated curved driveway paralleling the road except for a wide, flat section that branched off and ended in a two-car garage. Between the driveway and a hedge fronting a brick wall about five feet high was a narrow strip of lawn. The wall was split in the middle by a fancy, wrought iron gate. The ground must have dropped steeply on the other side because the wall and garage were the only visible structures. Way in the distance were the lochs of Pearl Harbor.

My hunch about the terrain was confirmed when I reached the gate. I found myself looking down a terraced slope at the roofs of three buildings on different levels. I rang the bell and was buzzed in almost immediately.

At the bottom of a stone stairway was a covered open area - the entrance hall to the main house. I was met there by a woman whom I recognized as Helen Magruder. She wore her blond hair in a loose way that hid her age. Her beige outfit flattered her figure.

"Oh," she said, "I was expecting my sister-in-law."

"Molly Gallagher? Great! That will make a nice party."

"Do you know Molly? I don't believe we've met."

"I'm Val Lyon."

"Val Lyon. Well, well. I suppose I should express my sympathy and then I ought to throw you out of my house. When Brian came to see us last week, he positively glowed whenever he talked about you. Kenneth, on the other hand, goes into a rage at the mention of your name. Do you have those effects on all men?"

"I don't know. I haven't met all men."

"Well, I am sorry about Brian. I hope you cared for him because I know he cared for you."

"I did care for him," I said. The words came out in a little croak and my eyes seemed to cloud over. "I was wondering about the funeral arrangements."

"They haven't been finalized. Mom and Pop Magruder have been notified in Europe. We expect them tomorrow. We won't complete the arrangements until they arrive. Molly and I were going to go over the details."

"And Frank, is he back?"

"Of course. He's been here all week. Now, he's a man who hasn't voiced an opinion about you. That's seminary training, I suppose. You would expect that being married to one twin, I'd understand the other, but I don't. However, it's all beside the point. I'm sorry about Brian. The funeral notice will be published in the paper, if that's what you came for."

"Actually, I have some business with your husband. Is he here?"

"Ah," she glanced quickly toward the back of the house. Turning back to me she seemed to realize that I'd caught the glance and said, "He may not have business with you."

"Why don't we let him decide that?"

A smile played briefly across her face. "Yes, why don't we?"

The house was largely open to take advantages of the breezes and the view. From the hall we went through the living area to a less formal family room separated by a low room divider. The divider held an assortment of video and audio components. I could see Ken at a table set outside on a lanai that was about three steps lower than the level we were on and a step or two higher than the level of the next unit of the house. His back was to me.

"Do you think I could use your VCR?" I asked.

The request was obviously a strange one to her. She considered it a moment and then said, "Sure, make yourself at home. I'll get Ken."

I put the tape in the VCR and pressed the power button. From outside came the sound of Ken's voice exploding in fury. His descriptions of me were loud and crude but not very creative. Jock's image appeared on the TV as Ken entered the room.

"What the hell are you doing here, Lyon? Get out this minute."

I paused the tape. "Hello, Ken. I have something here I think you should see."

Helen, who'd followed Ken into the room, a half dozen discreet steps behind, said, "Isn't that Jock Pfeifer on the TV? What is this about?"

"It's garbage," said Ken. "Do you think I haven't seen it, Lyon? What makes you think I want to see it again?"

"Last week, one week ago, today, to be exact, you said that you didn't know what Jock had on you. But, in fact, you had seen it."

"What is it, Kenneth. I haven't seen it," said Helen.

Ken's face paled and his eyes narrowed. "You don't want to see it, Helen. Go tend your garden."

"I want to see it," said Helen quietly.

"For God's sake, it's nothing but a tawdry blackmail attempt."

"Or a motive for murder," I said.

"Motive for murder?" asked Helen. "You're not suggesting…I mean you don't think that Ken was involved in Jock Pfeifer's death?"

"Not just Jock's but Sue Naito's and Brian's, too."

"Ridiculous!" said Ken. "Brian was my brother for God's sake. I did not kill him."

"You could have had him killed."

"I did not have him killed, Lyon. Nor did I have anything to do with the death of that baby-killer. I told you that."

"So you did. You claimed that retribution for her abortion work belonged to God and that you had no interest in revenging yourself for Windward Cove. I believe you on both of those. Let's talk about Nathan Pfeifer. Sue not only knew the facts, she knew the whereabouts of the boy - the one person on which the whole case rested. The only way Jock could make his allegations stick would be to produce the boy for questioning. If Nathan could be found and eliminated, Jock's allegations would fall apart."

"What allegations?" asked Helen.

In answer, I started the tape. Helen watched transfixed from one end of a long couch as Jock laid out his evidence and built his case. Ken sat down heavily in an armchair, refusing to look at either

Helen or the tape. Jock had just finished accusing Ken of being Nathan's father and was about to bring up the sexual abuse when the doorbell rang. Ken jumped from the chair to answer it. It was Molly Gallagher.

"Mol," he said, buzzing her in. "We have a situation here. Hurry up."

Molly entered the room and stopped short when she saw me. "Jesus God, Val," she cried, "you show your face here after all the grief you've brought this family?"

Ken paced back and forth. He said, "Val's also brought us a little posthumous greeting from Jock Pfeifer." He gestured at the TV. Jock was in the midst of his most serious charges, the sexual abuse allegation.

Molly marched to the TV and shut it off. "Why do we have to put up with this shit?"

Helen looked up at Ken, "Is any of that true, Kenneth?"

"Of course it's not true. Do you think I'm a pedophile?" Ken ceased his pacing a few steps from me. "What do you want, Lyon? Hush money? You're cut from the same mold as Pfeifer, only worse. I know you were screwing Brian. You had him totally deluded. He thought he was mad for you. He thought you loved him, too. I told him to drop you but he wouldn't. You couldn't get money from Brian so now you're trying to shake us down with Pfeifer's crap. Pfeifer was a blackmailer, but you're a tramp."

"Scheming, lying tramp!" screamed Molly. She launched herself at me, catching me unawares. I sidestepped away from the brunt of her attack, but her fingernails found their mark and left a burning trail down my cheek. I caught her wrist and dumped her on her ass.

"Sit down!"

Molly struggled to get up but I pushed her onto the couch. "Ken," she pleaded, "do something."

"How much, Lyon? What will it take to get that tape and to get you out of our lives?"

Molly said, "Ken, you can't give in to blackmail."

Ken looked at her. "What else can we do? If this gets out the family is finished. We'd never be able to face people in this state again. And Frank, the scandal would kill his career."

Blood pounded in my head. My cheek smarted where Molly had scratched me. I could feel little rivulets of blood run down my face, but I resisted the temptation to wipe it away.

"Frank?" I said. "You Magruders close rank pretty fast around Frank, but Brian was expendable, right? Why? Because he didn't buy into the Magruder mystique?"

Molly started off the couch but thought better of it. "You can't honestly think any of us killed Brian," she said. "He was our brother. It was an accident. If it hadn't been for your snooping -"

"Molly," warned Ken.

"Did Brian know about Nathan?" I asked.

"No," said Molly. "I'm sure Jean didn't tell him and no one here told him."

"So you were going to just let him hang out there in the hopes that he'd screw up and lead you to Nathan? Your own brother?"

"Kenneth," said Helen. "Tell me the truth. Did you kill Brian and those other people?"

"No. For God's sake, Helen. You know I was with you the morning Brian died. We were in Lahaina."

"I know. You were also with me the morning Jock Pfeifer was killed. What about Sue Naito? Where were you when she was killed?"

"I was playing poker, Helen. As usual."

"Now you're lying. You weren't at a poker game. You were with Myra Akuna. Why can't you tell the truth for once, Kenneth? I can put up with almost anything, but I can't stand it when you lie to me. For God's sake, Kenneth, after all I've given you, I deserve better than that."

Ken looked at me. "What do you want?" he asked. "Name your price. You've done enough damage as it is. You know I didn't kill my brother or anyone else. There's no point in dragging out this sordid affair."

I ejected the cassette and put it in my purse. "I don't want money. I've already given copies of the tape and Jock's documents to the media. This one's not for sale. There's nothing you can do to stop me. If anything happens to me, Laskowitz will tell them you were the last to see me."

"Do you know what you've done?" yelled Molly. "The police will think Ken did the killing. They'll never believe he didn't do it after this."

"Then give me the guy who did it. You know who killed Sue and Jock. You know who ran me off the road. I want him. I want the guy who wired my car."

Molly said, "Why, Val? Why can't you let it go? It won't bring Brian back. Nobody wanted it to happen, but it did. It's done. You could just forget it and go on. You're not the only one who's suffering."

"The guy who wired that car killed somebody I cared for," I said. "He ruined a part of my life."

"What you're asking will just cause more grief," said Ken. "For one last time, can't you just leave it?"

"No," said Helen. "I understand what Val wants. There was a time early in our marriage when I felt that if anyone were to harm you, I would hound him across the planet. It's too bad I don't feel that way for you now. I want you to get him, Val."

Ken walked to the window and stood looking out. "What makes you think we could do what you ask? Even if I could give you his name, you won't be able to find him."

"I'll find him. I found this, didn't I? I've got more, too. So if I don't find him, he'd better find me."

I shouldered my bag and walked out. At the door, I turned and looked back. Nobody had moved. "You've got my number, Ken. Or you can reach me through Leo Laskowitz." Only Helen turned to watch me go.

39 POLICE INTERROGATION

At my apartment I washed my face and applied an antiseptic to the scratches. They were not terribly deep, but they were ugly and they stung. They'd probably heal without scarring. Two or three days at the most.

As it was only 9:40, I drove to King's Bakery for a breakfast of French toast made with inch-thick slices of Hawaiian sweet bread. It came with a side of Portuguese sausage and hash browns. I floated everything in a thick glop of syrup and washed it all down with three cups of coffee.

Fortified, I drove a half dozen blocks to the police station on Beretania and ended up almost back at the bakery before landing a parking space. Oh well, after that breakfast the walk would do me good.

Hannigan looked up from a junk-laden desk as I entered the detectives' room. She whispered something to Nakashita who swiveled his chair around and crossed his arms over his chest. Otherwise his expression was completely impassive.

"Try to control your enthusiasm, Sergeant. People might get the wrong impression about our relationship."

"You are a material witness in a murder investigation, Ms. Lyon. You're out of jail on your own recognizance. Give me a reason why I shouldn't send you right back."

"You'd miss my delightful banter."

"Why don't you give me a sample of it, for old time's sake?"

"I can do better than that." I put Jock's tape on the corner of his desk. In contrast to Hannigan's, Nakashita's desk was clean and organized. No stacks of folders, no grungy coffee cups, no fast food wrappers. Only two photos of his family, a phone, and Jock's cassette.

"What's on it?" he asked.

"A motive. It ties things together."

"I'll set up a video," said Hannigan.

Nakashita held up his hand to stop her. He took a blank notepad out of his drawer and laid it on his desk. He laid his ballpoint next to it. "Let's take things in order. Sit down, Ms. Lyon." He indicated an armless office chair beside his desk at a right angle to Hannigan's. He waited until I was seated and had straightened my skirt. "Start with Friday night after you left Jock Pfeifer's. Where were you?"

"I took Nathan to Brian Magruder's apartment. I thought he'd be safe there."

"Did the two of you spend the night?"

"Of course. I was guarding Nathan."

"Were you also guarding Brian Magruder?"

"Yes. He'd received death threats. Someone had tried to run me off the road. They may have thought it was Brian in the car at that time."

"Is that what you believe?"

"No. I think the guy was after me. I'm sure the bomb was meant for me, too."

"Let's talk about the bomb," said Nakashita.

We went through the who, what, when, where and why of Saturday. Went through it three times. I came near to breaking down, but the black hole inside me sucked in every feeling I had.

Nakashita asked, "Did you get a look at the guy getting into the elevator?"

"No. Not enough to pick him out of a lineup."

"What makes you think he's involved?"

"All I saw was his back. All I can give you is that he limped. He could have gotten the limp when he left Naito's house after he attacked Sue and me. The EMT on the scene found the backdoor open and heard dogs barking. The dogs are next door. He could have gone out the back and jumped the hedge into the next yard. It's a long drop into the neighbor's. He might have hurt his ankle in the jump and set off the dogs at the same time."

"That's pretty far-fetched," said Hannigan.

"I know," I shrugged. "It's all I've got."

Nakashita sat tapping his pen on his teeth and staring at me. "It's not so far-fetched," he said. "Ms. L, here, knows from experience."

Hannigan raised her eyebrows. Wisely, I kept my mouth shut. Sometimes I surprise myself that way.

"That was the same route you took after you broke into Naito's house last Sunday."

"How do you know that, Wally?" Hannigan asked.

"Wood screws. We had a complaint from Davison yesterday that someone tried to break into his house. It seems his jalousies fell out because someone had removed the screws." Nakashita allowed just the trace of a grin to flicker across his face. Then he said, "So you think Naito was murdered and that it's tied to Magruder's murder?"

"Yes to both. Don't you?"

"Let's see the tape," he said.

We watched the tape twice in its entirety. When the second viewing had ended, Nakashita said, "Do you want to tell us where you got this, Ms. Lyon?"

"Jock hid it in the dog pen, inside the food bin."

"The dog pen," he said. "My man searched it. Why didn't he find it?"

"I don't think he was in the pen. His shoes were too clean for someone searching an area loaded with dog shit."

Hannigan turned away to hide her laughter. Nakashita scowled so deeply, I pitied the cop who'd screwed up. He tapped his teeth with the pen. "All you've given us is a reason why Ken Magruder wanted the boy. We can't tie him to any of the killings until we find the guy who actually did them. So, who wired the car, Ms. Lyon? Who pushed the button? Who killed Brian Magruder? Give us a name."

"I can't, Sergeant."

"You can't because you don't know, or you can't because you want the guy for yourself?"

"I don't have a name to give you."

"All right. Dana, get Ms. Lyon a cup of coffee. Take her to a room where she can be comfortable. Maybe the name will come to her."

Hannigan took me to a small room nearby. It was furnished simply with a table, four chairs and a wastebasket. "Black?" she asked.

"Yes."

While Hannigan was getting the coffee, Nakashita came in with several binders and a manila folder. He stacked the binders on the table and laid the folder next to them. The tab on the folder said, "Magruder, Brian Charles" followed by Saturday's date.

"These are photos of known felons. If Ken Magruder hired a hit man, he'd go for experience. I'd like you to look through them. Maybe something will click for you. Take your time. It'll take a few hours."

"And this other folder, Sergeant?"

"I won't make you look in there, Ms. Lyon. That's up to you."

Hannigan returned with coffee and they left me alone. I sipped the coffee and flipped idly through the first binder. The manila folder lay there on the edge of the table and the edge of my consciousness. Funny how I'd never known Brian's middle name. Brian Charles! I tried it out loud, "Brian Charles. Good morning, Brian Charles." The sound fell on dead air.

Nakashita obviously thought I knew who had killed Brian. It was equally obvious that he thought I couldn't resist peeking into the case file on Brian and that he hoped the contents would shock me into divulging the name. I was determined not to look.

Contrary to what Nakashita believed, I didn't know who had wired the car, or shot Jock, or tortured Sue. But I did know someone who limped - Art Spinoza. Spinoza had gone to the rally; Spinoza had developed his limp recently as a result, he claimed, of soccer. What about the threats? He'd spoken pidgin English around me, though the seminarian said he was usually articulate. Was he afraid I'd recognize his voice? It made sense to me that Ken Magruder would hire someone close to the family to do his dirty work. The Magruders had built their fortune on the strength of their close-knit family. Family was the key. I was counting on Ken, Molly or Frank to give up the guy who had killed their brother.

I went through the binders as Nakashita had asked. Art Spinoza's picture was in the second one. He'd been convicted of armed robbery sixteen years earlier, released from prison seven years ago.

Nakashita had been correct in thinking that I couldn't resist opening Brian's folder. My whole being recoiled from it, but it was more than curiosity that impelled me to open it. I had to convince myself that what I was going to do was correct.

The photos in the folder had been taken at the scene. I did not recognize the wreckage as belonging to my car. I did not recognize the remains as belonging to a human being.

Hannigan came into the room to find me retching violently into the wastebasket. "Will you be okay?" she asked.

"Eventually."

"I'm sorry you had to see that. Wally thought -"

"He can go to hell."

"Did any faces in the books mean anything to you?"

I shook my head.

"Too bad. Wally says there's no need to keep you if you can't identify anyone."

Outside, the late afternoon sun was low in the sky. It was close to four o'clock. I walked to where I had left the car. The parking meter had expired several hours before. I ripped the ticket in half and drove to the Halekulani.

The sour taste of vomit was still in my mouth. I poured an inch of Leo's Scotch and rinsed my mouth with it. I spat it into the sink and poured more.

"This came for you," said Leo.

He handed me an opened envelope addressed to him. Inside was another envelope addressed to me. I slit it open with a fingernail. It contained a photograph of Magruder with Jean and Helen. The photo was similar to Jock's in every way but one: Magruder and Jean appeared to be the intimate couple. On the back was a note for me. It said, "Val, Ken will call you. In spite of everything, he's my husband. I have to stand by him. Helen."

"You understand that, kid?"

"She believes Ken's innocent."

"The picture doesn't look innocent," said Leo. "The body language."

"Yes, I don't understand that." I put the picture in my bag. "I'd better wait for Ken's call at my place."

"If he doesn't call?"

"I'll go looking for Art Spinoza."

"Take this," said Leo. He gave me a Colt Detective's .38 Special and a clip on holster. "Know how you hate to carry a piece in your purse," he said.

I clipped the holster inside my waistband. With the gun snugged up against my belly, I went back to my apartment.

40 WHAT LOOKS GOOD ON A GUMSHOE

Jim Harbaugh had the Bears inside the Vikings' twenty on Monday Night Football when the phone rang. I grabbed it, expecting to hear Ken, instead I heard Lydia Pacaro.

"Miss Lyon," she said, "I found something I think you want to see."

"What did you find?" I asked.

"Please repeat."

Oh dammit! I didn't want to go through all this on the phone. "Where are you?" I shouted.

"I am at Mr. Pfeifer's house. Can you come soon?"

"I'll be right there."

It was quarter to ten. I pulled on shorts, a T-shirt, and a pair of Nike cross-trainers. I clipped the .38 inside my waistband and stuck a D-cell flashlight in my pocket.

At ten minutes after ten when I drove by, Jock's house was mostly dark except for a light burning behind the curtained front window. I drove down to the first cross street and turned right. A hundred yards from the intersection, I found a white pickup truck parked at the curb. It had a bar of spotlights on top. It was empty. I continued on to the next street, turned right again, and parked about midway down the block. From there I made my way on foot to the house directly behind Jock's. Luckily, the yard wasn't fenced. I skirted the house, keeping to the shadows and using my flashlight to get around obstacles. The last obstacle was Jock's fence. I went back five steps, took a short run and leaped for the top. Michael Jordan would have envied my air time. I caught the top of the fence, planted one foot in the middle and pulled myself over. A narrow gap separated the fence from Jock's shed.

Genghis began barking when I stepped across to the roof. He charged the fence and then ran into the shed and charged the door. I dropped to the ground beside the shed just as a light came on near the lanai door. Lydia emerged followed by Art Spinoza. He carried a gun loosely at his side.

"Shut that damn dog up," he said.

Genghis went wild.

Lydia approached the pen with Spinoza a few steps behind. I dropped into a crouch holding the flashlight and .38 in both hands. When they were about fifteen feet from the pen I flicked on the flashlight and swung the beam into his eyes.

"Art! Drop the gun!" I yelled above Genghis' barking.

He threw his hand in front of his face. "Lyon? Is that you? Cut the damn light. I want to talk."

"I'll shoot if you harm her, Art."

Suddenly from behind my shoulder another voice yelled, "Hey! What the hell's going on there? Shut that dog up or I'll call the police." He was in close proximity but on the other side of the fence. Nevertheless, his unexpected presence startled me and caused the light to waver from Spinoza's face.

Spinoza grabbed Lydia and spun her in front of him. "Get the fuck outa here," he yelled.

The guy behind me said, "Now look -"

"Do it," I shouted, "or he'll kill you."

"Cut the light, Lyon, or I'll shoot the maid."

I cut the light.

"That does it,' said the neighbor. "I'm calling the police." I heard him run off through his yard.

Spinoza put the gun against Lydia's head. She whimpered loudly enough to be heard above Genghis.

"I want to talk, Lyon. I want a deal. That's all I want. Are you listening to me?"

Lydia whimpered again. Genghis seemed to sense her distress and whimpered in response.

"I'm listening, Art. Talk."

"I can't talk with the damn dog. We're all goin' inside. You got a gun? Throw it down."

I gambled that he couldn't see me in the shadow and holstered the gun. I let my shirt hang out to conceal it. "It's down, Art. I've got a flashlight, nothing more."

"Turn it off!" I flicked it off. "Okay. I don't want to hurt anybody."

Spinoza backed Lydia to the house and I followed. When we were on the lanai, Spinoza swung Lydia around and made me go ahead. He marched us into the living room and motioned us to the sofa. It was the first time I was able to see Lydia's face. Her eyes were red and her face was tear streaked, but she seemed to be holding up well.

"I'm sorry," she said. "He made me."

"It's okay." I squeezed her hand. "What happened to the pidgin English, Art?"

"Shut up!" Spinoza paced agitatedly. The stress in his voice was like nails on a blackboard.

"How's the ankle, Art?"

"Fuck the ankle, Lyon! I should shut you up for good."

It would be pointless to remind him he'd already tried. "You said you wanted a deal, Art. What kind of deal could I give you?"

"You can talk to the cops for me. The Magruders are trying to burn me. I need you to cut me some slack."

"Why me? You killed Brian. I want you to pay for that."

"I'm gonna pay, I know it, but I'm not gonna go alone. Killing your boyfriend was an accident but the Magruders don't see it that way. They're trying to put the whole thing on me. It wasn't my idea to wire the car to begin with. And I didn't kill Pfeifer."

"Genghis seems to think you did."

"Fuck Genghis! I was there. I admit it, but I didn't kill him. All right?"

"Why don't you go to the police with the story?"

"Jesus! Do you think I'd be talking to you if I could? The Magruders are connected. Haven't you figured that out? Ken Magruder calls up a poker buddy and, whattya know, next thing there's a raid on Pfeifer's shop."

"You still haven't answered my question. Why me?"

"The cops'll listen to you. Even though your boyfriend got it, your head's still on straight."

I toyed with the flashlight in my hand, all the while listening for police sirens. I hoped the neighbor had called them. Spinoza waved the gun back and forth between Lydia and me. She was no longer crying. All that came from her was an intake of breath whenever he pointed the gun at her.

"What should I tell them, Art?"

Spinoza seemed about to cry. He said, "You have to tell them that I didn't have any part of that sick stuff. I swear, Lyon, Jesus help me, I go to church. I wouldn't have anything to do with what he did to that kid. Never. But people are going to think that I did unless somebody sets them straight. Jesus, God! Do you know what they'd do to me in prison if they thought I was part of that?"

I nodded.

Spinoza went on, "I didn't do anything to the kid. I'm not a mahu. You, I could fuck in a minute. The both of you, even."

"Pardon me, if I don't appreciate the thought."

"I don't need your smart mouth, Lyon. You'd appreciate it if I gave it to you. I'm telling you, I fool around with women, but I don't mess with boys. I wanted to be a priest, Lyon, but they kicked me out of the seminary for having pictures of girls. Poor moral character, they said. Who the hell were they to judge moral character? Now a priest does it with a boy and they hush it up."

Suddenly I realized what he was saying. I don't know why I

hadn't seen it before. "A priest? You mean Frank?"

"Of course, Frank. Monsignor Magruder. Honest, Lyon, I didn't know why they wanted the kid. They let me think it had something to do with Ken."

"Frank molested Nathan Pfeifer?"

Suddenly Lydia understood, too. She gasped loudly.

Spinoza said, "Yeah. That's why he wanted the kid so bad. But how was I supposed to know that? I didn't know about it until late Saturday when the bishop and the monsignor got to arguing about it."

"What were they going to do with Nathan if they got him?"

"They wanted to use him for leverage with the mother. The Magruders offered to set her up well if she would take the kid and move to a different country with a different name."

"In return for her silence."

"Yeah. They figured if she and the kid were out of the way, they could buy off Pfeifer for awhile. Later they would arrange an accident."

"But Jean wouldn't cooperate and Jock wanted too much."

"That's the size of it."

I heard a siren from somewhere off in the distance. It was followed by two more. Spinoza heard them, too. He said, "Shit, that bastard did call the cops." He grabbed Lydia's arm, yanked her off the couch, and swung the gun around at me. I was trying to get to my feet and to get the gun out at the same time but a waistband holster is not made for a fast draw. Lydia was faster. She bit down on his wrist. Spinoza yelled and knocked her aside. His gun went off and the bullet shattered the window behind the couch. I took a step towards him and swung the flashlight at his head, connecting solidly. Batteries arced through the air as the flashlight flew apart. Spinoza went down on one knee. Lydia had gotten to her feet.

"Run," I yelled at her.

She was already heading out through the back. I drew my gun and followed. In the kitchen, I stopped and looked back into the living room. Spinoza's gun lay on the floor where he'd dropped it, but Spinoza wasn't there. The sirens had gotten closer and finally stopped. I could hear voices outside and the crackle of police radios. I knew they were getting into position and they knew a shot had been fired. I had to tell them there would be no more shooting.

I moved cautiously back into the living room, but didn't see Spinoza. As I turned towards the front door, he rose up from behind the couch and leaped over it. He was on me before I could bring the gun to bear. The impact knocked us both to the floor. Spinoza rolled up on top of me. He pinned my right arm beneath his knee and seized my gun hand by the wrist. I tried to buck him off, but he had about forty pounds on me - all of it on my chest.

"I should've killed you sooner, Lyon," he sobbed. The side of his face was red and swollen. He drew back his free hand and aimed a punch at my head. I shut my eyes and managed to turn enough that the blow glanced off my cheek. I opened my eyes in time to see a large shadow charge into the living room. Genghis! Without pausing, he made a low growl and sprang at Spinoza. Spinoza screamed. The dog's momentum lifted him off of me and I rolled out of the way. Genghis pulled Spinoza across the living room, whipping him from side to side. Spinoza screamed in agony as he tried in vain to protect himself. "Get him off me. Oh God, get him off."

Spinoza turned a bloody face in my direction. "Shoot him," he begged. "For God's sake, Lyon, shoot."

I looked at the man who had killed Brian Magruder and Sue Naito and felt nothing. He looked done for. I could end his suffering quicker by shooting him, but mercy was not on my mind. I aimed my gun at the dog. Shooting Genghis would not help Spinoza much, but shooting Spinoza was still murder. And I was afraid that if I shot Spinoza, Genghis would turn on me. I needed a clean shot.

Genghis paused long enough in his mauling of Spinoza to give me the shot. I sighted down the gun.

"Miss Lyon! Do not shoot him."

I looked up to find Lydia and about five officers behind me. Lydia shouted some commands at Genghis and he backed away uncertainly. Two officers in protective gear rushed forward and pulled Spinoza away. One officer took my gun.

"I opened his pen," said Lydia.

41 MASS IS ENDED

Animal control officers took Genghis away. EMTs took Spinoza, unconscious, to a hospital. Lydia and I went to the police station to give our statements to the detectives on the night shift. Sergeant Nakashita, I was told, would probably want to speak to me in the morning. I was too tired to point out that it was already morning. Four o'clock, to be exact, on Christmas Eve.

I called Leo on leaving the police station and he was waiting for me when I reached his hotel. He'd ordered breakfast from room service. I filled him in while we ate.

"Did you tell the police about Frank?" asked Leo.

"No. I want to look at the pictures first."

Leo pushed aside the remains of eggs Benedict, fruit and coffee. He got out the picture of Jean, Helen and Ken from Jock's file. I put Helen's picture beside it. Leo handed me a magnifying glass. Through the glass, the little mush of scar tissue on Ken's chin was clearly visible in Jock's picture. There was no scar in Helen's.

"It's Frank," I said. "Jock was wrong."

"You gonna tell Nakashita?"

"He'll find out soon enough. This will be over before he finishes his breakfast."

I went to my apartment for a few hours of sleep and a

change of clothes. At eight I picked up Leo and at eight thirty we were at St. Ambrose Church.

"The Mass is ended. Go in peace to love and serve the Lord," pronounced the priest.

The choir struck up O Come, O Come Emmanuel. Monsignor Frank Magruder descended the altar steps, carrying the big red missal. At the bottom, he turned and waited for the acolytes to join him. They formed a line behind him and then, on some silent cue, Magruder and the acolyte holding the crucifix bowed, the acolytes flanking the crucifix genuflected. All four turned and made their way up the aisle in solemn procession.

They'd reached the vestibule doors when Frank spotted me and Leo. A look of desperation flashed across his face. He made a quick look over his shoulder. I thought, for a second, he might seek an escape through the church. But the congregation had begun filling the aisles behind him and there was nowhere that he could go. Instead he continued behind the acolytes into the vestibule. He nodded briefly to Leo. To me, he said, "I guess you're waiting for me."

"Spinoza's in the hospital, Frank. He's got a lot to say if he survives."

"He tried to kill Ms. Lyon," said Leo. "But you know about that don't you?" Leo was on Frank's left and I was in front of Frank. The three acolytes had stopped just inside the door and were now behind him.

Suddenly Magruder turned and threw the heavy missal at Leo, who staggered back and went down. Frank grabbed the staff from the acolyte and spun around to face me. I backed up a step. "Stay out of my way," he said. He swung the staff at my head and I ducked under it. The crucifix on the end was sterling silver with sharp edges. A hit with that could do serious damage. He jabbed with it at Leo, forcing him back. There was consternation among the congregation but none of them dared enter the vestibule. I saw one of the acolytes escape on his hands and knees. I took a step forward but Magruder swung it at me again. Whoosh. I retreated two steps.

He advanced on me. Whoosh. Wielding it two-handed, his athletic ability paying off. I ducked and dodged, looking for an opening with no luck. A forearm block would just get me a broken arm. Whoosh. He continued to force me back. The floor was terrazzo, polished to a high sheen. The vestibule was an open, airy space lined with low planter boxes about eighteen inches high. Magruder came at me with the staff again, only this time he jabbed at my midsection. I stepped back to avoid it and my heel contacted the planter box. I went down, twisting to avoid the crucifix. I heard my blouse rip and felt a sharp tug as metal scraped my side. I sat down hard on the planter.

Frank Magruder was out the door, vestments flapping, before I could extricate myself. I followed him. My side ached as though from a side stitch. Each time my left foot hit the pavement, I received a searing jolt. I spotted him halfway across the parking lot, still carrying the staff. Ever the priest, he wasn't about to commit the sacrilege of dumping the image of Christ. He had about fifty yards on me. There was pandemonium in the church behind me. I heard Leo telling someone to call the police.

Magruder ran between two classroom buildings and I followed. My side ached terribly and I had to pause for breath. I put my hand on the wound and it came away bloody. He was increasing the lead on me, heading to the rectory. I tried to head him off but a low fence blocked my way. I had to climb it and swing my legs over. It seemed harder than it should've been.

I rounded the corner of the garage, clutching my side, just as Magruder came out of the rectory door. He'd thrown off the chasuble but was still wearing the white alb, cinched up with the white cord around his waist. The stole flapped loose over his shoulder. He no longer carried the cross on the staff. It was leaning against the wall. He sprang for the garage door.

"Frank," I said, stopping to get my breath. "You can't get away, Frank. Spinoza'll talk."

He turned to face me. "If he lives. You said he might not. Nobody'll believe him anyway."

"They will if you run."

"I'm not running from the police, I'm running from you. You've got some crazy vendetta against me. They'll believe that. Now, stay away."

I was nearly spent and had no intention of getting any closer. The gash in my side throbbed mercilessly and I thought I would faint.

"You killed all those people - Sue Naito, Jock Pfeifer, and…and Brian."

"I didn't kill them. Spinoza did."

"You had them killed. Same thing. Your own brother."

"I'm sorry about Brian. He wasn't meant to die. It should have been you."

"It's what you did to Nathan that disgusts me. You took advantage of his innocence and trust to satisfy your own lust."

"We all stumble from time to time in matters of the flesh. He was an innocent in an adult body, not yet in tune with his sexuality. He was so much in need of guidance and had no one to guide him. I'm not making excuses, but I am asking forgiveness. I was trying to help him, believe me."

"You must have suspected you were his father, even if you weren't sure. Would you have everyone killed who discovered your secret?"

Magruder had the garage door open. "I'd do what I have to, Val. I've been called to an important position in the church. A weak moment should not ruin a life's work. Now stay out of my way." He got in the car and started the engine.

I grabbed the crucifix, the only object available, and took up a position in the driveway. I heard police sirens as I did so. Two cars, one in the vicinity of the church and the other one closer. I didn't know if Magruder heard them, but he accelerated backwards out of the garage. I swung the heavy cross at the car. The back window spider-webbed where I hit it. I rolled out of the way as he went past. He braked to a stop and then drove at me. I spun out of the way and jabbed the end of the staff at the passenger side window, shattering it. He braked again and started back at me just as a blue and white squad car pulled up, cutting off his exit.

The cop and Magruder were out of their cars at the same time. The cop had her gun drawn. "Thank God you're here, officer," yelled Magruder. "This woman's trying to kill me."

"I'm Val Lyon, I'm a private investigator. This man's a suspect in three murders."

"It's a lie," said Magruder. "She's crazy. She needs psychiatric treatment. Look at her."

I probably did look more than a little crazed. Wild hair, torn and bloody clothes. My blouse had come undone and was hanging open. I had a slugger's grip on the staff.

"Nobody move," said the cop. She swung her gun between us. "Drop the pole, sister," she said.

Magruder said, "No, it's a blessed object, give it to me."

The cop said, "Just lean it against the wall and move away."

I did as she said.

"I'm Monsignor Magruder." His voice rose shrilly. "This woman attacked me with that wild tale about murder. You can't believe her. I was trying to get away from her when you came."

"Is that right, lady?"

"My purse with my I.D. is back at the church," I said, as calmly as I could. "I'm pursuing an investigation."

"Lies! Look at her. She's probably got a weapon."

"Turn around, please," the cop said. "Hands behind your head."

"You're making a mistake," I said. "I'm not armed." Out of the corner of my eye, I saw Magruder snatch the staff with the crucifix. I yelled a warning, but too late.

Magruder brought the hefty staff down on the cop's arm. The bone snapped with a loud crack and she let out a scream that was cut off when he drove the staff into her throat. I dove for the gun. My fingers closed around the grip but I let go with a cry when Magruder smashed them with the cross. The gun skidded away from me to the edge of the pavement. Magruder swung again and I rolled away from the blow. The heavy cross slammed the pavement, where an instant before my head had been. Slammed it with such force that the staff splintered and the crucifix went flying into the grass. I rolled up to my knees, searching for the gun, but Magruder kept coming after me.

"You! You let Brian die in your place," he cried. He delivered a kick to my torn side that lifted me off my knees and landed me on my back. The left side of my body felt like it was on fire. A wave of blackness washed across my eyes. The blackness cleared and I caught movement off to my right. The cop was struggling to get up, to find her gun. It was just out of my reach. When I looked back to Magruder, he was standing over me, holding the staff above his head with two hands, the splintered end pointing down at me.

"It's all over, Frank. You won't get away." My voice was thick with fear, knowing the kind of damage it would do if he plunged it into me. People were coming but they wouldn't get here in time.

He said, "For what I am about to do, God forgive me."

The cop, with a last effort, pushed the gun into my hand. I swung it up and fired.

42 THE PEARL

Jean Pfeifer and I sat on the concrete lanai behind Carol and Annie's house in Hawaii Kai. Small clouds, pushed by brisk trade winds that had been absent for the past five days, scudded across a deep blue sky. It was the second week in January, two weeks after Brian and Frank had been buried together in a private, Catholic funeral. Carol's cats were inside at my insistence, but I kept an eye out for them just in case. Behind us, a green awning put half of the lanai in shade, but I had maneuvered my chair into the sunny part. The sun was pleasantly warm on my skin beneath my thin cotton dress. The gash in my side had healed to where I no longer needed a bulky dressing and the acne-like bloom on my face, a result of powder residue from the shot, had finally gone away.

Jean removed the cover from a plate of Chinese spare ribs, shoyu chicken wings, and skewered beef strips. A garden salad, a freshly sliced pineapple, and some cubes of cheese filled other plates on the table. "This is a far cry from jail fare, isn't it?" she asked. She had on a striped vest over a sage colored linen shirt and trousers. Her makeup was natural and understated. She'd cut and styled her hair so it was short and relaxed. She could have been modeling for a yuppie catalog instead of talking to a detective about the aftermath of tragedy.

"What can I offer you to drink?"

My choices were wine or beer. I chose white wine. Jean went inside the house and came out with a bottle of Gewurtztramminer. She poured a glass for me and one for herself. I wondered if Carol was watching from behind the curtains. Annie, I knew, was not home.

"Now help yourself," said Jean. She waited patiently while I filled a plate one-handed. My left hand with the three broken fingers taped together rested casually in my lap. I sipped the wine and tasted a spare rib. Both were good. Jean asked, "Did you go to the funeral?"

"No. It was just family."

"Of course. I suppose the manner of Frank's death, trying to kill you, poses problems for the church. To allow a public burial with the Mass and sacraments would create scandal, but they have to hold out the possibility that he repented between the time he committed the act and the time his life ended."

"The velocity of a .357 doesn't allow much time for an act of contrition."

Jean nodded. "That's the common sense view. The church, of course, gives him the benefit of the doubt."

"I think the church has been too much inclined to give the benefit of the doubt where Frank was concerned."

Jean sipped her wine and said. "You asked to see me, Val. What do you want to hear from me?"

"The truth. I'm trying to deal with my failure and my loss. I need to know what happened for my own satisfaction."

"Yes," she said. "You deserve that."

Jean went into the long history of her relationship with Frank. It began shortly after his ordination when he was a new assistant pastor. The period coincided with an early crisis in her marriage to Jock.

"I'd been away from the Church for a long time," she said. "But our marriage wasn't working out and I needed someone to talk to. I went to the parish and that was where I met Frank. He didn't act like any of the priests I knew. He was casual and friendly and he listened to me." Jean paused, toyed with her salad and went on. "He was such a change from Jock. Besides getting me back to church, Frank got me involved in parish activities. I worked on committees, went to social events, and met people. In a short time, I found myself visiting the parish office three or four times a week. Frank was always there."

"Where was Jock through all this?"

"He was building the business. You know, I have to give him some credit. At that time, nobody thought it was possible to make money renting videos. He really worked at it. Of course, that meant he wasn't around much, but we were having rough times so I considered that a blessing."

"So you and Frank got together?"

"Yes. He'd been in love with me since that first visit to the rectory. He told me that quite a bit later. All those times that we were together, he said, increased his desire until it became intolerable."

"And you?"

"I liked him. I admired him. He listened to me and he made me laugh. I was probably in love with him, too. Maybe not like he loved me, but I definitely had feelings for him, although I didn't think there was any hope of expressing those feelings."

"How did it happen?"

It happened, according to Jean, one weekend at the Magruder farm. The occasion was a luau for some of the active members of the parish. Jock was on the mainland and wouldn't have gone anyway. The Magruder farm was large and many of the guests spent the night. Frank insisted that Jean stay, too. Through some unspoken planning on each of their parts, they found themselves alone together.

"It was a beautiful night, I remember. It was easy to forget that he was a priest. Do you want a detailed description of what happened next?"

"No. I can fill in the blanks myself. Was it just that night or did it go on?"

"It went on. We were lovers for about eight months. We

weren't as discreet as we should have been and rumors reached the bishop's ears. He transferred Frank to other duties in the diocese and then sent him to Catholic University for some advanced study. I think it was a relief to Frank because he was having difficulty reconciling our affair with his vows. As it turned out, it was the start of Frank's career in the church hierarchy."

"Did you ever try to tell him about his child?"

"Not for some years. You see, I wasn't sure. For a long time, too, Frank and I had no contact. I think the bishop insisted that he not see me. But I did have occasional contact with the rest of the Magruders. Frank found out through them that Jock and I had divorced, so he called me one day. We had a great chat. I was pretty certain by then, that Frank was Nathan's father and I thought the two of them should meet. You see, I had a crazy idea that Frank would take Nathan under his wing, you might say, and do all the things for him that Jock hadn't done."

"Wait, you told Frank that Nathan was his son?"

Jean shook her head violently. "No. When Frank invited Nathan and me to the farm, I thought…I hoped . . they would become friends without my telling them."

"You trusted Frank?"

"Of course. He was a priest. I taught Nathan to trust him, too. Oh God, I had no idea that this would happen. No idea at all."

I had learned from Helen Magruder, the only Magruder who would speak to me, that an earlier incident involving Frank and an adolescent had been quietly resolved in the diocese. Pete Hagen at Pacific Economic News said he had heard a rumor to that effect. My efforts to reach Bishop Connor had so far been met with stony resistance. I asked Jean about it.

"I didn't believe it. I loved Frank, don't you see?" Jean's eyes clouded over. She seemed to me to be on the verge of crying, but then she steeled herself and wiped a drop of moisture away with her napkin. She picked delicately at a piece of beef and sipped her wine.

"Jean, out of all the attorneys you could have hired, why did you hire Brian?"

"I'd known him for a few years. He was a decent man. I thought he'd be a good attorney." She paused and looked off into a middle distance. "No, the real truth is that I thought, with Brian on my side, the Magruder family wouldn't be able to carry out their threats. I was so proud of myself. I'd pre-empted the Magruder family. I'm sorry. What more can I say?"

I convinced Jean that I should see Nathan regularly. Twice a week we went to Paki Playground to shoot hoops with Kalani and Moon. I took it upon myself to see that we made progress in our physical rehabilitation - his arm and my hand. Pam helped Jean arrange appropriate counseling for him. The counseling and the hoops went a long way towards rebuilding his self-esteem, but there was a lot more to rebuild.

My own self-esteem was in need of repair. Leo hung around until the end of January, helping me find office space and generally being a rock of strength. Any lingering doubts I had, he dismissed out of hand.

"You didn't fail Brian," he said. "Taking care of the kid was what he wanted. You did good work, kiddo."

I saw Pam daily, usually at her office, but sometimes at a beach or a bar. We were taking in the afternoon sun at Kaimana Beach on the first Sunday in February when the subject of Frank's disorder came up.

"Ephebophilia," said Pam, "not pedophilia, is the proper term for Frank's perversion. The ephebophile is attracted to youngsters in puberty. It's the innocence of a child in an adult body that they find appealing."

"That's sort of how Frank described it before I killed him. I still don't understand why he abused Nathan."

"And we may never know. We can speculate that he'd never gotten over Jean; that he'd seen Jean in Nathan; and that the surroundings of the farm where he'd conducted his affair with Jean stimulated his lust. A forensic psychologist might make something of that, but that's not my area. I deal with the living. Speaking of which, how's your pearl coming?"

The pearl was our metaphor for my healing process. We both knew the black hole that came with Brian's death would never go away, but I was dealing with it the way an oyster deals with something that irritates it. I was covering over the black hole inside me; I was making a pearl.

"It's coming along," I said.

"And you know this how?"

"Greg called."

"The gorgeous hunk?"

"The gorgeous hunk. He wants to take me sailing next week. Seven days around the islands. Just the two of us."

"And you said?"

"I told him yes."

Pam beamed. "Way to go, girlfriend. I would say the pearl is almost complete."

"I'm ready to find out," I said.

NOTE TO THE READER

Dear Reader,

Mahalo means "Thank you" in Hawaiin. So *mahalo* for choosing *Pilikia Is My Business*. I sincerely hope you enjoyed Val's adventure. You can find more of Val's stories at my website, http://www.marktroy.net. You can also find news there about an upcoming collection of short stories, in which you can share more of Val's adventures.

Connect with me online:

Hawaiian Eye Blog: http://hawaiian-eye.blogspot.com
Make Mine Mystery: http://makeminemystery.blogspot.com
Follow me on Twitter: http://twitter.com/Skywritermt

Aloha ka kou,
Mark

ABOUT THE AUTHOR

Mark Troy is a native of St. Louis, Missouri. He and his wife served as Peace Corps Volunteers in Thailand where they taught English and supervised student teachers. After the Peace Corps, the Troys moved to Hawaii for graduate school. They now live in Texas where Mark is an administrator and researcher at the Texas A&M University. Mark has degrees from Quincy University, Washington University and the University of Hawaii. The Troys have two sons a daughter-in-law, one granddaughter and one grandson.

Pilikia Is My Business is Mark's first novel. He is the author of numerous short stories, some of which feature Val Lyon. One story, "Teed Off" was named one of the 50 best American mystery stories of 2001 by Otto Penzler and James Ellroy.

When not writing, Mark runs marathons. He has completed 18 so far.

www.ingramcontent.com/pod-product-compliance
Lightning Source LLC
Chambersburg PA
CBHW071255170626
46809CB00001B/237